RISE OF THE KING

©2014 Wizards of the Coast LLC.

is protected under the copyright laws of the United States of America. Any reproduction or unau-
use of the material or artwork contained herein is prohibited without the express written permission
ds of the Coast LLC.

ed by Wizards of the Coast LLC. Manufactured by: Hasbro SA, Rue Emile-Boéchat 31, 2800
ont, CH. Represented by Hasbro Europe, 2 Roundwood Ave, Stockley Park, Uxbridge, Middlesex,
1AZ, UK..

GOTTEN REALMS, WIZARDS OF THE COAST, D&D, and their respective logos are trademarks of
rds of the Coast LLC in the U.S.A. and other countries.

characters in this book are fictitious. Any resemblance to actual persons, living or dead, is purely
cidental. All Wizards of the Coast characters, character names, and the distinctive likenesses thereof are
perty of Wizards of the Coast LLC.

inted in the U.S.A.

over art by: Tyler Jacobson
First Printing: September 2014

9 8 7 6 5 4 3 2 1

ISBN: 978-0-7869-6515-1
ISBN: 978-0-7869-6551-9 (ebook)
620A6634000001 EN

Cataloging-in-Publication data is on file with the Library of Congress

Contact Us at Wizards.com/CustomerService
Wizards of the Coast LLC, PO Box 707, Renton, WA 98057-0707, USA
USA & Canada: (800) 324-6496 or (425) 204-8069
Europe: +32(0) 70 233 277

Visit our web site at **www.dungeonsanddragons.com**

FORGOTT[EN]

R. A. SALV[A]
RISE OF THE

This boo[k]
thorized
of Wiza[rds]

Publish
Delém
UB11

FOR[GOTTEN REALMS]
Wiza[rds]

All
coi
pr[o]

P

(

PROLOGUE

Y E E'ER SEEN ANYTHING LIKE THAT?" King Connerad Brawnanvil asked the emissary from Citadel Felbarr. They stood on a small guard tower along the rim of the valley called Keeper's Dale, staring up at the dark sky. The sun barely penetrated the strange overcast. So little light came through the roiling and angry blackness above, in fact, that no one in the North had seen more than a wisp of a shadow in several days.

"None've seen anything like that, good king," the surly old veteran warrior named Ragged Dain answered. "But we ain't thinkin' it's a good thing."

"It's them orcs," King Connerad remarked. "Obould's ugly boys. It's them orcs, or the world's gone crazy and gnomes're wearing beards long enough to tickle a tall man's toes."

Ragged Dain nodded his agreement. That's why he'd been dispatched by King Emerus Warcrown, after all, because certainly the Kingdom of Many-Arrows had to be the source of this unseemly event—or at least, the dwarves of the Silver Marches were all betting that the minions of King Obould knew the source, at least.

"Ye heared from Citadel Adbar?" King Connerad asked, referring to the third of the dwarf communities in the Silver Marches. "Are they seein' this?"

"Aye, the Twin Kings are seein' it and looking to the Underdark for answers."

"Ye think them boys're ready for it, whatever it might be?" Connerad asked, for Citadel Adbar had only recently crowned a pair of kings, Bromm and Harnoth, the twin sons of old King Harbromm, who had ruled there for nearly two centuries until his recent—by dwarf accounting—death.

1

The twins had been raised well, but they hadn't seen much in the way of action or political intrigue in the quiet of the last decades.

"Who's for sayin'?" Ragged Dain replied, shaking his head solemnly. King Harbromm had been a dear friend to him and the others of Citadel Felbarr, almost as a brother to King Emerus Warcrown. The loss of that great leader, barely cold in the ground, could prove quite troublesome if this event, this darkening, turned as foul as it looked.

Ragged Dain dropped a hand affectionately to the shoulder of Connerad Brawnanvil. "Was yerself ready?" he asked. "When King Banak passed on and ye took the bridle o' Mithral Hall, did ye know what ye needed?"

Connerad snorted. "Still don't," he admitted. "Kinging looks easy from afar."

"Not so much from the throne, then," Ragged Dain agreed, and Connerad nodded. "Well, then, young King o' Mithral Hall, what're ye knowin' now after all?"

"I'm knowin' that I ain't knowin'," King Connerad said resolutely. "And not knowing's likely to get me boys in trouble."

"Scouts, then."

"Aye, a bunch, and yerself's to go with 'em, that ye'll be going back to Felbarr with what ye seen with yer own eyes."

Ragged Dain considered the words for a few moments, then offered a salute to the young King of Mithral Hall. "Ye're ready now," he said, and clapped Connerad hard on the shoulder once more. "Here's to hoping that the twins o' Harbromm catch on as quick."

"Bah, but there's two o' them," said Connerad. "Sure to be."

He looked back up at the sky, at the roiling clouds of smoke or some other foul substance that turned daylight into something less than moonlight and hid the stars entirely.

"Sure to be," he said again, more to himself than to his guest.

"I am a priest of Gruumsh One-Eye," the tall orc protested.

"Yes, and I was hoping that your standing would indicate some intelligence, at least," Tiago Baenre replied with a derisive chortle, and he walked off to the side.

"We have come to offer a great opportunity," Tos'un Armgo retorted. "Would not your Gruumsh be pleased?"

"Gruumsh . . ." the orc started, but Tos'un cut him short.

"Would not the god of orcs swim in the blood of humans, elves, and dwarves?"

The tall orc gave a crooked smile as he looked over Tos'un, head to toe. "Uryuga knows you," the shaman said, and Tiago snorted again at the typically orc habit of referring to himself by his own name.

"You speak of elves," Uryuga went on. "You know elves. You live with elves!"

"Lived," Tos'un corrected. "I was chased out, and by the same female who killed many of your kin by the holy cave."

"That is not the tale my people tell."

Tos'un started to respond, but just blew a sigh. His actions in that instance, with his wife Sinnafein by his side, certainly would work against him. He had abandoned her to the pursuing orcs in his quest to catch up to Doum'wielle and led her into the Underdark, but any of the orc survivors from that skirmish surely knew that he had not been fleeing from Sinnafein but traveling with her.

Uryuga chuckled and started to continue, but now it was Tiago who cut him short. "Enough," the son of House Baenre demanded. "Look above you, fool. Do you see that? We have blocked out the sun itself. Do you understand the power that has come upon these lands? If you or your stubborn King Obould will not heed our call, then we will simply replace you both and find another king—and another priest—who will."

The orc priest straightened his shoulders and stood up tall, towering over Tiago, but if the drow was intimidated, he certainly didn't show any signs of it.

"Ravel!" Tiago called, and turned to the side, guiding Uryuga's gaze that way, to see Uryuga—another Uryuga—approaching.

"What is this?" the orc demanded.

"Do you really believe we need you?" Tiago scoffed. "Do you hold yourself tall enough to believe that a plan to conquer the Silver Marches rests on the choices of a simple orc priest?"

"High shaman," Uryuga corrected.

"Dead shaman," Tiago corrected, his fine sword, a sliver of the starlit sky it seemed, flashing from its scabbard and rushing tip-in to rest against Uryuga's throat.

"I serve Gruumsh!"

"Want to meet him? Now?" Tiago flicked his wrist a tiny bit and a spot of blood appeared on Uryuga's throat.

"Answer me," the vicious drow prompted. "But before you do, think of the glorious sights you will miss when a sea of orcs swarm the mounds and dales and roll over the great cities of Luruar. Think of the slaughter of thousands of dwarves, and all without a swing of Uryuga's heavy mace. Because that is what we will do, with you alive or with you dead. It matters not."

"If it matters not, then why am I alive?"

"Because we prefer the priests of Gruumsh to partake of the war. The Spider Queen is no enemy to the great and glorious One-Eye and would welcome him in this great victory. But now I grow weary of this. Will you join or will you die?"

Put that way, and with a sword against his throat, Uryuga gave a slight but definitive nod.

"I'm not certain," Tiago said anyway, glancing back over his shoulder at the illusion of Uryuga worn by Ravel. "I think you look ugly enough to handle this task." As he spoke, he drove his sword forward, just a tiny bit, the fine blade easily cutting the orc's skin.

"Grab for it," Tiago said, turning back to face the shaman. "I would so enjoy watching your fingers fall to the ground."

Ravel began to laugh, but Tos'un shifted uncomfortably.

Tiago snapped his sword away in the blink of an eye, but came forward and grabbed the orc by the collar, yanking him low. "We offer you all you ever wanted," he growled in Uryuga's ugly face. "The blood of your enemies will stain the mountainsides, the dwarven halls will be filled with your people. The great cities of Luruar will grovel and tremble before the stamp of orc boots. And you dare to hesitate? You should be on your knees, bowing to us in gratitude."

"You speak as if this war you hunger for is already won."

"Do you doubt us?"

"It was drow elves who prompted the first King Obould to march upon Mithral Hall," Uryuga replied. "A small band with big promises."

Tos'un shifted uncomfortably. He had been among that quartet of troublemakers, though, of course, Uryuga, who was no older than thirty winters, could hardly know that distant truth.

4

"Gruumsh was displeased with that war?" Tiago asked skeptically. "Truly? Your god was displeased with the outcome, which offered your people a kingdom among the Silver Marches?"

"A kingdom we hold strong, but one that will be destroyed if we fail in our march."

"So you are a coward."

"Uryuga is no coward," the orc said with a snarl.

"Then let us proceed."

"They are seven kingdoms, we are one," Uryuga reminded him.

"You will not be alone," Tiago promised. He pointed back over Uryuga's shoulder, and the orc turned slowly, casting another suspicious glance the Baenre's way before daring to take his eyes off the dangerous drow. As he turned, though, his legs obviously went weak beneath him, for there in the distance beyond this high, windswept bluff circled a pair of beasts to take his breath away.

A pair of white dragons, ridden by frost giants.

They only remained in sight for a few heartbeats, then swooped away along a mountain valley between a pair of distant peaks.

Uryuga swung around, jaw hanging open.

"You will not be alone," Tiago promised. "This is no small band of dark elves stirring trouble. I am Tiago Baenre, noble son of the First House of Menzoberranzan and weapons master of House Do'Urden. The daylight is stolen by our power, to facilitate our march, and we have already spread our tendrils far and wide, a net to catch and enlist the battle-hungry. Dragons are always hungry, and the frost giants of Shining White are eager to finish what their Dame Gerti began a hundred years ago."

Uryuga shook his head, not catching the specifics of that century-old reference, apparently. But it didn't matter. He wasn't so stupid as to miss the implications of the reference: The giants would help in the war, and with a pair of dragons, it seemed.

Dragons!

"Go to King Obould," Tiago ordered. "Tell him that the time has come to find glory for Gruumsh One-Eye."

Uryuga paused for a few heartbeats, but then nodded and started away.

"A convincing illusion," Tiago congratulated Ravel when the trio of drow were alone.

Ravel reverted to his proper drow form and nodded.

"I meant the dragons," Tiago explained. "And with frost giants riding them. Well done."

"It will need to be more than an illusion if we intend to conquer Luruar," Tos'un put in. "This is no minor enemy, with three dwarf citadels, a forest full of elves, and three mighty cities."

"My sister will not fail in this, nor will Archmage Gromph," Ravel assured him, the wizard's tone showing great disdain.

"You have been here too long, son of Armgo," Tiago said dismissively to Tos'un. "You forget the power and reach of Menzoberranzan."

Tos'un nodded and let it go at that. But Tiago was wrong in one thing, he knew. Tos'un hadn't forgotten anything, not from the war between Many-Arrows and Mithral Hall and not from the war before that, when the legendary and godlike Matron Mother Yvonnel Baenre, the great-grandmother of this impudent peacock, had gotten her head cleaved in half by the dwarf king of Mithral Hall.

Saribel glanced nervously at Gromph Baenre. The priestess felt small indeed, surrounded as she was by a trio of blue-skinned behemoths.

Certainly the archmage didn't seem intimidated, and Saribel drew some confidence from that—until she reminded herself that Gromph wasn't her friend. Her ally, perhaps, but she'd never trust this old one enough to think of him as anyone she could rely upon.

The priestess pulled her furred cloak tighter as the mountain winds howled, chilling her even through the magical wards against cold she had placed upon herself.

She glanced at Gromph once more.

He didn't even seem to notice the wind or the cold. He walked at ease—he always walked at ease, she thought, supremely confident, never the slightest hesitation or self-doubt.

She hated him.

"Do you remember their names?" Gromph said then, unexpectedly, shattering Saribel's contemplations.

He had done that on purpose, she knew, as if he was reading her every thought.

"Well?" Gromph added impatiently as the flustered priestess tried to collect herself.

The archmage snickered derisively and shook his head.

"They are the brothers of Thrym, so we are to tell Jarl Fimmel Orelson," Saribel blurted.

"Three of the ten brothers of the frost giant god," Gromph said.

"Yes."

"Do you remember their names?"

"Does it matter?"

Gromph stopped short and turned to stare hard at Saribel. "For tendays now, I have been trying to figure out why Matron Mother Baenre decided to bless Tiago's choice of wife and thus bring you into the House proper. I have tried to justify it as an act to strengthen our ties to the new city of Q'Xorlarrin, to serve as yet another reminder to Matron Mother Zeerith that her world survives at the suffrage of House Baenre." He paused and gave a look and a nod as if that should suffice, but then added, "Truly, young priestess, even that pleasing reality does not seem worth the price of having to suffer your dim-wittedness."

Saribel swallowed hard and worked to keep her lip from quivering, all too keenly aware that Gromph could destroy her with just a thought, at any time.

"Beorjan, Rugmark, and Rolloki," she recited.

"Which is Beorjan?" Gromph asked and Saribel felt her fear rising once more. The giants were all the same size, fully twenty feet tall and with equally impressive girth and musculature. They all wore their hair the same, long and blond, all dressed in similar furs of the same cut, and all carried a gigantic double-bladed axe.

"Well?" Gromph prodded impatiently.

"I cannot tell them apart," a flustered Saribel blurted, and she thought she was uttering her last words with that admission.

And indeed, Gromph stared at her threateningly for a long heartbeat, until one of the giants began to laugh.

"Neither can I," Gromph admitted. "And I grew them." He, too, began to laugh—something Saribel had never thought possible. He clapped her on the shoulder and started them on their way once more.

"I am Rugmark, Fourth Brother of Thrym," the first in line recited.

"I am Beorjan, Seventh Brother of Thrym," said the one on the left behind the two dark elves.

"I am Rolloki, Eldest Brother of Thrym," said the one beside Beorjan.

And they believed their own words. The claims weren't true, of course. These were three giants Gromph had coerced to their cause at Matron Mother Baenre's request. A few spells of growth and permanency, a few sessions with Methil, the illithid imparting new identities to the trio that the slow-minded creatures couldn't help but believe, and the result: three living and walking doppelgangers of the fabled ten brothers of the frost giant deity, Thrym.

And three supremely powerful tools for Matron Mother Baenre to utilize.

"There is the doorway to the frost giant stronghold of Shining White," the archmage said, pointing up the path. "Just ahead and around the bend. Make a worthy entrance and play your role well."

"You are far better at this game than I," Saribel replied. "Are you sure that you will not join—"

"My dear wife of Tiago, consider this your worthiness test for House Baenre," Gromph said. He moved very near her. "You see, I can repair any damage your idiocy causes in the coming negotiation, or I can simply destroy Jarl Fimmel and replace him with a lackey more suitable to my needs if you fail to convince him. So I fear not for my own outcome.

"But you should fear for yours," Gromph added just as Saribel started to visibly relax. "If you fail me in this, well, there are many priestesses who would love to take Tiago Baenre as a husband, I expect, and many Houses more important to me than Xorlarrin, despite your ridiculous delusions of holding an independent city."

The giants around them began to chuckle, and one clapped his massive axe across his open palm.

"It would be unfortunate for you to fail me here, dear Saribel," was all that Gromph added, and he snapped his fingers and was gone, simply vanishing into nothingness, so it seemed.

Saribel Xorlarrin took a deep breath and reminded herself that she was a High Priestess of Lolth and the noble daughter of a powerful drow House—indeed, the princess of a city. These were just frost giants, bulky and powerful, but dim-witted and without magic.

She had set up a spell to teleport her almost instantly back to the cave where the drow had formed their base camp, but that notion now, given Gromph's last warning, didn't seem like such a clever escape should she fail here.

"Enough," she whispered under her breath, and to her three gigantic companions, she motioned forward and said determinedly, "We go."

"It is uncomfortable," Matron Mother Quenthel Baenre said, walking beside Gromph along a mountain pass high up in the Spine of the World.

"You are cold?"

"The light," she corrected. "The vastness of this unceilinged world."

"We are on the edges of Tsabrak's spell," Gromph explained. "It is darker in the midst of the Silver Marches."

"It is a foul place," said Matron Mother Baenre. "I long for home."

Gromph nodded, and couldn't really disagree. He led on with all speed, the appointed meeting place just ahead, around the next bend on a high and snowy plateau. The pair turned that corner and were assailed by high winds and stinging, blowing snow. So furious was the clime, whipping and blowing to near whiteout conditions, that it still took the pair a few more steps to see their counterparts, though those counterparts were huge indeed.

Huge and white.

And dragons.

Lesser beings than the Matron Mother and Archmage of Menzoberranzan would have fallen to their knees at that moment, or run in terror back around the bend.

"Is it not a beautiful day, wizard?" asked the larger of the pair, Arauthator, the Old White Death, one of the greatest of the white dragons of Faerûn.

"They won't think so, Father," said the other, a young male barely half the size of the other. "They are puny and the wind is too cold . . ."

"Silence!" demanded the Old White Death in a voice that shook the mountains around them.

It was hard to note a white dragon blanching, of course, but surely it seemed to Gromph and the matron mother that the young dragon, Aurbangras by name, shrank beneath the weight of that imperial tone.

"It is a beautiful day, to herald a glorious dawn," said Quenthel. "You understand the purpose of our journey here?"

"You will start a war," Arauthator said plainly. "You wish for me to join in."

"I offer you the opportunity, for the glory of your queen," said Quenthel.

The dragon tilted his huge, horned head, regarding her curiously.

"There will be much plunder, Old White Death," the matron mother went on, undeterred. "You will find all that you can carry and more. That is your charge, is it not?"

"What do you know, clever priestess?" the old dragon asked.

"I am the voice of Lolth in Faerûn," she answered with equal weight. "What should I know?"

The dragon growled, mist and icicles blowing from between his jagged teeth.

"We know that the word has gone out to the chromatic wyrms," Gromph interjected, "to gather their hoards of gold and jewels and gems." He paused and eyed the dragon slyly, and cryptically added, "A pile to reach the Nine Hells."

Arauthator rolled back on his haunches at that, his stare seeming as cold as any breath weapon he might produce.

"Yours is not the only queen who seeks to gain," said the matron mother. "The Spider Queen, in her wisdom, has shown me that your goals and mine intersect here in this land of the Silver Marches. There is opportunity here for us both, and in good faith do I come to you. Lend us your power, and share with us our plunder. For your queen and my own."

The dragon made a curious sound, as if a mountain had been inflicted with hiccups, and it took the two drow a short while to realize that Arauthator was laughing.

"I will make many trips south and back to my lair," the dragon informed them. "And each return will be laden with treasure."

"Your value will earn that," the matron mother agreed with a bow.

Gromph, too, wisely bowed, but he never stopped looking at Quenthel as he did. She had told him that this would be an easy acquisition, because of some stirring in the lower planes that held great interest and importance to the chromatic dragons of Toril.

Apparently, she had been correct, and on such a momentous matter as this, that served to remind Gromph yet again that he had helped to create a powerful creature in Quenthel. Not so long ago he had been plotting her demise, but now he would not even dare to think of such a thing.

"That one," Ravel said to Tiago, indicating a burly orc warrior strolling confidently across the encampment, as revealed in the scrying mirror.

"Impressive," Tiago murmured. "He would survive my first attack, perhaps, though I'd have him dead by the second thrust."

Ravel gave the pompous drow warrior a curious look out of the side of his eye, and even shook his head a bit. "If it plays out as we expect, that one—Hartusk—will be our best friend."

"In his small mind."

"That is all that matters," said Ravel. "Hartusk is a traditionalist, a war chief full of bloodlust, and he simmers for battle. Uryuga has whispered to me that Hartusk led several of the raiding bands that have attacked the humans, dwarves, and elves across the region. All secretly, of course, for this King Obould"—he motioned to another figure in the scene, sitting at the middle of a long feast table, bedecked in jewels, a fur-trimmed purple robe and a gaudy crown of beaten gold set with a multitude of semiprecious gemstones "—would tolerate no such activities."

"Uryuga said this pretend king would be trouble," Tiago said. "We offer him powerful alliances and grand conquests, and he shakes his ugly head."

" 'Pretend' king?"

"A king of orcs afraid of battle?" Tiago said with a dismissive snort.

"He is more concerned with the legacy of his namesake and the vision of the first Obould Many-Arrows," Ravel explained. "More than the glory of battle, Obould seeks the power of peace."

"What are these orcs coming to?" Tiago lamented.

"A change of mind," Ravel answered the quip with one of his own. The drow wizard smiled wickedly as another figure moved up near to Obould, and when they were close, the resemblance was unmistakable. "Lorgru, eldest son and named heir of Obould," he said.

"Belween, second bastard son of Berellip," Tiago corrected, for he knew the ruse, and knew too that the real Lorgru lay peacefully asleep in a mossy bed down by the orc docks on the River Surbrin, after hearing the soft and undeniable whispers of drow poison.

Ravel laughed.

In the orc encampment, the fake son of Obould moved up to his presumed father with the king's plate and drink, all properly tested by the court tasters—a precaution that had become critical in the last tenday or so, since the skies had darkened and rumors of—and calls for—war had begun cropping up all around.

The fake Lorgru saluted properly and moved off, and King Obould began to eat, washing down each bite with a great swallow of lousy wine.

"King Obould will be dead before the morning," Ravel said with confidence. "And so will commence the fighting among his many sons, since the heir will be blamed for this murder."

"And none of them will win," said Tiago.

"None will survive, likely," Ravel agreed, his smile showing that he would do his best to make sure of that very outcome. "Hartusk will claim the throne, and who among the orcs would dare oppose the powerful war chief when he is backed by the drow of Menzoberranzan and a legion of frost giants from Shining White?"

Tiago nodded. It had all been so easy. Saribel had not disappointed, and Jarl Fimmel Orelson had called out to other giant clans along the Spine of the World, coaxing them into the cause. They were eager for battle. The mere existence of the vast Kingdom of Many-Arrows had essentially cut the frost giant clans off from their traditional raids on the goodly folk of the Silver Marches, and the orcs certainly didn't have enough plunder or even livestock to make marauding worth the giants' time!

"It is better for us that King Obould did not agree with Uryuga's call," Ravel said, drawing Tiago from his private musing. The weapons master looked at his wizard friend and bade him continue.

"Obould would have ever been a reluctant leader," Ravel explained. "At any opportunity, where a city or citadel offered peace, he would likely have come to accept it as an appropriate feather in his cap and taken their offered treaty. He remains, and ever will, more concerned with his ancestor and the vision of a peaceful Many-Arrows than anything else. But Hartusk? Nay. He wants to taste blood, nothing less."

"But now the kingdom may be split," Tiago warned.

Ravel shook his head. "More orcs agree with Hartusk," he said. "The beasts are tired of the imaginary lines defining their borders. Particularly outside of Dark Arrows Keep, where King Obould keeps those most loyal to him and his cause, the orcs of the kingdom have been whispering about the Obould family living in luxury because of the deal they signed with the dwarves and the other kingdoms. There is deep resentment among the rabble, and there is . . . the hunger for battle, for victory, for blood. Hartusk's message will sound like the clarion horn of Gruumsh himself to many."

"Obould will be quickly forgotten, then," Tiago agreed. "Cast into the soot pile of history to be swept under the uplifted corner of a dirty skin rug, and spoken of with naught but derision."

"A hundred thousand orcs will march, with legions of giants behind them," Ravel said, his red eyes gleaming in the torchlight.

"We'll pull goblins and bugbears and ogres from every hole in the Underdark to bolster their lines," said Tiago, getting caught up in the excitement.

"And darker things," said Ravel, and Tiago laughed.

They had been sent here to start a war.

The drow were very good at that particular task.

PART ONE

UNDER SKIES OF GLOOM

HOW MUCH EASIER IS MY JOURNEY WHEN I KNOW I AM WALKING A ROAD OF righteousness, when I know that my course is true. Without doubt, without hesitation, I stride, longing to get to the intended goal, knowing that when I have arrived there I will have left in my wake a better path than that which I walked.

Such was the case in my road back to Gauntlgrym, to rescue a lost friend. And such was the case leaving that dark place, to Port Llast to return the rescued captives to their homes and proper place.

And so now the road to Longsaddle, where Thibbledorf Pwent will be freed of his curse. Without hesitation, I stride.

What of our intended journey after that, to Mithral Hall, to Many-Arrows . . . to start a war?

Will my steps slow as the excitement of adventuring with my old friends ebbs under the weight of the darkness before us? And if I cannot come to terms with Catti-brie's assertions of orc-kind as irredeemable, or cannot agree with Bruenor's insistence that the war has already begun in the form of orc raids, then what does this discordance portend for the friendship and unity of the Companions of the Hall?

I will not kill on the command of another, not even a friend. Nay, to free my blades, I must be convinced heart and soul that I strike for justice or defense, for a cause worth fighting for, worth dying for, and most importantly, worth killing for.

That is paramount to who I am and to how I have determined to live my life. It is not enough for Bruenor to declare war on the orcs of Many-Arrows and begin its prosecution. I am not a mercenary, for gold coins or for friendship. There must be more.

There must be my agreement with the decision to go to war.

I will enjoy the journey to Mithral Hall, I expect. Surrounding me will be those friends I hold most dear, as we walk the new ways together again. But likely my stride will be a bit tighter, perhaps a bit heavier, the hesitance of conscience pressing down.

Or not conscience, perhaps, but confusion, for surely I am not convinced, yet neither am I unconvinced.

Simply put, I am not sure. Because even though Catti-brie's words, so she says and so I believe, come from Mielikki, they are not yet that which I feel in my own heart—and that must be paramount. Yes, even above the whispers of a goddess.

Some would call that insistence the height of hubris, and pure arrogance, and perhaps they would be right in some regard to place that claim upon me. To me, though, it is not arrogance, but a sense of deep personal responsibility. When first I found the goddess, I did so because the description of Mielikki seemed an apt name for what I carried in my thoughts and heart. Her tenets aligned with my own, so it seemed. Else, she would mean no more to me than any other in the named pantheon of Toril's races.

For I do not want a god to tell me how to behave. I do not want a god to guide my movements and actions—nay. Nor do I want a god's rules to determine that which I know to be right or to outlaw that which I know to be wrong.

For I surely do not need to fear the retribution of a god to keep my path aligned with what is in my heart. Indeed, I see such justifications for behavior as superficial and ultimately dangerous. I am a reasoning being, born with conscience and an understanding of what is right and what is wrong. When I stray from that path, the one most offended is not some unseen and extraworldly deity whose rules and mores are inevitably relayed—and often subjectively interpreted—by mortal priests and priestesses with humanoid failings. Nay, the one most wounded by the digressions of Drizzt Do'Urden is Drizzt Do'Urden.

It can be no other way. I did not hear the call of Mielikki when I fell into the gray-toned company of Artemis Entreri, Dahlia, and the others. It was not the instructions of Mielikki that made me, at long last, turn away from Dahlia on the slopes of Kelvin's Cairn, not unless those instructions are the same ones etched upon my heart and my conscience.

Which, if true, brings me back full circle to the time when I found Mielikki.

At that moment, I did not find a supernatural mother to hold the crossbar to the strings supporting a puppet named Drizzt.

At that moment, I found a name for that which I hold as true. And so, I insist, the goddess is in my heart, and I need look no farther than there to determine my course.

Or perhaps I am just arrogant.

So be it.

—Drizzt Do'Urden

CHAPTER 1

SUMMER OF DISCONTENT

W HAT'RE THEM DOGS UP TO NOW?" KING BROMM OF CITADEL ADBAR asked when the scouts returned with their reports.

"No good, that's for sure as a baby goblin's shiny butt," replied his twin brother and fellow King of Adbar, Harnoth.

The twins looked at each other and nodded grimly—they both understood that this was their first real test as shared kings. They'd had their diplomatic and military squabbles, certainly—a trade negotiation with Citadel Felbarr that had almost come to blows between Bromm and King Emerus's principle negotiator, Parson Glaive; a land dispute with the elves of the Moonwood that had become so hostile the leaders of Silverymoon and Sundabar had ridden north to intervene; even a few skirmishes with the troublesome rogues of Many-Arrows, raiding bands that had included giants and other beasties—but if the scouts were correct in their assessment, then surely the twin Kings of Citadel Adbar had yet presided over nothing of this magnitude.

"Hunnerds, ye say?" Bromm asked Ragnerick Gutpuncher, a young dwarf, but one of considerable scouting experience.

"Many hunnerds," Ragnerick replied. "They're floodin' Upper Surbrin Vale with the stench o' orc, me kings. Pressin' the Moonwood already—been arrows flying out from the boughs and smoke's rising into the dark sky."

Those last three words rang ominously in the hall, for the implications of the eternal night sky locked over the Silver Marches were hard to ignore.

"They'll be pressin' Mithral Hall, to be sure," said Bromm.

"We got to get word fast to Emerus and Connerad," his brother agreed.

"Long way to Mithral Hall," Bromm lamented, and Harnoth couldn't disagree. The three dwarf citadels of Luruar were located roughly in a line, Adbar southwest to Felbarr, then an equal distance southwest from there to Mithral Hall, with most of the journey just south of the forested crescent known as the Glimmerwood. From one citadel to the next was a march of more than a hundred miles, at least a tenday's hike—likely twice that given the broken terrain. The three citadels were also connected underground, through tunnels of the upper Underdark, but even along those routes, any march would be long and difficult.

"We got to go," Harnoth reasoned. "We can't be sittin' here with our kin facing a fight—and might be that we're th'only ones knowing."

"Nah, Connerad's already knowing, I'm thinkin'," said Bromm. "He's an army o' orcs sitting on his north porch. He's knowin'."

"But we got to know what he's needin'," Harnoth said and Bromm nodded. "I'll take a legion through the tunnels to Felbarr, and if we're needed, we'll go on to Mithral Hall, then."

"Underdark," Bromm noted grimly. "We ain't been down there in years, excepting the underground way to Sundabar. Best make it a big legion."

"And yerself'll lock down Adbar," Harnoth agreed, nodding.

"Aye, she's already done, and might that I'll go out and have a better look, and might just chase them orcs from the Glimmerwood's edge. Next time we're arguin' with them elves over some land, we'll not be letting them forget our help."

"Hunnerds," Harnoth said grimly.

"Bah, just orcs," Bromm retorted and waved his hand dismissively. "Might that we'll skin 'em and use 'em to build soft roads from Adbar to Felbarr and all the way to Mithral Hall."

King Harnoth gave a hearty laugh at that, but he gradually dismissed the absurdity of the claim and allowed himself to picture just such a road.

"Ready to rumble!" General Dagnabbet, daughter and namesake of Dagnabbit, granddaughter of the great General Dagna, announced to King Connerad. They stood on a high peak north of Mithral Hall, looking down on the Upper Surbrin Vale, the mighty river dull and flat under the dark sky and the tall evergreens of the Moonwood portion of the long Glimmerwood dark in the northeast.

"Gutbusters're itchin' to hit something, me king!" cried Bungalow Thump, who led the famed Gutbuster Brigade as Connerad's personal bodyguard. All around the group came a chorus of cheers.

But King Connerad was shaking his head with every call for action. He looked at the swarm of orcs on the field far below. Something felt wrong.

The orc forces, opposing each other, rolled like swarms of bees, mingling in a great black cloud that turned the vale as dark as the sky above.

"Now, me king," Bungalow Thump pleaded. "The fools're fighting each other. We'll roll 'em into the dirt by the hunnerd."

He moved up beside Connerad to continue, but Dagnabbet intercepted him and eased him back.

"What're ye thinkin'?" the dwarf lass asked.

"What's yerself thinking?" Connerad asked of his general, who was soon to take command of Mithral Hall's garrison, by all accounts.

"I'm thinkin' that's been too long since me axe's chopped an orc," Dagnabbet replied with a sly grin.

Connerad managed a nod, but he was far from full agreement with the implications of the general's desire. He couldn't shake the feeling that something here was not as it seemed.

"We got to go soon," Bungalow Thump said. "Long run to the vale."

King Connerad looked to Dagnabbet and then to Bungalow Thump, and the eager expressions coming back at him made him worry that he was being too cautious here. Was he failing as a leader out of his own timidity? Was he seeing what he wanted to see so that he could avoid a risk?

Growling at his own weakness, the order to charge down to the vale almost left his mouth—almost, but Connerad bit it back and forced himself to focus more clearly on the chaos before him, and in that moment of clarity came his answer.

For the battle in the Upper Surbrin Vale, orc against orc, didn't seem to him to be a battle at all.

"Back to the hall," he said, his voice barely above a whisper, lost as it was in the midst of his gasp.

"Eh?" asked Bungalow Thump.

"Me king?" General Dagnabbet added.

"What're ye thinkin'?" Bungalow Thump demanded.

"I'm thinkin' that me king's smellin' a rat," Dagnabbet answered.

"I asked what yerself was thinkin'," Connerad said to Dagnabbet. "And now I ask ye again." He pointed down to the swirling morass of tiny orc forms below them.

Dagnabbet stepped out on the ledge before Connerad and stared hard at the mingling armies battling far below.

"They got no discipline," she said almost immediately. "Just a mob."

"Aye, seeing the same," said Connerad.

Dagnabbet spent a long while looking at the young King of Mithral Hall.

"Well?" an impatient Bungalow Thump asked.

A smile, somewhat resigned, perhaps, but also congratulatory, crossed Dagnabbet's face, and she nodded in deference to Connerad, her king, and replied to him and to Bungalow Thump, "Orcs o' Dark Arrow Keep fight better'n that."

"Eh?" the battlerager asked.

"Aye," Connerad agreed.

"They're thinking to lure us out," said Dagnabbet.

"Well, let's oblige 'em then!" Bungalow Thump cried, eliciting wild cheers from his Gutbuster Brigade.

"Nah," Connerad said, shaking his head. "I ain't seeing it." He turned to Dagnabbet. "Post a line o' lookouts, but we're back to the hall, I say."

"Me king!" Bungalow Thump cried in dismay.

Of course the battle-lusting Thump was blustering and sputtering, and Connerad didn't bother answering, knowing full well that the Gutbusters were, above all else, fiercely loyal. Connerad moved straight for the long stair that would bring him to the lower plateau just above Keeper's Dale where his army waited, waving his hand for Dagnabbet and the others to follow. From there, they would take secret doors that led to the descending tunnels that would take them back into the fortress of Mithral Hall.

It took a long while to descend those two thousand stairs, and the warning cries from the northeast beat Connerad's group to the bottom.

"Orcs! Orcs!" they heard with many stairs still before them. "Hunnerds, thousands."

King Connerad found it hard to breathe. He was not battle-hardened in this leadership role, and had seen little action that involved responsibility for anyone other than himself, but he knew then that he had narrowly avoided a huge error—one that would have left Mithral Hall reeling under the weight of staggering losses!

"Can't be!" General Dagnabbet cried. "Vale's too far!"

"A third orc army," Connerad replied. "The swinging door to close us into their box if we'd've gone out to the fake fight in the vale."

"Well, a dead third army then," declared Bungalow Thump, and he and his boys began bounding down the steps past Connerad, taking them three at a time despite the obvious peril along the steep stairway.

Connerad stopped and grabbed both railings, stretching out his arms and thus bottlenecking those still behind him. His thoughts whirled, imagining the trails back around the mountain to the Upper Surbrin Vale, estimating the time for such a march—a forced and fast march that had already almost assuredly begun, he realized.

"No!" he shouted to all those around him, particularly aiming his cry at Bungalow Thump and the rambling troupe of Gutbusters. "To the hall and shut the durned doors, I say!"

"Me king!" came the predictable cry of disappointment from Thump and his ferocious boys, all in unison.

"Them orcs're coming, all o' them," Connerad said to Dagnabbet behind him on the stairs. "Tens o' thousands."

The dwarf lass nodded grimly. He could see that she wanted to disagree with him, that she wanted nothing more than to go out and kill some orcs. But she couldn't and for a moment, he feared that it was simply because she could not bring herself to disagree with him. Like her father and grandfather before her, Dagnabbet was a loyal soldier first and foremost.

"If we could be done with this bunch and get inside, I'd be tellin' ye to go to the fight," she said as if reading his thoughts and wanting to put his concerns to rest. "But this group'll hold us down. That's their job, I'm guessin'. They'll come on a'roarin', but they'll fade back in the middle o' the line, they will. Again and again, just out o' reach. Aye, and we'll keep chasing and choppin', and oh, but we'll put more'n a few to their deaths, don't ye doubt."

"And then th'other two armies'll fall on us and we won't ne'er make our halls alive," King Connerad added with a nod.

Dagnabbet patted him on the shoulder. "Ye done the right call, me king, and twice," she said.

More cries rang out in the northwest, warning of approaching orcs.

"We ain't there yet," said Connerad, and he started down the stair with all speed. As he and the others neared the bottom, with perhaps a hundred stairs to go, they got their first glimpse of that third orc force, a black swarm sweeping around the rocky foothills.

"Worgs," Dagnabbet breathed, for a cavalry legion led the orc charge, huge orcs on ferocious dire wolves. When they came in sight of the dwarf army settled on the plateau, they blew their off-key horns and chanted for Gruumsh—and didn't slow in the least, roaring ahead and as eager for a fight as any Gutbuster.

Connerad thought to yell out for Bungalow Thump, but he realized that he needn't bother. Thump and his boys, too, had seen the orcs approach, and nothing the king might say would have made any difference at that point. The battle was about to be joined, and the Gutbuster Brigade, above all others, knew their place in such a fight. As one, they ran, leaped, and tumbled down the stairs, bouncing onto the plateau and charging ahead. Bungalow Thump cried out to the battle commanders of the garrison, ordering them to fall back, and those commanders readily complied, for they, too, knew the place of the Gutbusters—a place in the forefront, as the leading worg riders quickly and painfully learned. Cavalry, shock troops, depended on their ferocity and straightforward aggression to scatter lines and terrify enemies out of defensive positions. But for the famed Gutbuster Brigade of Mithral Hall, such a tactic inspired nothing but an even more ferocious response.

And with the Gutbuster Brigade fronting the line, the dwarf cross-bowmen neither flinched nor retreated, and they got their volley into the air just before the thunderous collision.

The worg riders were stopped cold by that wall of quarrels, and then by leaping dwarves in battle-ridged armor.

For the Battlehammers, the fight had started on a high note indeed. The pounding spiked fists of Gutbusters drew orc grunts and worg yelps. And that cavalry legion had gotten too far out in front of the charging infantry of orcs coming behind.

The army of Mithral Hall fell over them and slaughtered them, and cheers and calls for orc blood chased King Connerad down the stairs.

And might have chased him all the way out to the battle, but General Dagnabbet was right there behind him, whispering in his ear, and now it was she who urged greater caution.

Connerad at last leaped off the stairs to the plateau and ran with all speed to his garrison commanders, calling out orders for tight ranks. He ran past the back of the formation and shouted for those in the rear to begin their turn immediately for the hall.

"Go and get in and get clear o' the doors," he commanded. "Clear run to the halls for all."

Many disappointed looks came back at him—he would have been disappointed at any other reaction—but the dwarves did not argue with their king. Still cheering their brethren who had locked up with the leading orcs, the ranks at the back of the formation began their swift and orderly retreat.

King Connerad pulled up and whirled around. "Get to the door," he ordered Dagnabbet.

The dwarf warrior gasped in disbelief.

"I need ye there," Connerad told her. "We'll get all stuck shoulder to shoulder, and them that don't get in are to be murdered to death. Ye go and keep 'em movin'. Every one ye get in is one ye're saving."

Dagnabbet couldn't hide her disappointment and just shook her head.

Connerad leaped into her and grabbed her roughly by the collar. "Ye think any others'll hold the respect o' Dagnabbet?" he yelled in her face. "Ye think I can send an errand-dwarf and them damned doors'll stay cleared, and them that's running away—and what dwarf's wantin' to run away?—won't be stopping to look back? I need ye, girl, more'n e'er before."

Dagnabbet straightened and composed herself fully. "Aye, me king!' she said crisply. "But don't ye let yerself stay out there too long and get yerself killed to death. Ye're needin' me, and I'll do me part, but don't ye let yerself forget that Mithral Hall's needing yerself. More now than e'er if them orcs mean to stay about."

Connerad nodded and turned to go, but Dagnabbet grabbed him by the shoulder and pulled him around.

"Don't ye get yerself killed," she implored him, and she gave him a kiss for luck.

For luck and for more than that, they both realized to their mutual surprise.

Then both ran off, in opposite directions, Dagnabbet yelling orders to various dwarves to form guiding lines to the doors and Connerad calling his battle commanders together. It wasn't until he neared the front of the skirmish, that he was able to gain a wider view of the sloping pass that rounded the mountain, and when he saw that, the dwarf king had to force himself to breathe once more.

The orc armies out in the Upper Surbrin Vale had been large, but this force was larger still, and rumbling down among the swarms of orcs were huge blue-skinned behemoths, a full legion of frost giants.

Any fantasies Connerad might have had of standing their ground washed away in the face of that reality. If he could muster every dwarf of Mithral Hall out onto this field, fully armed and armored for battle, with a full complement of heavy war weapons—ballistae and catapults—and preset in proper formations, they simply could not prevail in this fight, not even if the two orc armies out in the Upper Surbrin Vale did not come in to join their kin and kind.

Connerad Brawnanvil had never seen so many orcs.

They blackened the trail and turned the entire side of the mountain into something resembling a writhing, amorphous beast.

Many times throughout that day, King Connerad reminded himself to remain calm, to lead with a steady hand. He didn't flinch when one of his battle commanders standing right beside him was crushed by a giant boulder. He suppressed his wail of anguish when Bungalow Thump and a band of Gutbusters fell amid a sea of orcs.

And he kept them moving, all of them, an orderly procession, one line breaking back and reforming as the next line broke and retreated behind them. With each step of the staggered retreat, fewer dwarves remained alive to take the next step, but for every downed dwarf, several orcs lay writhing and dying.

At one dark moment, it seemed to Connerad as if all was surely lost, for on came the giants, swatting orcs out before them as they bore down on the hated dwarves.

"Brace and go for the knees, boys!" he cried, and the dwarves cheered, and then all the louder as a volley of ballista bolts hummed through the air above their heads. Giants staggered, giants fell, and those behind the first line began a hasty retreat.

A shocked King Connerad spun around and spotted Dagnabbet immediately.

Beautiful and fierce Dagnabbet. Brave and noble and loyal Dagnabbet.

The line of dwarves continued into the hall through the doors in swift and orderly fashion, and somehow, even among that great responsibility, Dagnabbet had managed to get a quartet of spear-throwing ballistae out from the halls, and for just such an occasion as this, when the giants came on.

Mithral Hall lost three score brave dwarves that day, with thrice that number crawling back in with grievous wounds, including Bungalow Thump, who had somehow survived that swarm.

But they were secure behind their fortified doors now, and the moment of surprise had passed.

And hundreds of orcs and a trio of giants lay dead outside that northern door.

"Ye done good," Dagnabbet told him when the leaders of the hall convened in the war room. "Ye done King Bruenor proud."

Coming from the daughter of Dagnabbit, the granddaughter of the legendary Dagna, King Connerad knew that to be no small compliment.

He took it in stride, though, and knew that his trials were just beginning.

A great army of orcs was even then camping upon his doorstep.

CHAPTER 2

THE LINE BETWEEN LIFE AND DEATH

Drizzt could not get past the reality of where they'd ended up: a cave called Stonecutter's Solace.

A cave.

Out from the open front, which had only recently been widened by a team of determined masons, Drizzt could see the charred remains of the old tavern, its great hearth sitting lonely in the open air—a cairn, a testament to what had been and what was no more. The lowering sun behind it seemed fitting, Drizzt thought.

As he sat there recalling his adventures in this city, battling sea devils and helping the hardy townsfolk strengthen their borders and secure their beaches, Drizzt couldn't look on that hearth without a deep feeling of regret and a profound sense of loss. Stonecutter's Solace had been the common room to the whole of the city of Port Llast in the days of the struggle against the sahuagin. War parties had formed there to rush to the wall to battle the attacking monsters and the wounded had been brought there to be tended to by healers and clerics—indeed, Drizzt had helped hold down one grievously wounded man on a table while Ambergris saved his life with her divine spells. To the people of Port Llast in those desperate days, Stonecutter's Solace had been the promise of a better future.

And now it was gone, dead, burned to near-nothingness by the drow attackers, who had come, so it seemed, in search of Drizzt.

That fact echoed in Drizzt's thoughts, bringing him across the decades and the miles to when the drow had returned for him in Mithral Hall. And more recently, a band led by Tiago had gone to Icewind Dale in their hunt for him and in pursuit of a balor—a demon who chased Drizzt himself.

Drizzt glanced around at his companions, his gaze settling on Regis, who was looking quite debonair in his shining blue beret and fine cloak. Drizzt and the others often made light of the fact that Regis always seemed to be coming to them with trouble close behind. Long ago, working for one of the pashas of Calimport, whom Regis had wronged, Artemis Entreri had chased the halfling to Icewind Dale. And only recently, the lich Ebonsoul, pursuing Regis, had caught the companions on the road west of Longsaddle.

Looking out at the ruins of Stonecutter's Solace, considering the tumultuous waters that always seemed to roil in his own wake, Drizzt couldn't help but think that he, not Regis, should be the one with the reputation of towing trouble in his wake.

The drow ranger smiled as he considered that truth. In his younger days, such dark thoughts would have weighed heavily upon his shoulders, the anvil of guilt bending his mouth into a frown.

Now he knew better. Now, finally, Drizzt understood that the world was a wider place, and a dangerous place regardless of his chosen path—and indeed, for those who knew him as friend and ally, surely a more dangerous place without him. The dark elves needed no specific reason to invade any town, and surely any major demon set loose to walk the world of mortal men would wreak chaos whether in pursuit of Drizzt or not.

This was not about him. The destruction of Stonecutter's Solace was not upon his shoulders. Likely the place, the whole town, would have been abandoned long ago had not Drizzt and his former companions, Entreri and Dahlia and the others, driven the sahuagin back into the sea.

He thought of that other group now and glanced once more, one by one, to the Companions of the Hall. In many ways, the comparisons were quite apparent. Both this adventuring troupe and the last surrounding Drizzt could claim a competence in battle that few in the Realms could match.

But those comparisons ended there, at a very superficial level. His heart felt full. Beyond the ability to wield a sword or a spell, or even to battle side-by-side in true, devastating harmony, this group now beside him could not be more different than Entreri, Dahlia, and the others.

He laughed aloud as he thought of Afafrenfere and Ambergris among these very people, in the old Stonecutter's Solace. The dwarf had set the monk up as a prizefighter, and then collected bags of coins betting on Afafrenfere, who surely did not appear formidable. But with his martial training, focusing on battles with open hands, the tall and lanky Afafrenfere could easily defeat men much larger and stronger than he.

"What're ye seein' in yer thoughts, elf?" Bruenor asked. "And what's so durned funny?"

Drizzt just shook his head, never looking at Bruenor, for his gaze had drifted across the wide cave to Wulfgar. If Ambergris and Afafrenfere had come to this place now to set up their betting game, would Wulfgar accept the challenge?

And if he did, if Wulfgar squared up against the skilled monk, upon which combatant might Drizzt wisely place his own bet?

"Well?" Bruenor prompted.

"Wulfgar," Drizzt decided, answering himself and not the dwarf, and he nodded as he played out the fighting his mind. Even with Afafrenfere's undeniable skills, Drizzt had seen too much of Wulfgar's sheer power to ever bet against him.

"Eh?" the perplexed dwarf asked.

Drizzt just laughed again. How could he not? Even with the grim realities that had hit Port Llast so recently, no lament could hold, not when surrounded by the spirit of the town, the hardy folk full of life and cheer and celebration this night for the return of several citizens they had thought forever lost to the drow raiders.

More and more of the folk came into the cave as word of the rescue— and the heroic rescuers—spread far and wide.

"This was a mine?" Regis asked, sitting on the other side of Catti-brie from Drizzt.

"Quarry," Bruenor corrected, looking at the walls of the place and the sheer cuts. "Or might've been a bit o' both," he added, noting one snaking tunnel at the back of the wide chamber.

A great cheer rose up at the other side of this largest room, and all eyes turned there, to see Wulfgar downing a large flagon of foamy beer, prodded on by the roars of the patrons. The barbarian held up one arm and flexed, his muscles standing as tall and as hard as any rock a dwarven pick had ever chipped.

The cheers cascaded around and back to the other four heroes, a trio of patrons coming their way, hands full of flagons, faces full of smiles. They would celebrate throughout the night, so the town leaders had declared.

"Ambergris will be sorry that she didn't come north with us just a bit longer," Regis remarked, taking an offered flagon.

"She survived, then?" came a raspy voice from the side.

The companions turned to see a most remarkable creature: half-elf, half-tiefling, dressed in dark robes and carrying a staff made of bone with a tiny humanoid skull set atop it. Broken and twisted, the man seemed quite infirm at first glance. But that impression was quickly lost by any who could recognize the cut of his clothing and the clear power resonating in that staff. His skinny shoulders sat somewhat askew, left side back from the right, and with his left arm hanging limp behind him, almost like a tail that had sprung from his high back.

Drizzt's eyes popped open wide and he felt as if he were about to tumble from his chair.

"Effron?" the perceptive Regis and Catti-brie asked of the drow in unison.

Drizzt collected himself and sprang from the chair. "Effron!" he cried and rushed to clasp hands with the warlock. Drizzt pulled him in from there for a hug, one the tiefling—a former cellmate of Drizzt's in the home of Draygo Quick—gladly reciprocated.

"I had thought you dead."

"Very near," Effron said, pulling back to arms' length. "Filthy dr . . ." he paused and swallowed hard, then finished by altering the word to: "driders."

Drizzt nodded and let it go. Given the circumstances, had Effron said "drow," Drizzt would have agreed.

"I feared the same for you," Effron said. "We went in search of you on the mountainside in Icewind Dale, but we could not find your trail."

"For the better, in the end," said Drizzt.

Effron moved in a bit closer, putting his mouth near Drizzt's ear. "I am sorry for the way it ended between us all," he whispered, referring to that dark night on Kelvin's Cairn. "We even went to the dwarves in search of you, but they had heard no word."

"Against your mother's wishes, no doubt," Drizzt said, beginning with a smile, but one that fast faded as he remembered the end of Dahlia, Effron's mother.

Drizzt pulled back from him, and again offered a wide smile. He motioned to Wulfgar's empty seat at the table and bade Effron to sit.

"I have a lot to tell you," Drizzt said.

Effron hesitated, then said, "Tell me of my mother."

And a cloud passed over Drizzt's face, enough so that Effron had heard, at that moment, all he needed. Appearing unsteady on his feet, the tiefling warlock slipped into the chair.

Drizzt introduced his companions, even calling Wulfgar back to the table.

"This is Catti-brie?" Effron asked at one point. "Truly?"

"From the same forest as that in which we slept," Drizzt tried to explain. "Returned to the world, as were we, from a long slumber."

Effron eyed the woman up and down, his expression revealing his displeasure no matter how hard he tried to hide it. "You found your ghost," he stated rather dryly to Drizzt.

Catti-brie nodded. Drizzt could see the lump in her throat, for she knew that they—and more pointedly, that she—had to be honest here, and that the honest retelling of their recent adventures was certainly going to hurt this young warlock profoundly.

"Ambergris is alive, yes, and with Afafrenfere on the road south and then northeast across the inland sea," Drizzt explained as he recounted the recent journey to Gauntlgrym. "Entreri, too, survived the drow attack, but did not return with us. He may still be in Gauntlgrym for all we know, but I do not doubt that he's alive still— on his guard, few are more capable than Artemis Entreri."

"But they killed my mother," Effron said.

Drizzt sighed and started to reply, but Catti-brie interjected, "No," rather sharply, turning all eyes her way.

"I did," she admitted.

Now it was Effron who looked like he might fall off his chair, and beside him, Drizzt held his breath, expecting an explosion.

"They did worse than kill her," Drizzt tried to explain. "They told her you were dead. By Entreri's estimation, they broke her heart, and her spirit. She attacked Catti-brie—"

"I didn't want to kill her," Catti-brie said. "I didn't want to fight her at all. Dahlia was not my ene—"

"She was Drizzt's lover," Effron said, as if that point alone belied the woman's claims.

But Catti-brie shrugged as if that hardly mattered, and indeed, it didn't, not to her and not in any rational sense. "Was I to be jealous when my husband thought me a hundred years dead—indeed, when I had been a hundred years dead?"

Effron stared at her hard. He started to talk once or twice, as though fumbling over both the specific words and the tone he intended. But then, finally, he seemed to relax a bit.

"She was not my enemy," Catti-brie said again. "Never that. But it was not simply Dahlia I battled in the fire chamber of Gauntlgrym. She commanded jade spiders. She fought with a demonic eye possessed of Lady Lolth's spirit, while I was filled with the power of Mielikki. We were pawns of two goddesses—that much is clear to me. And in that event, Effron, I say to you with all confidence that your mother is freed now from a curse worse than death at my hands."

"The line between life and death," Effron muttered and lowered his eyes, and a single tear made its way down the taut skin of his thin cheek. "So fine, it seems, and so many times have those around me walked it of late."

"Given yer skull-headed staff and what th' elf's been sayin' about ye, ye should be knowin' that better'n most," Bruenor interjected.

Effron looked up at him and managed a self-deprecating shrug.

"They told her that I was dead?" he asked Drizzt.

The drow nodded solemnly.

"Then she died without hope," Effron lamented. "She had lost you . . ." He paused and gave a half-hearted chortle in Catti-brie's general direction. "Lost you to her. And then I was taken from her, so she thought—and I know well that pain. When we believed her lost to us in the home of Draygo Quick, and taken from me so soon after our reconciliation . . ." He sighed and could not continue.

"But surely, like these folk celebrating about us, the outcome of the drow attack on Port Llast is better than was expected," Regis interjected. "Many of those you thought dead are not, yes?"

Effron stared at him blankly, clearly unable to bring himself to that positive way of looking at the situation. Indeed, the tiefling seemed incredulous at that moment, and Regis shifted back in his seat.

Effron turned fast to Drizzt, as if an idea had come to him. "Where are Afafrenfere and Amber bound? South and then across the inland sea, you said. On the road to Suzail then?"

"Heading for the Bloodstone Lands and the kingdom of Damara," Drizzt answered. "To Afafrenfere's former home in the Monastery of the Yellow Rose, so they said. But it's a long and perilous journey, with many side roads, no doubt."

Effron planted his staff firmly beside his chair and pulled himself up quickly. "Then I bid you—"

"Come with us," Drizzt blurted, and the four others around the table widened their eyes at that unexpected remark.

"We seek the truth in a dangerous land," Drizzt explained. "We fear our blades may be needed, with the fate of many kingdoms in the balance."

Effron paused and looked around at the Companions of the Hall, as if taking a measure of each. He motioned to Drizzt and moved aside so the two of them could speak in private.

"My way of magic will not prove appealing to these companions of yours," he said when they were alone.

"They're a tolerant group," Drizzt assured him lightheartedly.

But Effron shook his head through every word. "Better that I find the monk and the dwarf, or that I walk my own road," he decided. "We are cut from different cloth, Drizzt Do'Urden, and so I bid you farewell. I do not doubt that our paths will cross again, and when they do, in whatever circumstance, know that I am not your enemy—never your enemy."

"And my friends?" Drizzt asked with clear skepticism, and he got right to the point when he added, "And Catti-brie?"

Effron's ensuing pause was telling, for of course it was Catti-brie's presence, and recent history, that had turned him away from the party. He hadn't carried his anger forward at that moment, and Drizzt could see that he was trying, at least, to accept her explanation.

But clearly it tasted as bitter oil.

"I believe her tale," Effron said at last.

Drizzt nodded, not because he was convinced, or even convinced that Effron believed what he had just proclaimed, but because Drizzt knew that it was the most the young warlock could emotionally offer at that painful time.

"Better that I go with Afafrenfere and Ambergris," Effron said quietly, and Drizzt didn't disagree. He patted Effron on the shoulder and gave him another hug.

"Well met, well parted, and well met again, on another road on another day," Drizzt said.

Effron nodded and left the cave serving as Stonecutter's Solace, and soon after, left Port Llast along the southern road.

"And how many nights do ye think it'll be taking him to avenge his Ma?" Bruenor asked when Drizzt returned to the table. The dwarf gave a great and disgusted shake of his hairy head.

"Drizzt asked him along to better watch over him," Regis said to the dwarf.

"Ah, but did ye, elf?"

Drizzt didn't answer. He slid back into his seat and sat exchanging stares with Catti-brie.

"Better that Effron goes with the others," she said quietly, and Drizzt nodded. "That pain is fresh—how could it not be? Perhaps as time passes, he'll find a better way to see it all."

"Well, elf?" Bruenor demanded and Drizzt looked at him curiously.

"Did ye ask him along to better look over him, then?"

Drizzt considered the words, and more pointedly, the dwarf's accusing tone, for a few heartbeats, then replied. "I asked him along because he is a friend."

"A friend who's Ma me girl killed," the dwarf retorted. "And one who's knowin' it!"

"So are we to look over our shoulder for that one?" Wulfgar asked.

"No," Drizzt blurted loudly, without hesitation and with all confidence. The four others leaned back at the unexpected outburst.

"No," the drow repeated more softly. He paused to consider his reaction, and thought back to the times he had spent with Effron and the others, and in Dahlia's arms. It was a complicated relationship between all of them—hadn't he first met Ambergris and Afafrenfere when they were trying to capture or even murder him and Dahlia, after all? In a brutal and bloody battle in which Drizzt had killed Afafrenfere's beloved fellow monk, Parbid?

But Afafrenfere had forgiven him.

Aye, that was the thing about his previous companions, Drizzt understood then. They lived on the edge of disaster and on the edge of morality, but to a one, Entreri included, they had always accepted the responsibility of their actions. As Afafrenfere had come to accept that Drizzt's defeat of Parbid had been simply an act of self-defense, and in a fight Parbid, Afafrenfere, and the other mercenaries of Cavus Dun had initiated. Afafrenfere had come to move past his anger and accept Drizzt as a trusted companion.

It would be the same with Effron, Drizzt was certain. The young tiefling who had known so much pain had surely kept his sense of justice about him. He wouldn't join them now because the wound was fresh, and no doubt every time he looked upon Catti-brie's fair face, he would be reminded of his dead mother.

Perhaps it would be different on another day, on another road, when the wounds had healed.

"You have met four of my companions," Drizzt said. "Let me tell you about them, and of Dahlia."

"I met her, too," Catti-brie reminded him.

"And I," said Wulfgar, "when your band of merry murderers traveled through the encampment of my people just before the spring equinox."

"Aye, and I knowed the crazy elf lass from before, or have ye forgotten that?" Bruenor insisted.

"Let me tell you more, then," Drizzt replied with a smile.

"I know Artemis Entreri better than you," Regis said. "I need hear no more about him."

But Drizzt was shaking his head. "You knew the man Artemis Entreri once was," he explained, and Regis rolled his eyes, and Catti-brie, who had once been captured by the assassin, didn't seem very convinced, either.

"This very town, Port Llast, exists today because of the efforts of those companions fighting beside me. Together we drove the sea devils from the shore, and together we strengthened the town in heart and arms. Speak the name of any of my former companions to any in Port Llast and you will hear a huzzah in response."

"Even after the drow came for them and laid waste to much of the town?" Catti-brie asked.

"Yes," Drizzt insisted. "We did well here, and we did good. Even Entreri, and without compensation." Drizzt was smiling—he couldn't help it—and nodding as he spoke.

"Might that yerself should be goin' to find them all, eh elf?" said Bruenor. "Seems ye're not needing us no more, then."

"I am quite content with my present company," Drizzt assured him.

"Then go get the skinny, twisted boy back, and we'll send Rumblebelly for the dwarf and monk and we'll all go find Entreri. With them four aside ye, ye'll clear Obould's dogs from the Silver Marches all on yer own, so ye're sounding."

"They were formidable, I'll not deny that," Drizzt replied against the biting sarcasm.

"Bah!" Bruenor snorted and threw up his arms, then swung around and called for the barkeep. When he couldn't get the man's attention, he hoisted his shield and reached behind it and brought forth a magical mug of hearty ale.

Catti-brie laughed, and Wulfgar pulled himself up, promising to go and fetch another round of drinks. "So we can toast your old companions," he said with a sly wink at the drow, the tension, what little there ever was, mostly broken.

Drizzt looked to Regis, though, and saw the halfling staring at him hard. No, not at him, he realized. Not really. Regis was looking past him, past them all, lost inside his own thoughts.

And indeed, Drizzt's story had hit the halfling hard, for Regis, too, had known powerful traveling companions, and before that, had known much more.

Regis almost wished they would send him after Ambergris and Afafrenfere as Bruenor had joked. What might happen if he rode the Trade Way once more and found himself beside Doregardo and the Grinning Ponies?

What might happen if he rode all the way to Cormyr and the banks of the Sea of Fallen Stars?

Looking across those waters, Regis's mind's eye would surely see House Topolino, and in his heart, he would be looking upon Donnola again. An inadvertent smile widened on his cherubic face, lifting the edges of his stylish mustache, as he thought of their sparring match, which had led them into each other's arms to tumble to the floor in passion.

"Regis?" he heard from afar, and he focused his eyes to see Drizzt and Catti-brie staring at him with curious expressions.

Regis just replied to that with a wistful smile, and said to Drizzt, "If you would trust them to ride with us, then so would I. Even the warlock."

And then the halfling rose and tipped his fashionable beret to the others and took his leave, wandering out of Stonecutter's Solace and onto the streets of Port Llast. The sun had dipped below the western horizon by then and the stars were just coming into view, and back to the east, a bright moon was rising.

Regis wondered if Donnola Topolino was looking upon that moon, as well. Was she remembering? Was she feeling his arms around her again, as he was surely feeling hers?

"We will watch the moonrise together again, my love," the halfling vowed, and started back to the cave that served as an inn.

But he stopped long before he got back to Stonecutter's Solace. "Not tonight," he whispered and turned away. This night wasn't for the Companions of the Hall, he decided. This night wasn't for Regis, but for Spider, the lad he had been in Aglarond.

Spider Parrafin climbed atop a nearby roof—coincidentally the same structure Artemis Entreri had scaled in the fight with the drow in Port Llast—and sat down on the edge, his feet dangling in the cool ocean air.

He didn't know it, but tucked under the eaves within his reach was a very special jeweled dagger, an assassin's weapon that could steal the very life force from a victim.

A dagger Regis knew all too well from his previous life, for in the hands of Artemis Entreri, it had once taken his finger . . .

CHAPTER 3

THE TEARS OF TARSAKH

Lorgru, Lorgru," Sinnafein lamented as she rested in a hidden tree house far up in a towering evergreen, out of breath and rubbing her aching legs. Normally the nimble elf would have had no trouble scaling the tree to this lookout perch, but she had been grievously wounded, her legs slashed by her husband.

Wounded and left to be slaughtered by a horde of angry orcs.

But that had not come to pass. Among that group had been Lorgru, the son of King Obould and likely heir to the throne of Many-Arrows. Very much an orc, Lorgru had wanted to kill her. She and her drow husband Tos'un had cut a swath of devastation through his fellow orcs of Many-Arrows as they had frantically pursued their daughter.

Still, and over the loud objections of many of his warriors, Lorgru had seen the benefits of keeping Sinnafein alive, and so had traded her back to her people in the Moonwood, the westernmost expanse of the great Glimmerwood, in exchange for a public apology, a promise of good will, and a fair amount of gold.

That had been but a few tendays ago, and now, for some reason Sinnafein could not decipher, Lorgru's mercy and subsequent actions seemed to make no sense at all. The orc armies had come to the borders of the Moonwood. They had crossed the Surbrin on several occasions, striking into the elven lands, felling great trees and starting fires.

And now this, Sinnafein lamented as she looked out from the eastern edge of the elven lands to the Cold Vale. Here, too, the orcs had marched, a sizable force milling about the foothills of the Rauvin Mountains. It made no sense. This seemed far beyond any excursion to test the defenses of the area, and certainly the swarms of orcs were too large to be some fringe tribe. Such a march as this had taken planning and coordination, and likely with battle plans set even before Sinnafein had found the bite of Tos'un's sword.

"They are Many-Arrow orcs," the fine young scout Myriel confirmed, scrambling up beside Sinnafein.

The elf leader winced at the news—she had been hoping that her scouts would determine this to be another tribe, instead of a warning sign that war with the vast orc kingdom had come in full. "You are certain?"

"There is no doubt, Lady," Myriel replied. "Some carry banners of Dark Arrow Keep. There was some confusion at first among our scouts, for we heard the name of King Obould not at all in those moments when we were close enough to discern their common prayers and battle chants."

Sinnafein looked at the young female curiously. Orc battlefield commanders who did not properly give thanks to the king with almost every sentence they uttered were often later seen impaled on a tall spike.

" 'War Chief Hartusk,' they cry," Myriel added.

"Hartusk?" Sinnafein whispered, more to herself than to the scout. She had heard that name before, though she couldn't quite place it. She stared out at the distant orc force, trying to make sense of it all. Not King Obould, but Hartusk? Where was Obould, then, and where was Lorgru, his son and heir?

A shiver coursed Sinnafein's spine as she remembered her days of capture among Lorgru's gang. The orc prince of Many-Arrows had been clear and decisive in his decision to return her to the Moonwood, but that decision hadn't gone over well with most of his ferocious charges. Indeed, on many occasions Sinnafein had thought her life forfeit as one of the lesser orcs approached as if to take her fate into its own ugly hands. By the time the orc group had reached the Surbrin, Sinnafein had heard open words of disdain aimed at Lorgru, and had been surprised by that level of discontent, and shocked by the boldness of the grumbles.

She couldn't help but wonder—and fear—that the mercy shown to her had been the final stone to crush the idealistic designs of the line of Obould.

The elf hated orcs and had never come to terms with this vast kingdom of the smelly, warlike creatures living in relative peace in the northern reaches of Luruar. She accepted the Treaty of Garumn's Gorge, of course, and did not openly condone the many bands of vigilante elves who had gone out to wage battle with rogue bands of orcs. But neither would she privately condemn their actions, and indeed had effectively pardoned all who had been caught at such activities, reducing their punishment to a trivial bit of work and a public apology.

Sinnafein understood the necessity of the treaty, but hated that reality nonetheless—and still, that reality was a far better sort, she had always believed, than the alternative.

But was that alternative, a full-out war with Many-Arrows, now on her doorstep? Had her excursion into Many-Arrows in pursuit of her daughter facilitated this impending tragedy?

Had she known that to be a possibility, even a remote possibility, at the time of her capture, Sinnafein would have fought the orcs with her bare hands, would have bitten them and spat upon them and forced them to kill her.

The western edge of the Glimmerwood cast dull shadows under the sunless sky upon the greatest army of orcs that had been collected in the Silver Marches, at least back to the days of the march of the original King Obould. And if that wasn't enough, a second sizable force had appeared on the other side of the deep forest.

"Oh, Lorgru," she whispered. "What have you done?"

She was startled from her introspection a moment later when Myriel dared to correct her. "Oh, Tos'un, you mean," the young elf scout said.

Sinnafein closed her eyes and took a deep breath to calm herself so that she didn't angrily lash out at the young scout. She was the leader of the clan, but the elves of the Moonwood were not the orcs of Dark Arrow Keep, and Sinnafein had always coaxed them to speak their minds honestly and without fear.

Myriel's observation had struck a deep chord of discontent within her; every word had poured like salt into the emotional wounds. Her son was dead, murdered by his sister Doum'wielle, and Doum'wielle was gone now, into the Underdark beside Tos'un. Tos'un, her husband for decades, her beloved, who had betrayed Sinnafein, hacking her legs so that she could not flee and would thus hold back the pursuing orcs while he and Doum'wielle made their escape into the deep tunnels.

Myriel had only spoken what they were all thinking, Sinnafein knew, and as horrible and painful as it was, when she looked into her broken heart, she could not deny the truth of the words.

Whatever this catastrophe was before her, it seemed plausible to her that Tos'un had played a role.

The elf shook her head, her expression grim. "There is nothing there for you," she told King Bromm, who was eight days out of Citadel, Adbar with a force of two hundred dwarves. "Go south, past the Rauvins and my people will meet you in the foothills and guide you through the forest to wide ferries that will speed you along the Surbrin to Mithral Hall's eastern gate."

"That'll put us ahead of yer royal brother," Oretheo Spikes, one of Bromm's commanders, remarked.

The dwarf king nodded. They had estimated just that morning that Harnoth's legion was a day closer to Citadel Felbarr than they, only, of course, Harnoth and his boys were making the trek via an underground route.

"We'd have to get word to him, then," Bromm reasoned, to the commander and to this elf who had come out of the Glimmerwood to intercept their march.

"Get word to Citadel Felbarr?" the elf maiden asked. "Easily accomplished. King Emerus is friend to my mother and we are all watching closely since the Darkening began."

"The what?" Bromm and Oretheo asked together.

The elf swallowed a bit too hard, perhaps, but Bromm didn't catch it. "The Darkening," she reiterated, pointing to the sky. "It seems a fitting name, does it not?"

"Aye, that'll do," said Bromm. "So ye're wantin' us to round south o' yer woods then, instead o' the north road?"

"The north road will leave you out alone for many days, and all you'll find is the Surbrin blocking your way and a horde of orcs across the water hurling their curses at you. The waters are too swift and strong up there with the spring melt for us to bring any suitable ferries to get you across."

Young King Bromm put his hands on his hips and turned to his commanders.

"What will you do then, good king of Citadel Adbar, so far from home and unable to advance?" the elf asked, as the dwarves stared and shrugged.

King Bromm turned a curious glance on the young elf maiden.

"Are ye mockin' me then?"

She shrugged and laughed as if it didn't matter. "I am telling you the way to battle, or to support Mithral Hall, if that is your choice—and my mother believes that it should be," she explained. "We will get word to King Emerus and your twin brother, of course."

"Puttin' both kings far from home," warned Chayne Mulish, one of the other dwarf commanders.

"Bah, Adbar's buttoned up tighter than the hug of a giant squeezer snake," the ferocious Spikes argued.

"Bah, yerself," said the first, and Oretheo scowled fiercely.

"I must be going," the young elf said when Bromm continued to mull his options, and she turned to leave.

"South?" Bromm called after her.

"The Rauvin foothills in the Cold Vale, then straight west into the Moonwood," she said.

"So says yer Ma?"

"Aye, so says Sinnafein, the Lady of Glimmerwood," she answered. "Tis the swiftest road to Mithral Hall."

"Aye, then we'll go," King Bromm decided. "And me best to Sinnafein, young lassie . . . ?"

"Doum'wielle," she answered with a smile. "I am Doum'wielle of the Moonwood."

"Well met, then," King Bromm called, and the elf lass nodded. "Ye tell yer Ma that Citadel Adbar's puttin' aside our unpleasantries and staying true to her friends."

The young elf nodded and smiled again, then rushed away, disappearing fully into the underbrush of the Glimmerwood in the blink of an eye.

"Double-time it," Bromm told Oretheo. "We'll get word to Harnoth to turn his force back for Adbar and we'll thicken King Connerad's garrison. I could use a bit of a fight."

"Aye," the dwarf commander replied, and most of the others nodded their agreement.

"So shall we go and relay to Sinnafein the brat Bromm's well-wishes?" Doum'wielle's drow father asked when she had gained their position, in a small clearing amid a line of thick pines not far from the forest's edge—close enough so that the dark elf sentry up in the tree could clearly watch the movement of the dwarf force beyond the Glimmerwood's borders.

Beside Tos'un, the wizard Ravel Xorlarrin snickered.

"He did seem concerned with her well-being," Doum'wielle played along, striking a perfectly contemplative pose.

Tos'un Armgo nodded and smiled, thinking that his daughter was making the adjustment to the ways of the drow with aplomb indeed. He reflexively glanced down at the sword hanging on her hip, suspecting that Khazid'hea continued to play more than a little role in that dramatically shifting attitude.

"The dwarves have turned to the south," came the hoped-for call from above.

"I expect that we're about to make quite the formal introduction, then," said Doum'wielle.

"I do believe that Arauthator will make that introduction for us," Ravel remarked and walked off.

Doum'wielle started to follow him, but Tos'un held her back, wanting a private moment with his daughter. "Well done, my Little Doe," Tos'un congratulated, and he gave his daughter a great hug. He looked past her as he did, though, into the Glimmerwood. He was thinking of Sinnafein and the life he had known here. Never had he been suited to such an existence, he told himself repeatedly.

But in the corner of Tos'un's heart, he couldn't deny the fine decades he had known here among the elves, or the love he had once known for Sinnafein, or his joy at the birth of his children.

He thought of Tierflin, his son.

Doum'wielle had slaughtered Tierflin, the end result of a contest that Tos'un had begun, a battle for the sword Doum'wielle now carried.

Why had he done that? Why had he begun something that almost assuredly would leave one of his beloved children dead, and likely at the bloodstained hands of the other?

Tos'un rubbed Doum'wielle's back and let his hand slide down her side to touch the hilt of Khazid'hea, and there he had his sinister answer.

But there, too, he found relief from his nostalgia and his pain, for with that touch, the sentient sword immediately dangled visions of glory and riches in his mind—they weren't even tangible images—a pot of gold, a cheering crowd, or anything like that—but rather a sensation in the mind of the old dark elf that his current road would lead him to greater joy than he had ever known.

"It's frozen, I tell ye," the dwarf scout shouted above the laughter of the others.

"How can it be frozen, ye dolt?" asked Oretheo Spikes. "It's midsummer."

"Aye, and how can the sky be black when it's midday?" the scout retorted, and the laughter drifted off uncomfortably.

"A frozen pond, ye say," King Bromm asked, shaking his head. "Well, let's us go and see what there's to see." He nodded to his commanders, who relayed the order with great efficiency and the dwarf force of three hundred started off in short order, marching hard through the rocky foothills of the Rauvin Mountains. Sometime late that afternoon, they had covered the ten miles to the location the scout had indicated.

They knew they were close from the pounding sound of a waterfall and soon came in sight of the cascading flow, leaping down from on high and disappearing behind a rocky spur of the mountain before them.

"Frozen," Oretheo Spikes said with a snort.

"They said that o' the pond, not the waterfall," Chayne Mulish reminded.

"How can the pond be freezin' if the water's falling?" Oretheo argued. "Colder up higher, course, and don't ye know?"

Even as his words left his mouth, though, the leading edge of the dwarf force climbed up to the apex of the rocky spur, and as one turned back to the main group and shouted out their surprise. King Bromm pushed his leaders forward, scrambling to the top of the stones, then looking down upon a frozen lake. The deluge of the waterfall splashed into the one open area, the resulting waves sending a film of water washing over the ice.

"Well I'm a bearded gnome," Commander Spikes remarked.

"Stupid one, too," Chayne Mulish added under his breath.

Bromm ignored them and led the way down to the water's edge. He motioned to a nearby sentry, who moved over and prodded his spear down hard into the water. The very top was liquid, but only as thick as a dwarf's fingernail, and under that, the spear hit solid ice. The dwarf stabbed again, scraping a bit, but this was no flimsy ice pack.

"How . . . ?" King Bromm started to ask, but he and the others jumped back in surprise as a burst of bubbles rose up from the lake around the edges of the ice pack and the loose water atop the ice immediately crystallized into a new layer of ice.

"Mage spell?" Chayne Mulish asked.

"Not for knowin'," Bromm and Oretheo said in unison. The two looked to each other and shrugged.

"Not for likin', neither," said King Bromm, and he turned to his commanders. "Move us around the lake, straight'n'fast for the Glimmerwood."

"Might that it'll hold us and we can slide right across," Oretheo Spikes offered, but clearly regretted the advice the moment it left his mouth, as a swarm of incredulous, even taunting, looks came back at him from all around, including from King Bromm.

"We'll go around," he agreed as Bromm started to explain it to him, and he hustled away.

The dwarf army looped along the northern back of the small lake, the Glimmerwood in sight to the north and to the west of them. They had gone more than halfway around the pond when the first cries rang out ahead of the main force.

"Orcs!"

"Bah, bandits," King Bromm said. "Kill 'em to death one and all."

"Not bandits," Chayne Mulish replied somberly, his tone drawing the attention of all nearby, and they followed his gaze across the lake to the southwest, where dark forms gathered around the bank.

Not bandits, indeed, Bromm and all the others understood, when they realized that the force that had come against them was considerably larger than their own.

"What in the name o' Dumathoin're them pig-faced rats doin' here in the Cold Vale?" the dwarf king asked. Those around him nodded. It was a good question, and to a one they wondered more about how such a force might have come to this protected place. The Cold Vale was surrounded north and west by the Glimmerwood, home of the elves, and on the south by the Rauvin Mountains, a land overseen by King Emerus Warcrown and his legions of sturdy dwarves.

King Bromm wondered if Citadel Felbarr still stood, and if not, then what trap might await his brother's march?

"No good, I'm thinkin'," said Chayne Mulish, drawing a curious look from King Bromm.

"Ye asked what them pig-faced rats're doing here," the dwarf explained.

"Rat-faced pigs, ye mean," Oretheo remarked.

"Vermin, howe'er ye slice 'em," Chayne declared.

"Shoulder to hip's me preferred way," Oretheo replied, hoisting his axe, and a chorus of cheers went up around him.

"Bah, but I'll take 'em two to yer one," Chayne Mulish declared, drawing a few heigh-ho's of his own.

"Bah, but yer mother's a bunny," Oretheo Spikes roared. "Three-to-one for meself."

They were nose-to-nose now, shouting their challenges back and forth, and each claim brought louder cheers than the previous.

King Bromm nodded his approval and let them continue for a long while. Few could rouse bloodlust in an army in the moments before a battle better than Chayne Mulish and Oretheo Spikes.

"Here they come!" cried a dwarf, and all eyes turned back to the orc force—now charging directly across the frozen lake, without reservation.

"Too stupid to know that lakes ain't supposed to be frozen in the summertime!" Oretheo cried.

He didn't add to that, but like most of the others, he hoped that was the case and the ice would shatter under their march and send them floundering in the cold waters. He feared something else, however. Had the orcs tapped into some magic to freeze the lake and aid them in this fight?

And if they were possessed of magic that powerful . . .

"Battle groups!" King Bromm ordered. "And don't ye go running out on the damned lake to meet 'em."

With great precision and the discipline infused through years of practice, the dwarven force settled into their organized brigades and formations, shield dwarves forming a wall in the front ranks of three squares, with crossbowmen behind, diligently cocking their weapons. Behind the middle square, the king's Wilddwarf Brigade, Citadel Adbar's version of the Gutbusters, drank their potent liquor and crashed against each other hard, "rising their blood," as they called it.

"We're breaking into fives then," called out the leader of the brigade, known simply—and for most of the Adbar dwarves, known only—as

Crunch. "Two for runnin' and three for flyin'."

"Flyin'!" every member of the king's Wilddwarves volunteered, and the crashing began anew with heightened vigor, as each vied for the coveted role. When the orcs met the defensive walls of the shield dwarves, some of the Wilddwarves, the runners, would charge between the squares, but many others would fly over the shield dwarves like living missiles. Indeed, pairs of "dwarf tossers" were already settling into place in the second ranks of the squares, each consisting of two young, strong dwarves holding a sturdy plank low and horizontal between them. A Wilddwarf leaping onto that plank would be "assisted" in his second leap, the one that sent him flying over the front line of shield dwarves.

King Bromm watched the jostling of the fierce brigade with a grin, and nodded with pride as he noted the precision of his superb battle group.

"Bolts at yer call," he shouted to Commander Chayne Mulish, who nodded back and began ordering the crossbows into action. Lines of deadly quarrels flew out from the lake's edge, sailing over the frozen pond. The orcs were still far away, but the powerful weapons showed tremendous range, and while it was difficult for any archer to be accurate at such a range, there were so many orcs charging, it was even harder to miss.

King Bromm nodded again as he watched orc after orc stagger and fall, and grinned wider to see fellow orcs, unable to stop their momentum on the slick surface, go tumbling over those driven down. He held no illusions, though, when looking at the approaching army compared to his own force. His dwarves were clearly outnumbered, by five to one or more, and the fact that such an orc force had somehow arrived in the Cold Vale unbeknownst to the elves of the Glimmerwood . . .

Or was this orc army, he wondered, the real reason Sinnafein had sent them here?

King Bromm chewed his lip bloody mulling that disturbing possibility, but quickly put it out of his mind. His dwarves would win here. He felt great confidence as he watched still more of the fast-closing orcs fall to a second brutal volley. Better armed, better armored, superbly trained, and battle-hardened, the Adbar legion would cover the lake with orc blood.

But then the first boulder hurtled down from on high.

It crashed down near the front rank of the left-most square, shattering three shields and two of the three dwarves who held them. No sooner had the grunts erupted in response to the unexpected explosion, then so did the cries of "Giants!"

Many dwarf voices raised in that chorus, with screams of warning for other rocks arcing out from the rocky spurs of the mountain. All around those higher trails and slopes loomed the gigantic blue-skinned humanoids, ferocious frost giants, who counted among their most-hated of enemies the dwarves of the Silver Marches.

At the sight of the behemoths and the thunder of the bombardment, the orcs began whooping and charging ahead with renewed energy.

Bromm's dwarves scrambled, their tight formations falling apart under the rain of stones. It didn't take long for the young King of Adbar to understand that he was facing utter disaster. Without the squares in place, the sheer numerical advantage of the orc army would overrun them in short order.

"Back! Tight lines and stepping back," he called out. "Get out o' the giants' range, me boys."

"For the love o' yer Ma's hairy back, back and stay tight!" Chayne Mulish added, and it proved to be the last word the dwarf commander ever spoke as a giant-hurled boulder splattered his brains all over his shiny armor.

Despite the confusion and the rain of boulders—and there were many giants up there on the slopes, the dwarves quickly realized—the skilled veterans of Citadel Adbar held tight their formations and held strong their courage. The Wilddwarves darted around, helping the wounded, dragging them back as the squares stepped back, double-timing it to get out of range of the deadly boulder rain.

The lead orcs made the lake's shore, sliding from the ice into a dead run at the retreating force. Their presence hardly slowed the giants, however, and boulders fell on orc and dwarf alike as the forces came crashing together.

"Keep backing as ye kill 'em!" King Bromm cried and his commanders echoed, up and down the line. With every step, the boulders were more likely to hit the orcs, he knew, and so did the orcs. When Bromm looked up to the slopes, he realized that the giants were catching on as well. Many of them had stopped their barrage to rush down the long, winding trails.

King Bromm nodded and glanced over his shoulder to the north, to the Glimmerwood. He was confident that he could get his boys under that canopy before the giants could join in the fight. If a sizable number of elves were about, they just might turn the tide.

But first, the dwarves had to disengage these stubborn orcs and break off in full retreat, and Bromm knew just how to do that. He called for his Wilddwarves, thinking to gather them into a horde of dwarven hammers and send them blasting into the orcs to break the line and drive them back.

As they assembled, though, there came a low rumbling beneath Bromm's feet. Dwarf and orc alike paused in their slaughter and glanced around, and the ground began to shake more violently.

Bromm recognized the point of origin then, and turned his gaze to the frozen lake, just in time to see the ice breaking apart far out from the bank, a great sheet tilting up , throwing orcs into the sky, sending them sliding and tumbling all over each other, weapons and armor tangling. For a moment, King Bromm's heart soared, as he believed that some great rescue was upon them. Perhaps his twin brother and the dwarves of Felbarr had devised this trap for the orcs with some cunning machinery or magic.

But no, he realized a heartbeat later, and then his heart skipped more than a few beats as he came to understand the true source of the icy upheaval, and of the ice itself, as the gigantic head of a white dragon appeared above the tilted and broken sheet.

Two hundred dwarves cried out at once, and a thousand orcs cheered—despite their brethren trapped out on the lake, many dead and many wounded, and many floundering amid the now-shattered ice sheet, they cheered.

Up into the air went the great white wyrm, ice and water falling from its shining leathery wings.

"Me king!" more than one dwarf called, and Bromm only had one answer in that awful moment.

"Run away!" he cried at the top of his lungs. "Run away! To the forest. Oh, run!"

The dwarves broke ranks and sprinted to the north, except for the king's Wilddwarves, huddled together and nodding grimly. They knew their place, and willingly accepted their fate. "Crunch!" they cheered in unison, and while the main force retreated, they charged, throwing themselves with abandon into the orc ranks, thrashing and biting and kicking and punching, and a hundred stabs couldn't stop any of them.

King Bromm didn't want to flee. Indeed, for a long while, he stood his ground, yanking those retreating dwarves past him and shoving them along to the north.

"Ye got to go, me king," Oretheo Spikes said to him, rushing up and grabbing him by the arm.

"Fifty boys dead, and fifty more to fall, if we're lucky," Bromm lamented.

"And if one o' them fifty's King Bromm, then Adbar's knowin' a darker day," the commander insisted, pulling him along.

Bromm resisted only a bit, then finally nodded in resignation, turned, and began his sprint.

Just a few strides later, though, a shadow came over the pair, a darker spot in the dull darkness of the near-blotted sunlight, and that shadow grew, reaching wide to either side as the dragon descended.

"Right and left," Oretheo yelled to Bromm, and he pushed off the king and scrambled out to his right while Bromm broke left. Oretheo turned as he went and began hurling insults at the dragon, wanting it to swerve at him that his King Bromm might escape.

But the beast did not, locking onto the other form and swooping in with such speed that the air thrummed around it.

"Ah, ye nasty, wormy fish bait!" Oretheo Spikes cried desperately as the beast bore down on King Bromm, but the last word caught in his throat indeed when he realized that the dragon wasn't alone.

There was a rider.

A drow rider.

The dwarf's mouth gaped as the dragon's maw opened and a cone of white frost blew forth, a cone strong enough and cold enough to freeze a lake in summertime, a cone powerful enough to blow poor King Bromm to the ground and freeze him there.

The dragon soared past, but its rider dropped from it and gently and magically floated down to the ground. The great wyrm issued a mighty shrieking roar that had all around, dwarf and orc and giant alike, covering their ears in terror.

Oretheo Spikes stumbled and cried out for his king, running, scrambling, crawling even, until he could get his feet back under him. Across the way, the drow, too, approached, but with no apparent urgency.

"Ah, ye dog!" Oretheo cried, leaping over Bromm, axe high.

The drow smiled and easily side-stepped cleanly. He never even bothered to lift his strange, translucent shield, and the overbalanced Oretheo went sprawling. The dwarf jumped up and spun around, and his heart sank even more. The orc horde closed in now, with most of the fighting to the south finished, and the drow stood calmly waiting, very close to King Bromm, who lay quiet under a coating of icy crystals.

"Run away, dwarf," the drow said. "Run away and tell your kin that the drow have come, that Many-Arrows has come, and that the land is ours."

Oretheo Spikes replied with an unintelligible, growling sound, and threw himself at the drow once more.

This time, the dark elf did not sidestep. Up came his shield, its edge magically rolling as he raised his arm, the shield growing with each turn. Oretheo's axe slammed in hard, but the impact was dulled somehow by the magic of that shield. And when the dwarf tried to retract, he found his blade sluggish and stuck as if he had driven it into a vat of heavy syrup.

His surprise and delay cost him. The drow's weapon, a sword that seemed as if it had captured the nighttime stars within its translucent glassteel confines, cut across and up perfectly, taking the dwarf in the wrist and hand, and forcing him to let go of his trapped axe.

He heard the orcs howling; the dragon screeched again.

The drow, so quick, had moved behind him somehow, Oretheo realized. Only the blink of an eye before he felt the pain as that fabulous sword slashed across the back of his legs.

He found himself kneeling. He didn't know how. He didn't know why.

"But Hartusk didn't get the kill," Doum'wielle reasoned to her father and Ravel as they watched the gruesome scene unfolding from the edge of the Glimmerwood. Out in the field, halfway to the lake, the orc army chanted Hartusk's name and the legion of giants laughed as the burly war chief bent over the fallen form of King Bromm.

"Perhaps he will," Ravel interjected, pointing out to the scene. When Hartusk kicked at the prone dwarf, the thawing diminutive fellow seemed to move a bit in reaction.

War Chief Hartusk seemed quite pleased by that development. He eagerly bent low over the form, slapping Bromm's helmet off to the side. He took the dwarf's thick hair in hand and tugged his head back hard, exposing the neck below. Around went Hartusk's other hand and he worked his serrated long knife savagely, tearing out the king's throat to the howls of approval from his legions. The ferocious orc didn't stop there, digging and ripping the blade back and forth, unrelenting until he took the head from the dwarf king's shoulders.

Hartusk sprang to his feet, holding the severed head up high, blood falling from the torn neck, so all could see and all could cheer.

Above the throng, the dragon, Arauthator, roared again and dipped into another air-shaking swoop, and the white hair of Tiago Baenre flew wildly in the rushing dive.

"He does enjoy his pets," Ravel Xorlarrin remarked.

"Tiago or Arauthator?" Tos'un Armgo asked.

"Yes," Ravel replied with a laugh.

Hartusk carried the head over to the prisoners, including the dwarf commander, and even from this distance, the trio of elves could hear the war chief's shouted demands.

"Go tell the dwarves of Adbar to stay in their hole!" Hartusk yelled in the dwarf's face. "If you come out, you are in the domain of Many-Arrows, and you will die!" He pushed the dead king's severed head right into the face of Oretheo, then swung around and roared triumphantly. Other orcs gathered up the wounded Oretheo, stripped him naked, bound his hands behind him tightly, and shoved him off to the north.

He staggered and fell more than once, and Doum'wielle could see that he was crying, and could see him wince, time and again, as another of the captured dwarves was horribly executed behind him.

She shook her head in disgust, but in her mind, Khazid'hea told her that it was all for the best.

So lost was she that she knew she had to believe the sword, and so she clutched desperately at the thoughts it imparted. To do otherwise was to step back and widen her view, to see her role in this, from the murder of her brother Tierflin to her journey to the Underdark and back, and that, her conscience could not survive.

She swallowed hard.

She felt the gaze of Ravel upon her and knew she was being judged, and knew that if she showed weakness that she and her father would surely suffer.

"Idiot dwarves," she said, and she spat upon the ground and walked deeper into the Glimmerwood.

RISE OF THE KING

The heavy picket gates of Dark Arrow Keep groaned and creaked as they swung wide for the approaching legion, a dozen strong orcs bending their backs on each. No word came down from the wooden watchtowers above; the whole of the gathering remained strangely quiet at this unexpected approach.

Tensions had run high in Dark Arrow Keep since the murder of King Obould. The fighting had begun almost immediately among his many sons, including among those who claimed without evidence to be of his lineage, bastard children of unnamed mothers. Through it all, many of the orcs had looked to Lorgru for guidance, as the named successor to the throne, but of course, many others had looked the other way.

In whispers, Lorgru was spoken of as the murderer. That in itself wouldn't have necessarily disqualified him from the throne, but adding to those whispers were reminders of Lorgru's recent show of mercy—to an elf!

Now the war drums were beating, and against the people of Sinnafein, whom Lorgru had released back to the Moonwood. And Lorgru opposed those war drums, but in the heightened tensions, their cadence had grown in strength and volume, aided by the stamp of thousands of heavy orc boots.

Now came the return of War Chief Hartusk, so claimed the pennants flying over the dark force marching to Dark Arrow Keep, and for a long while after those banners had been sighted, the orcs argued about whether or not to even open the gates for Hartusk, for the war chief who had defied Lorgru's expressed commands and took an army into the field.

Inside the grand circular main building, the would-be King of Many-Arrows was not amused.

"Do not open the gates," Lorgru commanded his lieutenants.

"Then they will be torn asunder," Ravel Xorlarrin calmly replied.

Lorgru slammed his hands down on the arms of his throne and started to rise.

"Hartusk returns with a legion of giants," Ravel explained. "And how do you think he crossed back through the Glimmerwood and across the Surbrin with such speed?"

"Drow trickery, no doubt."

Ravel shook his head, smiling wickedly.

At that very moment, one of Lorgru's loyal underlings burst into the chamber unannounced, a severe breach of conduct.

"What is it?" the would-be king demanded.

"My . . . king," the orc stammered and gasped, trying to catch his breath. "They have . . . dragons. Hartusk has returned with dragons!"

Gasps erupted around the chamber, and Lorgru fell back into his throne, his expression blank, his jaw hanging open.

An ear-splitting shriek rolled down from high above and reverberated around the room.

"Dragons," Ravel teased. "And giants. Oh, and drow . . . have I mentioned that Menzoberranzan has thrown her not-insignificant resources behind Hartusk?"

"I will have you killed!"

"You cannot begin to kill me," Ravel confidently replied before the would-be king had finished the sentence. "I can be gone with a snap of my fingers, but why would I? Nay, I would fill this room with flames and burn you down on your throne. Be reasonable, son of Obould. Your time has passed. Your line is no more. Your people reject the way of . . . of farmers. They will taste the blood of humans and dwarves."

He led Lorgru's gaze around the room, where, undeniably, so many of the throne guards were licking their lips with an eager gleam in their yellow, bloodshot eyes.

Lorgru stood up defiantly and drew his sword. "Then let us, you and I, be done with it." he said.

Ravel laughed at him. "My dear Lorgru, are you so certain of your way that you are ready to meet Gruumsh?" the drow wizard replied easily. "You see, I am told by the priestesses of Lolth that Gruumsh is not pleased. The line of Obould has gone too far. To send an elf queen back to her forest, and after she had murdered orcs of your kingdom, indeed, of your own patrol?"

It was Lorgru's weak heel, clearly, and he slipped back into his throne.

"Is your tale done then, Lorgru? Or have you more to write?"

"What do you mean?"

"I offer you a way out," Ravel explained. He brought forth a wand, pointed it at the side of the throne and uttered a command word. A doorway appeared, black and swirling at first, but gradually clearing to reveal within its multi-dimensional frame a small encampment somewhere high in some rocky mountains.

"The Spine of the World," the drow explained. "Through this door, you find exile, though permanent or temporary is yours to decide. Perhaps you will come to see a better way—a more appropriate extension of the vision of Obould that century ago. One that is more fitting with the realities of Luruar beneath the dark sky."

"Hartusk will fail," Lorgru declared.

"Perhaps he will," Ravel said with a bow. "And in that case, my people will look to you to return and bring some calmness and order to Many-Arrows. As I said, is your tale fully told, or not? If you wish to meet with Gruumsh, then I can oblige—and if not I, well, Hartusk has returned with powerful allies, as you now understand."

"My guards," Lorgru said. "My . . ."

"Take them," Ravel interrupted. "The door to freedom is open. But be quick, for it will not linger long after I am gone. And now, I fear, I am gone."

He clapped his hands together and disappeared, simply vanishing.

But not of his own doing, despite his bravado and acting. Gromph and the illithid Methil had been watching, ready to pluck Ravel from the room.

"Well played," Gromph said in congratulations when Ravel materialized in a small chamber in the tunnels beneath Dark Arrow Keep. On the wall before the archmage, a tall mirror showed the scene Ravel had left behind. Lorgru and his guards jostled and argued, many peering repeatedly into the magical doorway to the mountains Ravel had created.

Finally, Lorgru instructed one to go through the door. The orc went hesitantly at first, dipping his leg through, then disappearing.

The smiles on those watching from the throne room showed that they saw their scout and that he seemed quite all right.

A great horn blew.

"Hartusk enters Dark Arrow Keep," Ravel said.

Gromph nodded, then smiled when Lorgru sent more of his guards through the door, and called many females to his side as he, too, went through.

"Dismiss the doorway," Gromph instructed, even though more orcs were moving for the magical portal. "Hartusk should enjoy the taste of some blood for his fine service."

"What of Lorgru?" Ravel asked. "Should Tiago and I commandeer the dragons and destroy him in the mountains?"

"Let Lorgru live—he is of no matter at this time," the archmage replied. "Perhaps we will find use for him in the future, perhaps not."

Ravel nodded and stared at the archmage, who rested back in his chair, watching the mirror with great amusement.

Soon enough, Hartusk and his burly guards stormed in, the war chief carrying a spear with the head of King Bromm of Citadel Adbar spiked upon it.

Many of Lorgru's remaining loyalists fell to their knees and cheered Hartusk. Those that hesitated were dragged down and torn apart.

Gromph Baenre seemed to enjoy that part, Ravel noted with a shudder. After the murdering had ended, Ravel started to speak, but Gromph silenced him with an upraised hand, and following that, Ravel noted the scene in the mirror, with Hartusk approaching the throne.

"And so Hartusk becomes king," he said.

"No," Gromph quietly replied.

And indeed, Hartusk lifted his great double-bladed axe as he approached the throne, and proceeded to smash it to pieces.

"No king," Gromph predicted.

The ferocious orc reduced the great throne of Many-Arrows to kindling in short order.

"Warlord Hartusk!" the orc's minions cheered.

In a chamber far below, viewing the scene through the magical mirror, a most satisfied Gromph Baenre turned to Ravel Xorlarrin, nodded, and said, "Much better."

CHAPTER 4

MATRON MOTHER DARTHIIR

Filthy beasts," Saribel Xorlarrin remarked with a crinkled face and disgusted expression. She heaved a great sigh and brushed some maggot-like larval creature from the sleeve of her fine gown.

The drow band had expelled some orcs from a cluster of crude houses just north of Dark Arrow Keep, though for the cultured drow nobles, the word "houses" hardly seemed to describe these hovels. They were no more than piled stones along this wall or that, with a living tree serving as an anchor for another wall, and nothing more than the curving side of a hill completing the structure. Ragged skins and hides closed in the walls and roof, crudely pinned together with splintered sticks.

Saribel chortled again and looked up at the drooping hide serving as a ceiling for this part of the domicile, guessing correctly that the maggot had fallen from there. Caked in dried blood, this was from some recent kill, peeled off the dead or dying creature and just thrown up to patch the ceiling without the orc even bothering to clean it.

"Curse these wretched orc beasts," she said, not even trying to hide her disgust from the orc female in the room, who had been kept on as a servant. "When we are done with them, I'm sure I will enjoy feeding a score of them to the dragons."

The orc female wisely kept her eyes lowered to the dirt floor as she moved past the powerful priestess, and didn't dare utter a sound of protest or surprise.

"We are here for the Spider Queen," one of her attending priestesses reminded. "I would suffer being devoured by maggots for the pleasure of Lolth."

"I can easily arrange that," the angry Saribel replied. There was no hint in her voice that she was joking, and when the attending lesser priestess inevitably backed away, she found little support from the other two drow females in the room.

They each moved out from her on either side as if expecting Saribel to cast a devastating spell over the impudent young priestess at that very moment.

Indeed, so did the young priestess, as she revealed when she jumped nearly out of her shoes as the hide flap serving as the hovel's door flew aside and Gromph Baenre swept into the room, nearly tripping over the orc slave as she skulked about. With a snarl, Gromph hit her with a simple spell, a gust of wind, a spell any minor mage could cast.

But not like this. Not with the power of the Archmage of Menzoberranzan behind the burst. It caught the poor orc like a tornado, sweeping her up and spinning her sidelong, hurling her straight back from Gromph to crash into the unfortunate attendant priestess on that side of the room. Both tumbled down in a tangled heap, but Gromph paid them no heed at all.

"Gather your husband, and be quick," Gromph snarled at Saribel. "You are recalled."

"Recalled?" Saribel replied before she could find the good sense to just do as the archmage had ordered. "The war is only just begun. The armies have barely left Dark Arrow Keep."

Gromph looked at her with what seemed to be a mixture of disgust and pity, and it was clearly not an expression Saribel enjoyed.

"Shall I inform Matron Mother Baenre that you choose otherwise?" the archmage said evenly.

Saribel swallowed hard. "Tiago is—"

"Over with the legion from Shining White," Gromph interrupted. "He fancies himself a dragon rider, it would seem."

"He handled the great beast with—"

"Oh, shut up," Gromph told the insufferable witch.

Saribel's eyes widened and she even inadvertently reached for her snake whip. Yes, he was the Archmage of Menzoberranzan, but she was a high priestess, a noble female, and he should not address her with such irreverence, particularly not in front of her attendants.

"I will create the portal on a count of eight-legs-ten," he said calmly, using a common drow time reference. A count of "eight-legs" to the drow meant counting to eight, then seven, then six, and all the way back to one, for a total of thirty-six. Eight-legs-ten, therefore, meant a count of three-hundred-sixty, or a span of one-tenth of an hour.

"Join me if you will," the archmage went on. "If not, I will give your condolences to the Matron Mother of Menzoberranzan, who rules the House of Saribel Baenre."

The reminder of her new surname—for against drow custom, it had been Saribel and not Tiago who had changed her name and House, of course—had Saribel stammering for an answer.

"One," said Gromph, and the cold reminder of the dripping hourglass had four priestesses, scrambling.

They rushed past Gromph and pushed through the door in such a tangled way that they tore the hide down from the ceiling post above it.

"Idiot," Gromph muttered under his breath, silently cursing his sister for allowing Tiago to bring the bumbling Xorlarrin waif into their esteemed House.

He was glad, then, that it wouldn't be for long—not outwardly, at least.

He wished he could just leave the both of them here, for while he was anxious to return to Menzoberranzan and his studies, he knew that the arrival of these two impertinent children would spark outrage and intrigue in the drow city.

Now it was Gromph's turn to sigh, for there was nothing he could do. Matron Mother Baenre had spoken.

This couple was needed for the coming-out party, to take their place in Quenthel's grand scheme.

Matron Mother Mez'Barris Armgo of Menzoberranzan's Second House impatiently took her seat at the end of one of the two longest legs of the arachnid-shaped table.

She saw the chair placed to her right, between her seat and that of Matron Mother Baenre, and she knew that the conniving Quenthel was up to something foul.

Five other matron mothers sat behind the lesser six limbs of the table, with only the seat of the Eighth House left open. The seat for House Do'Urden, so Matron Mother Baenre had told them at the last gathering of the Ruling Council.

High Priestess Sos'Umptu Baenre entered the chamber, and Mez'Barris noted the nods of the lesser matron mothers. They thought she was still named as Matron Mother Do'Urden, Mez'Barris realized, and indeed, only Mez'Barris did not gasp or widen her eyes when Sos'Umptu moved not to the grand seat for the Eighth House but to the unremarkable chair set between Baenre and Del'Armgo.

Stone-faced, the disciplined Baenre priestess betrayed nothing with her expression. If she had been demoted, House Do'Urden taken from her rule, then she seemed not at all unhappy about it.

Mez'Barris turned her stare to the Matron Mother Zhindia Melarn of the Sixth House, who was not so clever at disguising her emotions. Among the most fanatical of the matron mothers in her service to the Spider Queen, Zhindia was surely no shrinking myconid, as the old saying went.

Matron Mother Melarn stared at Sos'Umptu with open contempt. Surely Zhindia among all the ruling matron mothers had been the most angered by Matron Mother Baenre's decision to recreate House Do'Urden and place it at the eighth rank in the city, thus affording the chosen matron mother a seat on the Ruling Council—one that would serve as an echo to Matron Mother Baenre, all of the other six knew.

For ambitious Zhindia, it had been a terrible blow. She had wanted House Duskryn elevated one rank and placed as the Eighth House when House Xorlarrin had departed the city for their new sister city. It wasn't that Zhindia held any fondness for House Duskryn, Mez'Barris knew. Quite the contrary. Indeed, Zhindia had plotted with House Hunzrin, the most powerful of the city's families not on the Ruling Council, to make short work of House Duskryn.

But now it was House Do'Urden in that coveted spot, and the matron mother had made no secret of House Baenre's open alliance with the newly reconstituted Do'Urdens—and indeed, Sos'Umptu, Matron Mother Baenre's sister, had been installed as the Matron Mother of House Do'Urden, albeit temporarily.

Clearly that time had come to an end, as Sos'Umptu had taken the unusual seat away from the Council Chamber.

"High Priestess," Matron Mother Zhindia dared to remark, "or shall I call you Matron Mother?"

Dedicated and disciplined Sos'Umptu, of course, did not respond.

Mez'Barris somehow kept the smile off her face as she noted Zhindia's tightening lips—had Matron Mother Quenthel Baenre been too clever? House Melarn, filled with fearless devotees to the Spider Queen, was not to be taken lightly, nor was House Hunzrin, with whom the normally reclusive Melarni had only just begun to formulate a loose alliance.

Yes, Zhindia Melarn was itching for a fight, Mez'Barris could see; Zhindia remained outraged that House Baenre had swept clean the corridors of the vacated House Do'Urden, which Zhindia had been secretly using to harbor her private elite warriors, including several driders.

One insult after another, Mez'Barris noted. The boldness of Quenthel appalled her, but she couldn't deny her surprise and even admiration for the matron mother. Mez'Barris Armgo had known Quenthel Baenre for centuries, and never thought this one had such tricks and courage within her.

Matron Mother Baenre as last entered the room, pulling her spidery lace robes close about her as she strode confidently—defiantly even—to her chair at the head of the table. She was tall and undeniably beautiful, among the most physically striking of all the matron mothers. That, combined with her position as the first matron mother of the city, had all in the room, even her allies, looking at her with a great measure of envy.

Mez'Barris knew that keenly as she looked upon the faces of the matron mothers of the Third, Fourth and Fifth Houses, supposedly allies of House Baenre.

All Mez'Barris had to do was find some way to exploit that deep-seated hatred . . .

Matron Mother Baenre brought the meeting to order and bade Sos'Umptu to lead them in prayer. When it was finished, Sos'Umptu quietly sat back down in her chair, which brought more than a few curious looks her way.

"Why is she there?" Zhindia Melarn finally asked.

"She is a High Priestess of Lolth, who leads the Fane of the Goddess," Matron Mother Baenre replied.

"She is the Matron Mother of House Do'Urden, you mean," Zhindia replied, and she turned to the empty chair diagonally across the spider-shaped table from Matron Mother Baenre, the least seat among the Ruling Council.

"No more," Matron Mother Baenre corrected. "The Matron Mother of House Do'Urden has been revealed to me, to be formally introduced this day."

"Then why is Sos'Umptu Baenre in this chamber?" Zhindia Melarn pressed. Rarely would any of the matron mothers so push Matron Mother Baenre, but Zhindia, fanatically devout and a strict traditionalist, showed no signs of backing down. She leaned forward in her seat, elbows on the table, her expression as sharp as a jade spider's fang.

"Revealed to you?" Matron Mother Mez'Barris asked to deflect the confrontation. As anxious as she might be to see others turning against the miserable Quenthel Baenre, she was more interested in having all of the facts laid bare.

"In Q'Xorlarrin," the matron mother explained.

"The Xorlarrins are no more of Menzoberranzan," Zhindia argued, and Matron Mother Baenre shot her an incredulous and dismissive look.

"The truth would be revealed to us, so I was assured, and so it has been," Matron Mother Baenre calmly replied to Mez'Barris. She turned a sharp look over Zhindia and added, "And the Matron Mother of House Do'Urden is no Xorlarrin."

The smugness of her expression and tone brought Matron Mother Mez'Barris full circle. "You have not explained the presence of High Priestess Sos'Umptu," she said, just hoping to take some of that arrogance away.

Matron Mother Baenre straightened in her seat. "Today I renounce my position as Mistress of Arach-Tinilith," she said, and that had the other six matron mothers sitting up and taking notice indeed. Quenthel's sister Triel had broken tradition by keeping that title even after ascending to lead House Baenre, and Quenthel, after succeeding Triel, had helped secure this dual power as the new tradition. That she would willingly abdicate it, that she would give up such power, seemed truly astounding.

The others began whispering and exchanging looks all around, but Mez'Barris sat back in her chair and spent the moment considering the possibilities. Unlike many of the others, Mez'Barris wasn't as bothered by Triel Baenre's power grab, nor with Quenthel Baenre's insistence on keeping the dual titles. To Mez'Barris's reasoning, Mistress of Arach-Tinilith was more a ceremonial title than anything else, since the power structures within that web of intrigue shifted continually. And to have Matron Mother Baenre, this one or the previous, with her attention diverted away from the Ruling Council, could only be a good thing.

Perhaps Quenthel had realized the same.

"And your sister . . ." Matron Mother Zhindia started.

"High Priestess Sos'Umptu Baenre," the matron mother quickly cor-rected. "Mistress of the Fane of the Goddess, First Priestess of House Baenre, Matron Mother of House Do'Urden until this very day."

"Your sister," Zhindia insisted.

"Sister of the Matron Mother of Menzoberranzan, then," Baenre agreed, turning the notion right around. "Another impressive title, would you agree?"

Zhindia's eyes flared threateningly, but she fell back in her seat.

"So you ask the council to vote on this appointment of Sos'Umptu Baenre to serve as Mistress of Arach-Tinilith?" Matron Mother Byrtyn Fey of House Fey-Branche, the Fifth House of Menzoberranzan.

Mez'Barris sat up and took note of that remark, and realized that it had been rehearsed. Quenthel had arranged for Byrtyn to introduce the formal notion, knowing full well that she had already secured the votes of all the others, excluding Zhindia, of course, and Mez'Barris.

"More than that," Matron Mother Vadalma Tlabbar added. "Matron Mother Baenre is, I believe, asking us to vote for a seat on the council for High Priestess Sos'Umptu, who has served Lolth so well by creating the Fane of the Goddess."

Gasps could be heard in the council chamber, but only from Zhindia Melarn and Mez'Barris herself.

So there it was, Mez'Barris realized, the complete domination of the Ruling Council by Quenthel Baenre. And now so much more was coming clear to her. Zeerith Xorlarrin, were she still on the council and still within the city, would never have agreed to such a move as Vadalma had just, by design, brought forth. Zeerith and Mez'Barris would have defeated such a proposal before it could have ever been brought forth. Eight was the number of the Spider Queen, not nine.

But Vadalma Tlabbar, now seated as Matron Mother of the Third House, was in debt to House Baenre. More than a century before, House Faen Tlabbar had been attacked by the upstart Oblodrans, and Matron Mother Yvonnel Baenre, Quenthel's mother, had utterly destroyed the Oblodrans.

And now, to add to that debt, Quenthel had conveniently rid the city of the Xorlarrins—and to her benefit in that regard, as well—thus elevating House Faen Tlabbar to the coveted position of Third House, and, in the same move, had removed Faen Tlabbar's greatest rival, the Xorlarrins.

Only a short while back, Mez'Barris had heard rumors of a quiet alliance developing between House Faen Tlabbar and House Melarn, perhaps the two most fanatically devout Houses in the city.

No more, though, clearly, and the anger was not well-hidden on the face of Zhindia Melarn.

Quenthel Baenre's victory was complete. Quenthel would win the appointment of Sos'Umptu to lead Arach-Tinilith, and by extension, the Academy, and would put a ninth chair on the Ruling Council for her sister.

Could she have done anything more to prove to Mez'Barris Armgo and Zhindia Melarn that resistance was futile?

Matron Mother Mez'Barris got an answer to that question soon after the vote confirming the ninth council seat, when Mistress Sos'Umptu, in her last act as Matron Mother of House Do'Urden, introduced her replacement, leading a surface elf named Dahlia into the chamber for confirmation.

A surface elf!

Matron Mother Darthiir Do'Urden.

The magical gate at the appointed spot in the black bowels of House Do'Urden flickered to life, and with a glance over his shoulder, the Bregan D'aerthe warrior quietly slipped through, traveling back to Luskan.

This time, though, the door remained open just a bit longer, and a pair of dark elves came through the other way.

"It is strange," Beniago said as Kimmuriel closed the gate, "but I am less comfortable in this, my natural form, than in the guise of a human."

Kimmuriel Oblodra gave him a sidelong glance, but otherwise did not respond. He was sure that Beniago Baenre's discomfort could not begin to compare with his own, for he did not like returning to this city—ever.

Kimmuriel's House and family had been obliterated by Matron Mother Yvonnel Baenre in the Time of Troubles, and while the cerebral Kimmuriel had no affection for, and therefore no resentment regarding, the loss of his family, he knew that in this place, he could never find security, or be left in peace to his studies. If discovered by any of the powers that be, he would be used either as an offering to Lolth or a bargaining piece in some subterfuge between rival Houses.

He found neither proposition very appealing.

"We should have brought Jarlaxle to Luskan to meet with us," Beniago offered as they moved into the more inhabited sections of the newly-formed House, many curious stares falling over them from dark elves who were not of their mercenary band.

"Jarlaxle is being watched closely. His absence would be noted."

He is sending through a mercenary every day, Beniago protested, using the drow sign language so that he was not heard. *And replacing veterans with Houseless rogues he is pulling from the dregs of the city.*

Kimmuriel returned an incredulous look, silently asking why anyone would even care, and Beniago backed away from the argument.

They found Jarlaxle soon after, in a fabulously decorated room he had taken as his own. He looked up from the flesh of the young female he was bedding, his face brightening at the sight of his partner and their top lieutenant.

That hopeful smile became a look of concern quickly, however, for what issue could coax Kimmuriel to return to Menzoberranzan? Nothing good, likely.

Jarlaxle leaped up from the mass of pillows and limbs on the bed—enough limbs showing among the pillows for Kimmuriel and Beniago to realize that there was more than one other drow buried under there.

"Another room?" Kimmuriel both asked and ordered as Jarlaxle pulled on his trousers and then, still naked from the waist up, plopped atop his head his gigantic wide-brimmed hat with its garish diatryma feather.

"For you?" Jarlaxle replied. "Anything." And he led them from the bed, where the pillows continued to roll and bounce around, to a small door that led into a more formal study, and one that Jarlaxle had turned into an office.

Kimmuriel entered last, psionically waving behind him to slam the door shut. "There is news from the surface—from the higher Underdark, actually—that I thought might be of interest to you," the psionicist said.

"Important news, I would surmise, to bring the two of you here," Jarlaxle replied, fishing through the drawers of his desk until he at last found a blousy white shirt he could pull on. "News that will draw me from the boredom of this place, I pray."

"You did not appear very bored," Beniago quipped, glancing back at the door.

Jarlaxle shrugged. "Even that in too great abundance . . ." he lamented.

"You will want to leave," Kimmuriel assured him, "though how you might facilitate that is your concern, not mine." He looked to Beniago and bade him to explain.

"Drizzt Do'Urden has returned," Beniago began. "And with his great friends of old. They paid a visit to Q'Xorlarrin to free Artemis Entreri from the clutches of Matron Mother Zeerith's children."

Despite his discipline and determination to never tip his hand, Jarlaxle was already leaning forward, his mouth agape.

Beniago continued, divulging all that he had learned of the capture of Entreri and the others, and the daring rescue by Drizzt and his friends, including the murder of Berellip Xorlarrin. He had just relayed the fate of Dahlia, dead under a cave-in, when there came a knock on the door.

Jarlaxle motioned the others to a far corner, behind a screen and bade the knocker to enter. In walked one of Bregan D'aerthe's most promising young scouts, Braelin Janquay. He followed Jarlaxle's gaze and nod, then hesitated when he noted the unexpected visitors coming out from around the dressing screen.

"High Captain?" he asked, for rarely had he seen Beniago in his natural drow state.

"I've not the time for formalities," Kimmuriel intervened. "What do you want?"

The Bregan D'aerthe scout swallowed hard and reported. "The city is in uproar. Matron Mother Baenre has announced her choice to serve as the Matron Mother of House Do'Urden."

"I will prefer it, in any case, if it gets that wretched Sos'Umptu out of this House," Jarlaxle quipped.

"Darthiir," Braelin said, using the drow word for their hated surface elven cousins, and the clever grin disappeared from Jarlaxle's face. "Matron Mother Darthiir Do'Urden, an elf," Braelin clarified, and paused and locked eyes with Jarlaxle as he explained further, "An elf named Dahlia."

Few things could render Jarlaxle speechless. He was quite old, and had lived a life of twists and turns beyond what most drow families would know throughout several generations.

This, though, had him quietly sliding down into his chair behind his desk, his mind whirling as he tried to sort out the implications of any of this. He looked to Kimmuriel more than once, but the stoic psionicist offered nothing.

After many moments of uncomfortable silence, for Jarlaxle, who had history with Dahlia, could not begin to figure out what this might mean for him, the mercenary leader turned to Kimmuriel once more. Hadn't Kimmuriel and Beniago just told him that Dahlia had been slain? So many questions bounced around in Jarlaxle's thoughts at that confusing moment, but one notion overrode them all.

"I must be away from this place," he decided.

"As if my day could get worse," Jarlaxle lamented a short while later, when Tiago Baenre and Saribel stormed into House Do'Urden.

"Oh, it will," the brash young warrior assured him.

"Should I bother to ask what that might mean? Or are you just in a foul mood of your own because Gromph pulled you from a battlefield where you could impress yourself by killing weaklings?"

It took a moment for Tiago to unwind that remark, but when he did, his eyes narrowed and his sword hand went to the hilt of his fabulous weapon. He even jerked Jarlaxle's way just a bit, attempting to elicit a flinch from the mercenary leader.

Jarlaxle stifled a yawn.

"You do not even realize that your day is past, do you?" Tiago said. "A new era has dawned on Toril and a new generation of great drow will rise, led by me."

"And yet, here you are, by the power of the oldest drow in the city and to the call of the matron mother," Jarlaxle replied. "A weapons master in a House that barely finds a seat on the Ruling Council. Your claim of greatness rings hollow."

Tiago's eyes narrowed again and his jaw clenched, and Jarlaxle knew that the violent upstart was fantasizing about killing him then.

"Fear not, however," Jarlaxle goaded, "for one day, should House Do'Urden fail, perhaps I will find a place for you in my band. But then, perhaps not."

He turned to go, but Tiago made a strange little sound that pulled him back around, to see the young warrior's face shifting through a range of emotions, from anger to confusion to a look of dread.

Yes, Jarlaxle knew, his fantasy was playing out in his thoughts, an imagined duel with Jarlaxle. And now, poor Tiago was seeing his own death at Jarlaxle's hands.

Archmage Gromph Baenre came into the room then, jolting Tiago back into the present. The archmage stared at the brash young weapons master briefly, noting his unsettled look, then turned an accusing eye on Jarlaxle, who held his hands up innocently.

"How long am I to be imprisoned here?" Tiago demanded.

"An odd choice of words for a weapons master of a noble House," Gromph replied.

"Weapons master?" Tiago echoed incredulously. "I should be leading the armies in the Silver Marches to glorious victory. And only then, after the glory, should I take my rightful place as Weapons Master of House Baenre."

"Matron Mother Quenthel favors Andzrel for that position in House Baenre, it would seem," Jarlaxle quipped, for no better reason that to anger Tiago.

To his credit, Tiago didn't even glance the mercenary's way.

"I should not have come," Tiago insisted.

"I didn't give you a choice," said Gromph.

Now it was Gromph's turn to see the threatening stare of the impudent whelp. Yes, Jarlaxle was enjoying this, particularly the way Tiago soon shrank back.

A withering smile spread across Gromph's face, like a crack in the facing of a glacier right before a pile of cold death buried the helpless witness.

Tiago swallowed hard.

"That war was mine to win," he declared.

"That war is only your concern if the matron mother says it is your concern," Gromph calmly corrected. "You duty is here now, and so here you are."

"I have ridden a dragon!" Tiago protested.

"I have eaten a dragon," Gromph replied.

I have slept with a dragon—two! Jarlaxle thought, but did not say, though he couldn't avoid a grin at the pleasant memory of the wonderful copper dragon sisters, Tazmikella and Ilnezhara.

He thought he was about to witness a pleasant memory right then, too, for Gromph was surely about to put Tiago in his place, but then, to his surprise and to the surprise of Gromph, the harsh words came from another source.

"Stand down and shut up," Saribel said to Tiago, pushing in front of him and jabbing her finger into his chest.

He stared at her incredulously, beautifully so.

"First you insult Jarlaxle of Bregan D'aerthe and now dare question the archmage?" she yelled in his face. "Learn your place, fool, or I will be a widow by my own hand."

Tiago continued to stare at her with the most dumbfounded expression. "You?" he managed to stutter.

Saribel laughed at him. "Oh indeed, you held the upper hand, and so you enjoyed it," she said. "For the sake of my family, and for respect of House Baenre, I granted you that."

"Granted?" he asked, and he looked to Gromph for support.

But none came.

"I am Baenre now, have you forgotten?" Saribel said. "I am named as the High Priestess of House Do'Urden, but also a noble priestess of the families of Baenre and Xorlarrin. And you? You are just a male."

Gromph smiled and Jarlaxle laughed aloud.

Saribel snapped a glare over the mercenary. "As are you," she warned.

"Oh, do not make that mistake," Gromph quietly told her, and she wisely focused her ire back on Tiago. She held up her left hand, the hand he had clasped in their ceremony of marriage.

"I am Baenre," she said. "Of your own making. Were you to undo that, then Tiago and not Saribel would be cast aside by the First House."

Tiago looked to Gromph, who merely shrugged.

"She has a point," Jarlaxle had to remark.

"And now you are both Do'Urden," the archmage reminded. "Brought here to prepare the House for the coming of the new matron mother. If you are done wasting my time, do be on about your duties."

"You need to get me out of here," Jarlaxle told Gromph as soon as the happy couple left the room.

"Because of your history with Dahlia?" he asked.

"More than that," Jarlaxle replied. "There are great happenings in the world above. Bregan D'aerthe . . ."

"Is capably led by your companion Kimmuriel," Gromph interrupted, and he nodded at the grand tapestry hanging on the far wall, behind which "secretly" stood the psionicist.

"These are matters politic, of which Kimmuriel has little interest or understanding," Jarlaxle replied, and he was not surprised that Gromph knew of Kimmuriel's presence, even though Kimmuriel was psionically hidden as well as out of physical sight. Jarlaxle had long ago stopped being surprised by the things his older brother knew.

"Archmage," Jarlaxle pleaded, "do you see the possible gains here?"

"Gains for which I care little."

"Even gains to the city?"

"Especially to the city."

It was true enough, Jarlaxle knew. All Gromph wanted was to be left alone . . . or perhaps . . .

"You enjoy the presence of Methil," Jarlaxle said. "You are glad that the illithid is returned to us."

"He is a useful tool."

Jarlaxle was shaking his head, staring slyly at his brother. "No, it is more than that," he said. "You have conquered the mysteries of Mystra's Weave—are there any spells left to learn which might interest you?"

"You should not refer to the web of magic in such a way in Lolth's city," Gromph reminded dryly. "Not at this time."

Jarlaxle nodded, conceding the point, for the Spider Queen, was, after all, trying to steal the domain of magic.

"There is no secret in magic left for you, is there?" he asked rhetorically. "Oh, the occasional spell to be discovered, or a new fantastical creature to add to your menagerie, perhaps. But even that grows boring to one so accomplished as the mighty Gromph."

"If there is a point to your rambling, do get to it, for I assure you that you are more boring than anything of which you pontificate."

"Conceded," Jarlaxle replied, and he began a slow walk around the archmage, sizing him up with every stride. "But I know you, brother Gromph, and I understand your dilemma—oh, so quite well, which is why I long to be out from this place and on the road for my own adventures once more."

"Are you thinking that I might join your pathetic band?"

"No, no, of course not," Jarlaxle replied—though, of course, in the back of his mind, he did see that as a future possibility. "But I am thinking that there is only one place left for the brilliance of Gromph to explore, and that is why you are pleased that Methil is among us once more. The illithids own the secret of another magic, a purer magic, a magic of pure thought."

"Shall I polymorph myself into a mind flayer and join the hive, then?" Gromph asked dismissively, but there was a kernel of truth in that wild claim, Jarlaxle knew.

"No need," Jarlaxle answered, and he turned to the tapestry where Kimmuriel was hidden. "I know one who might take you there, to the place of pure magic. Surely you have the intellect for it."

"Psionics are more than a matter of simple intellect," Gromph reminded.

Jarlaxle nodded, knowing well that truth, for he considered himself as smart as any, and yet, the powers of psionics had eluded him, despite quite a bit of training with Kimmuriel. "But you must know," he teased.

"You try my patience."

"Train with Kimmuriel," Jarlaxle offered.

"In exchange for your freedom from Menzoberranzan?"

"Bregan D'aerthe will need my oversight in these perilous and exciting times, no doubt, particularly with Kimmuriel serving your desires."

Archmage Gromph didn't respond, and didn't blink as he stared at Jarlaxle for many heartbeats.

Then he gave a slight nod and started away—to visit with their sister, Jarlaxle knew.

As soon as he left the room, Kimmuriel came out from behind the tapestry.

"You bargain with dangerous partners," he said.

"We live in dangerous times. And Gromph will be a grateful student, I expect, whatever the outcome."

"Why do you suppose that I am speaking of Gromph?" Kimmuriel asked, and dryly—and when had this one ever put an inflection in his voice?

Jarlaxle stared in surprise, for this was the closest he had ever seen Kimmuriel come to actually threatening him.

"I cannot stay here," Jarlaxle explained. "Not with Tiago . . ."

"Tiago will not go against you," Kimmuriel interrupted. "Not now."

Jarlaxle nodded, for he and Kimmuriel had just played out that meeting with the brash young weapons master to perfection. When Tiago had begun his fantasy of attacking Jarlaxle, Kimmuriel had subtly and telepathically imparted upon him the brutally realistic images of a most unfortunate outcome should he ever try.

"Not with Dahlia," Jarlaxle admitted.

"Not with Drizzt, more likely," said the psionicist and Jarlaxle looked at him curiously.

"Your fascination with him is obvious, and greater now, no doubt, since you have learned that his old companions have somehow been reborn to his side."

71

"A gift of a god, right before us to witness," Jarlaxle agreed. "And not just Drizzt."

"Artemis Entreri, yet again," Kimmuriel said, and the mercenary leader nodded his agreement.

"So many moving parts," Jarlaxle said. "It pains me that they move without my hand near the lever. This is a great time, my friend. I feel it—and so do you. I must be free of this place, to witness the hand of the gods upon the wider world."

"I heard similar echoes in the thoughts of Tiago," Kimmuriel replied. "He will not be held here forever, not when Drizzt Do'Urden is known to be about on the surface world."

"And not when Drizzt plays a hand in the war of the Silver Marches, as we both know he will."

"Tiago's fascination with the rogue exceeds your own. He will have his battle."

Jarlaxle wondered how Quenthel would take the news when Drizzt cut her beloved Tiago into little pieces.

"I would not be so sure of that," Kimmuriel warned, and Jarlaxle looked at him curiously, for he had said nothing aloud.

Jarlaxle's eyes narrowed and he adjusted his magical eye-patch, the item he used to keep psionicists, magic-users, and priests, one and all, out of his private thoughts. He had to assume that he had worn his thoughts on his expression, and Kimmuriel had simply caught the look.

He had to hope that was it, at least.

CHAPTER 5

CROSSINGS OF THE REDRUN

A LARGE FIRE BURNED IN THE HEARTH OF MITHRAL HALL'S AUDIENCE hall, even though the sixth month of Kythorn neared its end, with the midsummer heat of the month of Flamerule whispering over the rising sun's shoulder each dawn.

King Connerad Brawnanvil crushed the parchment into a ball and kept it in his tightly clenched fist. He swung his flagon to his lips, but barely tasted the foam before he threw the whole of it, foaming ale and all, across the room to smash against the stones of the hearth.

That brought a communal gasp, to be sure, for what Battlehammer King had ever thrown a good tankard of ale?

"Good news, I'm thinkin'," Bungalow Thump said slyly. The tough Gutbuster stood strong at his king's side once more, for he had almost fully recovered already from the many wounds he had suffered in the skirmish north of Mithral Hall.

"Aye, that'd be me own guess," agreed General Dagnabbet.

Ragged Dain of Sundabar, who had just returned from the tunnels connecting Mithral Hall to his homeland, seemed less than amused.

"Crossings o' the Redrun?" he asked King Connerad.

The king nodded and threw the crumpled parchment in the same direction as the previously flying tankard.

"I seen the Silverymoon knight pacing around in circles in yer antechamber," Ragged Dain explained. "I'd come to tell ye the same grim tale. Ye heared o' Redrun Ford?"

Bungalow and Dagnabbet exchanged curious glances and a shrug.

"Easiest way to put an army across the River Redrun," Ragged Dain explained, referring to the great tributary to the River Rauvin, one of the two main rivers of Luruar. The River Rauvin flowed out from the Rauvin Mountains to the southwest, with the Redrun tributary joining it from the northwest just north of the great city of Sundabar. "Ye'd be trackin' many days back to the north and west if ye meant to go around the Redrun—and she's runnin' fast this summer—for there ain't no bridges for taking war engines across to the south. Fine place for a crossing, and fine place for an ambush."

"Many-Arrow orcs," King Connerad elaborated. "Moving south past the mountains east o' here, south o' the Glimmerwood and right past Felbarr's closed gates."

"Orcs're heading for Sundabar, then," Bungalow Thump reasoned.

"Aye, and the Knights o' Silver out o' Silverymoon seen it coming and thought they had had them orcs cut apart," said King Connerad. "They thinked to catch the whole o' the band at the Redrun and send 'em running."

"But they found more orcs than they thinked," General Dagnabbet reasoned.

"Six to one," Ragged Dain confirmed, shaking his head. "Many-Arrows breaked their forces into three groups, so we're all sayin', and ye see one o' them outside yer own doors. But even with that, the Knights in Silver found themselfs outnumbered six-to-one or more, and with hordes o' giants aside them stinking orcs."

"And with a dragon," King Connerad added grimly. "Same dragon that killed King Bromm, I'm guessin'."

"And hopin'," said Ragged Dain. "Hate to be thinking them orcs got more than one."

"Who's knowing what to think?" King Connerad asked. "Whole o' the Silver Marches're smellin' of orc."

"Eh?" Bungalow Thump remarked, and when the others looked to him, they followed his gaze to the crushed parchment, then to the door, beyond which waited the Knight in Silver emissary from Silverymoon.

"They're to be blaming us, ain't they?" Bungalow asked. "Blaming Clan Battlehammer for the darkness that's come roarin' down from the north."

King Connerad stared at the Gutbuster leader hard, but didn't refute the claim.

Bungalow Thump rushed to the door and pulled it wide. "Get in here," he ordered the Knight in Silver, who casually strolled through the door a few moments later, grim-faced and clearly not intimidated.

By that point, Bungalow had retrieved the parchment and pulled it open, grunting as he read through its flowing letters. After a nod from King Connerad, General Dagnabbet was there beside him, reading the harsh condemnation from the leaders of Silverymoon.

"By the hairy gods, what fools ye be!" Bungalow Thump roared at the knight, who stood impassively.

"Be at ease, me friend," King Connerad cautioned him. "Them boys o' Silverymoon took a beating and are smartin' good."

"I'll be givin' another o' them a beatin' if he makes a bad word about me clan and King Bruenor," Bungalow returned angrily, his fierce expression turned wholly on the Silverymoon emissary with every word.

"You cannot deny . . ." the knight began.

"Shut yer mouth," Bungalow warned.

"For meself, I canno' deny that Silverymoon and Sundabar and all the rest wouldn't stand with King Bruenor," Ragged Dain intervened. "I was there, long afore yerself was born, at the Treaty o' Garumn's Gorge. Weren't no choice given Bruenor and the Battlehammers. Only me own home o' Felbarr thought to stand aside 'em if they went to finish the war. Even the dwarves of Adbar said no, and no voice was louder against the fight than that of Lady Alustriel o' Silverymoon."

The knight snorted and looked to King Connerad.

"If ye're thinkin' to call me a liar, then do it here and now," Ragged Dain demanded. "And if ye're thinkin' that me words're wrong, then ye're a fool. Not Silverymoon, not Sundabar, not Everlund, not Nesmé, and not Adbar. Not a one. They left King Bruenor and Mithral Hall sittin' here in the middle of a vast horde o' orcs. So th'orc kingdom was staying, war or not, and so here we be, fighting a war a hunnerd years in the waitin'."

"The treaty allowed them the room to wait and grow," the knight argued. "Because of that treaty, the filth of Many-Arrows is much stronger in this day."

"And yerselfs was all for that treaty—demandin' it o' King Bruenor!" Ragged Dain shouted back. "I was there, ye dolt. I seen it!"

"Enough!" King Connerad demanded angrily, though he offered a nod of gratitude to Ragged Dain, and indeed, Bungalow Thump walked over and patted the visitor from Felbarr on the shoulder in appreciation.

"What's done's done," the King of Mithral Hall decided. "Done a hunnerd years and more. We're better talking o' what's next, not what's past."

"We must understand the culpability, that we do not—that you do not—make the same mistakes this time," the knight insisted.

King Connerad narrowed his eyes, his bushy eyebrows practically swallowing the gray orbs. "Yer lips're flappin', but all I'm hearin' is Silverymoon's desire to stand on her own," he said evenly.

The knight stammered in reply, but hadn't managed to piece anything decipherable together before Ragged Dain interjected, "Nah, good king, they're askin' indeed. That's what else I come rushing back to tell ye. They're wanting King Emerus to empty Felbarr and chase them orcs all the way to Sundabar's gate." He cast a sly look at the knight. "And likely, they're about to ask ye . . . nay, to order yerself to send all ye got running south. Course, ye'd have to break through the army on yer door to take the first step."

King Connerad digested Ragged Dain's words for a few heartbeats, then turned to the knight and asked, "Well?"

The man, obviously uncomfortable, cleared his throat. "Well, it is clear that you will need some time to break out of your hol . . . home, so your delay will be forgiven."

"Forgiven?" Connerad, Bungalow and Dagnabbet all gasped together.

"Clear?" Ragged Dain asked. "Aye, so clear that yerself had to crawl through the tunnel from across the Surbrin to even get here. Ten thousand orcs on Battlehammer's door, and ye're asking them to go running to help ye do yer fightin' in the south?"

"Should you not be organizing Felbarr's march?" the knight quipped at Ragged Dain. "Silverymoon stood in your defense along the Redrun, and where was King Emerus? Knight-Commander Degar Mindero battled bravely. The river earned its name anew, the Redrun, and now running red with the blood of orcs."

He paused and winced, clearly in great pain, and added, "And with the blood of several hundred Silverymoon Knights. The Crossings of the Redrun will be remembered for a thousand years in Silverymoon as a dark day of great gallantry."

He paused again, but this time his face screwed up with obvious anger. "And as a day when Citadel Felbarr did not come to our aid against the common horde of enemies. A day when King Emerus failed his allegiance . . ."

"Shut yer trap, ye dolt," Bungalow Thump demanded, and he started past Ragged Dain for the knight, but the old veteran from Felbarr held him back with an upraised arm.

"Ye're thinkin' we even knew?" Ragged Dain asked. "Our eyes were north o' the mountains, where King Bromm fell. Ye think we knew o' yer Knight-Commander Mindero?"

"You'd not have come anyway, would you?" the knight accused. "Safe in your hole . . ."

"Mindero's the fool," Ragged Dain said, and the knight's hand went to his weapon hilt.

"If you draw, your body will be floated down the Surbrin," King Connerad warned, his tone showing clearly that he meant every word. "Perhaps your kin will find it, perhaps not."

"Mindero's eyes filled with false hopes o' glory," Ragged Dain pressed, and now it was Bungalow Thump holding him back instead of the other way around. "Oh, but I'm knowin' that one—seen him afore prowlin' about the Cold Vale."

"Protecting Felbarr. And Sundabar," the knight insisted.

"Making his name," Ragged Dain retorted. "He didn't even tell Sundabar, eh? King Firehelm's no coward, and yer knight-commander could've bringed the thousands o' Sundabar's garrison aside him, and could've telled King Emerus to close the door on them orcs from the north. Aye. But then, where's the glory if Mindero's to be askin' for help, eh?"

The knight tensed even more, and for a moment, it seemed as if he meant to spring at Ragged Dain. But then he calmed, and stood upright with an air of superiority about him.

"The orc hordes are sweeping past your citadels," he said to King Connerad. "One army will soon press Sundabar, no doubt, and Silverymoon and Nesmé will find clouds gathering all around. Silverymoon asks you to come forth, with all speed and with the whole of your garrison."

Connerad didn't answer, and slowly turned to Ragged Dain.

"The same will be demanded of Citadel Felbarr," the knight went on. "And with all haste, to catch the horde before it can lay siege to Sundabar."

"Ye sent a note akin to that to King Emerus, did ye?" Ragged Dain asked.

"An emissary was dispatched," the knight confirmed.

Ragged Dain snorted, and locked stares with Connerad, and in that silent exchange, it quickly became clear to all in the room that the dwarves weren't about to go flooding out of their defensive fortresses any time soon.

"You test the alliance," the knight warned, apparently catching on.

"Yerself tests me patience," said Connerad. "Ye're seein' tens o' thousands o' orcs swarming across the lands, and ye're thinking that's the whole o' Many-Arrows. Ye dolt, don't ye know that orcs take to tunnels? If I'm emptyin' me halls, then I'm surrenderin' Mithral Hall to Obould's dogs. Same for Emerus and Citadel Felbarr. That what ye're wantin'?"

"The fields are black with orcs."

"And ye're afraid, and ye should be," King Connerad said. "I'll lose half me dwarves trying to break out into the army that's campin' on me doorsteps. Better for all, better for Silverymoon, that so many o' Obould's dogs got themselves stuck here in siege, keepin' us in."

The knight stiffened, then snorted derisively. "Aye," he said, "as we've come to expect from Battlehammer dwarves."

He gave a curt bow, spun on his heel, and swept out of the room.

"King Emerus ain't to go out," Ragged Dain assured King Connerad. "Not now. Not after what happened to King Bromm and his Adbar boys."

"Might be that them orcs are just goadin' us all," King Connerad warned. "They're lookin' like they be heading for Sundabar and Silverymoon, when might be that they'll turn right around if we come forth. Three treasures for them orcs above all, Felbarr, Adbar and Mithral Hall, and woe to me and me fellow kings if we let th'orcs have 'em."

"King Harnoth o' Adbar's still in Felbarr," Ragged Dain replied. "He's wantin' a thousand orc heads on pikes around his doors for the murder o' his brother."

"Adbar's farthest from the hordes," Connerad reasoned. "But I'm still thinking Harnoth's better off behind his iron gates."

Ragged Dain nodded. "I got to take me leave, good king," he said with a bow. "I'm fast bound for Felbarr and me own King's side."

"Aye, and I'm to come with ye," King Connerad announced, and he motioned to his two advisors, Bungalow Thump and General Dagnabbet, to gather their traveling gear. "Might that we'll get there afore King Harnoth's left, that we're all talkin' with one voice."

Ragged Dain nodded, and the smile that crossed his weathered old face was one of clear admiration, as if to assure the young King of Mithral Hall that he had just made a wise choice.

On the First of Flamerule, the seventh month of Dale reckoning 1484, the three dwarf kings of Luruar gathered with their commanders and trusted advisers in the war room of Citadel Felbarr.

The meeting began solemnly, with many muted toasts to King Bromm, the fallen twin brother of King Harnoth of Citadel Adbar. Several rounds of potent ale later, the toasts became more hearty, led by Harnoth himself, who recounted the good days he and his brother had shared under the tutelage of their legendary father, King Harbromm.

Toasts to salute Bromm became toasts promising retribution against the orcs of Many-Arrows, promising full payback for the disastrous Battle of the Cold Vale.

Flagons clapped together, foam flew from the side of tankards, and many a beard turned white as drinks were upended with too much vigor, and many a sleeve grew wet from wiping the foamy beards.

And so it began as a celebration, for Bromm, for the dwarves of Luruar.

That ended abruptly, though, as if all the puffing boasts expired all at once, when the clanking, the slurping and the cheering ceased, and an uneasy quiet settled over the room.

"Yerself takes the lead, out o' respect," King Emerus told King Harnoth, and the leader of Citadel Felbarr surrendered his chair at the head of the table to his friend from Citadel Adbar.

"Well, ye know that I'm wantin' to kill every orc in the Silver Marches," Harnoth began as he settled in. "And to line me porch with pikes topped in giant heads."

A couple of cheers arose, but they were muted, for Harnoth's voice was subdued, and it rang clear to all listening carefully that he was about to offer a rather large caveat.

"But I'm not for sending out me boys," he said. "Not until we're knowin' what foul powers're behind the orcs' march. Giants, aye, and that's to be expected, but me few boys who found their way home from the murder in the Cold Vale spoke of a dragon, a real one and a big one. And more than one saw himself a few dark elves."

He looked directly at King Connerad as he spoke the last part, and the King of Mithral Hall could only nod in acceptance, if not agreement, for indeed, Mithral Hall among all the dwarf fortresses had more history with the dreaded drow elves.

"Th'orcs ain't pressin' us," Harnoth continued.

"They be pressing me," Connerad interjected. "Not coming against me doors, but keepin' me doors closed, don't ye doubt."

"Aye," Harnoth conceded. "But still the biggest force crossed the Redrun, movin' south of all o' us."

"Aye," agreed King Emerus, who also looked to Connerad. "Ragged Dain told me about yer meetin' with the Knight in Silver. Sure that ye're to be hearin' the calls from the human lands to the south, playing their great butt-eyeball vision against the treaty."

King Connerad nodded grimly.

"I ain't takin' to hearing the name o' Bruenor Battlehammer tossed about like that," King Emerus promised. "The humans are writing new words into the history books, looking to send blame where they shouldn't."

"Battlehammers don't care what the durned fools o' Silverymoon and Sundabar're saying," Connerad insisted, but his tone, of course, showed that he did care, quite a bit, and that he wasn't amused.

"Well, Felbarr's caring, don't ye doubt," Emerus replied emphatically. "I was there with me friend Bruenor, and I'm knowin' that it near killed him to put his mark on that treaty. Felbarr ain't blaming Mithral Hall for this, ye should know."

King Connerad nodded in gratitude.

"Nor's Adbar!" King Harnoth shouted, and slammed his flagon down on the table. "Aye, not by a hair o' me thick beard. Me Da told me many the tales o' King Bruenor. Weren't no coward, yer old king. And I'm not taking well to hearin' that the fools to the south're shoutin' at ye about a hunnerd years past."

"Not just at me and me boys o' the hall," Connerad said, and nodded to King Emerus.

Emerus Warcrown nodded, grim-faced, and Connerad, who knew well that Silverymoon was hurling insults openly at Citadel Felbarr for not rushing out to the Crossings of the Redrun, returned the look and nod.

"Aye, and with all respect to yerself and yers, King Connerad," Harnoth said, "the cries from the south calling the dwarves o' Felbarr cowards're angering me even more than the slight to yer King Bruenor. One thing to go back and change the truth o' the past for yer own feelings, but to call me friends . . ."

"Ye're in no need o' explaining," Connerad interrupted. "And aye, when the emissary from Silverymoon spoke ill o' Bruenor, he got me words o' wrath. When he spoke ill o' me boys for not breaking out to rush south, he got a shake o' me head, the fool. But aye, when he spoke ill o' me kin'n'kind o' Felbarr, he near got me fist and a wad o' spit for his faceplate."

"Aye and so King Connerad did, and so'd his Gutbuster, Bungalow Thump. Huzzah and heigh-ho to King Connerad and the boys' o' Mithral Hall!" Ragged Dain, who of course had been in Mithral Hall for that very meeting, agreed and cheered, and the flagons came up with a rowdy cheer of solidarity, three dwarf citadels standing as one.

"So what're we to do, I'm asking?" Connerad said when the commotion died away. "Seems we're agreed that we're standing as one."

"Three as one," said Harnoth, and Emerus nodded.

"How rough's yer breakout?" Emerus asked Connerad.

"I got more orcs about me doors than I e'er seen," the King of Mithral Hall admitted. "I can punch 'em in the mouth, true enough, but they'll be yapping at me heels anywhere I'm meaning to go."

"If me and me boys crossed the Surbrin north of ye and come running down, and Emerus and his boys came to the bridge aside ye're eastern door and kept the orcs in a skirmish there, we might be swatting them good," King Harnoth said, and Connerad nodded, thinking it a proper plan.

"Aye, but what o' them orcs that ain't there?" asked King Emerus, by far the eldest and most experienced of the three. "They split into four armies, so we're hearin', counting the one on Mithral Hall's door."

"Heading south," said Harnoth.

"So we're guessing," Emerus replied slyly.

"Ye're thinking they're layin' a trap to lure us out," Connerad said, for he had mentioned the same possibility back in Mithral Hall. Orcs would prefer the dwarf citadels to the feeble human cities, no doubt.

"The prize for the orcs's got to be the dwarf homes," Emerus reasoned. "We got the mines, the forges—Citadel Adbar's providing the war ordnance for all o' Luruar."

"They'll not get Adbar," Harnoth strongly replied. "We got oil a'plenty ready to dump into the maze if them ugly orcs try."

The others in the room, king and commoner alike, nodded at that proclamation, for the defenses of Citadel Adbar were quite legendary among all the people of the Silver Marches, and greatly respected by the dwarves of Felbarr and Mithral Hall. Of the three dwarf strongholds,

Adbar had by far the most access to the surface world. The citadel itself was actually constructed above ground, and a sizable portion of the populace were housed under dwarf-made ceilings instead of tons of rock. But those realities didn't make Citadel Adbar vulnerable to enemies on the surface—not at all. The surface fortress itself lay in the center of a maze of rings of towering stone wall, mostly natural, but with added dwarven touches, like the multitude of strategically placed gates that could be lifted at a moment's notice to send a deluge of burning oil among any of the rock channels, and great stone bridges cleverly designed to drop at the pull of a lever from the guard towers, or even worse for the invaders, designed to swing down into the oil-filled channels.

Orc hordes had attacked the jewel of Adbar no less than five dozen times over the centuries, and the place had been besieged by armies numbering in the tens of thousands.

Adbar had not fallen, and would not, to orc hordes.

"Aye, but how well will yer rings and oil protect ye if the orcs get through one o' the other citadels to the underground tunnels?" King Emerus reminded, for indeed, the dwarves had done a fine job of connecting the three fortresses with subterranean passageways.

"Aye, if one falls, th'other two are more vulnerable," King Connerad agreed. "And more alone. Only way anything's getting into or out o' Mithral Hall right now's through the tunnels, and if I'm needin' to shut them down, the place'll grow tight about me boys soon enough."

"No trade, no support," said Emerus. 'Winter'll come soon enough."

"And I'm not for thinking that Sundabar, Silverymoon, Everlund or any o' the rest'll march north to help any of us," Connerad added. "The Knights in Silver didn't go runnin' to the Redrun for to help Felbarr— nay, if that'd've been the case, they'd have told King Emerus they were coming, aye? They went for glory, and fought on the ford to protect Sundabar, I'm thinking. The tall folk're thinking of each other above us, as has always been, and so for meself I'm o' the mind that we ought do the same."

"Aye, three tankards lifted as one," King Harnoth replied, and he hoisted his drink to tap the raised mugs of Emerus and Connerad.

"I'm not for thinking that there's any gain to us in breaking out now," King Emerus said after a giant gulp of drink, foam still hanging thick around his beard. "Sit tight and let me play me own counsel."

"And tighten the underground ties," Connerad added. "Armies set in place along the connecting tunnels, ready to run to one or th'other if the orcs try to find their way in."

"So ends Luruar and the Confederation o' the Silver Marches," King Harnoth warned, and the others couldn't disagree, for they all understood that if the dwarves didn't come forth now and the great cities were attacked, the anger would run deep. The sole King of Adbar shrugged as he finished and digested the responding looks, for in truth, Adbar had been the last to join the confederation, and was the farthest removed, geographically, from the wars that had now begun to boil.

"Were it e'er really there, then why's an orc army sitting atop Mithral Hall?" asked Connerad.

"Aye, and how'd the orcs get an army through the Glimmerwood to ambush yer brother in the Cold Vale?" Emerus agreed. "And why weren't them boys from Silverymoon knockin' on me door, that we could put a plan to fight aside each other? Bah, but there ain't no Luruar. Never been one."

He slammed his flagon down on the table, foam and ale flying everywhere, and wetting his beard and cheeks in such a way as to make the old warrior look even fiercer in the torchlight.

"If I'm getting one more letter blaming King Bruenor, may his beard smell o' Moradin's fine beer, then might that me boys'll come out and march aside them orcs in breaking the southern cities!" King Connerad roared, and so the toasts began anew, to Bruenor and to Mithral Hall.

Late the next day, the contingents from Mithral Hall and from Citadel Adbar shook hands in the tunnels below Citadel Felbarr, and each set off for home, Connerad to the west, Harnoth to the northeast.

When each arrived in their respective stronghold, they were met with the news that mighty Sundabar, the great city on the eastern bank of the River Rauvin just two days' march from Citadel Felbarr's southern gate, was under siege by a vast army of orcs and their dark allies. A thousand giant-thrown boulders flew over the walls each day, so it was rumored, and great dragons had been seen circling high above the city.

A flurry of correspondences rushed to and fro between the three dwarf strongholds over the next tenday, and when it was done, it was decided that they would send supplies through the tunnels to support the besieged citizens of Sundabar.

But they would not march to break the siege.

Frantic pleas from Sundabar, Silverymoon, and Everlund came back with every returning dwarf caravan.

But the dwarves stayed tight behind their iron walls and stone mountains.

The Confederation of the Silver Marches lay in ruins, and soon too, it seemed, would mighty Sundabar.

CHAPTER 6

THE BELCHING HORN

FROM THE HIGH ROAD ATOP THE ROCKY SEASIDE SOUTH OF PORT LLAST, Effron looked back to the towering stone ridges that surrounded and harbored the city he had left behind.

So much had he left behind.

A part of him wanted to rush back to the cave of Stonecutter's Solace, to find Drizzt and join in with the drow ranger and his new companions. A very substantial part of him, and that surprised Effron more than a little. He had come to trust Drizzt, to like Drizzt, and indeed, to look up to the courageous rogue. Drizzt had escaped his trials unscathed, it seemed, at least in comparison to Effron.

But now Effron had come to believe that he could scale those same emotional heights as the drow who had become as a hero to him, that he could straighten his way and heal his heart. Because of Drizzt and the others, because of the circumstance that had put him face-to-face with Dahlia, and because of Dahlia's graciousness toward him, her willingness to admit her errors, her willingness —nay desire, nay desperate need—to apologize to him, the road of hope and health lay before Effron.

At this moment, though, his heart was heavy, both from the news of his lost mother and from having to walk away from Drizzt. He knew it was the best course, though, and he reminded himself of that with a determined nod and started off along the south road at a strong pace. For some reason, Effron sensed that Ambergris and Afafrenfere were more

85

suited to serve as his companions in this leg of his personal, spiritual journey.

He paused as that notion struck him profoundly, and oddly. He looked back once more to the north, his steps slowing, then stopping all together as he reflexively eased around.

"They are as troubled as I am," he said quietly. "They too seek a truer road." He heaved a great sigh, one that sent his dead arm behind his back swinging, and nodded—it would not be fair to throw his personal turmoil into the group with Drizzt and his friends. He had heard enough about that troupe to realize that he didn't belong with them. Not yet, and perhaps not ever. Surely they had more important tasks to accomplish than helping a wayward and confused young half-tiefling warlock find his way.

"She would not approve," he said with a laugh as he considered his bone staff. What might the reaction of Catti-brie be the first time Effron performed his, to her eyes, unsavory magic?

He nodded again, more convinced that he had done the right thing, for himself and for Drizzt, by departing Port Llast. With what he thought a last glance, he turned around once more.

A magic alarm went off in his thoughts.

Traveling alone down a dangerous road, Effron often enacted such divination spells, and now his magical ward, a spell to detect living creatures, told him that something, someone likely, was nearby.

He scanned carefully, but saw nothing. He quietly cast a spell to reveal invisible beings, but that, too, showed him nothing.

He completed a slow turn, ending with him facing out to the sea, looking out over a sheer drop. Slowly, he inched up to the lip of the low cliff.

Effron leaped back as a tall, red-haired man came over that lip, suddenly and so easily.

"Well met," the man said, "again."

Effron stared at him hard, unable to place him. He thought he had seen this man before, but under very different circumstances, likely, for in this place, in this time, he could not recall.

"Again?" Effron asked, leaning on his staff, and ready to put the powerful item into action.

"I know you, Effron son of Dahlia, even if you do not recognize me," the stranger said. "Several times have you come through my city."

The way he spoke the last two words, my city, sparked a bit of recognition in Effron. "High Captain Kurth?" he asked as much as stated.

"Good, you recognize me," the red-haired man replied. "That saves me the trouble of convincing you that I am one worthy of your time and attention."

"It was a guess," Effron said, for the two had never actually met. But Effron had seen this man from afar. After he, Drizzt, and the others had been rescued from Draygo Quick's dungeons by Jarlaxle, they had gone through Luskan, and in that journey through the streets to a waiting wagon north of the city, he and the others had passed by Closeguard Isle. This man, or one who looked very much like him, had been watching them intently from the bridge, and Drizzt had whispered his name to Effron.

Effron's eyes went wide, though, as he placed the man, for that had been before he had gone into the enchanted forest on the banks of a lake in Icewind Dale.

That had been nearly two decades earlier, yet this man standing before him would have been but a child . . .

The twisted warlock backed away a step and brought his staff before him. "Who are you?"

"You just said."

"Who are you?" Effron demanded.

"I am Beniago, more commonly known as High Captain Kurth, as you stated."

Effron shook his head, muttering, "It has been two decades, yet you seem a young man still."

"Ah, I see," Beniago said, and he gave a bow. "I am half-elven."

Effron narrowed his eyes doubtfully.

"You left Drizzt in Port Llast?" Beniago asked.

"Your presumptions do not impress."

"Please, must we play this game?"

"You could leave, or I could kill you," Effron replied.

Beniago's casual and amused smile warned him that such a task wouldn't likely prove easy, but Effron kept faith that this one didn't understand the truth of the dark power he was now facing. Surely most people underestimated this broken and frail-looking tiefling when first they saw him.

"When Jarlaxle pulled you from Draygo Quick's tower, when Athrogate led you and Drizzt and Ambergris to the waiting caravan, who do you think . . . arranged all of that?" Beniago asked.

"Jarlaxle."

Beniago laughed and conceded the point with a bow.

"Do you know who controls Luskan?" he asked.

"High Captain Kurth," Effron said, his tone one of mocking disrespect.

"Jarlaxle," Beniago admitted, and when Effron's eyes betrayed his surprise, the red-haired man merely shrugged.

"It was Jarlaxle who told me to return the jeweled dagger to Artemis Entreri and fashion the deal with Drizzt when he and Entreri came north to Luskan," Beniago explained. "On the command of Jarlaxle, I arranged your transport to Icewind Dale those many years ago. And still I serve our drow friend, and by his bidding am I here now."

"What do you want?"

"Where are you going?"

"South."

"Why? Did you not leave Drizzt and his companions in Port Llast?"

"If you know, why are you asking?"

The red-haired man rubbed his face with obvious exasperation. "Come," he said. "I do not wish to delay you. We will walk together."

"I prefer to travel alone."

"It is not your choice."

Effron cocked an eyebrow at that, and at the obvious change of tone.

"I am Jarlaxle's eyes and ears in the north," Beniago said bluntly. "I fear his wrath more than yours, I assure you, and also . . ." He glanced back to the south, and Effron turned around, to see a contingent of drow soldiers on the road. Beniago then turned north, leading Effron's gaze back that way, and to another group of dark elves who had appeared there, seemingly out of nowhere.

"Let us walk," Beniago said. "My associates will remain at bay."

Effron stared at him hard, his reservations clear. "Half-elf?" he asked sarcastically, and Beniago laughed as if it did not matter.

"Jarlaxle has earned your trust," Beniago reminded him. "Many times over. Jarlaxle seeks information. It is how he survives. It is how he is able to know when he is most needed, as in the castle of Draygo Quick, yes?"

Effron couldn't deny that, and he felt his visage soften a bit.

"Besides," Beniago added, "perhaps I can be of some assistance to you, young warlock. Once I know more of your destination and your plans, you will find that I am no enemy—indeed, were I an enemy, you would be on your way to Luskan now, in chains stronger than iron, and you would tell me anything I wished to know . . . eventually."

It wasn't a threat, but it hung there like it might become one. Effron looked at the drow soldiers behind, and those ahead, and knew he was woefully overmatched. He thought to assume wraith form and slip away into the stones, and perhaps make an escape.

But these were dark elves, and a shudder coursed his spine as he considered the damage and destruction this very band had exacted upon the castle of Draygo Quick, a warlock many times more powerful than Effron could hope to be.

And also, he considered, there was more than a kernel of truth to Beniago's words. Jarlaxle had never been anything but an ally, and given the dark elves all around, and given that High Captain Kurth had come out to find him, the only sense he could make of this was the explanation Beniago had just offered.

He started off, Beniago at his side, the dark elves disappearing from sight, and soon the two were talking like old friends, without reservation.

The companions lingered in Port Llast for many days, begged to stay by the people of the town, who feared another drow raid—and not without some reason, given the explosive breakout from Gauntlgrym. A sense of duty and responsibility had forced them to remain in the vulnerable city, despite Bruenor's constant grumbling against that course—for the dwarf's sense of duty wanted him on the road to finally resurrect, redeem, and put to rest Thibbledorf Pwent. And more importantly, Bruenor felt as if he had been called by his gods to the road to Mithral Hall.

The days became a tenday, then two, and with no signs that the dark elves were coming for retribution, Bruenor finally got his way. Regis on his fat-bellied pony, Drizzt on Andahar, Catti-brie on her summoned spectral mount and Bruenor and Wulfgar trading stories and taking turns guiding the wagon, the Companions of the Hall set out from Port Llast, riding north.

They stayed along the coast road for a short while, seeking a trail Drizzt knew to take them more easily through the rolling hilly region of the Crags. The air was light, the weather fine, and the five companions made the most of the journey, sharing songs and tales, and even engaging in some sparring as they set their nightly camps.

"The new Wulfgar's so much akin to the old," Catti-brie remarked to Bruenor, sitting by the fire one night. The barbarian had just battled Drizzt in a wild back-and-forth affair, countering the drow's superior speed with brute force and a much longer reach. The fight had ended with Wulfgar hoisting Drizzt up in one arm, Wulfgar seemingly at an insurmountable advantage—and all three of the onlookers cried out in surprise that Wulfgar had bested Drizzt.

But alas, when the combatants unwound, the last to be revealed was the drow's arm, bent back behind his shoulder at a seemingly impossible angle, and yet a perfect angle to hold the fine edge of Twinkle against Wulfgar's throat.

"Fightin' better, I'm thinking," Bruenor replied. "Seems to me the boy had the drow there."

"Many the dead enemies thinked they had the drow there," Catti-brie said with a grin, her blue eyes sparkling as she studied the lithe form of her dark elf husband.

Bruenor's teeth showed through his orange beard as he looked at his girl. "Ye're talkin' like a Battlehammer, girl," he said.

It was true enough, Catti-brie could not deny; being around Bruenor again was bringing out the brogue.

"Yerself should get into the ring," Bruenor remarked. "Yer magic's all fine and good, but might be the time when ye're needing a bit o' the fist, or the blade. Have ye forgotten that ye was once a fine fighter? And trained by the best of all?"

Catti-brie thought back to her time in the floating city of the Shade Enclave, when she was in training under the tutelage of Lady Avelyere and her sisterhood known as the Coven. Those sorceresses relied fully on their magic and their wiles, and Avelyere had taken Catti-brie to task when she watched the gruff young battle-mage at her furious play, as often kicking an opponent as blasting it with magic.

"I've not forgotten a thing," the woman replied.

"Then go and fight," said Bruenor. "Rumblebelly's waitin'."

"Aye, and he's waiting for yerself," Catti-brie replied. "I'll be tangling with Drizzt later."

Bruenor's face became a scowl for just a moment, a reminder that he was still her father, as he replied, "Aye, but I'm talkin' about fighting."

"Well, dwarf?" Regis called from the other side of the fire. He held his rapier up in salute. "Have you rodents in your beard needing to be plucked?" He finished with a flourish and sudden stab of his slender blade, poking it in Bruenor's direction several times in rapid succession.

"Bah, but I'd find more challenge in downing me mug o' ale," Bruenor yelled back, and made no move to stand. "Ye go and kick the little one around," the dwarf quietly offered to Catti-brie.

"They'd be small rodents, I am sure," Regis added. "Have to be, to hide in a beard so thin and short."

Walking to the dwarf and Catti-brie, both Wulfgar and Drizzt burst out in laughter.

And Bruenor didn't even seem to move, but he had indeed, flipping to his feet so quickly that he had gathered up his axe and shield before Catti-brie even realized that he was no longer sitting beside her.

"I'll be keepin' me boot up yer arse until it grows thicker then, Rumblebelly," Bruenor grimly promised, and he banged his many-notched axe against his shield and stomped off, pushing roughly between Drizzt and Wulfgar and kicking the edges of the campfire so that sparks and embers leaped into the night air.

Drizzt collapsed onto the ground beside Catti-brie, breathing heavily.

"I go to tend the horses, and to fetch a bit more wood," Wulfgar said, his words coming in bursts that showed he, too, had been exhausted by the match.

"Not too far, I hope," Drizzt replied. "You would wish to see this, I expect." He nodded to the combatants across the fire.

"Aye, I'll move around to the other side in the trees," Wulfgar said with a wide grin, "to keep those two with the fire behind them."

"He fights well," Drizzt said as soon as he and Catti-brie were alone. "Better than I remember, even."

"He lived in Icewind Dale to be a very old man," Catti-brie reminded him. "It is a place full of battle, and so his experiences grew as his body weakened."

"That was a long time ago."

"Not so," Catti-brie replied. "Not for him. A couple of days in the forest and he was given a new body. A new body, but with the experiences of an old warrior. He trained, from the beginning of his new life, I expect, as did we all."

She turned to the match across the way. "It is all we had."

Drizzt kept looking at her for a long while, absorbing her words. What must it have been like to be trapped in a child's body with the memories of an old warrior? They had described to him the sensation of simply trying to control the movements of a finger in their earliest days of rebirth. Was it a hopeful experience, where the conquering of movements came quickly, to be celebrated? Or was it a tenday of frustration for every minor victory, a moment of control separated by endless hours of unanswered demands?

"With determination," Catti-brie said, drawing him from his thoughts, and Drizzt gave her a puzzled expression.

"How we got through it," Catti-brie explained. "That's what ye were thinking, aye?" She turned to face him directly, a knowing grin on her face.

"Determination," she said, and she nodded across the way, drawing Drizzt's gaze to the joined fight.

And what a row it was.

Bruenor rolled around, axe arm extended in a great sweep. He pulled up short and launched into a bull rush, so suddenly and brutally that Drizzt was sure he'd bury Regis where he stood.

But no, the halfling was too quick, and beautifully balanced. He darted to the right a step, tapped off three quick thrusts, jabbing his rapier into Bruenor's leading shield, then cut back the other way, forcing Bruenor to skid to a stop and whirl around to keep his shield in line.

"The cadence," the drow heard himself say.

"What?"

"Regis tapped his blade to set a cadence for Bruenor, and only for that," Drizzt explained. "He knew he could not get through Bruenor's perfect defense, so he coaxed him like a drummer's march, goading him forward enough for Regis to get beside the charge."

"Determination," Catti-brie repeated. "Our little Regis is all grown up."

"He fights brilliantly," Drizzt agreed.

They two went through a series of thrusts and sweeping cuts, and every time Bruenor bulled forward with his shield, Regis was quick enough to disengage. Clearly he had surprised the dwarf, as Bruenor's frustration shined in the firelight, his toothy grimace clear within his beard. He wasn't expecting this, for he was remembering Regis—nay, Rumblebelly—and did not know this creature before him, this Spider Parrafin.

But still, this was Bruenor Battlehammer, who had sat on the Throne of the Dwarven Gods, who had basked in the light of Moradin, who had heard the whispers of Dumathoin, who had bathed in the blood of

92

Clangeddin Silverbeard. He hadn't found a way to get at Regis, perhaps, but neither had the halfling found a weakness in the dwarf's skilled defenses and solid balance.

They moved in to close quarters then, the dwarf waving his axe in short cuts, Regis poking and prodding, seeking an opening.

Bruenor rolled his shield arm forward, but Regis sidestepped. Out flashed Bruenor's axe, but out came the halfling's dagger at a perfect angle to intercept.

Now Regis came forward with a thrust, but Bruenor's axe wagged back in close, slapping it sidelong.

The halfling rolled his blade and Bruenor turned his axe, the weapons winding and wrapping around each other in a confusing blur.

"Take care," Drizzt whispered, for the two were putting each other off-balance, and in such a twisting clench . . .

The rapier slipped free, too fast for either to react, and Regis's weight was forward, and so forward went the blade.

Bruenor cried out and fell back.

"Regis!" Catti-brie shouted, for the rapier had stabbed the dwarf in the neck, and a thick line of blood ran down Bruenor's throat, disappearing behind the metal collar of his breastplate.

"Ah, ye rat!" Bruenor howled, and he leaped forward, bulling and chopping wildly.

Regis got his blade up at the correct angle to intercept the leading shield, and used the collision to help propel him back from the charge.

But on came Bruenor again, furiously, howling and spitting curses, bearing down on Regis like a swooping eagle descending on a helpless rabbit.

Catti-brie sucked in her breath and Drizzt winced, both thinking their little halfling friend was about to be clobbered.

Bruenor thought so, too, as was evident by the expression on his face when Regis disappeared, simply disappeared, warp-stepping ahead and to the side as the dwarf skidded past.

"Aha!" the halfling cried, and he swatted Bruenor across the arse with the side of his blade. "Victor . . ."

He almost got the word out before Bruenor swung around and shouted, "Tricksters are we?" And the dwarf reached behind his shield and produced a flagon of ale, and promptly flung the foamy contents into Regis's face.

His ensuing bull rush connected this time and sent the halfling flying.

"Bah, but I'll be takin' a bit o' yer hide, Rumblebelly!" the dwarf cried as he charged in behind the living halfling missile.

Regis panicked, clearly, and cried out in terror. He flicked his dagger arm forward, though why the others could not tell.

Bruenor's charge ended abruptly, instantly, and he flew the other way and over backward, axe flying free, hand coming to his throat.

And behind him, the specter loomed, tugging the snake garrote.

"Regis!" Catti-brie and Drizzt cried together.

Clearly, the halfling understood his mistake, for he leaped forward and stabbed over Bruenor's shoulder, stabbed the spectral assassin so that it disappeared into blowing smoke. Bruenor gasped and fell flat.

"Oh, but ye're to pay for that," Bruenor promised, slowly rolling up to a sitting position, then staring hard at the halfling as he started to his feet.

Regis wanted no more of him. Not then. With a shriek, the halfling sprinted off into the trees.

Up leaped Bruenor, grabbing his axe as he ran by, off into the darkness in pursuit. Even as the dwarf disappeared from sight, Wulfgar walked into the firelight, trying futilely to suppress his laughter.

"Better than the entertainment in any tavern in Baldur's Gate," the barbarian declared, and he and Drizzt laughed heartily.

"There could be monsters lurking out there in the forest," Catti-brie reminded.

"Let us hope so!" Wulfgar cried, and all three laughed then, and laughed all the harder when Bruenor roared and Regis shrieked.

A long while later, Bruenor walked back into the camp, and his hands were not red from wringing a halfling's neck.

"The little ones are adept at hiding in the forest, so I'm told," said Wulfgar, who was alone in the camp, as Drizzt and Catti-brie had wandered off.

"Bah, I should've blowed me horn," the dwarf said with a grumble. "The little rat."

"When we join in battle with real enemies, your feelings about Regis's newfound skill might be different, I expect," said Wulfgar, and Bruenor managed a smile and conceded with a nod.

"Little one's quicker'n I'm remembering," the dwarf admitted.

Not sure of his bearded friend's remaining simmer, Regis thought it best to wander around the forest a bit longer. Silent as a shadow, weapons in hand, and the campfire in sight through the boughs, the halfling was not afraid.

When he heard a noise beyond a ridge the other way, he didn't flinch and didn't hesitate. He fancied himself a scout, and it seemed that there was scouting to be done. As he neared, when he heard the ring of a blade, he only clutched his own weapons tighter and moved with more determination and speed.

He slid up over the ridge on his belly, worming in between a pair of bushes, and there before him, on the banks of a small stream, stood Catti-brie and Drizzt, each holding one of the drow's scimitars.

They too were in practice, he realized.

They passed with a ring of metal, each turning, scimitars lifting between them. Then back again the other way, Drizzt quickstepping and Catti-brie taking a simple step back to let him harmlessly past.

Regis marveled at their dance, at the harmony of it, for even when they were engaged in sparring, these two blended together so well, and even when they struck at each other with weapons, the movements seemed more the dance of love than the fury of battle.

This was an exercise more to achieve harmony of movement than to become quicker and more clever with the blades, a dance more than a fight indeed, where the couple were using the battle to find unity in their movements, to anticipate, to tease with a dodge, to tickle with a touch.

Regis rolled on his back and slid back down the far side of the ridge, not wanting to further spy on a dance they had made private. He remained on his back and stared up at the stars, his heart full from the love he saw in his two dear friends.

He thanked Mielikki with all his being for the chance to experience this again. All of it, from Bruenor's spitting fury to Wulfgar's seeming amusement with life, to the bond between Drizzt and Catti-brie, indeed, the bond between them all.

He heard laughter from the other side of the ridge and could imagine the couple tumbling down together into the soft sand at the stream's edge.

Regis, too, had sparred like that, danced like that, and with a woman as dear to him as Catti-brie was to Drizzt.

His heart ached for Donnola, but there was more warmth than pain as he remembered the sparring that had led to their first lovemaking.

That thought jolted Regis back into the present, and he hustled away, not wanting to intrude on Drizzt and Catti-brie's private moment.

When he came back into the camp, he found Bruenor and Wulfgar scratching out a game of Xs and Os in the sand, each with a mug of beer. Bruenor looked up at him sternly and gave a little growl, and Regis skidded to an abrupt spot.

"Bah, ye little rat, pull up a log and I'll get ye a beer," the dwarf said. "Just ye promise me that when we find us some orcs, ye'll fight just as well."

"Better," Regis promised, pulling up a seat and plopping down beside his friends, as Bruenor drew forth another mug from his strangely enchanted shield. "I was merely playing with you, for I did not wish to humiliate a proud dwarf before his friends."

Bruenor had just begun to reach out with the beer when the taunt hit his ears, and he pulled the tankard back.

Wulfgar's laugh jumped right to the dwarf, though, and then to the halfling, and the three lifted their tankards in a clinking, foam-flying toast.

On midsummer's day, bright and sunny and particularly hot, the group at last came in sight of the town of Longsaddle. Many cheers and waves followed them as they wound their way through the town to the gates of the Ivy Mansion on the hill, but no folk followed them, most reclining in the shade and enjoying the heat as if it was an excuse for a bit of laziness.

Regis surely shared that notion.

"Word has already been sent forth for those who will help us," Penelope Harpell assured them when they presented her with the cracked horn containing the spirit of Thibbledorf Pwent. "Our clairvoyants have been watching the road for your approach."

She offered them all the hospitality the Harpells could muster, which was surely a considerable amount. Catti-brie soon went back to her old spot in the House library, brushing up on her old spells and seeking some new magical combinations she might employ, and old Kipper joined her, demanding that she entertain him at length with tales of their daring adventure in Gauntlgrym.

Regis was granted a special place at a small pond in the house's back courtyard.

"Fish to your content," Penelope bade him, smiling wide. "But be wary and quick, I warn, for you never know what you might hook in the pond of the Harpells."

Regis grinned from ear-to-ear—until he fully realized the actual implications—this being a Harpell house—of what she had said. Then he looked at his flimsy pole a bit suspiciously, and it took him a long while to muster the courage to actually drop a line into the bright waters.

For Bruenor, the day was full of impatient pacing, and Drizzt stayed by his side, reassuring him and helping him plot their course of action upon their return to the Silver Marches. Was Bruenor to announce his true identity immediately to Clan Battlehammer? And if he did, what implications might such a remarkable revelation hold for King Connerad? Connerad was indeed King of Mithral Hall, and not merely a Steward in Waiting.

The hypothetical exercise was more to keep Bruenor calm than anything else, for Drizzt knew that they'd find unexpected allies and enemies when they returned to the Silver Marches, and he suspected that any plans they might now make would be altered by necessity in short order when the reality of the situation, whatever it might be, confronted them. Still, such planning was a positive and constructive way to pass the time.

And that was the point, for they all needed to pass the time busily that they didn't dwell on the expected conclusion. They were awaiting a priest to properly finish their job.

A priest to destroy the vampire. A priest to destroy Thibbledorf Pwent.

Too many emotions and opposing thoughts punctured their patience whenever their minds were idle.

So they kept busy, planning, playing, studying, or whatever else they could find as a diversion.

"I thought I would find you out here," Penelope Harpell said when she turned a corner around a trellis of grape vines to come into view of Wulfgar.

The barbarian smiled at her, a bit of wistfulness there as he, like Penelope, remembered their last encounter in this garden.

"It is cooler inside," she added.

"I grew up in Icewind Dale, and so I have learned to appreciate the hot days," Wulfgar replied. "And, too, I lived for many years in Mithral Hall, and so the sun shines all the brighter to me."

Penelope grinned and walked off to the side, glancing at Wulfgar out of the corner of her eye and muttering something he could not make out.

A moment later, she spun on him, and threw her hands his way and called out the final words of a spell she had quietly enacted.

Wulfgar's expression went from curiosity to surprise to shock as a large volume of water appeared in the air above his head and splashed down upon him, and Penelope laughed riotously.

"What?" he sputtered, and shook his head, his long blond locks flying wide and throwing water around. He leaped at Penelope reaching for her hands, for she was into her spellcasting once again.

And she kept going when he caught her, and a second flood of conjured water appeared above them both and splashed down upon them.

Both were laughing then, and Wulfgar pulled back to wipe his face. His mirth ended abruptly, though, when he could not help but notice the effect of the water on Penelope's thin blouse.

He swallowed hard.

And then again when Penelope came to him and took his hands, and went up to her tip-toes to kiss him. A sweet kiss it was, and Wulfgar wanted to pull away, but found he hadn't the strength. Penelope Harpell was in her late forties, but he couldn't deny her attractiveness, and it was a beauty that grew greater to him every time the intelligent wizard uttered a word. He lifted the woman in his arms, crushing her tightly against him, and pressed his lips into hers with a passion he had not known in a long, long while.

But then he broke free and pushed her back, stammering, "I . . . I cannot."

"Of course you can," she said, coming forward, and Wulfgar backed to keep distance between them.

"I cannot cuckold your husband," he said, and Penelope was laughing before he finished the thought.

"Did you not once tell me that the aim of living was pleasure?"

"Not at the expense of . . ."

"There is no expense," Penelope said, and she rushed up and caught him around the waist. "I exact no promises from Dowell, and he none from me."

"He is your husband."

"And I love him, and he loves me. And I would kill for him or die for him, and he for me, but this . . . this is simple play, and it is unimportant to us."

"I am truly flattered," Wulfgar said dryly.

"Not that," Penelope laughed. "Fidelity is not a course we choose. We are loyal in spirit, but we indulge the flesh." She pressed a bit closer, and laughed, clearly understanding that she had Wulfgar more than a little uncomfortable.

"Fear not, wonderful Wulfgar," she whispered. "I do not ask for loyalty from you."

"Then what do you ask?"

"Adventure," she answered and kissed him again, and wearing a mischievous grin, pulled him down to the wet grass.

Candlelight filled the dark, thick-walled basement chamber beneath the Ivy Mansion, the dancing light reflecting off the glassy sheen of the many inks marking magic circles of protection.

"Shouldn't we be doing this out in the daylight?" a nervous Regis asked.

"The sun would torment him terribly, and might even destroy him, before the spell was completed," Kipper Harpell answered.

"Well, near sunlight, then?" offered the halfling. "A curtain or closed door away?"

Kipper laughed and turned away, and Penelope offered the halfling a comforting smile.

"I expect that Regis has seen enough of the dead of late," Drizzt put in dryly, "chased as he was across the lands by a particularly nasty lich."

Drizzt smiled as he finished, enjoying the tease of Regis, but that grin went away when he noted Penelope and Kipper exchanging what seemed to him to be a nervous glance. He made a mental note to inquire about Ebonsoul, the lich they had trapped in the phylactery the Harpells had prepared for Thibbledorf Pwent, before they left. He turned his attention to Catti-brie and Bruenor, who stood at the side of the room, quietly talking and both staring at the broken silver horn as Bruenor rolled it over in his hands. With the phylactery occupied by the spirit of the lich, the magical horn in Bruenor's hand had come to serve as the vampire Pwent's prison.

Wulfgar sat on the stone floor in the corner behind them, his gaze repeatedly going to Penelope Harpell, Drizzt noticed. Drizzt had a good idea of what that might be about, but he wasn't going to dwell on it in this important moment. He scanned to the right, across the room, where a robed priest whispered incantations as he traced the magic circle. The old man bent, dipped his fingers in a pot of ash, and drew a glyph of runes above the symbols etched into the floor. This circle of protection had been designed to ward demons or devils, Penelope had previously explained to Drizzt, but this priest Kipper had brought in could alter it to strengthen its effectiveness against cursed undead beings.

After a long while, the priest stood up and brushed his hands together, then stretched his back, turned around, and offered a grim nod to the others.

Drizzt swallowed hard. It was time. He knew in his heart that this was certainly for the best, particularly for Thibbledorf Pwent, who was clearly losing his battle, indeed losing himself, against the unrelenting curse of vampirism.

But still . . .

It hurt. A lot. More than Drizzt expected, surely. He remembered when he had left Pwent in the cave in the Crags, just outside of Neverwinter. Holding faith in the tough dwarf, Drizzt had expected the coming dawn to be the end of Pwent, and he had accepted that and had moved on.

But still . . .

He watched as if in a distant dream as Penelope went to Bruenor and escorted him to the edge of the magical circle and bade him to enter it.

The dwarf's hand trembled visibly as he lifted the silver horn to his lips, and he had to pause there and collect his breath, steadying himself as best he could and swallowing hard against the lump that had come into his throat.

"It is for Pwent," Catti-brie said, and Drizzt glanced her way, to see Wulfgar beside her, his arm casually draped across her shoulders. On Penelope's motion, Wulfgar walked from Catti-brie's side to Bruenor.

He should go to Catti-brie, Drizzt knew, but he did not, instead turning his gaze back to Bruenor as the dwarf lifted the instrument to his lips.

The note he blew was not clear and melodic, as had come from the horn before. Far from it. The whole of the note vibrated discordantly from the crack the capture of Pwent had put in the instrument, the effect sounding more like the low and shivering rumble of a naval foghorn.

Or the rumble of a dwarf too full of Gutbuster and spicy foodstuffs, Drizzt thought, and he held back his giggle—an inappropriate bit of mirth, surely, and yet, a thought that helped him then, undeniably so.

Gray fog poured from the horn, floating down before the dwarf king. It started to spread wider, but the edges of the magical circle contained it fully as it took the shape of Thibbledorf Pwent.

"Me friend," Bruenor said quietly when the vampire dwarf materialized, and he dropped his hand on Pwent's shoulder.

"Me king!" Pwent cried happily, but his expression changed immediately and he looked around, his face darkening. "Me king?"

Across the room, the old priest began his powerful spell.

"Wulfgar," Penelope whispered.

"Eh?" Pwent said, and he growled then, his eyes going wide with apparent fury—and with pain as the old priest's cadence and volume increased.

When Bruenor made no move to back away, and seemed incapable of doing anything in that terrible moment, Wulfgar reached into the magical circle, grabbed the dwarf king by the shoulder, and tugged him across the edge of the protective circle.

And Pwent followed, leaping for the pair, shouting, "Ye treacherous dogs!"

If he had run into the side of a building, he would not have stopped any faster, for a wall of bright, holy light leaped up from the runes before the leaping vampire, burning at him and blocking his course. He staggered backward, clearly in pain.

Then Thibbledorf Pwent seemed more like a rabid animal than a dwarf. He leaped and spun around, spitting curses and rending the air. He darted this way and that, but the circle was complete, unbroken, and walls of brilliant light leaped up before him to defeat his progress whenever he drew too near the perimeter.

"Ah, but ye're a liar and a fool!" he yelled at Bruenor.

Drizzt started to his friend, but stopped, for Bruenor steadied himself and stared back at Pwent without blinking. "Once ye would've given yer life for me, yer king," he said. "And I'd've given me own for the likes o' Pwent. And so now ye're being told to do just that, and for yer own sake, ye iron-gutted, stone-headed battlerager."

Pwent stood in place and seemed to be battling against intense pain. "Ye . . . ye catched me and ye killed me to death . . ." he stammered angrily.

"Ye're already dead, ye fool!" Bruenor shot back.

The old priest lifted his voice and the vampire was driven to his knees.

Bruenor fell back, but did not turn away. None of the Companions of the Hall turned away, knowing their duty to witness this, as friends to Pwent and to each other.

It went on and on for a long while, and with every word the old priest uttered, Pwent was clearly shot through with pain, the holy enchantment piercing the animating power of vampirism. Pwent continued to curse and to thrash. More than once he found the strength to hurl himself at Bruenor, only to be intercepted and rejected by the magic of the rune-etched circle of protection.

Still it went on, the priest unrelenting, and more than once Drizzt fought the urge to run over and stop the old man's devastating chant.

Pwent's agony could not be denied; it seemed as if he was being tortured here, brutally so, his face twisting, his words garbling as surely as if he had been staked to a post and jabbed with glowing hot pokers.

The vampire dwarf remained on his knees. He couldn't begin to get up, obviously. He did manage to get his hands up over his ears, pitifully and futilely trying to block the magical intonations, the blessed chanting, that so profoundly pained him.

Finally the priest stopped, abruptly so, his last notes echoing off the stone chamber's walls.

The glorious lights of the holy circle of protection died away, and there was only candlelight once more.

Pwent remained in place, and only after a long, long while did he bring his arms back down and manage to look up at Bruenor again. He didn't cry out in rage, though, but in a very weak voice asked, "Me king?"

Bruenor didn't even wait for permission, but pulled free of Wulfgar and leaped forward into the circle once more. He fell to his knees before the sobbing dwarf.

"Oh, ye forgive me, me king?" Pwent asked weakly, and he seemed to be aging with each word, his vitality falling aside as the protective cloak of vampirism dissipated into nothingness. "I weren't strong enough," he whispered, and he slumped forward and Bruenor grabbed him and hugged him close.

"Ye're the strongest I e'er knowed," Bruenor said to him. "And most loyal, and know that there's to be a statue o' Pwent in Mithral Hall, in a place of honor beside the kings. They still know ye, me friend. In Mithral Hall, aye, there's still many the huzzahs for any mention o' Thibbledorf

Pwent, though ye ain't been there in many the decade. I heared them meself, I tell ye and I'm not for lying to ye. Not now, no."

He pulled Pwent back to arms' length—he wanted Pwent to see the sincerity on his face as he reassured him.

But alas, Pwent wasn't seeing anything.

Bruenor pulled him close and hugged him again.

They buried Pwent in a cairn behind the Ivy Mansion the next morning—a temporary grave, for Bruenor assured the Harpells that he would return to collect the body so that it could be properly interred in a place of honor in Mithral Hall, as soon as he had set things in order among Clan Battlehammer. Few words were said as Pwent was lowered into the stones, and other rocks piled atop him, but as they neared the end of the solemn moment, Bruenor held up the silver horn and declared, "Know that I'll blow it in me darkest battles, me old friend. And I'll know yer spirit's aside me, and woe to them standing afore me."

He started to lower the horn, but Regis grabbed him by the arm and motioned for him to blow, and that seemed a fitting way to end the interment of Thibbledorf Pwent.

And so, on a sunny and hot summer's day, the discordant blast of the broken silver horn sounded in Longsaddle, drifting on the slight summer breeze. And drifting, too, came a grayish fog, and all the friends watched, confused, as that fog formed into a familiar figure indeed.

"Pwent," Bruenor breathed as the battlerager formed and began hopping around wildly, snarling "Me king!" repeatedly and clenching his fists as if looking for something to hit.

"Penelope!" Drizzt cried, drawing his blades. The leader of the Harpells rushed up beside him, shaking her head, clearly at a loss.

Pwent continued to hop about, glancing this way and that, but made no move to approach any of them. Finally, he turned to Bruenor and held up his hands as if at a loss, and faded to gray fog, which was collected once more by the silver horn.

"Oh grand," Regis exclaimed.

"It wasn't Pwent," Catti-brie said. "Not his soul, but . . . " She looked to Penelope, who looked to the old priest, who could only shrug.

Kipper's laughter brought all eyes upon him.

"The horn!" he cried and clapped his hands together. "Old magic dies hard, it would seem."

"You don't mean . . ." Wulfgar remarked.

"A rather unique berserker, I expect," Kipper said. "Yes, King Bruenor, blow your horn when battle is joined, and find the strength of your old shield dwarf ready to defend you."

Bruenor looked at the horn incredulously, then around at his friends. "It ain't him?" he asked Catti-brie.

The woman shook her head. "Thibbledorf Pwent has passed on from this world," she assured him. "Truly. He is at peace."

"What you summon is the magic of the horn," Penelope agreed. "It is the embodiment of the fighting spirit of Pwent, fashioned corporally by the magic of the horn. Nothing more."

Bruenor rolled the horn over in his hands and glanced to Wulfgar. "How many?" he asked.

The barbarian shrugged. "I found as many as ten allies in the notes of that horn."

"Ten Pwents?" Bruenor asked with a wicked grin.

Kipper laughed. "Just the one, I would presume," he explained. "Then ten previously expelled were the embodiments of ten different slain barbarians, I believe."

"Bah," Bruenor snorted, a wide smile showing under his red beard. "Ye give me ten Pwents and I'll take down the whole lot o' Many-Arrows in short order."

Drizzt laughed aloud, as did the others, as did Bruenor. For the Companions of the Hall, there could not have been a better or more fitting way to end the funeral of Thibbledorf Pwent.

Except, of course, for hoisting a tankard of ale in toast to the fine fellow, and Bruenor very quickly took care of that little detail.

PART TWO

UNDER THE DARKENED SKY

I HAVE LIVED THROUGH TWO CENTURIES, AND MUCH OF THOSE YEARS have known conflict—battle and war, monstrous ambushes and unexpected dangers.

Yet if I add together all of the actual fighting I have done in my life, that total measure of time would pale against the number of practice hours I might devote to my fighting in a single tenday. Indeed, how many hundreds of hours, thousands of days of time, have I spent in turning my weapons against imaginary opponents, training my muscles to bring the blade to bear as fast as I can manage, in perfect balance, at the right angle, at the right moment?

In a single session of training, I might execute a middle thrust more times than in all the fights I have ever known, combined. This is the way of the warrior, the only way, and the way I have come to know as truth, of anyone and everyone who deigns to rise to excellence, the way of anyone and everyone who seeks perfection even while knowing that there is no such thing.

For there is no perfect strike, no perfect defense, no perfect form. The word itself defines a state that cannot be improved, but such is not the case, is never the case with muscle and mind and technique.

So there is no state of perfection, but to seek it is not folly, nay, for it is that very seeking, the relentless journey, which defines the quality of the warrior.

When you see the journey and focus not merely on the goal, you learn humility.

A warrior must be humble.

Too often do people too greatly measure their lives by their goals, and, subsequently, by that which they consider accomplishments. I have reflected on this many times in my life, and so the wisdom of years has taught me to constantly move the goal just beyond my stretching reach. For, is the downside to achievement complacency? I have come to believe that too often do we name a goal and achieve it, then think the journey at its end.

I seek perfection, with my blades, with my body. I know there is no such thing, and that knowledge drives me forward, every day, and never inspires frustration or regret. My goal is unattainable, but the truth is that it is my journey to that goal that is more important.

This is true of every goal of every person, but rarely do we see it. We seek goals as if their achievement will grant magical happiness and unending fulfillment, but is that ever the case? Bruenor would find Mithral Hall, and so he did—and how many years subsequent to that achievement did my dwarf friend seek ways to un-discover the hall? At least, to remove himself from the goal he had set, as he sought new adventures, new roads, and new goals, and ultimately abdicated his throne in Mithral Hall entirely.

As this is true for the king, so it is true for the commoner, so it is true for almost everyone, living their lives in a mad rush for the next "if only," and in doing so, missing the most important truth of all.

The journey is more important than the goal, for while the goal might be worthwhile, the journey is, in fact, the thread of your life.

And so I set an unreachable goal: perfection of the body, perfection in battle.

That lifelong quest keeps me alive.

How many times have I narrowly escaped the bite of a monstrous maw, or the murderous edge of an enemy's blade? How many times have I won out because of the memory within my muscles, their ability to move as I need of them before I register the thought to move them? The relentless practice, the slow dance, the swift dance, the repetition of repetition, ingrains carefully considered movements to the point of mere reflex. When I dance, I see in my mind's eye the angle of my opponent's attack, the balance of his feet, the posture of his form. I close my eyes and put the image there in my mind, and react to that image with my body, carefully calculating the proper response, the correct parry or riposte, the advantage and opening.

Many heartbeats will pass in that single imagined movement, and many times will many heartbeats pass as the movement is executed again and again, and altered, perhaps, as better angles present themselves to my practiced imagination. Over and over, I will do this same dance. The pace increases—what took fifty heartbeats will take forty-nine, then forty-eight, and down the line.

And when in real combat my eyes register the situation pictured in my mind's eye during practice, the response will happen without conscious thought, a flicker of recognition demanding reflexive counters that might be fully played before the time span of a single beat of my heart.

This is the way of the warrior, honing the muscles to act correctly upon the slightest call, and training the mind to trust.

Aye, there's the rub of it all. Training the body is easy, and it is useless if the mind, too, cannot be properly conditioned.

This is the calm of the hero.

From my experiences and encounters, from speaking to warriors, wizards, priests, from watching incredible courage under incredible duress, I have come to believe that in this regard, there are three kinds of people: those who run from danger, those who freeze when in danger, and those who run into danger. This is no great revelation to anyone, I expect, nor would I expect anyone to believe of himself or herself anything but the latter of those three choices.

But that reaction, to run to danger, to face it forthright and calmly, is the least likely among all the races, even the drow and even the dwarves.

The moment of surprise stuns the sensibilities. Often will a person caught in a sudden emergency spend too long in simply processing the truth of the moment, denying its reality as that very reality overwhelms the onlooker.

"It cannot be!" are among the most common of final words.

Even when the situation is consciously accepted, too many thoughts often blur the reaction. When faced with a grievously wounded companion, for example, a person's fears of unintentionally doing something harmful can hold back the bandage while the friend's lifeblood pours forth and stains the ground.

When battle is joined, the situation becomes even more complicated, for there is also the matter of conscience and fear. Archers who can hit a target from a hundred paces often miss an enemy at much closer range, a much easier shot. Perhaps it is conscience, a flicker of a person's soul telling him that he is not a killer, that he should not kill. Perhaps it is fear, since the consequences of missing the mark could soon thereafter prove fatal to the shooter.

In the drow martial academy of Melee-Magthere, when I began my training, one of our first classes involved an unexpected attack by duergar marauders. The raiders burst through the doors of the training hall and took down the instructors in a matter of eye-blinks, leaving the students, young drow all, to fend or to die.

I witnessed dark elves of noble Houses fleeing out the back of the chamber—some threw down their weapons as they went, screaming in terror. Others stood dumbfounded, easy kills for the enemy gray dwarves—had it been an actual ambush.

A few leaped in for the battle. I was among that group. It wasn't courage that drove my feet forward, but instant calculation—for I understood that my duty, my best chance for doing the greatest good for Menzoberranzan and my fellows at the Academy, and indeed, my best chance for surviving, lay forward, in the fight, ready to do battle. I don't know how, but in that moment of sudden and overpowering stress, my mind overcame my heart, my fears fell away beneath the call of my duty.

This expression and reaction, the masters of the academy called "the calm of the hero," and we who faced the duergar properly were acknowledged, if not applauded.

For those who ran or froze, there came angry recriminations, but none were summarily dismissed from the Academy, a clear signal that the masters had expected as much. Nay, those who failed were trained—we were all trained—hour after hour, long day after day, endlessly, relentlessly, brutally.

This test was repeated many months later, in the form of another unexpected battle with a different enemy in a different location.

Now many more of us had been taught what some of us had instinctively known, and relying on that training, few fled and fewer froze in place. Our enemy in that battle in a wide tunnel just outside the city, was a band of goblins, and this time, unlike with the duergar, they had been instructed to actually attack us.

But this time, unlike with the duergar, the ambushers met a force that had trained under skilled masters, not just physically, but mentally. Hardly a scratch showed on black drow skin when the last goblin fell dead.

Those dark elves who fled or froze, however, would get no more chances in Melee-Magthere. They were not possessed of the mind of a warrior and so they were dismissed, summarily.

Many, I later learned, were also dismissed from their Houses and families in shame.

In the cold and heartless calculations of the Spider Queen and her wicked matron mothers, there is no place in Menzoberranzan for those who cannot learn the way of the warrior.

Watching Regis these last tendays reminded me of those days in Melee-Magthere. My halfling friend returned to mortal life determined that he would rewrite the impulses in his heart and brain, that he would teach himself the way of the warrior. When I consider my own experiences, and the progress of those many dark elves who failed the first encounter with the gray dwarves, but fought well against the goblins, I nod and understand better the truth of this new and formidable companion.

Regis sometimes calls himself Spider Parrafin, the name he found in this new life, but in the end, he is Regis, the same Regis we knew before, but one who through determination and the pursuit of an unattainable goal has found confidence enough in himself to walk the road of the warrior.

He has confided to me that he still has doubts and fears, to which I laughed.

For that, my halfling friend, is a truth universal to all the folk of all the reasoning races.

—Drizzt Do'Urden

CHAPTER 7

TO THE EDGE OF GLOOM

DRIZZT CRESTED A RIDGE ON A HIGH JUT OF ROCK AND LOOKED DOWN to the east, where the snaking waters of a small river, the Shining Creek, wound through the grassy plain. The drow had noted storm clouds in the distant east, or at least he had thought them storm clouds, but now that he was up high and with a wider view, he wasn't certain at all.

There loomed a darkness there, in the sky beyond the Shining Creek and the Surbrin River, but even from this distance, it appeared like no storm Drizzt had ever seen. The whole of the land beyond the river was dark, as if in a starless night, and not shadowy as if speckled by the daytime clouds. From this high perch, Drizzt could see the late morning sun shining in the sky to the east, but those rays found no way through to the land beyond the rivers, it seemed.

The strangeness of the sight accentuated just a moment later, as the sun continued its travels, moving far enough beyond the blackness of the clouds, or whatever they were, to send its light and warmth to the waters of the creek. Drizzt watched the shadow retreat to the east, then blinked against the sting as the snaking river lived up to its name, a brilliant line of winding silver.

Bruenor charged up to him, huffing and puffing as he hopped from stone to stone. "Ye won't get away, elf," he called, for he had foolishly challenged Drizzt to a race over the rocky hill. He came up laughing, ready to leap past, but he skidded to a stop and his grin disappeared when he, too, looked to the unnatural darkness in the east.

"What in the Nine Hells?" Bruenor asked.

Drizzt shook his head. "I guess from your expression that the sky in the east didn't look like that when last you came west from Mithral Hall."

"Never seen a sky lookin' like that," said Bruenor. "Ye thinkin' that's even the sky?" He shook his head, clearly at a loss. "Looks more like someone stole a patch o' the Underdark and plunked it down o'er me home."

Somewhere below on the hillside, Wulfgar whistled.

The pair turned back and glanced down, but their friends were not in sight. "He's thinking we're bein' followed," Bruenor explained.

"Shadowed," Drizzt corrected. "You remember these hills?"

Bruenor nodded. "Surbrin Hills. Uthgardt land."

Drizzt pointed to an expanse of taller green grassy hills southeast of their position. Between two rounded tops, a thin line of smoke drifted lazily on the light winds.

"Sky Ponies?" Bruenor asked. He and Drizzt had come this way before, long before. Before the Spellplague, before the Time of Troubles, before Bruenor had reclaimed Mithral Hall for Clan Battlehammer, even. They had left Icewind Dale alongside Wulfgar and Regis, determined to find Bruenor's ancestral home, and just north of these very hills, they had been taken captive by an Uthgardt Tribe known as the Sky Ponies.

Drizzt shook his head. "Griffon's Nest," he explained, referring to the village of the Uthgardt Griffon tribe. "It is well-known to travelers about the region these days, for unlike the Sky Ponies, the Griffons are traders."

"Aye," Bruenor said, and he nodded as the reference incited old memories. Mithral Hall had traded with Griffon's Nest on a couple of occasions during Bruenor's reign. "They still know ye?"

Drizzt nodded, but then seemed unsure. "It has been many years since I visited with them. Likely most of those who showed me hospitality are gone now to the halls of their gods."

"I'm wanting to be home anyway," Bruenor grumbled. "Straight east to them clouds . . . to whatever that darkness be."

"The Uthgardt Griffons will likely know something of it," Drizzt pointed out.

Bruenor looked to the wafting smoke. "Not like them Sky Ponies?" he asked, as if needing the assurance, for his visit with that other Uthgardt tribe had not been a pleasant one.

Drizzt grinned and glanced down the hillside behind them, where the other three of their troupe had come into sight. With his long legs, Wulfgar easily bounded up to join the pair.

He, too, wore a puzzled look as he glanced to the east, to the darkened skies. Regis, too, when he arrived, but the most profound reaction came from Catti-brie, who stared out that way with a look of clear concern. She didn't say anything, but neither did she blink.

"Do you know what it is?" Drizzt asked her.

"Mystra's Weave?" Regis added. "Unwinding again? Or thickening? Or . . ."

"It has nothing to do with Mystra," Catti-brie said definitively.

"What're ye knowing, girl?" Bruenor demanded.

"That it is unnatural," she replied, and she finally pried her eyes away to turn her look, not to Bruenor, but to Drizzt. "And that it is connected. I can sense it."

"Connected?" Drizzt asked.

Catti-brie glanced around to their companions one at a time, leading the drow.

"Connected to us," Regis reasoned. "To us coming back."

Wulfgar looked to the east. "Mielikki?" he asked.

"Th'other one, I'm bettin'," Bruenor said, staring hard at his daughter. "Are ye sure, girl?"

Catti-brie shrugged and shook her head. "The coincidence," she explained, still helplessly shaking her head.

"To Griffon's Nest," Drizzt said. "Let us gather our wagons and mounts and be on our way for that settlement marked by the smoke. The tribe will have answers for us." He started off even before he finished speaking, the others falling into line behind him. They were a solemn procession, mostly, but Bruenor managed more than a few growls about "whacking orcs" along the way. Every bump along the rough trail that jolted the wagon elicited another curse from the now-surly dwarf. The others couldn't blame him, as that unnatural darkness hovered right over Bruenor's beloved homeland.

Near the rounded top of a wide, grass-cloaked hill, the companions found their destination, marked by a high palisade of thick, stout logs. Several farms lay scattered outside the settlement and large humans, male and female, watched the curious procession of a drow on a unicorn, a robed woman on a spectral unicorn, a halfling on a fat pony, and a dwarf and a huge man driving a wagon.

Looking past one trio of onlookers, to the right side of the trail leading up the hillock, the friends caught movement of a more serious matter, for a cavalry patrol, long-legged barbarians looking out of place on short ponies, was shadowing them and beginning to swerve in to intercept along the road, it seemed.

Drizzt and Catti-brie slowed their pace to let the wagon and Regis's pony catch up.

"Hurl no missiles, verbal, axe, or hammer," the drow said, then looked at Regis and added, "or hand crossbow quarrel or choking snake."

"I should speak for our group," said Wulfgar. "They are Uthgardt, my people."

Drizzt nodded, and motioned to Catti-brie, and the couple guided their unusual mounts to the back of the wagon, letting Bruenor and Wulfgar take the lead.

Only a short distance later, the pony cavalry came rushing out to block their way on the road, a score of barbarian riders with javelins resting easy on their shoulders, ready to throw.

"Well met, brothers of Tempus," Wulfgar said, standing and reaching across with his right fist to thump himself on the left breast. "I am Wulfgar, son of Beornegar, of the tribe of the Elk of Icewind Dale."

The pony riders spread out a bit, and one man with long black hair, tied and braided with feathers over each shoulder, eased his pony mount forward.

"Greetings, Wulfgar," he said, and similarly thumped his left breast. "I am Keyl, son of Targ Keifer, chieftain of the Griffon." He gave a slow visual inspection of the other four. "You travel with strange companions."

"Your father will know me," Drizzt interjected. "Though he was but a child when last I visited Griffon's Nest, no doubt. But then again, perhaps he will not, for I didn't stay long."

A smile creased the pony rider's face. "You are Drizzt Do'Urden," he stated.

"Well met, Keyl, son of Chieftain Targ Keifer," Drizzt replied. "I am humbled that you recognized me."

"Not many dark elves are known to be riding about the surface world on a unicorn," the barbarian replied, and the tension, what little there was, fell away. Behind and about Keyl, the others laughed and lowered their javelins as Keyl turned back to Wulfgar. "What brings you to Griffon's Nest, son of the Elk?"

"We are returning to Mithral Hall," Wulfgar answered, and he pointed to the east, to the dark sky in particular. "The way seems amiss."

Keyl nodded grimly. "Come," he bade them. "I will grant you an audience with Chieftain Targ Keifer."

A short while later, the companions found themselves seated at the side of a long table, with many barbarians flanking them and seated across from them. Children hustled about with plates of food and tankards of mead—good mead, which made Bruenor smile. Keyl's patrol had gone back out, but he had remained behind, sitting beside Wulfgar and asking about life in Icewind Dale.

The small talk went on for some time, until at last, the great Targ Keifer entered the room. All the barbarians leaped to their feet and gave the chest-thumping salute, and the companions followed suit. Targ Keifer took his place directly across the table from the companions, a sturdy and handsome middle-aged woman with thick black hair and heavy dark eyebrows taking her seat beside him. As she did, she motioned to the other woman who had entered the room beside the chieftain, to sit to her left. This woman did not appear to be of the Griffon tribe. She was strong and solidly built, but not as big-boned as the Uthgardt people. She was dressed in riding garb and covered in the mud of the road, so that her long and dark brown hair was matted, and her light gray eyes shone even more starkly against the ruddy texture of her round face.

Targ Keifer waved his son around the table to sit at his right. Keyl slid into his seat and began hurriedly whispering to his parents, explaining and introducing the newcomers.

"I remember your name, but not you," Targ Keifer said to Drizzt, apologetically. "But welcome again to Griffon's Nest. To all of you."

"We have not come for trade," Wulfgar said. "We did not intend to disturb your village at all."

"Hardly a disturbance," the chieftain replied.

Wulfgar nodded. "We changed course when we crossed the hills, for from the higher ground . . ."

"You saw the darkening," Targ Keifer interrupted. "Clearly. And you are hardly the first bound for the Silver Marches who have turned to inquire at Griffon's Nest."

He leaned forward and looked to his left, motioning for the woman with the light gray eyes to speak.

She turned her roving gaze over the companions, settling on Drizzt, and didn't seem overly eager to engage in any discussion.

"He is Drizzt Do'Urden, friend of Mithral Hall, friend of Silverymoon, friend of Luruar," the chieftain explained.

"Friend of Many-Arrows?" the woman asked suspiciously.

"Bah, filthy orcs," Bruenor growled. "Knowed it had to be them."

"Drizzt Do'Urden is known to Nesmé," the woman said.

"Nesmé?" Bruenor huffed. "Yerself's from Nesmé? Ah, but here we're goin' again."

"It was Drizzt Do'Urden who brought about the kingdom of Many-Arrows, the scourge of Luruar," the woman stated. She was breathing in labored gasps, as if her mounting anger threatened to simply overwhelm her, as she continued in a low and seething tone, "And it is House Do'Urden that has darkened the sky above the Silver Marches, that has incited the minions of Warlord Hartusk."

Many barbarians about the table slammed their hands down at that, and Chieftain Targ Keifer and his wife and son all turned suspicious stares upon the drow.

"There is no House Do'Urden," Drizzt said calmly.

"The orcs speak of Matron Mother Darthiir Do'Urden," the rider from Nesmé accused. "I have heard it myself. Do you call me a liar?"

Drizzt wore a helpless and perplexed expression. He looked to his friends and shook his head, having no idea what any of this might be about. His House, his family, had been wiped out more than a century before!

"What do you know of this?" Chieftain Targ Keifer demanded.

Before Drizzt could answer, Bruenor slammed his palms down on the table and drove himself to his feet. "Enough, I tell ye!" the dwarf bellowed. "I ain't for hearing another word down this line o' applesauce. I ain't for knowing what ye're babbling about, girl, and I ain't for caring."

"And who are you?" the chieftain's wife asked.

"Of the royal line o' Mithral Hall," Bruenor answered.

"A son of King Connerad?" the rider from Nesmé demanded, and the way she spat the name of Mithral Hall's king showed her to be none too pleased with Connerad and the boys of Mithral Hall, either.

Bruenor snorted at her, but didn't bother answering. "Th'orcs're out o' their hole, are they?" he asked the chieftain. "I expected as much. Aye, but we'll be leaving now."

He started to stand, but all the barbarians about the table leaped to their feet, as if to stop him.

"Ye wantin' to play this game?" Bruenor asked.

"Where will you go," Chieftain Targ Keifer, who had not stood up, asked calmly.

"Trouble's that way," Bruenor said, pointing to the east. "So that's where I be headin'. And if ye're thinking o' stopping me . . ."

The chieftain patted his hands in the air to calm Bruenor and his own tribesmen. He looked left and right, patting more emphatically to get his minions to sit back down.

"What is House Do'Urden?" he asked Drizzt.

"I was born unto House Do'Urden," the drow admitted. "But that was two centuries ago. There is no House Do'Urden."

The chieftain looked to the rider from Nesmé.

"I only know what the orc raiders we captured claimed," she explained. "Would they concoct such a name without cause or prompting?"

"Even if there is such a House as you state, then it is not connected to this dark elf you see before you," Catti-brie interjected. "Would we have come in here, were that the case?"

"If you did not know that I would be here," the woman said.

Before anyone could respond, Regis gave a little laugh, then stood up and walked over to Drizzt. He whispered into his friend's ear and placed his blue beret upon Drizzt's head.

A moment later, Drizzt's skin lightened and his white hair became a lustrous golden hue, more so than that of the young woman, even. In mere moments, he looked like a surface elf.

"I give you an emissary of the Moonwood," Regis explained.

Drizzt pulled the beret off and handed it back, immediately reverting to his drow appearance.

"So you see? It would have been no trial at all to disguise our companion," Regis explained. "But why would we? The name of Drizzt Do'Urden is well known in these reaches, and throughout Luruar, he is welcomed. As are we all."

Chieftain Targ Keifer looked to the rider from Nesmé. She started to protest, but he hushed her immediately.

"Is the darkened sky spreading?" Catti-brie asked.

"It did to its present state," Targ Keifer replied. "But it has not widened in several tendays."

"It is a pall over all of Luruar!" the woman from Nesmé added.

"Then to Luruar we must go," said Drizzt, "with all speed."

———— ⌒⌒ ————

"Shadowing us," Regis whispered to Drizzt, walking his pony up beside the majestic Andahar.

Drizzt nodded.

"The woman from Nesmé?" Catti-brie asked, and the drow nodded again.

"She would not be much of a scout if she did not, I suppose," said Drizzt.

"Go and tie your pony to the wagon," Catti-brie said with a clever smile a few moments later. "Past time for you to take a nap, I believe."

Drizzt looked at her curiously, then turned to Regis, who was smiling widely and already turning his fat-bellied pony about.

"You would have him confront the woman?" Drizzt asked his wife when he finally caught on.

"He's the least intimidating," Catti-brie said. "If no longer the least formidable."

Drizzt nodded, then his eyes widened as he digested the second part of her statement. With a grin of his own, he turned back to regard Regis, who was already in the back of the wagon, tying up his pony.

"Down there," Catti-brie said, drawing his attention back to her, then following her gaze to a copse of trees just ahead along the winding road. "Under that cover, so our shadow doesn't see."

As they neared the cluster of trees, Catti-brie eased her spectral mount's pace and slipped off to the side of the trail. She nodded to Bruenor and Wulfgar as the wagon rumbled past her.

"So what're ye about, girl?" Bruenor asked. "And if ye're heading back there, then rouse the lazy little one."

"Not lazy," Catti-brie assured him with a wink. She walked her mount right up behind the wagon and quietly cast a spell, cloaking the waiting Regis with magical invisibility. As soon as she was finished, she trotted her spectral mount back out and around to rejoin Drizzt at the front of the procession, whispering the plan to Bruenor and Wulfgar as she passed them by.

The companions came out of the trees in that order, the drow and his wife leading on their magical unicorns, the dwarf and the giant barbarian laughing and swapping tales as they drove the wagon, and the halfling's pony tied behind it, with the little one apparently asleep inside.

Except, Regis wasn't asleep or inside any longer.

"I'm thinkin' we turn north and stay far from the Trollmoors and the town o' Nesmé, elf." Bruenor called as they cleared the trees, and he was making no secret of it. "Bah, but I'm thinking Nesmé's worse than the durned Trollmoors. Sure that they ne'er went out o' their way to greet a Battlehammer or a drow, eh? Bwahaha!"

"North," Drizzt agreed, again, turning back to regard the drivers. "It will be good to see the walls of Mithral Hall once more."

"Huzzah and heigh-ho!' Bruenor cried. "And good king Connerad's only to be good if he's got a flagon o' ale waiting for me thirsty lips."

He gave a great laugh and spurred the team on.

"Damned to have a drow nearing my town," Giselle Malcomb muttered as she guided her horse into the copse of trees, having watched the companions ride out the other side, eastbound.

"He's not so bad a fellow," came a voice from above and the woman from Nesmé stopped her mount with a slight pull on the reigns. She froze, not daring to reach for her sword or the bow she had settled across her saddle. Only her eyes moved, scanning up into the boughs to spot the stylish halfling, in his fine shirt and breeches, black traveling cloak, and that blue-flecked, remarkable beret. He sat comfortably on a thick branch, his feet crossed at the ankles and dangling free, fine black boots catching the speckles of sunlight coming through the trees from the west.

"Indeed, many would call him a hero, particularly those who know him best," the halfling went on.

"I have heard his name," Giselle admitted. "It is not spoken with fondness in Nesmé."

"True, but that is only because the folk of Nesmé won't look beyond their own noses for heroes."

The woman straightened and glared at him.

"I am Spider Parrafin of Aglarond," Regis said.

"You were introduced at Targ Keifer's court as Regis of Icewind Dale," Giselle retorted, and she smiled knowingly as the halfling winced. "Ah, of course, but you were not present when the Griffon guard came to us in our private audience and announced your arrival, so you would not know that."

"It is another name I carry," the halfling stuttered. "A complicated tale . . ."

"One I care nothing about," the rider replied, and now she did move, easily lifting her bow. "My experience tells me that fools who carry more than one name are always thieves or worse."

She blinked then, just as she went for an arrow, thinking to arrest this one and interrogate him more forcefully, for from nowhere, it seemed, the little one had drawn a curious weapon, a crossbow, only much, much smaller than any such weapon Giselle had ever seen.

He extended it with one hand and pulled the trigger, and the woman jolted as a small dart stabbed her in the left shoulder. Almost immediately, she felt the burn of poison.

"Ah, murderer!" she cried, and though her arm grew heavy and her shoulder throbbed, the veteran warrior kept her wits enough to grab for that arrow.

But again the clever halfling moved first, this time thrusting his hand out to Giselle, throwing something small. Instinctively, she got her hand up to deflect, but the item—at first she thought it a length of cord no longer than her forearm—hooked about her thumb.

Only then did she realize that it wasn't a cord at all, but a living snake. With a yelp, she tried to brush it away, but the thing moved with uncanny speed and agility, sweeping over her shaking hand and rushing the length of her arm, and as she turned, dropping her bow back across her lap so she could slap at the creature, it darted under her slap, or perhaps she had struck it, but not hard enough to dislodge it, and rushed up and about her neck.

Both hands went in to grasp at the living noose, but even as Giselle grabbed at the coil at the front of her neck, something yanked at it from behind, and with supernatural strength, throwing her backward, pulling her from the saddle. She crashed down to the ground hard and awkwardly, one foot still caught in the stirrup, and thrashed about helpless, too concerned with being unable to draw breath to even realize how much her twisted leg pained her.

She grasped and slapped at the living garrote, flailing futilely.

Her vision tightened, darkness creeping into the edges of sight.

She felt herself falling, falling, far from the world of the living.

"Welcome back," came a woman's voice, calm and steady.

Giselle Malcomb felt the bump and roll of a bouncy road, the jolting along with the call gradually easing her back to her senses. She opened her eyes, then reached up to rub them, and as she found her focus, she saw the woman, Catti-brie, above her, kneeling beside her.

Immediately, Giselle tried to rise up on her elbows, but a wave of pain laid her low.

"Be at ease, rider of Nesmé," Catti-brie said. "You took a tumble and badly twisted your knee. I've given you some healing magic, but it will take just a bit of time to get you up on your horse again."

"My horse!" Giselle exclaimed, and stubbornly, she forced herself up to her elbows. She was in the back of their open wagon, she realized, and she noted the halfling ambusher—Regis, or Spider, or whatever his name might be—sitting easily in the back corner of the wagon bed, feeding carrots to his pony and her horse.

"A fine animal," the halfling said.

"Careful," Catti-brie remarked to Giselle, "or Regis there will make your fine mount as fat as his pony. He bribes with food, does that little one, so typical for a halfling."

"Regis? Or Spider?" Giselle managed to ask, her tone accusatory, her eyes narrowed on the halfling.

"Both," Catti-brie answered. "But always Regis to us."

"I didn't want to shoot you," Regis added.

"Or to throw some demonic serpent upon me?" the woman asked.

"Or that," Regis replied. "But I just wanted to stop you—your arrow would have skewered me front to back and more."

"How can there be more?" Catti-brie asked, and from the other way, up above her head, Giselle heard the laughter of a dwarf.

"Or are there really two of you, then?" Catti-brie went on. "One Regis and one Spider, one ever invisible and both taking turns to confuse folk?"

"Bwahaha!" the dwarf howled.

The halfling walked over and knelt beside the woman of Nesmé. "Pray forgive me," he whispered to Giselle. "I had no choice."

"You could have just remained with your friends instead of ambushing me on the road," Giselle retorted, and now another voice came from above her, and the huge golden-haired barbarian twisted about and leaned back so that she could see his face above her.

"That you might set the Riders of Nesmé upon us?" he asked. "Or do something stupid yourself, and then we would have had to kill you? We left the halfling behind to speak with you, to learn your intent, to insist that we are not your enemies, but like so many of your kin—aye, we've met them before, in another time, another age even—you are too full of pride to hear any such suggestion. So you are here, our guest, and you will be fully healed soon enough, and returned to your horse with all of your belongings."

"I do not . . ." Giselle began to protest, but the barbarian cut her short.

"And if you come against us in any way, then know that you'll not feel the bite of the halfling's hand crossbow," he insisted. He held forth his huge warhammer for her to see it up close, and indeed, it seemed an impressive and powerful weapon. "But instead, the weight of my throw. And after that strike no magic will awaken you."

His severe tone had Giselle off-balance, and even the barbarian's friends seemed taken aback somewhat.

"This is Nesmé land . . ." she tried to argue.

"We are crossing this land," he cut her short, "on our way to Mithral Hall. And if you or any others of Nesmé deign to stop us or even delay us with anything other than an offer of a fine meal, then you will be a meal for the birds, the worms, and the daisies."

"Enough, boy," Giselle heard the dwarf say.

But the barbarian shook his head, scowled even more fiercely, and lowered down so that he was closer and more imposing to the wounded and helpless woman. "I have been to Nesmé, so many years ago. I did not much like the people I found there on that occasion, and so the impression seems to hold true today. So mark my words and mark them well. You will find me less merciful than my companions."

With that, he turned around, and Giselle swallowed hard.

"Listen to him," Regis added solemnly, and his tone and demeanor showed that he was clearly shaken by the barbarian's grim warning.

Giselle rested back, turned away from the others, even bringing an arm up to shield her eyes, and said no more.

"Surely unnatural," Catti-brie said to the others, except for Drizzt and Regis, who had gone ahead to scout. They had come under the dark blanket that was Luruar's sky, and as soon as the roiling blackness had gathered above them, it seemed as if night had descended in full. Looking back to the west, they could still see the sun, low and near the horizon, but its light was a meager thing indeed; they could stare at it with unshielded eyes, not even squinting. It was just an orange dot, far, far away.

"I could have told you as much," Giselle said from the back of the wagon. She was sitting up fully now, and feeling much better.

"Aye, but ye didn't," said the dwarf called Bruenor—and Giselle thought it the height of presumption that a dwarf had named his child after that long ago king, and the height of absurdity that any dwarf of any clan would want to take the name of the dwarf who had imperiled the whole of Luruar out of such cowardice!

"So busy are ye with throwing yer insults and yer threats, ye've not bothered to tell us anything worth hearing," the dwarf went on. "So much akin to yer stupid ancestors. Bah!"

"What would you know of that?" Giselle retorted, for clearly, this dwarf was younger than she!

"Yeah, ye keep thinking that, stubborn fool," the dwarf mumbled and turned away.

Giselle stared after him and started to throw an insult, but Catti-brie spoke first. "Let your anger pass, both of you," she begged. "There is no point to it. We are not enemies."

"Ain't friends," Bruenor insisted.

"And no need to be," said Catti-brie, and she turned to Giselle.

"Just give me my horse and I will gladly take my leave," the Rider of Nesmé said.

Catti-brie shook her head. "Not yet, I beg. The halfling's poison is a potent brew. The slumber might return, in mid-ride even. Just a bit longer, and I'll renew my spells upon you, and you can safely go. Besides, our road is your road for a bit longer if you mean to return to Nesmé, in any case."

"I prefer a quieter road," Giselle replied, and she stared at the back of the dwarf's hairy head.

"As would I," said the huge man called Wulfgar, and he turned back to regard Giselle. "So would you please shut up?"

Giselle glared at him, but he didn't blink and didn't back down. Indeed, a sly smile spread on his face, as if he knew something she did not, and under that intense gaze, Giselle felt herself blushing.

Tucked into the leaves of a high branch, Regis looked upon the encampment with trepidation. The orc encampment, he believed, judging by the cut of the tents and the hunched forms he saw silhouetted against the central bonfire. Dark Arrow Keep lay many miles to the north and east, for he was on the very western edge of Luruar, a place not known for orcs.

Or had the minions of Obould spread so far and wide, spilled from the borders of what had been their granted kingdom, expanding their lines with the sheer weight of numbers? Regis didn't think that likely, particularly given the odd sky above and the rumors he had heard in the mead hall of Targ Keifer.

The notion, however, inspired a memory of Bruenor, sitting about a campfire one long-ago night, in the days of the first King Obould's great invasion.

"Bah, but they breed like bunnies in a field o' clover," the dwarf had said. "And who'd think it, for who'd want to breed with a thing so ugly?"

The halfling turned back in the direction of the wagon and his companions, thinking he should go and tell them.

But where had Drizzt gone off to?

And what would he tell them, exactly?

He looked back to the encampment. His mind drifted back across the years, to what he had been, to what he had determined he would be, to what he had become.

He tapped his blue beret, settling it more firmly upon his head and called upon its magic. He closed his eyes and tried to remember. He hadn't encountered many orcs, but having seen one or two up close on occasion made it a hard image to forget. He pictured the lupine ears and the dry and rough skin—was it green or gray?

"And the tusks," he whispered to himself, and imagined a boar's face. He brought his hand up to where his hat had been, and now found long and stringy black hair.

He reached into his pouch and brought forth a small mirror, but in the dim light, he couldn't be sure of the disguise.

He looked back to where his friends might be, full of doubt, but then turned resolutely to the camp, bent low and grasped the tree, then rolled under the branch, holding to his full length by his hands before dropping easily to the ground below.

Regis tucked his mirror away, hoping he now appeared very much like a small orc, and no halfling.

He set out immediately for the camp, quietly reciting and recalling the Orcish tongue, a language he had not spoken in this lifetime, though one he had known—not fluently, but well enough—in his previous existence.

The ground was more open between him and the encampment and he knew that he'd have a hard time indeed in getting to the orcs without being seen. He crept to the edge of a small cluster of trees and tucked in close to one, peering around and trying to pick his path.

A branch snapped behind him and Regis froze.

An orc grunted out an indecipherable blurb, and Regis realized that his knowledge of the language might not be as strong as he had hoped.

Slowly he turned, to see the ugly creature coming up beside him, muttering curses—yes, Regis recognized a few of those colorful words—and carrying an armload of firewood.

"Bricken brucken spitzipit!" the orc demanded, or something like that.

"Spitspit?" Regis echoed in puzzlement.

The orc called him a name he did not know, though nothing positive, he could tell, and lifted a small log free of its armload. With a grunt and snarl, the orc cocked its arm and flung the missile at Regis, who nimbly dodged aside.

"Bricken brucken spitzipit!" the orc demanded, pointing to the log with its free hand.

Spitzipit . . . firewood!

Regis snorted and grumbled and ran to retrieve the log, then darted into the trees to collect more as the grumbling orc ambled out of the copse and made for the distant encampment.

It occurred to Regis that he could catch up to this one easily enough, and dispatch it before it even came to realize that he was no ally. He would return to his friends with blood on his blade, and surely they'd think him no coward!

But he shook his head and looked to the encampment, and knew there were more important tasks right here before him. Besides, he realized, despite his revulsion at the mere sight of the filthy, slobbering creature, he wasn't even sure if these orcs were enemies. Many-Arrows was a legitimate kingdom in the Silver Marches, one established by Bruenor despite the dwarf's recent change of heart.

He quickly collected an armload of firewood, hustled out of the trees, and made for the camp. He saw other orcs similarly burdened with firewood paralleling his course and knew that he could not turn back without causing a commotion.

He entered tentatively, trying not to look as nervous as he felt, and fell into line behind the others depositing their firewood beside one of the main bonfires in the encampment. The wood-gatherers then went to a steaming pot off to the side, where a most ugly orc ladled some foul-smelling stew into shallow bowls for them. Regis glanced around as he dropped his armload, and noted that all of the wood-gatherers were going for their meal.

Not wanting to direct any attention, the halfling-turned orc moved over and picked up a bowl and spoon, and successfully stifled a retch as the filthy stew was plopped onto his plate.

He moved aside, rolling the contents with his spoon to make it look like he was interested in the meal as he weaved his way through the orcs that were milling about. He was the smallest in the area, and by quite a lot. Orcs came in various sizes, of course, and many were half-goblin, making them smaller than the average. But even though the magic of the beret now made Regis appear taller, the top of his head barely reached the shoulders of any orc he passed by.

That fact alone got him shoved a few times by the bullying brutes, and he knew that it was only a matter of time before the unwanted attention turned rougher.

He moved to the far side of the camp, where the firelight was less, and sat down upon a fallen log, hoping that his seated posture would draw less attention. Then he lowered his eyes and went at the gruel with his spoon, shifting it about and occasionally looking up and pretending to chew, as if he had taken a mouthful—which he most certainly had no intention of doing!

And mostly, he listened.

The word he heard most and actually recognized was "Nesmé."

This was no hunting party out beyond the borders of Many-Arrows, he soon discerned. Nor was it a rogue band of raiders.

No, this was the western flank of an army, an orc army marching to lay waste to the town of Nesmé.

Regis glanced about, looking for some way to slip off into the darkness and make his escape. When he turned back to the campfire, though, he found his plans altered, as an orc walked over and sat down beside him, glowering at him.

The brute muttered something Regis couldn't understand, and when the poor and confused halfling-turned-orc didn't respond, the orc slugged him in the shoulder.

The jolt nearly dislodged Regis from the log, and he bit his tongue so hard that he could feel the warmth of blood in his mouth. The orc motioned to the shallow bowl and uttered another growling demand.

Regis looked to the gruel and caught on, and immediately, obediently—and ultimately happily—handed the wretched stew over.

The orc pulled it from his grasp and thrust its own platter, licked clean, into Regis's hands, then went at the new bowl furiously, slobbering and spitting the contents all over itself. With the orc engaged, the halfling slipped off the far side of the log and started out, picking a shadowy route to the field and tree line.

An argument gave him pause, though, for he recognized a different language than common Orcish. Indeed, it was a goblin speaking, he believed, and he quickly recognized that he understood that language much better than the tongue of the orcs. Despite his very real fears at getting caught and thrown into the next batch of ugly stew, Regis crept about to the corner of a nearby tent and eavesdropped.

He spotted the goblin—a shaman, judging from the tattered and garishly-colored robes it wore, along with a necklace of assorted teeth and feathers and small bones.

"We do not attack until the others come," the goblin insisted.

"Farmers! Outside the walls," the orc counterpart argued, speaking the goblin tongue as well.

"Coordinated!" the goblin cried, wagging a finger at the orc, who, to Regis's surprise, did shrink back a bit. "We go when we are told to go."

"And if they see us?"

"Then we are hunters and well met. Well met, human folk. We will not kill your cows and sheep. No, we eat wolf, and many wolfs will we take for pets. Yes, glad you will be that we came here. Your night is full of wolfs," the goblin recited, and it was clearly a practiced speech.

The orc growled and spat upon the ground, but it was obvious that the goblin held the upper hand, amazingly. Perhaps it was because of the shaman status, but in any event, it became evident to Regis that this group was not independent, and that someone of a higher rank had determined that the orc should listen to the goblin.

That was a good thing, the halfling thought, though he wasn't sure of why until he found himself inexplicably creeping behind the goblin as it moved along the avenues between the many tents and into a wide boulder tumble.

A boulder tumble that contained a deep cave, burrowing under a hillock, Regis discovered. With a glance around, the halfling tapped his beret once more and became a goblin, then slipped into the cave without a whisper of sound.

The tunnel broke into three, forking left and right and continuing straight ahead into a deeper room where torches blazed. Regis crept ahead and flattened himself beside a rock, gaining a good viewing angle. A score and more of goblins moved about a small pool of water, carrying bowls of similarly disgusting stew, while others danced and prayed and still others sat in the shadows against the far wall sharpening their spears.

A noise from the left hand side tunnel behind him froze Regis in place, and he pressed himself more fully against the stone.

A group of goblins came into the intersection behind him and headed out.

"Take food," he heard a voice down the side passage tell them, and it sounded very much like the shaman he had seen outside. "More will come, yes?"

"More," one of the departing goblins replied. "Two tribes, but the tunnels are deep and they will not be here this day."

"Two tribes," Regis mouthed silently. He held his place for many heartbeats, then slipped back the way he had come and eased down the left-hand tunnel.

The tunnel ended only a short way down, around a sharp bend, with an oval natural chamber lying before him and a second one off to his right. He crept up to the makeshift, ill-fitting door and peered in.

There stood the goblin shaman, the goblin leader, it seemed, fiddling with stones set in lines on rough shelves along one wall, arranged like some crude abacus. In the center of the room, a ladder protruded from a hole in the floor.

"Deep tunnels," Regis silently recounted, and he realized that this was a hole into the Underdark, likely, and that the goblins were gathering reinforcements.

He moved to the other room, noted the makeshift cot and bedroll, and with a glance behind, crept in.

He found a bundle of parchments, written in stylish letters and rich ink, neither of which could have goblins as its source. Flipping through, he noted rolls, names, and orders.

And noted, too, the signature of the author: Tos'un Do'Urden.

The halfling-turned-orc-turned-goblin's jaw dropped open. He knew of one named Tos'un, but that drow was surely no Do'Urden!

Regis swallowed hard, not knowing what to make of all of this.

He heard the shaman coming his way.

There were no other exits.

CHAPTER 8

EYES TO THE EAST

O H, THEY WILL HEAD EAST, NO DOUBT," BENIAGO SAID TO JARLAXLE .
The pair walked the streets of Luskan one warm evening. The wind blew off the water, offering a bit of relief to the muggy and hot weather that had settled over the Sword Coast this midsummer month of Flamerule.

Jarlaxle looked out at the boats bobbing in the harbor and shook his head. Drizzt and the Companions of the Hall returned and together again, youthful and ready for adventure.

And ready to go to war, no doubt, and likely Quenthel's war in Luruar.

"What word from the Silver Marches?" Jarlaxle asked.

Beniago shrugged and shook his head. "I have spent the last tendays reorganizing the Bregan D'aerthe soldiers you slipped out of House Do'Urden and have sent my way. And in hunting down the stragglers from Entreri's group, as you asked."

"The Darkening has been cast, to full effect?"

"That much I know, yes," Beniago confirmed. "And there are rumors that the orcs have marched in force."

"And what of Entreri?"

Beniago snorted and wore a perplexed expression, and Jarlaxle took a deep breath and steadied himself. He was all over the place, his questions bouncing back and forth with little logical guidance.

"I am relieved to be out of Menzoberranzan, and out from under the thumb of dear Matron Mother Baenre," he said calmly in explanation.

"And I am relieved to have you back in command," Beniago replied, and he dipped a respectful bow. "To your question, Artemis Entreri got out of Gauntlgr—Q'Xorlarrin. This much I know, and I have been told by one of the Xorlarrin commoners that Priestess Berellip was murdered in her bed. Matron Mother Zeerith has whispered it to be the work of Drizzt Do'Urden, but I think not."

"Entreri," Jarlaxle stated more than asked, and Beniago nodded.

"So he is out and about, though as to where, I cannot begin to guess," Beniago went on. "He has not found the trail of Drizzt and the others, it would seem, and did not go to or through Port Llast. Of that I am certain, or as certain as one can be with the likes of Artemis Entreri. Beyond that, however, I can find no sign of him. Perhaps he winds his own road to intercept Drizzt at some future, agreed-upon place."

"And Drizzt's trail?"

"Through the forest and the east road to Longsaddle. Perhaps he and his companions remain there, or perhaps they have already moved on farther to the east. They have not come back west, I am sure."

The pair approached the bridge to Closeguard Isle and the castle of Ship Kurth. Just to the side loomed the walled ruins of Illusk, the ancient city that predated Luskan. Kimmuriel was there, Jarlaxle knew, deep down in the catacombs of old Illusk with Gromph. Jarlaxle nodded farewell to Beniago and veered to the ruins. He picked up his pace, anxious to find answers.

So many answers to so many questions.

He was twelve years old. He could barely hold level the spear which had been thrust into his hands, its large tip continually dipping, though the boy gallantly leaned back to try to counterbalance its weight.

He was twelve years old and he had no experience with battle.

His sister stood beside him before the parapet of Sundabar's south wall, her helmet far too big and constantly falling over her eyes, her short sword seeming more like a bastard sword in her tiny hands. She was younger by two years, though almost his size.

"Stay alert!" came a barking command, and young Giles Wormack knew that the recrimination had been aimed at him. That one was always yelling, always criticizing, always telling Giles and the others that any mistakes would cost the city, their home, dearly.

That one, Aleina Brightlance, Knight-Captain of the famed Knights in Silver from Silverymoon, was relentless indeed, both in ferreting out any and every able-bodied man or woman to take up arms, and in patrolling the length of Sundabar's walls, yelling at anyone who seemed less than perfectly vigilant. She was not of Sundabar, but had taken over the garrison at the request of King Firehelm when nearly all of his military officers had been killed in a tragic bombing.

"They will come against us today!" Aleina shouted.

"They come against us every day," Giles muttered quietly.

"Be quiet," said his sister Karolina. "The Knight-Captain is speaking."

"The Knight-Captain is shouting," Giles corrected under his breath. "The Knight-Captain is always shouting."

Thoroughly miserable, the boy who was not yet a man took a deep breath and stared off into the darkness south of the city. To his right, the Rauvin River ran dark under a starless sky, a night so dark that only the sound of the rushing water confirmed to Giles that the river was still there.

Before him, to the south, lay darkness and silence, a fact for which he was truly grateful as the sounds of battle erupted anew back behind him, as the Many-Arrows orcs came on yet again. Soon enough, the ground shook under their charge, the cacophony of horns rent the night air, and when he put his hands against the stone of the wall, Giles could feel the vibrations of the impacts, as flying boulder, both giant-hurled and catapulted, crashed against the northern reaches of the circular walled city.

Every night and most days, those walls shook.

The field north of Sundabar lay thick and black with orc bodies, red with orc blood. The charge of the orcs this night resounded with the sickly squishing of boots stomping on bloated corpses. But still they came, and their numbers did not seem diminished, each charge seeming thicker than the last, and each charge getting nearer to the walls, inflicting more damage and more death on the beleaguered city and its desperate citizens.

"One night, they will send a second force around to the south, to attack under cover of the battle at the north wall," said a voice suddenly beside Giles, and he nearly jumped out of his boots and turned to see Knight-Captain Aleina Brightlance standing beside him—and the mere fact that she had gotten there without his noticing shamed him and screamed at him to stay alert. "When that happens, will you be ready, boy?"

She stared down at him severely.

"Yes," he answered, a response made more out of fear of this imposing warrior than out of any real conviction that he would be ready, or that he even could be ready.

Ready for what? Ready to fight against a savage orc warrior? Wielding a spear he could hardly lift and with armor so ill-fitting that a strong wind would blow it free?

The wall shook then, so violently that Giles nearly tumbled, and his sister would have, had not the Knight-Captain caught her by the arm and held her steady. Before Giles could react, before Karolina could even thank the powerful woman, Aleina Brightlance was gone, bounding down from the wall and screaming orders to those across the way to "Close that breach!"

Giles glanced back and swallowed hard. A huge stone, hurled from a mighty catapult no doubt, had taken down a sizable section of the north wall. Even from this distance, scanning through the taller buildings, Giles could see the commotion as orcs poured into the breach, holding long logs to be used as an impromptu bridge across the moat that flowed between the stone barriers of the double-walled city. They were met hard by the Sundabar garrison. Torches danced in the hands of running men and women, and flew through the air and across the narrow waterway into the midst of the attackers.

"Drive them back!" Aleina called, and to another group, she yelled for temporary barricades.

The commands sounded so familiar in the ears of Giles Wormack. Every night there came a breach now, as the walls withered under the unending barrage, and only the courage and skill of the Sundabar garrison, and the hard and determined work of the masons and mages had kept the city clear of orc vermin.

"Eyes to the south, all of you!" Aleina Brightlance screamed at Giles and the other curious sentries upon that southern wall.

Giles spun around, managed a glance at his sister, who was sniffling and trying to hold back tears, before turning his vigilant gaze back to the dark southern reaches.

And trying, so hard, not to give in to the fear that an orc would creep up behind him and lop off his head.

———◦⟨∽⟩◦———

A short while after leaving Beniago, Jarlaxle caught up with Kimmuriel in the ruins of Illusk, the ancient city below the mainland section of Luskan just off Closeguard Isle, only to learn that his brother the archmage had returned to Menzoberranzan immediately following their first psionic training session.

"Do tell," Jarlaxle bade the Oblodran psionicist.

"Tell what?"

It seemed fairly obvious that Kimmuriel was not in the best of moods. "The Archmage," Jarlaxle explained, though he knew he didn't really have to. "How did he fare?"

Kimmuriel stared at him for a long while. "He has promise."

"Good."

"Many have promise," Kimmuriel reminded. "Few will see it bloom, as you yourself know well."

"Oh, believe me when I say that I hope Gromph's promise does not bloom into psionic prowess," Jarlaxle explained. "It is bad enough that I have to constantly ward against your prying telepathy. Adding the meddling archmage to that list of subtle dangers would be maddening."

"Then why . . ."

"His promise will keep him engaged with you," Jarlaxle cut him short. "Gromph engaging with you means he needs you, and so he needs me, and us. Even if you quickly discern that he cannot access the psionic powers, do not let on so quickly, I beg. There are so many moving parts now with the end of the Spellplague, the ambitions of Lolth's priestesses and of the Spider Queen herself, that the more we keep Gromph at our side, and the less we allow him to be beside Quenthel, the better for us."

Kimmuriel stared at him hard, in what passed as a great frown from the emotionless drow.

"Be hopeful and of good cheer," Jarlaxle laughed at him. "Perhaps if Gromph's promise turns into something more, you'll not be so alone in your strange magic."

Kimmuriel's visage didn't soften at all. Indeed, he seemed angrier at the possibility.

Jarlaxle shrugged and put on a curious expression. "If this task was not to your liking, why did you agree?" he asked. "We are partners, and you need not obey . . ."

"My acquiescence had nothing to do with you."

Jarlaxle's expression grew perplexed.

"Other than your idiocy in suggesting it to the archmage before consulting with me," Kimmuriel explained.

It took Jarlaxle a heartbeat or two to unwind that, but then a great smile creased his face. "My dear Kimmuriel, you're afraid."

"Not of you."

"No, but of Gromph."

"He is the Archmage of Menzoberranzan," Kimmuriel replied as if that should explain everything, and indeed, there was an undeniable truth to that line of reasoning.

"Still, I don't recall that I have ever seen you fearful."

"Not of you," Kimmuriel reiterated. "Perhaps you would be wise to remember that."

Jarlaxle laughed. He knew that Kimmuriel was joking—but then recalled that Kimmuriel was never joking. He cut the laugh short with an embarrassed cough.

"When will Gromph return?" Jarlaxle asked, changing the subject. "I had hoped to find him here."

"A tenday? Two? He will return at his leisure, as he informed me."

"I need you to exact a promise from him."

"No." The psionicist's flat reply left Jarlaxle stunned.

"This is not a simple request," Jarlaxle explained. "It is a necessity. I am in need of the services of Gromph and I have no leverage with which to gain them. You do, and so I need you to . . ."

"No."

Jarlaxle took a deep breath, leaned back in his chair, and put his booted feet upon the desk, staring curiously at Kimmuriel the whole time.

"It is a favor for Bregan D'aerthe, not for Jarlaxle," the mercenary leader said at length.

"There is nothing I can ask of Gromph. He will refuse me, if only to let you know that your control over him is less than tentative, less than existent, even."

"How can you know until you ask?"

Kimmuriel's responding expression was one of pure pity, as if he was looking down upon a truly inferior intellect.

"What?" Jarlaxle demanded.

"I have been teaching the archmage the power of psionics, the power of looking into the mind of another," Kimmuriel explained, speaking slowly, as if he was talking to a child.

"And so I have witnessed his thoughts and his honest attitude," Kimmuriel explained, but Jarlaxle, having caught on, waved his hands to silence the drow.

"I need him," Jarlaxle said. "There are no others I would trust in the spells I require. There are great happenings in the land of Luruar, the Silver Marches, and we must stay abreast of the news from there."

Kimmuriel nodded.

"And so I need to go there."

"I have taken you places before. Psionics is not without its own form of teleportation. And indeed, I have already been there."

"More than just going there," Jarlaxle explained. "There are many places to visit, many situations to explore. Gromph knows the layout of the orc army—he directed much of it. He knows of their allies, indeed facilitated many of those alliances, like the frost giants, lured into alliance with Many-Arrows through his own tricks. Our ranks include many wizards, yes, but none I would trust for so many great teleports—and to unknown places."

"I have been there," Kimmuriel repeated.

"Your psionic methods of teleport are limited," Jarlaxle reminded.

"Take off your eyepatch," Kimmuriel instructed, and Jarlaxle eyed him suspiciously.

"My proxies are in place," the psionicist explained. "I know more of the events in the Silver Marches than does Gromph. I have been there, in the midst of the orcs, and through them I have traveled to Adbar and Felbarr, and Mithral Hall, even."

The mention of Mithral Hall surely piqued Jarlaxle's curiosity, though he wasn't quite sure what Kimmuriel was talking about. "Through them?" he asked quietly.

"My proxies in Luruar infect all they contact, orc to dwarf, dwarf to dwarf, orc to human."

"Infect? What are you talking about?"

"Take off your eyepatch. I'll not ask again, and if you choose to miss this opportunity, then know that you have severed the bonds of trust between us—and those bonds are all that keep us in harmony as co-leaders of Bregan D'aerthe."

It took Jarlaxle many heartbeats to realize that he had just been threat-ened, but then to unwind that notion enough from his instinctive reaction to realize that no, Kimmuriel did not threaten. Kimmuriel only warned, and warned honestly.

Jarlaxle took off his eyepatch.

"Do not resist my intrusion," Kimmuriel explained. "I will join with your consciousness and take you . . . to see."

Before Jarlaxle could even ask for clarification, he felt the intrusions of Kimmuriel Oblodra into his mind. Reflexively he resisted—no rational, reasoning being would ever surrender identity in such a way, with defenses based purely on instinct; indeed, the very notion of basic survival rebelled against such a violation. But Jarlaxle wasn't any subject here. He was old, centuries old, and hardened by experience, and wizened by an insatiable curiosity and a desire to know—everything.

He fought back, then, ferociously, but not against Kimmuriel. No, he fought back against his own natural revulsion. He let Kimmuriel in.

Almost instantly, Jarlaxle understood the psionicist's references to proxies, and believed Kimmuriel's claim that he knew what was transpiring in the Silver Marches, for almost instantly, Jarlaxle found himself looking through the eyes and hearing through the ears of a young man, a boy really, pressed into service on the south wall of Sundabar. He knew it was Sundabar immediately, for he "knew" what the boy knew, immediately!

The great city was besieged and battered. The orcs had come on, every day. The walls shook under bombardment, every day, all day. The field outside the city lay black with bodies and carrion birds, but the houses of healing within the city bulged with patients, and lines of dying men and woman lay outside the doors, awaiting their time with the clerics—if they were fortunate enough to ever receive any healing.

The cries of battle began anew. Thunderous retorts resounded from the shaking walls. The air filled with the stomp of thousands of boots, the war whoops of tens of thousands of orcs, the orders and cries for assistance from dozens of locations along the crumbling wall of Sundabar.

Jarlaxle felt the boy's fear, palpably. And then he felt a curious twist in his own thoughts as the child pulled information from his consciousness as he had pulled from the boy's.

Then curiosity, the boy becoming aware that something was very much amiss!

It all went for naught a moment later, however, when above it all, a great screech rent the air.

"Oh good, they have a dragon," Jarlaxle heard himself say.

Two, he heard Kimmuriel reply in his thoughts.

Jarlaxle nearly fell out of his chair as he flew from the scene in Sundabar, to find himself in a dwarf cavern—for a moment, he thought it Mithral Hall. But no, he realized as he found the memories and sensibilities of his new host. He was in Adbar, in the Court of King Harnoth, in the body of a dwarf named Oretheo Spikes, a great warrior who had been sorely injured in the battle of the Cold Vale, where his king, Bromm, brother of Harnoth, had fallen.

"'E's out again," one of the other dwarves in the room said, and the conversation began, the dwarves talking about, lamenting, that their young King Harnoth, so full of despair over the loss of his brother, kept going out of Adbar looking for orcs to slaughter. Sometimes he went with a raiding group, but often, he went alone.

Many of the dwarves in here were gravely concerned—could Adbar survive the loss of both her kings?

All that Jarlaxle felt from Oretheo Spikes, though, was regret—regret that he was still too injured to go along with the angry young King of Adbar.

Oretheo Spikes wanted to kill orcs, and dark elves, and dragons.

The dwarf silently cursed the name of House Do'Urden.

Clever Quenthel, Jarlaxle thought, and it pained him greatly to think that Lady Lolth was indeed getting her revenge on Drizzt and his goddess.

Giles Wormack felt dizzy, and violated, though he had no idea of how that might be possible. It was as if someone else was in his thoughts, or something strange like that—but it was far beyond the boy's experience to understand.

Except the violation part—that he knew and felt keenly.

And now the screech and he fell out of his contemplation and nearly fell over entirely as the scene before him came into view. He turned fast to his sister, but she was not looking back at him. Her bulging eyes looked to the north.

Her expression, one of abject horror, prompted Giles to spin that way.

"Giles, run!" he heard her say, but distantly, even though she was standing right beside him!

It wasn't that someone was inside his head again, no, but rather, the sight before him that pushed any thoughts of Karolina aside, and that froze him in place with terror.

He had never seen a dragon before.

He had fancied that one day he would like to see a dragon.

Now he saw a dragon, and knew that he never wanted to see a dragon.

Now he heard a dragon, and that was even worse, if there could be an even worse.

And then he saw the dragon better, bigger and closer, as it dived across the field north of Sundabar, as it skimmed over the north wall, hind legs clipping men and throwing them into the air, and knocking over stones as easily as Giles blasted through pillows on the bed when he and Karolina were at play. He saw the dragon and he knew doom, utter doom. They could not defeat this beast—no army could stand against the magnificence of this dragon. Its horns could skewer a dozen men, and even holding them atop its head wouldn't slow its biting maw. The monster shined white even in the dim light of the darkened sky, its eyes glowing bluish-white with inner cold, its teeth, most as long as Giles' arm, glistening with their icy coating, catching and reflecting with crystalline clarity the meager sparkles from the bonfires about the city. A single flap of its great wings as it soared across the city nearly extinguished any of those nearby fires, bending the flames away as if they, too, cowered in fear as the godlike creature passed.

"Giles, run!" Karolina cried again, but he couldn't really register the words and couldn't obey the command in any case. How could he turn from the glory of this spectacle? Why would he run when there was, after all, no hope at all?

All he could do was stand there and watch.

The steeple of a tall building exploded into flying stones as the dragon crashed through, hardly bothered or slowed by the obstacle.

"Giles!"

He knew he was dead. He could not move, but the dragon was coming . . . coming for him!

Despair stole his strength, fear locked him in place, the magnificence of the beast thrilled him even as he knew that he would die.

He felt hands against him, but hardly understood.

Then he was flying, to his left and forward, to pitch off the wall and into the courtyard. He rolled over and crashed into a wagon, tumbling and bouncing to the ground.

The dragon roared.

The dragon breathed.

Giles saw it as the great beast swooped past, a burst of whiteness spewing forth from its fanged maw, striking the ground not far from him, rushing to the base of the wall and up and over as the dragon soared beyond the battlements, flying out into the night.

And in that breath was coldness, killing frost, leaving a scar upon the ground and upon the wall, and encapsulating several men on the ground, and a pair of sentries up on . . .

Karolina.

"Karo!" Giles cried. He pulled himself up from the ground, ignoring the waves of nauseating pain sweeping up from his twisted leg, and from the ribs he had surely broken in his fall. He stumbled and staggered to the nearest ladder and stubbornly tugged himself up, crying out for his sister with each movement. On the walkway, he stumbled and fell, then crawled, and his hands stung like burns when they touched the ice.

So cold.

He propelled himself into a short slide, crashing into the form of his sister, who was half lying, half-standing as she leaned against the parapet.

"Karolina!" he cried, and he tried to touch her, but he could not feel her through the cocoon of ice the great dragon had breathed upon her. He scratched at it, clawed at it, punched at it, but she did not move, stuck fast.

Then he felt the wetness, for already the summer warmth began to melt the ice. Initially, that only made things slipperier, and Giles almost slid once more from the wall.

"Here, boy," said a man he did not know, grabbing him by the collar and pulling him back to steadier footing.

"My sister," he sniffled.

"She's gone, boy," the man said, roughly yanking him aside. "She's gone."

Giles stuttered for an answer, a cry, a retort, a denial—anything to take him from that awful moment, anything to deny that awful image. He choked on the lump in his throat and could make no decipherable sound, and he looked at her—she seemed to be sleeping peacefully—under the dragon cocoon, and he knew.

He knew.

Like so many in besieged Sundabar, Giles knew that his life would never be the same, that the hole in his heart would never fill. She had saved him because he had failed. She had saved him by pushing him from the wall, and the effort had cost her her life.

"Karolina," he whispered, and now even his own voice sounded distant in his ears.

He was a guard in Dark Arrow Keep, a burly orc warrior standing in the great circular throne room, great spear in hand.

He saw the Warlord and knew it to be Hartusk.

The killer of King Bromm of Citadel Adbar, he who drove away the line of Obould.

Looking through the burly orc's bloodshot eyes, Jarlaxle realized that he was witnessing the rise of the king, a new king.

A new king, or warlord, dedicated to the old ways.

Jarlaxle listened to the banter between Hartusk and the shamans and battlefield commanders. The orcs had sent forth a great force, splitting it three ways around the hub of the encampment they had built in the Upper Surbrin Vale, surrounding Mithral Hall and locking the filthy dwarves in their hole. Now they struck at Sundabar—Jarlaxle had seen that—and Silverymoon, and with another force marching to crush Nesmé and curl back in from the west.

"The fool King of Adbar is beyond reason," the orc before Hartusk explained. "He comes forth with his war bands to strike at any and all. Give me a sly and deadly force, Warlord, and I will bring you the head of Harnoth!"

Jarlaxle watched as the orc leader mulled over the request, then slowly, and wisely, shook his head.

"Let Harnoth have his small victories for now," he replied. "Send enough patrols, strong patrols, to keep him fighting, and make those fights difficult—perhaps he will be killed, perhaps not. It does not matter. If the dwarves sate their bloodlust revenge with small strikes, then they will remain in their holes."

Warlord Hartusk stood up and spoke loudly to all in the room. "And if Mithral Hall, Felbarr, and Adbar stay in their holes, then Sundabar will fall."

The crowd cheered; Jarlaxle heard his own throaty cheer pouring forth from his host orc.

"Then Silverymoon will crumble beneath our war machines."

The cheering grew louder.

"And Nesmé will be flattened under the tramp of our boots. And three armies become one will destroy Everlund." Orcs began chanting the name of Hartusk, the guards banging their spears on the wooden floor.

All but the poor fellow inhabited by Jarlaxle and Kimmuriel, at least, for this one was too internally tousled to begin such a coordinated movement as that.

"And the dwarves will still be in their holes when our armies return— return wearing the armor of the Knights in Silver, and carrying the swords of the Sundabar garrison. The bearded fools will know their folly then, that they should have come forth while their allies drew breath. But what will be left for them when the great cities of men and elves are thrown down, when the Glimmerwood is burned and harvested?

"Naught, I say. There will be nothing left for them but their tunnels and their mines, and we will have those soon enough. The Silver Marches will be ours. Gruumsh!"

The wild cheering commenced, and this time even Jarlaxle's orc managed to clap the butt of his spear on the wooden floor. It seemed like it would go on for hours, an orc orgy of screams and shouts and cheers, but just when Jarlaxle was ready to flee this body, in a most interesting twist, a contingent of much more refined warriors entered the room.

Ravel Xorlarrin, Jarlaxle realized, and almost inadvertently prompted his host to say. And with Tos'un Armgo and Doum'wielle beside him.

And in walked Tiago Baenre.

Jarlaxle forced himself, willed himself, into a fast retreat, and he opened his eyes back in Illusk, beneath the coastal city of Luskan, seated across from Kimmuriel.

"That is brilliant," the mercenary leader congratulated, and Kimmuriel nodded his acceptance of the compliment, as if it was surely deserved. "How many of these hosts do you have?"

"Five in the region," Kimmuriel matter-of-factly explained. "These are momentous events. Bregan D'aerthe would be ill-served if we were not informed of the every turn in Luruar."

"The Matron Mother has struck with brutal efficiency," said Jarlaxle. "Orcs . . . and a dragon."

"Two," Kimmuriel reminded. "And a horde of frost giants to back the orc lines."

"She may win," Jarlaxle remarked, and he sounded surprised, because he was.

Kimmuriel nodded. "As of now, it seems likely."

"The human kingdoms will find allies."

"There are none. War is general across the land, as factions vie for control. A void of power invites war, and so the invitation has been answered, in many lands."

Jarlaxle sat back in his chair and brought his hands up before him, his fingers tap-tapping as he tried to look long-term.

"There are few drow there," he remarked.

"Not so few. Enough to be present at every battle, and to be at Hartusk's court commonly. This reinvented House Do'Urden is formidable, it would seem."

"There are more there . . ."

"All under the banner of House Do'Urden," Kimmuriel explained. "All. Even proud Barrison Del'Armgo. Even the nobles and wizards of House Xorlarrin, who are no longer of Menzoberranzan."

"Why?" Jarlaxle asked, as much to himself as to his partner, so out of proportion did this all seem.

"The Matron Mother serves Lady Lolth," Kimmuriel said. "The Spider Queen is angry."

"Drizzt."

"She tried to seduce him, but she failed. She lost him to Mielikki."

"He is just a mortal drow. Why would she care?"

Kimmuriel gave him an incredulous look.

"She doesn't care," Jarlaxle answered his own question. "She cares only for her wounded pride. She needed a war, and so she found one. She needed her people united at this time, that she can wrest the Weave of Magic to her own domain. She would . . ."

He paused and sighed. "Ah, the gods," he said. "And we are their playthings."

"Does Jarlaxle really believe that?" Kimmuriel asked, and when Jarlaxle looked up, he was surprised to see his pragmatic partner grinning at him.

"Jarlaxle believes they are meddling puppeteers and nothing more," the mercenary leader returned.

Kimmuriel just smiled.

"I need to travel, and quickly."

"Shall I get you a fast horse?"

Jarlaxle gave him a sour look.

"Where would you go?"

"Where is Drizzt?"

"I know not, but I would expect that he and his friends will soon become enmeshed in the battles of Luruar," Kimmuriel answered. "They were bound for Mithral Hall, so we believe, and the happenings in that region would spur them forward if their past actions are any predictor."

"And the others? Effron, the dwarf and the monk?"

"On the east road in the south, the latter two bound for the Sea of Fallen Stars and to the Bloodstone Lands, the former trying to catch them—or at least, he was."

"Yes, yes, but where exactly? Do you know?"

"Of course. You bade Beniago to find them, and so he did."

"Then get me a horse fast enough to catch up to them."

Kimmuriel looked at him curiously.

"Oh, get me there, you fool," Jarlaxle pleaded. "Or find me a wizard who will."

"What are you thinking?" Kimmuriel asked.

Jarlaxle stared hard at Kimmuriel, then slowly lifted his eye-patch, inviting the drow into his thoughts.

"Truly?" Kimmuriel heard himself remark, and there was more emotion than usual in his steady voice.

Before the sun had set that very same day, Jarlaxle sat on a bare-topped hillock near the Trade Way, looking back to the west, awaiting the arrival of the tiefling, the dwarf, and the monk.

CHAPTER 9

WELCOME HOME

H E HAS NOT RETURNED," WULFGAR PROTESTED, CLIMBING UP ON THE bench beside Bruenor after hitching the team.

"Not now, boy," the dwarf quietly replied.

Wulfgar leaned back and studied his hairy friend. What did Bruenor know? Why were they getting ready to break camp when Regis had not yet returned from his scouting?

"Keep yer hammer ready," Bruenor whispered.

"What are you whispering about?" Giselle Malcomb demanded from the back of the wagon. "And where are the others?"

Bruenor turned around and glared at her. "Just shut yer mouth."

Wulfgar considered the dwarf's tone—deadly serious. He, too, wanted an answer to that second question at least, for only then, in glancing about, did he realize that Drizzt and Catti-brie were nowhere to be seen. Their mounts had not been summoned, of that he was sure, and yet, neither of them were anywhere in sight.

With a soft snicker, Bruenor set the team to walking along the rough path, winding slowly through the trees. Tied to the back of the wagon, Giselle's horse and Regis's pony plodded along.

But then the pony, a veteran of many battles, lifted its head and snorted on alert, and at the same moment Bruenor tugged back the reins and quickly tied them off, going for his axe.

Wulfgar understood when the first orcs appeared, arrayed for battle and rushing out onto the path before them. Another was also on the move, in mid-air, actually, jumping down from a branch along the left-hand side of the trail, leaping for the driver of the wagon.

But that driver knew it was coming—indeed, that driver had only started the wagon rolling to draw out the ambushers he had known to be about. And now Bruenor was up and swinging, taking the orc out in mid-air with a well-timed blow from his powerful axe.

Wulfgar, too, leaped to his feet, bringing Aegis-fang back over his shoulder. He studied the three orcs on the trail ahead just long enough to discern that one held a bow, and he let fly even as the orc loosed its missile.

The arrow shot past Wulfgar, the wide edges of its devastating head cutting the inside of his left arm and drawing a deep gash along his chest as he tried to dodge. Somehow he had avoided a direct strike, one that would have surely killed him, but he had not escaped unscathed.

But neither had the orc archer. It futilely tried to block the spinning warhammer with its bow and arms, but Aegis-fang blasted through, splintering wood and bone with ease. The orc fell away with the head of the warhammer embedded in its chest.

Wulfgar started forward, thinking to spring to the horse team and leap out over them to charge into the other two orcs before they could even realize what was happening.

A cry from behind him brought him to an abrupt halt.

Another enemy had come upon them, a large ogre rushing in from the side and swinging at the desperately diving and dodging Giselle.

Over the bench went Wulfgar, a leap that brought him crashing into the ogre's shoulder just as it reached back that arm, holding a heavy club. The barbarian grabbed on and twisted, for the monstrous brute, thrice his weight, did not stumble aside under the force of the collision.

Thrice his weight, but not thrice the strength of mighty Wulfgar. He set one foot on the edge of the wagon rail and heaved and turned with all his strength, then reversed, driving forward powerfully, bending the ogre sideways.

The brute started to fall and Wulfgar leaped and tugged away from the wagon, twisting the ogre as they went down in a confused tumble.

Now they clenched and crushed, squeezed and twisted. Wulfgar punched out, smacking the brute in the face, but to little avail as the ogre merely tried to bite his hand, then raked him with its filthy fingernails.

And the brute tried to wriggle free, and Wulfgar knew that if it managed any separation, that heavy club would cave in his skull.

He hung on. For all his life, he hung on.

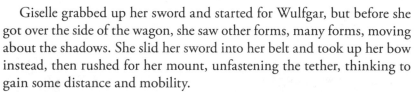

Giselle grabbed up her sword and started for Wulfgar, but before she got over the side of the wagon, she saw other forms, many forms, moving about the shadows. She slid her sword into her belt and took up her bow instead, then rushed for her mount, unfastening the tether, thinking to gain some distance and mobility.

She had just got into the saddle when the first arrow struck the horse. The steed reared in pain, but Giselle hung on, and started away.

A spinning hand axe cracked across the side of her head, dazing her, and only good fortune brought the spinning weapon upon her with the back side of the head!

Still, she felt the warmth of her blood and it took her many heartbeats to set her vision straight, and even then, the world seemed to swim as the horse leaped and darted.

A ball of flames exploded behind the tree line, and the poor horse reared again—and was hit with a spear this time, burrowing into its flank. Now it staggered sidelong, then turned around and darted back for the camp, but then stumbled again and fell over, throwing Giselle hard to the ground.

She knew she had to get up. She still had her bow, but no arrows. Instinctively, she went for her sword while rising, leaning on her bow for support.

She heard a horn, discordant and painfully off key, and took it to be an orc battle call.

Indeed, it had to be, she thought, for they were all around her now, with a trio of orcs rushing out of the brush, spears leveled and forcing her back. But the other way came another ogre, huge and ugly and holding a club that resembled an uprooted tree with giant spikes stuck through it.

Giselle cried out and spun desperately, and saw another enemy in a branch above her, a giant black panther, all muscle and claws and killing teeth.

The cat leaped for her, and she cried out again and knew she was doomed.

Except that the panther went right over her and flew between the orcs, touching down behind them, and by the time it had landed and turned back around, two of the orcs lay on the ground, one squirming and spouting a fountain of blood, the other already still in death, for the panther had neatly taken out the throats of both!

The third orc wheeled about and got buried as the cat sprang again.

"Me king!" came a cry at the same time, and Giselle noted another newcomer to the battle, the strangest looking dwarf she had ever seen, dressed in ridged armor and with spikes protruding from hands, elbows, knees, toes, and a huge one straight up from his strange helm. He bounded in a supernatural manner, springing with a lightness that defied the solid appearance, each hop seeming more like a bounce, and each taking him up as high into the air as Giselle's wide eyes.

He came at her, great leaps and sprinting, and sprang up above her so fully that it seemed to her as if he had simply taken flight.

She heard the ogre groan behind her and spun around to see the brute with a kicking and flailing dwarf embedded firmly into its chest. The ogre staggered backward, grasping at the dwarf, punching at him, trying to bring its heavy club in to swat him away.

But that strange dwarf moved with amazing speed and fought without fear, yanking his bloody helmet spike free and scrambling around the brute, punching and biting and kicking, grabbing on tightly and grinding his ridged armor against ogre flesh—anything, any movement, that might inflict pain.

Giselle didn't know what to make of it, or of any of this. She spun back to the panther, to see it finishing off the third orc. The magnificent feline turned her way and roared, and the blood drained from her face as she feared that she would be next!

But the cat sprang away, far away, disappearing from view within the thick brush, and almost immediately there came the shouts and terrified cries of more orcs caught in the path of the killing cat.

The Rider of Nesmé grabbed up her bow and ran for her horse, which was up again and hobbling gingerly. She comforted the animal with soft words and worked her way around it, wincing as she noted the wounds, knowing in her heart, though she couldn't admit it, that the spears and arrows would surely prove mortal to the loyal mount. Determination and anger replaced and erased her fear, and Giselle calmly reached for her quiver set behind the saddle on the horse's right flank. She pulled forth an arrow, scanning the trees as she set it, determined to pay back the ugly orcs.

With a sudden burst, Wulfgar twisted and drove forward, ducking his head so that he tumbled right across the prostrate ogre's face. He rolled to the ground and over to his feet, quick-stepped ahead and away from the beast, where he skidded to a stop and spun around.

The ogre was halfway up, in a crouch and swinging about, club sweeping in.

But Wulfgar was quicker, and Aegis-fang was back in his hand, magically returned to his grasp. The ogre came in from the side, but Wulfgar went straight ahead, inside its reach, and drove his warhammer into the ogre's forehead as the brute tried to fully stand. Wulfgar's muscles corded with the brutal hit, the weapon vibrating as profoundly as if he had struck granite instead of flesh and bone.

The powerful weapon tore through that flesh and smashed through the skull, splashing ogre brains all around, and the brute went down to a confused jumble on the ground. Spasms twitched its limbs and rolled its eyes, but it was already dead.

And Wulfgar was already gone, running out after enemies he saw scrambling through the brush.

He realized his error only as the spear entered his left side when he passed the nearest large tree.

With amazing reflexes, Wulfgar's hand clamped down on that stabbing shaft before the orc could drive the spear tip in too deeply. The barbarian dropped Aegis-fang, turned, and grabbed the spear with his other hand as well, driving down with his left, yanking up and in with his right, and thus snapping the feeble weapon cleanly.

He grabbed the piece still held by the orc, ignoring the end stuck into his side, and heaved up and about, taking the monster with his turn, lifting it right from its feet.

The orc was smart enough to let go before Wulfgar could launch it away, but Wulfgar had anticipated that. He twisted right, stepped left, to the orc as it landed, and batted across with the spear shaft.

The orc's head snapped to the side, blood and teeth flying from its mouth. Dazed, it staggered, but somehow managed to hold its footing.

But Wulfgar came on, infuriated by the violation of his body. Hands wide on the spear handle now, he drove it under the orc's chin, then growled and pushed out and upward, turning the orc and lifting it off the ground as he pressed ahead to slam it against the tree. With a growl he drove on, thinking to crush the creature's muscled neck. But the spear shaft broke again around the orc's throat, and as Wulfgar stumbled forward, the orc kept its wits enough to throw its face forward as well, head-butting the barbarian hard.

Wulfgar accepted the blow and ignored the wave of dizziness and the coppery taste on his lips. Out to the side went his arms, then in and up, just as the orc reached for him.

The splintered ends of the weapon shaft served as short spears, each driving in hard through the orc's ears.

The creature shuddered and jerked violently, and Wulfgar roared and held on, driving it back against the tree once more.

He twisted and pressed, but he needn't have, for the twin spears had torn the orc's brains apart.

Wulfgar threw the beast aside and stumbled over to retrieve his war-hammer. He brought his arm across to wipe the blood from his broken nose, then closed his eyes and shook the cobwebs from his sensibilities.

"Over here, boy," he heard Bruenor call, and he turned just as an orc burst from the brush, not charging at him but running from the mur-derous dwarf.

The orc noticed the hulking barbarian a stride later, its eyes going wide, its hands coming up, but too late to block the two-handed swing of Aegis-fang.

Wulfgar stomped on the squirming creature's face and stalked off to find his dwarf companion.

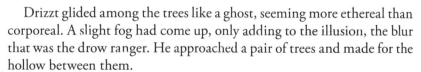

Drizzt glided among the trees like a ghost, seeming more ethereal than corporeal. A slight fog had come up, only adding to the illusion, the blur that was the drow ranger. He approached a pair of trees and made for the hollow between them.

But the extra sense that had guided this veteran warrior through a thousand battles warned him of the course. At the last moment, he tossed one scimitar through the gap, while rolling around the other way, going about the thick trunk of the tree to his left.

He came upon the orc pressed against the bark preparing the ambush, the orc that was now looking curiously at the scimitar that had come flying through. The oblivious beast even leaned out to look more closely, to peer back through the hollow.

Drizzt's remaining blade crashed down upon the back of its neck, severing its spine, and as it dropped straight and fast to the ground, the drow noted its companion across the way, pressed against the other tree and staring back at him wide-eyed.

With a howl that orc lifted its spear and let fly.

With his enchanted anklets enhancing his speed, Drizzt could have easily side-stepped the clumsy throw, but instead he moved just a bit and brought his curved blade back across his body, the flat of the weapon smacking against the spear tip, stealing the missile's momentum. Before it bounced away, Drizzt's free hand nabbed it out of midair, and he deftly flipped it about.

In the space of all those movements, the orc had come on, but only a step, and now it dug in its heels to halt its momentum when it noted the drow holding a scimitar in one hand and its own spear in his other!

The orc stepped back, awkwardly swung about and stumbled off.

To its credit, it actually got a couple of running strides from the drow before its own spear violated its back.

The orc staggered to one knee, but kept pressing forward. It had allies close by, it knew. If only it could get to them . . .

Darkness fell in the form of a scimitar, creasing its skull, and a second blade fast followed, for Drizzt had been quick enough to retrieve it in his fast pursuit, stabbing the orc through the throat.

And the hunting ghost swept on, noting movement ahead, but up in the trees.

Away went the scimitars, and out came Taulmaril.

A macabre dance filled the woods about Catti-brie as a trio of orcs rushed about, flapping their burning arms wildly. Three others lay dead from her fireball, and flames licked at many of the nearby trees.

It occurred to the woman that perhaps she should not have used that particular spell in this particular location, for now, surely, enemies far away would see those flames.

Another orc came tumbling down from the boughs, though, crashing through the branches to fall dead at her feet. It still clutched its bow.

The woman nodded, changing her mind. That was the third archer she had inadvertently taken down with the blast, for she had been aiming only at the quartet who had come at her on the ground.

So yes, she thought, perhaps the fireball had been the correct response after all!

She glanced about, thinking it best to move along, but a volley of spears came flying out at her from the brush ahead. She winced and dodged instinctively, but she needn't have, for of the four missiles, the two that were on target rammed against her magical shield and were defeated.

Behind those throws came another foursome of orcs, however, and the woman moved fast, calling upon her divine powers this time.

Blue swirls of magical energy curled out of her robe's right sleeve, twisting about her and mingling with the swirl that had come from the spellscar of Mystra on her left forearm.

One of the orcs slowed and nearly toppled forward, its boots grabbed by the remaining grasses. Two others stopped completely as tree limbs reached down to enwrap them.

The fourth got through, drawing a short sword and leaping in for the kill.

Catti-brie lifted her spread hands before her, thumbs touching, and met the charge with a fan of flames. Even as they sprouted from her fingertips, the woman fell off to the side.

The orc barreled through, blinded and burning, and swinging wildly with downward chops and desperate thrusts. It staggered for many steps, tiny flames licking at its clothing and hair, before it could stop its rush and swing about.

More flames appeared on the creature, not biting at its flesh but outlining it clearly for the enemy who stood against it.

"I need to get a weapon," Catti-brie lamented, and she began casting yet another spell, and a quick one, for the orc soon realized that this faerie fire wasn't hot and stopped slapping at it, instead renewing its charge.

One, two, three, four went the magic missiles, singeing the creature, burrowing into the creature. It kept coming forward, but out of momentum and not conscious thought, Catti-brie realized.

She crouched low and swung up and around with a timed circle kick to the dying orc's face just for good measure.

The creature proved too heavy for her to fully block its advance, however, and so Catti-brie ducked and dodged as it crashed past. She rolled up under its still-lifted arm and caught hold, and managed to extract the orc's sword from its dead hand before it ever hit the ground.

She shook her head at the pathetic balance of the weapon and put it through a quick practice swing, or tried to, until a tremendous cracking sound spun her about.

Unbeknownst to the priestess, her entangling enchantment had caught another victim, so it seemed, bigger than an orc, bigger than an ogre.

Catti-brie swallowed hard as she watched the frost giant extricate itself from the grabbing tree, by ripping the heavy limb right off the trunk!

Now it held the broken branch like a giant club, and with a look of grim satisfaction, it strode to the woman.

Wulfgar winced as he batted aside the thrusting spear, for the movement painfully twisted the spear tip that was embedded in his side. He could feel the blood streaming from the wound, and worse, he could feel it pooling inside of him.

The orc before him swept the spear back in, but Wulfgar moved inside its reach and the shaft banged harmlessly against his hip. He locked it in place with his right hand and punched out with Aegis-fang in his left.

The orc ducked the blow and returned a stinging punch to the big man's face, but he accepted it and spat blood as he let go of the spear and brought his hand up frighteningly fast, clamping it about the orc's throat.

But the powerful humanoid tightened its jaw, flexing its considerable neck muscles against the pressure. It punched out again, repeatedly, rapidly, snaking its hand about Wulfgar's attempts to block, pummeling him again and again. No novice to warfare, the orc also used the barbarian's self-imposed disadvantage, for both his hands were engaged, one with the warhammer, trying to block the punches, the other grabbing at the orc's throat. So the orc's spear was free, and the monster brought it up fast to clip the barbarian's already bloody face. The orc threw its arm back and loosened its grip, sliding the spear back to shorten its forward length.

Now it could thrust under the barbarian's arm and score a kill.

Except that the orc did not understand the power of Wulfgar, the sheer strength of the man. Wulfgar had accepted the punishment in order to get the orc rocking forward, which it did then as it tried to stab.

But Wulfgar spun around, yanking the orc around with him, and he heaved the monster through the air, sending it spinning into the trunk of a tree.

"Behind ye, boy," he heard Bruenor shout from the side, and indeed, Wulfgar too had seen the second orc rushing in to join the fray.

Wulfgar rolled his left arm down and under, launching Aegis-fang into a spinning flight. He leaped around to see the charging orc collide with the hammer, and stumble forward, and he slapped the creature's sword aside, grabbed it by the hair and helped it on its way, launching it into a forward pitch to crash into its dazed companion.

"Bwahaha!" Bruenor howled, and Wulfgar turned to regard him just in time to see the dwarf bury his axe through the collarbone of his ugly opponent.

"Tempus!" Wulfgar growled, calling his hammer back to his hand. He leaped forward, towering over the two tangled orcs and began to chop mightily.

He didn't aim, didn't try to sort one out from the other. He just brought the hammer down with two-handed chops, turning flesh, muscle, and bone into mush.

He didn't know how many strikes he had landed, a dozen at least, when he heard Bruenor's cry for him.

"Boy!" the dwarf bellowed. "Boy, get down!"

But Wulfgar was already jumping about, and still standing straight.

He saw the arrows coming, but had no time to react defensively. One drove into his chest just under his right breast, a second jabbed right through his left shoulder. Wulfgar felt the explosions, dull at first, then burning with fire. The strength left his legs and he began to sink, and he saw two orc archers coming out of the brush, setting arrows and sneering at him.

He saw them draw back.

He saw . . .

Giselle could feel her heart thumping in her chest. She had known many battles before, but mostly against goblins or orcs, or even annoying trolls that had slithered out of the Trollmoors. And on those occasions, she had been among fellow Riders of Nesmé, skilled and coordinated and well-practiced in their movements.

She had never seen a true giant before. To her, an ogre or a troll had seemed an incredibly powerful beast, but measured against the frost giant she discovered in the forest, even those formidable foes seemed no more than puny goblins!

She noted the woman, Catti-brie, launching another magic missile barrage at the behemoth, which winced but didn't even slow its pursuit. Around a tree Catti-brie rushed, cutting back under some low branches.

Out came the giant behind her, simply tearing those branches from the trees as it passed, then hurling them forward at the dodging and scampering woman.

Giselle swallowed hard and lifted her bow, and with a determined grimace, she let fly. Her aim proved true—how could it not when it seemed to her as if she was shooting at the side of a mountain?—and the arrow caught the behemoth in the upper arm.

It didn't even flinch, didn't even turn to take note of her!

The woman looked at her quiver. She had but five arrows remaining, and what use might they prove?

But she had to help. She thought of drawing her sword and realized that she would stand only momentarily before this brute.

Her mind whirled. She felt helpless, felt like a coward!

Catti-brie had gained some distance, she noted, and Giselle's heart skipped, thinking the woman might get away. But then Catti-brie had to cut back to the side, rushing back into the thicker brush and trees, and the giant angled and gained ground quickly.

For a moment, Giselle didn't understand the turn, but then she noted the orc, moving slowly, tearing each foot up from the grabbing grasses. She saw its two companions then, as well, back a bit, caught by tree limbs, but struggling and wriggling to get free.

The woman calmed herself with a deep and slow breath, and leveled her bow.

The nearest orc tore free its boot and stepped forward.

Giselle shot it dead.

She nodded grimly. Determined to open the escape route for Catti-brie, she took a quick look at the giant, then advanced for a clearer shot at the remaining orcs.

"By the bearded gods!" came a roar from the side. Bruenor leaped out of the shadows. He sent his battle-axe spinning out before him, the weapon twisting and rolling with little chance to take out an orc.

But it did crash in before the pair, disrupting their shots. One arrow fell harmlessly aside, the bowstring twanging uselessly. The second orc got its arrow away, though the angle was wrong, and the shot aimed for Wulfgar's chest stabbed into the big man's thigh instead.

Behind the axe came a leaping Bruenor. The nearest orc drew out a long knife and turned to meet him.

The dwarf didn't slow, springing high, taking the hit in exchange for burying this enemy beneath him, and the pair went flying away into the brush.

The other orc charged ahead following its shot. It saw weakness there, in the huge barbarian, who swayed as if he could barely stand his ground.

And indeed, nauseating waves of pain had Wulfgar teetering. Blood streamed from his side, from his chest, from his shoulder, from his thigh. He raised his hammer to meet the charge, and let fly with a cry to his warrior god.

The weapon flew past the charging orc, however, for Wulfgar had spotted a more important target, as another orc appeared near the brush where Bruenor wrestled the first. So intent on lining up a strike with its axe on the rolling dwarf, the orc never saw the warhammer coming and made no move to dodge or even block.

It wouldn't have mattered anyway, and Wulfgar nodded in grim satisfaction that he had given his friend a fighting chance at least before he himself was slain.

He set himself for the orc's charge, knowing his only hope was to get in close, to use his superior strength to choke or crush the orc before it could bring its short sword to bear.

But the orc was no novice. Like many of the orcs of this kingdom, it had waged many fights and many raids against the peoples of Luruar, even against fellow Many-Arrow orcs. It pulled up short and slashed hard at Wulfgar's reaching hand, and though he retracted, he did so with a painful gash from forearm to palm.

The barbarian shrank back and the orc smiled wickedly, even laughed aloud as it began to circle slowly.

"A thousand cuts and you die in your blood," the orc teased.

Wulfgar shrugged.

Aegis-fang came back into his hands.

The orc's yellow eyes went wide and it made a strange squeaking sound and Wulfgar now came forward, jabbing ahead with his mighty warhammer. The barbarian rushed forward, his weapon now sweeping in great circles, around and around and the orc did well to keep its weapon back from that killing flow.

It looked for an opening; it tried to go left, then right, seeking an angle to get inside the devastating cuts of the warhammer.

Surely the big man, blood pouring freely, would tire!

But Wulfgar merely let go of the warhammer on the next spin, and though it wasn't an exact or well-aimed throw, he was standing just a few feet from his opponent.

Aegis-fang smashed and crashed in, twisting and turning the orc, and Wulfgar leaped in right behind it. He drove his right forearm under the orc's chin as he stepped beside the beast, strategically placing his right foot behind the orc's left to prevent it from stepping back even as he forced it backward.

The barbarian's left arm slapped at the orc, catching hold about its torso and pinning its right arm, and that sword, in tight.

Wulfgar pressed down and forward, laying the orc out flat—it would have fallen to the ground, but the barbarian drove his knee up into its back.

The move cost Wulfgar his breath, as the orc collided with the arrow still sticking into its chest. But the barbarian held on, pressing down against the orc's throat with his right forearm, driving and bending the orc backward over his knee.

The orc punched at him with its free left hand, pinched him, scratched him, but Wulfgar, knowing that he might soon simply faint away, pressed on with every bit of his remaining strength. He couldn't quite get the leverage to break the creature's backbone, but neither could the orc draw breath against his weight.

So it became a game of attrition, a test to see which would hold on longer.

The orc got its hand up to claw at Wulfgar's face, and he took a scratch but bit off one of the orc's fingers in response.

The hand came back in stubbornly, but then held there and hovered, trembling as the orc at last expired.

Wulfgar let it fall to the ground and staggered back, but found himself unable to fully stand up from his half-kneeling posture. He glanced to the brush to see Bruenor rise up from the bushes, and with a great tug, the dwarf lifted up the orc's head as well.

Bruenor had a dagger, Wulfgar noted, and only realized that it was the same knife the orc had drawn to meet Bruenor's charge.

The dwarf jerked the orc's head back and cut out its throat. He staggered backward a few steps and turned around, calling for his boy.

And Wulfgar saw that Bruenor had not escaped unscathed, for the blood on his face and the side of his neck was indeed his own.

Wulfgar managed a smile and a nod, but both were cut short by a flash of fire off to the side. The pair turned to see a ball of roiling flames hovering about the trees, far from the ground. A huge shadow rushed under it and the flaming ball reached down to form a pillar of fire, and in that light, they saw the frost giant.

"Me girl," Bruenor breathed and he dashed about frantically, finally finding and hoisting his axe, and running off to the distant battle.

Wulfgar nodded again and tried to rise.

The giant tore through some branches, batting them aside, plowing ahead. "Where'd yer go, girl?" it whispered, but that voice still sounded like a small landslide.

And then it roared in shock and anger and pain, for as it came out of the tree tangle, it stepped right under the suspended ball of fire, and that enchantment shot downward in a painful flamestrike, the divine fires of Mielikki biting at the behemoth. It staggered and stumbled out of the line of fire, batting at its hair and beard, the skin on its face blistering already, its blue skin shining an angry red.

That spell would have destroyed many creatures. No orc would have survived it, perhaps not even Catti-brie's own companions.

It had slowed and stung the giant, but the brute was far from defeated.

It spotted Catti-brie and charged, or started to, until an arrow arced out and drove into its cheek. With another howl, the behemoth snapped the arrow shaft and rolled its jaw, then spat out the arrowhead as it turned its focus to Giselle, who knew she was doomed, who couldn't find the strength to even run away from the bared fury and power of the frost giant.

The behemoth took a huge stride at her, and started a second, but another arrow hit it, and this one, streaking like a lightning bolt, surely hurt it.

The giant stumbled backward as a second silver-streaking arrow rushed in, and another behind it, and a whole line streaming in behind that. The giant jerked and swatted futilely, trying to turn, trying to flee as missile after missile drove into its heavy jerkin and through the padded armor to bite at its thick flesh.

Behind the barrage came a running form, speeding along, drawing his scimitars. The giant noticed him at the last moment and brought its huge tree club to bear, but the agile newcomer darted off to the side, disappearing into the brush.

Magic missiles hit the giant from the other side, and it whirled about, noting Catti-brie once more and taking up the chase.

Barely two steps later, out of the trees came the speeding form, came Drizzt Do'Urden, leaping from a branch to speed across the giant's midsection, his scimitars slashing and stabbing viciously. He landed past the behemoth, but cut back immediately the other way, stabbing his blades at the brute's fleshy thighs as he rushed past, hoping to be ahead of the club strike that would surely flatten him.

He made it, just barely, when another living missile came out of the trees, from higher up.

"Me king!" the specter of Thibbledorf Pwent yelled, leaping down from the top boughs, inverting and lining up his helmet spike to impale the giant through the skull.

But the giant had heard the cry, and whipped its club up and about with perfect timing, batting the dropping dwarf with a tremendous swipe, one that would have sent him flying a hundred strides, it seemed.

Except that there was nothing to launch, for the impact destroyed the specter dwarf, reducing him to gray fog instantly, as if he had simply exploded into nothingness!

The giant gave that lost enemy no further attention, leaping after the woman once more.

And once more, the drow rushed past, stinging its legs with his nasty little blades.

"Arg, but yer won't kill me with yer pigstickers!" the angry giant roared, turning to pursue.

And now came another foe, another dwarf, out of the darkness behind it, rushing up and expertly driving his many-notched axe into the giant's knee.

The brute tried to curse the dwarf, but merely howled instead and dropped down to clutch the torn knee.

And in came the dwarf, leaping and crying for his gods, inside the reach of the tree club.

The giant swatted him aside with its open hand, and though the brute took an axe-bite on the forearm, accepted the sting and the gash in exchange for putting that nasty bearded one into the brush.

Now the giant collected its thoughts and stood up straight, fighting through the pain. "Come out and play, dark elf!" it bellowed and it puffed out its massive chest in defiance. Truly it was a battered thing, with singed hair and half its beard melted away, with smoking holes from the lightning arrows, and a dozen cuts about its midsection and legs. But still, this was a true giant, and it looked far from defeated.

The brush moved before it, across the small clearing, and out leaped a form, but it was not the drow.

And a warhammer spun for the behemoth, and it heard the call to a name it recognized, the god Tempus, the war deity of the Uthgardt barbarians.

Aegis-fang slammed hard into the massive chest and the brute grunted.

"Come along," said the thrower, a curious-looking tall and huge and young human with long blond hair and wearing the silver hide of a winter wolf—and sporting several arrows, protruding from different spots on his body.

The giant started forward. Out of the brush beside the man came the dark elf, and the behemoth grimaced.

And growled, and started forward again.

But then it grimaced some more from a sudden and unexpected pain. It was down to one knee, unsure why, but feeling a strangeness in its chest, right where the warhammer had struck it.

And had cracked the rib, and had driven that rib into the giant's heart.

The frost giant looked at the barbarian and the drow curiously.

A ball of fire appeared in the air above its head and as it fell face down, a second flamestrike lashed down to curl its flesh.

But Catti-brie needn't have bothered, for the behemoth was already dead.

Out of the brush came Bruenor, shaken and unsteady, but holding his axe as if he was ready for battle.

"Where's yer damned cat, elf?" he asked, spitting leaves and twigs with every word.

"Some orcs ran off and she went in pursuit."

"With a durned frost giant here?" Bruenor asked incredulously, brushing away Catti-brie and motioning to Wulfgar as she tried to tend him.

"I didn't know about the giant. Better that no orcs return to alert their encampment."

"Encampment?" Giselle asked with concern.

"Huge," Drizzt answered. He turned to Bruenor. "And so I expected a visit this night from one of the many scouting parties such a camp would deploy."

"Aye, and they likely saw some of the fires, or heard the roars, or noting the lighting of yer arrows," said Catti-brie. She looked Wulfgar in the eye, nodded, and jammed the arrow the rest of the way through his shoulder, pulling it out the back.

Wulfgar nearly swooned, doubling over, and had Catti-brie not caught him, he would likely have fallen to the ground.

"So we should be goin'," Bruenor said to Drizzt, and the drow nodded.

"But where is Regis?" Wulfgar asked, gasping every word.

All eyes went to Drizzt, but the drow had no answers for them.

CHAPTER 10

INSIDE INFORMATION

WHY ARE YOU HERE?" THE GOBLIN SHAMAN SHRIEKED WHEN IT SAW Regis, now disguised as a goblin, in its private chambers, and near a pile of sensitive and confidential communiqués from the drow leaders!

Regis turned slowly and smiled crookedly at the shaman.

"Orc spy!" the goblin cried, and Regis took a step for him and tossed something his way, but then disappeared, or seemed to, leaving the goblin shaman to stare in puzzlement, and to ponder the remnant the intruder had left behind: a small length of rope, or was it a small branch, or . . . a living serpent?

The goblin shaman batted frantically at the living missile, then sucked in its breath when it felt the point of a dagger against its back. And the snake—and oh, it was a snake—wrapped about a finger of that slapping hand, and before the goblin could react, sped along its arm, to the shoulder, to the throat.

The goblin did a good job of jumping forward and turning around, instead of simply recoiling, which would have driven the dagger deeper into its flesh, and started to cry out again as it stared at the intruder, facing it.

The halfling-turned-goblin smiled crookedly as that cry was fully stifled, for the enchanted serpent got about the shaman's throat. A heartbeat later, the leering face appeared, the specter tugging the garrote so brutally that the goblin shaman lost one of its shoes as it flew over backward to the floor.

A short while later, a goblin climbed off the ladder and into the adjoining chamber, his tooth necklace clattering. He straightened his shamanic robes, and with a glance around to ensure he was alone, went to the small basin of water set off to the side of the room. It was hard for Regis to make out the details in the dim light, but he was pretty sure that he had managed the look of the dispatched shaman pretty well.

He glanced back to the hole and recounted his steps in the tunnels below, hoping he had also done well in properly stashing the body.

He heard a commotion on the ladder then and reflexively started for the exit.

"No," he whispered and he held his ground, and he cast a stern glance at the goblins coming up from the Underdark, one after the next, and all of them offering a deferential nod, even a motion of supplication, his way.

"Shaman Kllug," one said with a deep bow.

Regis grunted in reply and motioned the goblin away. He hid his grin as the goblin departed, for that name, "Kllug," was the same one written in the greeting on the communiqués in the other room. The disguise had worked.

He went back into the other room. He had some reading to do.

When Regis emerged from the chamber, from the cave and from the boulder tumble back into the orc encampment, he did so with his eyes wide open and his heart thumping in his chest.

A commotion in the camp and shouts for Shaman Kllug from other goblins had drawn him outside, but the source of his current discontent had more to do with what he had read on those parchments, which were now rolled and tucked safely under his robes.

He made his way along, following the shouts and the shoving, with goblins falling in behind him, whispering his name. They were afraid, he realized, as goblins often were when immersed among bullying orcs. They came to the southwestern section of the camp, near to where Regis had initially entered in the guise of an orc with an armload of wood, way back when the moon had first climbed into the eastern sky.

That moon had begun its descent in the west, Regis realized. The night had turned to early morning, only a short few hours from dawn.

He was about to bark out some demands for an explanation as he led the goblins—his goblins, he knew—to the gathering orcs, when he found many answers on his own. Off in the distance, far to the west, a fiery blast erupted, a line of flames cutting through the darkness. Regis didn't need to get his bearings and do any calculations to understand the source of those divine fires.

Those were his friends, surely.

And the orcs were mustering into battle groups, an army readying to march.

"No!" he said to the orc leader when he came upon the ugly creature, pushing and shoving its minions into formation.

"Our patrol," the orc argued, pointing off into the distance, where all seemed quiet and dark once more.

"Whatever it is has passed," Regis said.

"We cannot leave them!"

"We have to leave them. And hope they did not tell our enemies of the greater plan." Regis hopped around. "Fires down," he ordered orc and goblin alike. "Dark and quiet, all."

"What are you doing?" the orc leader demanded.

"If those who battled our patrol are still alive and they find this encampment, they will warn Nesmé," Regis explained. "Nesmé cannot know of the cloud gathering before its walls until it is too late."

"We will crush them," the orc said. Looking around at the size of this force, then comparing it against what he remembered of the small town of Nesmé, Regis didn't think the claim an idle boast.

"Yes," he agreed, realizing that he had to calm this down quickly. "But we must be fast and it must be clean. The drow have told me. We are needed in the east when Nesmé is destroyed."

"We go," said the orc, and around it, other brutes cheered.

"No!" the goblin shaman shouted back. "Tomorrow night when the sun first sets."

The orc stammered and pointed off in the direction of the flames and battle.

"An incident, a patrol, nothing more. Orc raiders and Nesmé farmers, nothing more," Regis answered, improvising as his plans solidified. He too looked to the west and tried to calm his fears, trusting that his friends had handled whatever had come against them.

"Fires out, tents down," he ordered, and the orcs all looked at him incredulously. "And all go into the cave, into the tunnels. The fools of Nesmé will not know their doom is upon them until it is too late."

The orc stared at him hard, and turned a doubting expression to its companions, none of whom seemed convinced.

"Our kin," the orc muttered.

"A giant, Thorush," another orc said, and Regis couldn't help but wince at the news that his friends had apparently tangled with a formidable band. Still, he had to trust Drizzt and the others, he knew, for his options were few indeed.

"Break the camp and go hide in the tunnels," he said to the orc leader. "I will go and learn of this fight. Gruumsh is with me." He ended with a shake of his toothy necklace for effect, and to remind the orcs that he had been put in charge here—as he had learned from the communiqués—for a reason.

"I go, too," the orc said, staring at him hard, an expression full of distrust.

Regis nodded, figuring he'd sort out that problem when he had to. For now, he just wanted to learn the fate of his companions.

Giselle fought back tears. She tenderly stroked the shaking neck of her horse, the mount inevitably sinking down to the ground, the light fading from its pretty black eyes.

Just to the side, Wulfgar sat in the back of the wagon, Catti-brie working her healing magic upon him. He winced repeatedly, despite the warming waves of comfort and magical salve, as Catti-brie determinedly worked at removing the barbed arrowheads.

"You'll be lying down for a long while," the woman said to him, nodding as she looked at his badly ripped side.

Wulfgar shook his head. "Take it out."

"She'll take half yer belly with it," Bruenor remarked.

Wulfgar shrugged as if it did not matter.

"I'll tend all the other wounds first, then we'll know," Catti-brie conceded. She moved her fingers to feel the hole in the big man's shoulder and closed her eyes, beginning a minor healing spell.

Wulfgar interrupted her. She looked up at him curiously and he nodded to Giselle.

"I've not much more to offer," she replied to his plaintive look.

"You'll have more tomorrow, and I'll still be here."

"Girl?" Bruenor asked, not catching on to the deeper meaning of the curious exchange.

Catti-brie looked to him, then past him to Drizzt, who understood the quieter implications and nodded his agreement with Wulfgar.

Catti-brie kissed Wulfgar on the cheek, promising to be right back, then went to Giselle and her wounded horse. After a quick inspection, the priestess of Mielikki put her hand against the most serious wound and softly chanted a spell of blessed healing.

"Good thing ye seen 'em coming in, elf," Bruenor said, the dwarf, Drizzt and Wulfgar gathered at the back of the wagon.

"I knew they were about," Drizzt answered. "The encampment to the east is no small hunting party."

"The group we fought was no small hunting party," Wulfgar added, his voice a bit raspy as he was still clearly in pain. "And a giant with them?"

"Aye," Bruenor replied. "And where's Rumblebelly?"

Wulfgar and Drizzt exchanged nervous glances.

"Go and find him, elf," the dwarf said. "I ain't likin' him out there with so many stinkin' orcs about."

"Trust in him," Drizzt answered, but his tone didn't sound as confident as any of them, Drizzt included, would have wanted.

"Perhaps the war you foresaw has come in full," Drizzt added. "Nesmé?"

The drow shrugged. "Get mended and get the group moving," he instructed. "Continue to the south—and stay along the tree line."

"I'm wantin' to get to Mithral Hall and not Nesmé," Bruenor reminded.

"Take what we can," Wulfgar said, and coming from him, with so many wounds evident, the advice carried more weight. "I doubt we'll find a straight road home, and surely not a clear one."

"South," Drizzt said again. "I will find you along the tree line after I see what I can learn."

"Find Rumblebelly," Bruenor instructed.

The drow nodded and slipped off into the darkness.

As he departed, Catti-brie and Giselle returned to the wagon, the latter leading her horse, which was moving much better, the light of life back in its dark eyes.

"Give all the blessings ye got left on me boy," Bruenor said to Catti-brie, and he pointed to Wulfgar, who, despite his stoic resolve, occasionally winced and lurched against the pain in his side.

Catti-brie nodded, but she didn't seem overly pleased when Bruenor added, "We're moving right out."

She didn't argue, though. They couldn't stay here, despite the injuries.

Anyone and anything nearby had surely heard the sounds of battle, and seen the blasts of fire and lightning arrows.

Catti-brie found herself glancing off nervously into the distance where Drizzt had disappeared. Her magic was all but exhausted. Giselle's horse would live, but could not be ridden anytime soon. Wulfgar would no doubt rise up to meet any new challenges, but he had not fared well in that last battle, and he still had a large, barbed spear tip embedded deeply into his side, where any jostling could start the blood flowing anew.

She looked back to the darkness and before she began her formal prayers to Mielikki, she offered a silent hope that Drizzt would keep them clear of enemies.

The halfling's plans were not playing out as he had imagined. He had gotten out of the orc encampment, but not alone, and in no position to come out of his goblin shaman disguise. He suspected they were coming into the area where his friends had been, and so perhaps Drizzt was nearby, but that brought him little comfort.

How would Drizzt or any of the others know it was him, after all? And if the drow ranger was nearby, ready to strike, wouldn't an enemy shaman be among his primary targets?

Regis swallowed hard as he imagined a silver-streaking arrow rushing out of the darkness to blast his little skull to pieces.

Fear inspired him, then, and he held up his hands to stop his companions, a ragtag group of goblins and orcs. Before they could even begin to question him about the delay, the phony shaman began to chant quietly—and in gibberish—and to dance about, as if in sudden and deep spellcasting.

Regis, Shaman Kllug, stopped as abruptly as he had begun, his body frozen in a defensive crouch, his head swiveling back and forth, eyes darting around for dramatic effect.

"What?" barked Innanig, the orc who had demanded to come along back in the encampment.

"They are close," Shaman Kllug announced in a harsh whisper that seemed on the edge of desperation.

"Enemies?"

Regis considered that for a moment, trying to improvise, looking for some way out. He imagined again silvery arrows, or maybe even a spinning warhammer, blasting him from life. He feared that some of his friends were dead at the hands of the scouting party they had obviously battled.

So many thoughts swirled at him, biting at his sensibilities, paralyzing him with terror.

"Drow," he squeaked. "Our drow friends are close."

Orcs and goblins alike began dancing in circles, looking off nervously into the darkness at that surprising and nerve-wracking announcement.

"Where?" Innanig demanded, and he moved nearer and towered over the diminutive shaman. Despite his intended intimidation, Regis had clearly heard the tremor in the orc's voice.

Still, the orc shoved him and growled, and the halfling knew that his life was on the very edge of disaster, both from within his party and without.

Yes, Regis understood this moment all too well, for he had lived it many times over in his previous existence and even in this new incarnation, on the streets of Delthuntle. When the halfling thought about it, Innanig and his ilk weren't much different from Bregnan Prus and the other bullies the young Spider Parrafin had suffered daily. Surely a teen-aged Bregnan Prus was not as formidable as the brutish orc standing before him, but then, Regis had been but a small child at that time.

"Innanig," he said slowly, calmly, and he lifted a pointing finger and even dared to tap the brute in the chest, "you do not please Gruumsh." As he did that, Regis cleverly pulled his other arm right back through the robe's loose sleeve inside the robe. Innanig slapped his finger aside, of course, and in the distraction and sudden movement, Regis pulled forth a small weapon, brought it up tight against the robe and pulled the trigger, moving right against the orc as he did.

Innanig jerked and grunted at the sting as the hand crossbow bolt ripped through the fabric and pinched him in the chest.

Confused, the brutish orc reacted violently, of course, shoving the shaman, and Regis was ready for it, turning before the orc ever slapped at him and bringing his other hand back across to deftly take the dart from the orc's chest as he went. He spun and hopped and rushed back, putting ground between himself and the brute, where he stood pointing at Innanig and crying, "Gruumsh is angry. Gruumsh will not forgive!"

All around him, goblins and orcs began jostling, pointing fingers and weapons and hurling curses one way or the other. Regis worried briefly that he might have started a battle here, orc against goblin, but mixed in with that trepidation was a measure of hope that he had indeed done just that. Maybe he'd find his escape in the coming commotion.

For now, though, he focused on Innanig, standing before him and staring hatefully at him. The orc hunched his shoulders forward and clutched his chest—he could feel the burn of poison, no doubt, the disguised halfling knew.

"Gruumsh is not happy!" the fake shaman cried loudly, demanding the attention of all as he pointed repeatedly and accusingly at Innanig. "Gruumsh is mad at you!" he shouted and hopped, and skittered backward as he landed, for now the large orc straightened.

"Succumb," Regis muttered, prayed, under his breath.

Innanig took a step toward him, and fell over on his face, just dropped straight to the ground and lay in a heap, very still. He looked quite dead, but he was not, Regis knew, only sleeping, so soundly, under the influence of the infamous drow poison.

The fake goblin shaman breathed a sigh of relief. He almost swooned with relief at dodging that moment of near disaster, but realized that he still had a lot of work to do.

"Gruumsh! Gruumsh! Gruumsh!" he yelped, hopping about and pointing accusingly at this orc or that goblin, using the god's name like a blunt weapon to slap his minions into obedience. And with Innanig, the strongest of the orcs, lying so still on the ground, the results proved immediate and effective.

The group calmed around him, and looked to him for orders.

"I will go find our dark elf allies," he informed them. "Stay in group. Here!" He looked around, still improvising, and pointed to the fallen Innanig, whom he feared might start snoring at any moment!

"Tend to him and when he awakens, remind Innanig that Gruumsh rules, not Innanig."

He hustled out of the ring of orcs and goblins, rushing into the darkness, hoping that his friends were indeed nearby.

He knew that some of the ragtag band he had left behind were likely watching him, that perhaps a couple of Innanig's closest allies were even following him out for a bit, and hardly trusted him. He wanted to get out of this disguise, though, and as soon as possible, and certainly before he came upon his friends, particularly a certain dark elf and a rather nasty bow the ranger carried.

He glanced back many times, looking for quiet pursuit, and finally dared to dart across an open patch of ground that brought him into a tangle of trees. At the near edge, he stared back across the long open expanse, and at perfect angle to note any silhouettes moving across the lea, even in the meager light of the darkened night.

He saw nothing.

He was clear of them and could become Regis once more.

He reached for his beret.

He was too late.

He got hit hard in the side and was launched through the air sidelong, flying to the ground.

Barely aware, but enough to know that he was surely in the last moments of his life.

CHAPTER 11

TRAVELING COMPANIONS

T HE BOAT ROLLED OVER A WAVE AND SPLASHED DOWN JARRINGLY, WHITE spray flying around the front of the deck.

"Salty bath," Afafrenfere said to Ambergris as the dwarf spat out a considerable amount of water.

"Bah to any bath," she replied, but cheerily.

"We bathe often at the Monastery of the Yellow Rose," the monk said. "It will be expected of you, as well. The desired state of cleanliness . . ."

"Baths make ye sick," Ambergris finished with a dismissive wave of her hand. "More'n these waves e'er could."

Almost as if in response, the prow rose again to climb another large wave. The sky above was clear, the day quite warm, but dark clouds gathered to the east above the Sea of Fallen Stars, the portent of quite a storm if these leading swells were any indication.

The captain of the boat was not concerned, though, for he expected to make the mouth of the River Vesper and the great port city of Calaunt before the weather turned.

The boat crashed down and Ambergris stumbled forward, catching hold of the guide rope just before she pitched forward, which would have landed her in the arms of another dwarf who came around the mainmast at the same time, a dark-bearded and slender fellow whom neither of the companions had noted before.

"Ah, but it'd be a great catch to have ye fallin' into me arms, eh?" he greeted the female dwarf heartily and he moved to help steady her.

"Ain't got me sea legs," Ambergris replied, a bit embarrassed.

"Aye, and ye'll get 'em just as we put in to dock, not to doubt." He laughed a bit too exuberantly then, drawing curious looks from Ambergris and her human companion.

"Well met, then, Lady Ambergris!" he said and held out his hand.

Ambergris looked at it, then at him, skeptically. "Aye, well met, then, and who ye be?"

"A friend."

"A friend?" Afafrenfere echoed, coming forward and on his guard. "We have been aboard this boat a tenday, and seen all there is, and all there are, and there aren't many."

"One more, now," said the dwarf. "Came aboard in Procampur when I saw ye weren't getting off."

Ambergris and Afafrenfere shared puzzled and concerned looks as that curious remark sank in.

"And who might ye be, then, what's lookin' for us?" Ambergris asked.

The dwarf rocked on his heels as if taken aback. "What, ye don't know me, then?" he asked incredulously and shook his head, but then brightened . "Bah, but it's me accent—good one, though, eh? Bwahaha, if I told ye that ye're owin' me yer lives, ye both, would ye guess me name then?"

The companions shared another skeptical look.

"Or if I called ye Amber Gristle O'Maul o' the Adbar O'Mauls?" the dwarf asked.

"You're from Adbar?" Afafrenfere asked.

"He's not one from Adbar that I'm knowin'," Ambergris insisted.

"I am from many places," the dwarf answered, and his accent disappeared, "though I cannot claim Citadel Adbar as one of them. I have been to Mithral Hall, however."

He glanced around, then smiled and hopped off to the side, moving behind some tied barrels. When he came out the other side, he was no longer a stranger to the two, indeed, no longer a dwarf.

The sight of Jarlaxle aboard this ship in the northern reaches of the Sea of Fallen Stars had both Ambergris and Afafrenfere rocking back on their heels indeed!

"Well met again," Jarlaxle said with a bow and tip of his gigantic hat.

"Of all the folk I might expect to be seein' out here, yerself ain't one," Ambergris remarked.

"That is my secret, good dwarf. Always by surprise, you see?"

"Would that include murder?" Afafrenfere asked.

Jarlaxle laughed. "Am I deserving of that remark? From you, good brother? From you, whom I might once have wheeled into a town square as a resting spot for pigeons?"

The reminder of their previous meeting, when Afafrenfere had been turned into a statue by Draygo Quick's pet medusa, had the monk stammering and at a loss for a reply.

"Doesn't mean we trust ye," Ambergris dared to say.

"I have earned a bit of that, I expect."

"Why are you here?" Afafrenfere asked directly.

"In search of Effron, and of Artemis Entreri."

"Ain't seen Entreri since Gauntlgrym," said Ambergris. "And Effron? Got himself killed in Port Llast, we're hearing."

"Not so," Jarlaxle corrected. "Indeed, he was on the road to find you when he learned of your escape, from those who rescued you, in Port Llast. It would seem that he wasn't quite fast enough to catch you."

Afafrenfere and Ambergris looked to each other, and nodded and smiled, clearly glad to hear that Effron had survived.

"Might that he found Entreri, then," Ambergris offered, and Jarlaxle shrugged.

"They'd both have lost our trail at the coast, I'm guessing, as we were fast out to the sea."

"Aye, so I learned in Suzail," Jarlaxle replied.

"Long way behind us, Suzail."

"Indeed, but since I have no idea of where those two might be, and I knew that you two were aboard this fine vessel, I decided it would be worth my time to pay a visit," Jarlaxle explained. "I've business in Damara, in any event, so why not share the road?"

The two exchanged yet another look.

"You can disembark in Calaunt, as you've planned," Jarlaxle said, "though you'll find a difficult hike through the Earthspurs and across the Glacier of the White Worm, no doubt."

"Last stop," Ambergris replied.

"Or you can sail on to Mulmaster," the drow finished.

"Boat's not going to Mulmaster," said Ambergris.

"And we've been warned against traversing that particular city," Afafrenfere added.

"I've convinced the captain otherwise, so yes, we will sail next to Mulmaster," the drow replied. "And fear not, for I can navigate the streets of Mulmaster quite easily, I assure you. The place is known to me, and knows of me."

Once more, Ambergris and Afafrenfere glanced to each other for support.

"And I've news and stories to share, and some to hear, I hope," Jarlaxle added.

The two paused and seemed hardly convinced.

"If not Mulmaster, then know that you've erred," the drow told them. "You would have been much better off disembarking in Procampur than at the port of Calaunt soon before us. Your intended destination is a longer road from Procampur, but one more traveled and one far safer."

"I know the Earthspurs," Afafrenfere replied. "It is high summer and the passes are not that difficult."

"You knew the Earthspurs," Jarlaxle corrected. "Before the Sundering. Much has changed, much has grown darker, in the decades since you have traveled here."

"It was just a few years . . ." Afafrenfere started to argue, but he cut himself short as he remembered the little fact that he had been asleep in an enchanted forest for nearly two decades. He gave a great sigh and shook his head. The events of the last few tendays of his consciousness were still too confusing!

"So, Mulmaster, ye're saying?" asked Ambergris.

Jarlaxle nodded. "The captain will take us there."

"And ye can get us through?"

Jarlaxle nodded again.

"Why would ye?"

"Why would I not?" Jarlaxle answered. "I prefer to share the road when I find good company and strong companions. As I told you, I seek Effron and Entreri, and they may be seeking you. And besides," he added, tossing a wink at the dwarf, "if we are overwhelmed by enemies, I know I can outrun you."

"Aye, and I believe ye'd do just that," said Ambergris, but now she too was smiling widely. As the shock of seeing Jarlaxle way out here had worn off, Ambergris had to remind herself that this drow was indeed no enemy.

He had saved her from certain death at the hands of drow assassins in Luskan. He had rescued her friends from Draygo Quick, and had put them all on the road to the north. And no doubt, he had done all of that at no small personal risk. Drizzt had explained Bregan D'aerthe to her as an organization still tied to Menzoberranzan, and among those assassins seeking her in Luskan, Ambergris had learned, had been none other than a noble of the greatest House of that drow city.

She recalled that dark night then, muttering, "Poor Stuvie," as she considered the young dwarf she had escorted out of a tavern, and who had been murdered on the street beside her.

She came out of her memories nodding. "Mulmaster," she agreed. "And glad I am to share the road, a drink and a few good tales beside ye, Jarlaxle."

She looked to Afafrenfere as she finished, and the monk nodded.

"Oh, I expect you'll be gladder still as the road grows long," the drow mercenary said, and he wore that little smirk that was so typical of Jarlaxle, the one that conveyed the likely truth that he knew more about the situation, whatever the situation might be, than the person to whom he was speaking.

The troll slogged through the muck, long arms reaching about to grasp at skeletal dead trees and pull itself along.

The hungry beast knew that its prey was near. Acrid smoke curled about the trees, mixing with the ever-present fog of the quagmire known as the Evermoors. A foul odor to most, to the troll it smelled like a fine supper.

Long green fingers with claw-like nails grasped the darkened trunk of a dead tree and the troll yanked itself forward, tearing its thin legs and enormous feet from the muck. It pulled itself past the trunk and came to drier ground, then loped along, propelled by its insatiable hunger as the curling smoke thickened.

A pointed tongue flickered eagerly through sharp yellow teeth, and the troll gasped quickly so that its breathing sounded like raspy laughter, and behind that, the monster whispered, "Come out. Come out."

"Huffin' and puffin', I hear me a troll," came a grumbling voice from the underbrush ahead. "So I'm swingin' me balls to give it a roll! To drop it down low, snap legs like they're twigs, and stop it from growin' with the feet o' me pig! Bwahahaha!"

Leaping out from the brush came a most curious sight, a black-bearded dwarf, his beard braided three ways and tipped with dung, sat atop a large boar—but not any boar, for this one had smoke coming from its nostrils and puffs of flame exploding from its stamping feet. The dwarf held a pair of heavy glasssteel morningstars with spiked heads bouncing about at the end of adamantine chains.

The troll's eyes lit up, its tongue flicking hungrily, and as the dwarf kicked his war pig into a charge, so too did the monster launch itself forward.

They came together in a wild tangle, troll hands clawing, troll teeth biting. The ugly beast came in fearlessly, knowing that any wounds the dwarf and his meaty hell boar might inflict would heal quickly.

That look of eagerness and hunger changed quickly, though, when the morningstars swung about, for one was coated now, magically so, with a peculiar oil that exploded mightily when it connected against the troll's side. Before the monster could dig its claws into the dwarf, it was flying, sidelong, launched by the weight of the strike and the power of the oil of impact.

It broke through a dead tree, splintering the wood, and impaling itself through its hip on the broken remainder of the trunk. With a snarl and a wad of green spit, the troll looked back at the dwarf and began to lift itself straight up, sliding free of the trunk.

Almost free, for the dwarf came on, the war pig galloping and snorting fire. They wouldn't reach the troll in time, so it seemed, but then the boar drove its front hooves into the muck and bucked hard, launching the dwarf from its back—and the dwarf didn't look the least bit surprised.

Indeed, he seemed rather exuberant as he arced forward, both hands on his mighty flails, held up high over his head. He had spun them about each other, so they seemed like a singular two-headed weapon. Down he came and down the weapon came, crashing mightily on the troll's shoulder and back and driving it back down hard on the sharpened spear of the broken tree.

The troll went into a frenzy, clawing and biting and spitting green bile. One sweeping hand caught the dwarf on the cheek and dug a deep line through his beard, red blood pouring.

But the dwarf proved as fearless as his enemy, and he didn't flinch and didn't shy away at all.

He just sang and rhymed and swatted tirelessly. The morningstars, swung deftly into two weapons once more, crunched troll bones and tore at the beast's skin. One troll arm stopped working in short order, dangling uselessly, but at last the troll managed to extract itself and rise up to its ten-foot height, towering over the dwarf.

But over the dwarf came the war boar, leaping right into the troll's chest and knocking it backward and to the ground. With its good remaining arm, the troll threw the goring and biting beast aside, but as it tried then to stand up, in came the dwarf, leaping from the broken tree trunk, up high and descending quickly.

Down came the dwarf.

Down came the morningstars.

"Bwahahaha!" he cried, and then came a retort as sharp and loud as a large tree snapping in half.

Skull shattered, head pulverized, the troll continued to flail and strike out, as trolls were wont to do. Trolls do not die as most creatures might. If a troll was cut into ten pieces and scattered about, they'd wriggle and crawl together. And if they could not reconnect, each would grow into a new troll, so powerful was the troll regenerative process!

A severed troll hand could fight. It could not see, but it could claw and it could burrow.

And so the troll thrashed and fought on, and the dwarf's powerful arms pumped repeatedly, driving the heavy morningstars down with punishing force. And the dwarf laughed, for he knew the secret.

A troll was hard to kill, aye, and would grow back and mend faster than almost any living creature—unless its wounds were sealed with fire.

And this dwarf had a war boar, a red-skinned hell boar, actually, and the fire of its hooves was no illusion, but true, biting flames.

The magical boar scrambled over and began its work, hopping around the fallen troll, puffing out flames that bit at troll flesh and bubbled troll blood, and killed the bits of troll life that normally would not die.

For a long while, the dwarf pummeled the fallen creature, crushing and stomping any part that moved. Then he stepped back, admiring his work, and summoned his hell boar to climb atop the monster and begin its fiery hopping once more.

Flames rolled out from smoking hooves and bit hard, and caught on, and soon the boar leaped away, and the troll lay there, burning, unmoving, destroyed.

"Well come on then, Snort," he called to his pet boar. "Lights o' the town're in me eyes and we've not long left to ride."

As he climbed atop the magical steed, Athrogate muttered more than a few curses at Jarlaxle for sending him to this forsaken place. "Trolls, trolls," he muttered, looking back at the latest in a long line of smoking troll corpses he had left in his wake in skimming the northern end of the Evermoors, a place also known, and rightly so, as the Trollmoors.

"And here, we part ways," Jarlaxle said at the bottom of a long climbing path. Up ahead and far to the right, the south, loomed the towering ice wall of the Glacier of the White Wyrm, and directly up the trail, the trio could just make out the crenulated top of the highest stone keep of the large structure known as the Monastery of the Yellow Rose. "Though not for long, I hope."

"And my hope was to escort you into the monastery beside me," Brother Afafrenfere replied, "As my guest. There is much of interest to see within those walls, a vast repository of knowledge."

"You are not returning to the monastery in good standing," Jarlaxle reminded.

"Aye, he's got a point," said Ambergris.

"And I doubt that bringing along a drow elf would do much to engender the trust of the Brothers of the Yellow Rose," Jarlaxle added with a laugh.

Afafrenfere nodded, conceding the point, and he seemed genuinely dismayed.

"Make me the offer again when such a visit will not threaten your own standing within the order," Jarlaxle said. "You will have no trouble convincing me to visit if the libraries of the monastery are as I remember, and your brethren will have me."

Afafrenfere brightened at that and happily nodded.

"Hold then! What?" Ambergris said, however, and she added incredulously, "As ye remember?"

Afafrenfere looked at her curiously, then back at Jarlaxle, catching on to the reasoning. "You have been there before?"

The drow laughed and pulled out a small onyx figurine, dropping it to the ground at his feet. "I am Jarlaxle," he explained. "I have been everywhere." With that, he summoned his magical hell horse and pulled himself up onto the saddle.

"I have business in Heliogabalus," he explained. "It could be finished quickly, or perhaps it will take me tendays to sort it out. In any case, I will return to this place and send word to you, and if you choose, perhaps we will have roads yet to travel together. Perhaps I will have news of Effron and Artemis Entreri, as well." He tipped his hat.

"If ye won't go into the place, then how'll ye send word to us?" Ambergris asked.

The dark elf laughed. "I am Jarlaxle," he answered, as if that explained everything.

It did.

"Stand and be recognized!" the guard shouted down from Nesmé's high and stout southern wall.

"Bah, ye're not to know me," retorted Athrogate, who was walking now, having dismissed his hell boar back to its home on the lower planes before coming in sight of the town. He doubted that riding up on a fire-snorting pig would create the trust he needed to be allowed into the famously xenophobic city.

"Then perhaps you would do well to introduce yourself, good dwarf," said another voice, a woman this time, "before we shoot you dead where you stand."

"That so?" Athrogate asked, hands on hips. He took a deep breath even as he spoke the words, though, and glanced over his shoulder at the tangled morass that bordered the town. He could well imagine that these hardy folk battled trolls every tenday.

"Name's Athrogate o' Felbarr," he called out. "Though I ain't been there in a hunnerd years and more."

"And is that where you're headed?" the woman asked.

"Nah, Mithral Hall's more likely."

"You are friend to King Connerad, then?"

"Nah, ne'er met him, but he'll be letting me in, don't ye doubt. I called his predecessor me friend once."

"His predecessor?"

"Aye, King Bruenor," Athrogate boasted, thinking the name would buy him some political capital. He didn't quite get the response he was expecting.

"Then Mithral Hall will be welcoming you," the woman called, and she seemed clearly annoyed. "So be on your way."

"Eh?"

"Be gone," the other guard said.

"I been walking through the muck for tenday," Athrogate protested. "Left a dozen trolls dead in me wake."

"Then they are probably moving close behind you even as we speak," the woman said.

"I'm knowin' enough to burn the damned things." Athrogate turned around and pointed to the southwest. "Left one dead there, not a thousand steps back. Go and see."

"Perhaps we will."

Athrogate shrugged and plopped down in the dirt, sitting with his arms crossed. He began singing to himself, nonsensical rhymes mostly, including a few he improvised to insult guards at unwelcoming gates.

Within a few heartbeats, the gate cracked open and a trio of riders came forth. As soon as they exited, the gate was closed once more, but Athrogate had made no move for it in any case.

They rode right up to the dwarf, staring down at him from their tall horses.

"What?" he asked.

"You said you killed a troll nearby," said the tallest of the group. "Show us."

"Ye did'no bring me a horse."

The man smirked, but made no move, and didn't offer his hand.

With a sigh, Athrogate pulled himself to his feet. He thought of walking, but only briefly before deciding that it really didn't make any difference, given their dour demeanor. Maybe showing them a bit of the power he possessed would be a good thing.

He pulled out the onyx figurine of his hell boar, a gift long ago from Jarlaxle, and with a nod at the guards, dropped it to the ground and called for his mount.

The horses reared and stepped back, snorting in fear, when the diabolical beast appeared, all puffs of fire and snorting meanness.

"See if ye can keep up," the dwarf said, sliding onto the saddle and kicking Snort hard in the flanks. The boar leaped away.

By the time the foursome returned to Nesmé's south gate, they were laughing and swapping tales of killing trolls, and the guards walked Athrogate right into the town, even bade him to keep his hell boar around for a bit so that others could see the wondrous thing.

Indeed the dwarf had made quite an entrance, and the people of Nesmé, reputedly—rightfully, as wary of visitors—held a bit of gratitude for any who killed a troll or ten, especially those who destroyed the beasts correctly, so they couldn't regenerate!

Still, it wasn't all open arms and friendship for Athrogate, for the guards kept him near to the gate.

"Why have you come?" asked one, and Athrogate recognized the voice as that of the woman who had questioned him from the wall.

The dwarf pointed up at the darkened sky. "Heared there be things not right in the Silver Marches," he said. "Come to see what's what for me old friends, the Battlehammers."

"Your friends are not much appreciated in Nesmé," the woman said.

"Aye, ye told me as much."

"Nor in Everlund," said another. "Or Sundabar or Silverymoon."

"I'm listenin'," Athrogate assured him when he stopped.

"The orcs have marched from Dark Arrow Keep, in force," the woman said.

Athrogate nodded as the woman continued, though it was all coming clear to him. He knew about the old treaty of Garumn's Gorge, had even read it on the pedestal on the bridge across the chasm in Mithral Hall that had given the treaty its name, and so he wasn't surprised that those looking to escape responsibility would glance back a century and point to it as the impetus for their current problems.

"You'll not get near to Mithral Hall," the woman ended, and the words jolted the dwarf.

"It is besieged by a great orc army," she explained, "as are Sundabar and Silverymoon. We have been fortunate here in Nesmé thus far, but there are rumors of orc forces moving about the trails to the north of here. We may know war soon, dwarf, and siege. When it comes . . ." She paused and nodded her chin at the morningstar balls bouncing about behind him, the weapon secured in place on his back.

"Aye, ye'll have me bludgeons," Athrogate promised. "Only thing better'n killin' a troll's killin' an orc, bwahahaha!"

"Come along," the tall man from the patrol decided then. "The Lord of Nesmé will see you, and we'll give you your assignment."

"Assignment? Bah, so I'm workin' for me food and bed, am I?"

"You object?"

"Bwahahaha!" Athrogate roared, and he waved his hand, indicating that the man should lead on.

CHAPTER 12

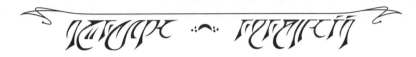

TRICKSTER

Teeth. Just teeth. Big teeth, sharp teeth, shining teeth, killing teeth. Teeth, and a low growl rumbling between them. Teeth that could kill him with a single bite, and a growl promising that the monster was about to do just that.

It went on and on, it seemed, interminably so, but in that moment of terror and confusion, enough sensibilities returned for the victim to utter one word.

One name that saved his life.

"Guenhwyvar?"

The teeth receded and the halfling-turned-goblin saw the whole frame of the panther's beautiful face.

The low growl continued, though now sounding more curious than ominous.

Regis tried to slowly slide his arm up to tap his beret and dispel the illusion, but he had barely started moving it when the panther snarled and slapped a huge paw onto his elbow, painfully pinning the arm to the ground.

"Guen," he said softly, calmly. Then the halfling swallowed hard as a bow swiveled into view, or more particularly, when the pointed end of an arrow set to a bow shifted right above his eye.

"Drizzt, it's me. It's Regis," he squeaked.

The bow went away and Guenhwyvar backed off. As soon as his arm was free, Regis reached up and tapped his magical beret, dismissing its enchantment. He had always before thought it a good thing that the magic of the beret secured it tightly to his head, that it wouldn't fall away if he was jostled, but in this instance, he wasn't so sure of that!

As he blinked through his shifting eyes, he saw a familiar hand reaching for him, offering to help him up. He grabbed on and started to rise, but a wave of weakness and numbness dispelled that notion and he crumpled back down.

The panther had hit him harder than he had realized.

Drizzt bent down over him, studying him and looking closely, his expression one of concern. "Where?" he asked.

"My side, my back," the halfling realized, and he reached over and tried to stretch through the tightness and pain.

The drow reached into a pouch and pulled forth a small vial. He flipped the cork off with his thumb and moved the potion of healing—one that Regis had brewed and given to Drizzt—to Regis's lips.

The halfling felt better immediately as the warm liquid poured into him, its magical healing properties spreading quickly. He lifted one arm for Drizzt to take and this time, they managed to get him sitting up.

"We have a lot to talk about," the halfling explained.

"You joined in with a group of our enemies, I take it?"

"I was in the camp," Regis explained. He reached inside his vest and pulled forth some rolled parchments, handing them to Drizzt.

"This is more than a rogue band or a hunting party, or even a raiding party," Regis explained. "Bruenor predicted a war and it looks like he walked right into the middle of it."

Drizzt clutched the parchments—he didn't have enough light to read them, and he wasn't about to light a torch out in the open. He stood up and extended his hand to the halfling. "Come," he bade, and when Regis grasped his hand, he helped the halfling to his feet. "Let us go and find our friends."

"Not yet," Regis replied. He was a bit shaky on his feet, but felt better already and knew it would pass.

"Our friends are bound for Nesmé now," said Drizzt.

"So are the orcs," Regis grimly replied. "And they are numerous enough to easily overrun that town, even with us helping the defenders."

Drizzt paused and stared at the clever halfling spy.

"You come with me," Regis explained to that quizzical look. "I have an idea."

The halfling wore a wry grin, a plan formulating. The communiqués had outlined a three-pronged attack upon Nesmé, with the camp Regis had entered as the westernmost of the attack groups—and apparently the first of the three groups in position to strike. The orders had called for proper restraint and patience, and finally a coordinated charge to pressure Nesmé on three sides simultaneously.

The orders had come from a dark elf, clearly.

Perhaps a dark elf could change those orders.

Athrogate sat along the front wall of Torch, a boisterous common room in southwestern Nesmé, a tavern and inn that sported a staircase that led directly to the southern parapet of the city wall. Nesmians gathered here in large numbers to drink and eat and share tales bawdy and adventurous. The noise of such partying had lured Athrogate here while he waited for word of his audience with the leader of the town, and he hadn't been disappointed upon entering, to see a sign that instructed him to keep a weapon in one hand and a drink in the other.

And in the event of a call to arms, to "swallow the drink and run for the stairs."

At the base of that wide staircase was a large box filled with torches, and a fire was always burning at the top landing before the wall, just before the exit.

Go to the parapets armed, and armed, too, with the weapon the hated menace of the Evermoors feared the most: fire.

Yes, Athrogate liked the feel of this place, thinking it the perfect mix of drink and battle. Almost as if a dwarf had designed it!

He sat by the window staring out into the streets and ways of Nesmé, a fair-sized city of three thousand hardy souls, which thrived, despite bordering the Evermoors, as the gateway to the west for the trade merchants of Luruar. Almost all the goods bound west, and almost all coming in from the west, from Mirabar and Waterdeep and Luskan, went through the Nesmé markets.

But of late, with word of the march of the Kingdom of Many-Arrows, those markets beneath the unnatural dark skies of Luruar had become sparse indeed.

Along the empty ways, then, Athrogate could see the western gate. He lifted a loaf to his mouth and tore off a large bite, then chased it with a hearty swallow of ale. He thumped the tankard down on the table and leaned forward when he noted a commotion at that gate.

The portal swung open and a wagon rolled in.

Athrogate's mouth fell open and the half-chewed loaf tumbled out, and the old dwarf understood then the real reason Jarlaxle had sent him to Nesmé—and that reason wasn't about the problems with the marketplace as Jarlaxle had said, oh no!

He saw them, come to life, the Companions of the Hall. He had heard the whispers of their resurrection from Beniago back in Luskan, but the reality hadn't registered to him.

But there they were, Bruenor and Catti-brie, and the large barbarian sitting beside them had to be Wulfgar of Icewind Dale.

The dwarf shook his head, trying to argue against the reality before him. The dwarf on the wagon was young, while Bruenor had been an old dwarf when Athrogate had met him, on the road to the Spirit Soaring. But it was him, Athrogate knew in his heart and could not deny. It was Bruenor Battlehammer right down to the fiery orange beard and the one-horned helm, to be sure.

And surely that was Catti-brie beside him, younger now than when Athrogate had last seen her in the midst of her Spellplague affliction.

"Perhaps her daughter," the dwarf tried to tell himself, but then he thought about it, and how could it be so? Catti-brie had no daughter that he had ever heard tell of, and if so, any daughter of Catti-brie would be a hundred years old now!

No, it was her, really her, in all her beauty.

"The Companions o' the Hall," he whispered.

A crooked smile came to his face, and he snorted, then giggled, then laughed a bit more, for some reason finding himself quite enchanted and amused by the prospect.

"Don't you go all bat-dancing on us now, you fool," came a voice from behind, and Athrogate swung about to see the approach of one of the guards he had met at the wall.

He chuckled again and nodded, hoisting his tankard in toast.

"First Speaker Jolen Firth will meet with you," the guard replied. "Now."

Athrogate stood up, drink in hand, and moved to follow.

"Chug it down and leave the mug," he said. "You'll find better drink in the First Speaker's Hall."

"Bah, better drink's usually meanin' weaker drink," the dwarf said, and he glanced back to take another look out the window.

He had a feeling he might need some strong drinks.

"Here's hoping that these orcs aren't well informed of the truth of me," Drizzt whispered to Regis as the two approached the scouting group that had come out with the goblin shaman to investigate the apparent battle.

Regis, back in his disguise as Shaman Kllug once more, shrugged and replied, "There are only a dozen of them, so if they figure it out, they will be a dozen fewer we have to kill from Nesmé's wall."

Drizzt smiled. He quite enjoyed this halfling's new attitude.

They moved into the group of goblins and orcs, one in particular coming up and trying hard, and futilely, to appear unafraid.

"Innanig," Regis whispered to Drizzt.

The orc stood right before them.

"This is . . . Ragfluw Do'Urden," Regis said, stuttering and clearly—and badly—improvising.

"Ragfluw?" Drizzt mouthed silently.

"Back to the camp at once!" Shaman Kllug cried, waving his arms to the north, herding the group to set off with all speed ahead of him.

"Ragfluw?" Drizzt quietly asked Regis as they fell in at the back of the fast-moving procession.

"I had to come up with something."

"Ragfluw?"

"Say it backward."

Drizzt stared at him curiously, then groaned as he considered that the fate of the land might well rest on the cleverness and improvisation of his little friend!

They made the orc encampment a short while later, striding in with a confidence that surely contradicted the knots in the bellies of Drizzt and

Regis. Scores of brutish orcs greeted them, along with hundreds of goblins and more, for apparently another of the tribes had arrived through the Underdark tunnels.

An orc came to the forefront and conversed quietly with Innanig for a few moments before stepping up to stand before Regis and Drizzt. Regis recognized him as the brute who had been arguing with Shaman Kllug when Regis had first come into the encampment, then disguised as an orc.

The orc started to address Regis, the shaman, but Regis held up his hand and deferentially stepped back behind the drow, then moved out to the side.

The orc didn't seem to like that much, as it conveyed with its glare as its eyes followed the goblin shaman.

"Ragfluck?" the orc asked.

"Ragfluw," Drizzt corrected, taking keen measure of the dangerous scene about him. His hand came up then, faster than the orc could block, faster than the orc could even notice, and he slapped the brute hard across the face. "You will call me Master. Fail in that again and I will kill you."

The orc seemed angry, but more than that, the orc seemed afraid.

Just the way Drizzt had to have it.

"Who are you?"

"Korock," the brute growled in Drizzt's face. "I lead . . ."

"You saw the fires and the lightning of the battle?" the ranger interrupted, and he pointed out to the southwest.

The orc nodded, as did many of the others nearby, within earshot of the conversation.

"We encountered a group of the terrible Riders of Nesmé," Drizzt said, loudly enough for all to hear, "in the midst of vicious battle with your scouting party. The Riders are dead now."

A burst of cheers and hoots went up around him.

"But so are many of your scouts, including the giant," Drizzt finished, silencing those triumphant hoots and eliciting a chorus of gasps in response. Korock actually growled a little bit, seeming much less than pleased.

"On whose word did a giant go out so boldly?" Drizzt demanded.

The orc's ugly head swiveled about and it stared at the goblin leader. "On order of Shaman Kllug," it said. "Patrols of Kllug!"

Drizzt turned to glower at Regis as well. He gave a slight nod when his gaze met the disguised halfling's, tipping his friend off to the needed response.

"I said patrol," Regis protested. "I said strong patrol. You chose the giant!"

Drizzt turned his glare upon the orc, who stiffened, but stood strong, chest puffed out.

"Kllug chose," it insisted.

"Korock!" the halfling-turned-goblin shouted back.

"Kllug!"

"Korock!" Regis yelled back, just as forcefully.

The orc turned and took a step Regis's way, its hand going for the sword hanging at its hip.

"Who do you believe, drow?" Regis cried, and he put enough desperation in his voice to let Drizzt hear his fear.

Drizzt put his arm out to block Korock, who turned back on him angrily. The drow knew how his Menzoberranzan kin would react to such impertinence, surely, but the thought did not sit well with him. Still, when he noted the other orcs about, all crowding in eagerly as if ready to leap to the aid of one or the other arguing leaders, the drow understood his choices to be severely limited. He had to be quick, he had to be decisive, and he had to end this before it could escalate.

The drow's blocking arm went down to his opposite hip and grasped Twinkle too quickly for the onlookers to keep up with the movement. That arm came back up so fast that the onlookers, including Korock, only then registered that the hand had gone to the hip in the first place.

And across came the backhand, perfectly aimed, and Korock's head fell free to the ground as the others only began to realize that the drow had drawn his blade. The gasps included shouts this time.

Not far away, the shaman Innanig began to protest, but a look from Drizzt silenced him and had him fading back into the crowd.

Drizzt stood there, bloody blade in hand, eyes set in a dangerous glower as he scanned the crowd, locking eyes with the most forceful of those protesting, silencing them with a look. After a while, the tumult became an anticipating hush, and Drizzt knew that he had played the role perfectly, exactly as a dark elf commander would discipline his inferior goblin forces.

He pointed to Innanig. "You, come here."

The shaman stepped out tentatively, remaining in place right before the others.

"Out here," Drizzt commanded, and when the orc didn't move, he shouted, "Now!"

Innanig glanced around, but those near to him stepped back. They wouldn't go against the drow, Drizzt realized.

"You will lead the orcs," he told the shaman. "And you," he said, swinging back to Regis, "will lead all."

"Lead where?" the phony Shaman Kllug said, playing his part in the ruse.

"Nesmé," Drizzt explained, and that brought a cheer. Nothing could unify a group of goblins and orcs faster than promising them a chance to destroy a town, it seemed.

"We go to Nesmé!" Innanig roared to his people, and the orcs began their battle chants.

"Not now!" Drizzt called above it all and the gathering quieted. "No, they are ready now. It is night and they too have seen the fires of battle."

"When?" Shaman Kllug demanded, boldly coming forward. "My people are hungry for blood. We were promised blood!"

The goblins began to howl and the orcs joined in, and Drizzt let them go for a bit, for their cheers were in support of Regis, after all, and he needed his friend supported, particularly since he was going to leave Regis alone with this murderous group in short order!

"Tomorrow," Drizzt said after the commotion died away.

"Tomorrow night!" Innanig roared, but Drizzt cut him short.

"No," he said. "Tomorrow under the dull midday sun."

The reaction was immediate, a communal gasp of disbelief. Battling in daytime, even under the muting effects of the darkening was not the preferred situation for orcs, and favored the goblins even less. These were creatures of darkness, murderers whose greatest advantages were found when the infernal orb had set—and particularly so with this particular group, since most of the goblins standing behind Shaman Kllug lived almost exclusively in the near-lightless Underdark!

"Every morning, the garrison of Nesmé slips out to the south, to fight the trolls my people have sent against the city," Drizzt explained. "They expect that any attack of orcs and goblins will come at night, and so the town is weakest in the day. Too weak. Attack at midday and most of the Nesmé warriors will not be there. We will overrun the city in one assault, and when the troll hunting groups return, we will slaughter them from the battlements of their own walls."

Innanig had begun nodding about halfway through the commands, an eager look coming over him right when Drizzt had lied about the Nesmé patrols.

Drizzt wasn't surprised, for he knew the truth: though bloodthirsty, orcs and goblins weren't really fond of battle. No, they were fond of the spoils of battle, of the pain they could inflict upon the defenseless when the fight was won. He thought of that now, considering it in light of his arguments with Catti-brie and Bruenor about the nature of orc-kind, and he found that his insights seemed to bolster the arguments of his friends more than his own.

Drizzt didn't want to believe that Bruenor and Catti-brie were right, that orcs and goblins and the like were irredeemably evil to their heart and soul. A big part of him, the part that had led him out of Menzoberranzan, rebelled against such a notion.

Or wanted to.

"Midday tomorrow, you trample Nesmé," Drizzt said, looking alternately to Kllug and Innanig. "I will look for both of you on the field of battle, and if either is missing, the other will be . . . punished." He looked down, drawing all eyes to the headless orc lying at his feet as he said that.

"No more fighting among the goblins and orcs," he said. "My people will not accept it. Not now. Not when there are greater enemies to slay."

With that, he turned and started to the south.

"Where are you going?" Innanig demanded.

"To prepare the trolls," Drizzt said without slowing. "They will lead the Nesmé hunters far from the city." He stopped and swung about, to dramatically add, "Just far enough to hear the dying screams of their kinfolk, and yet too far to get back to save them."

Orc and goblin alike licked its lips at that remark, so full of deliciousness was it to their twisted sensibilities.

Drizzt turned and ran off. He hated leaving Regis behind with these brutes, but he had to trust in his friend—it had been Regis's plan, after all!

And he had to get to Nesmé and prepare the defense, or more correctly, the ambush.

"I will go to the wall to await Drizzt and Regis," Catti-brie said to Bruenor and Wulfgar when, exhausted, they fell into chairs around the same table Athrogate had used at the inn called Torch.

"That rider girl went to the First Speaker," Bruenor reminded. "He'll be wantin' to talk with us."

"First Speaker Firth," Wulfgar remarked. "Firth! But there's a name I never desired to hear again."

Bruenor nodded at that, remembering well the Rider of Nesmé known as Galen Firth, who had so rudely treated them when they had first come through this town many decades before, on the journey to find and reclaim Mithral Hall. Nesmé wasn't a small town, but other than the markets, it was somewhat isolated, and most of the families living here had been here for many generations. It was quite possible, likely even, that this First Speaker Jolen Firth was a direct descendant of the ill-mannered man of old.

"You go to speak with him—he won't need all three of us," Catti-brie replied. "Our friends are out there, and sure to be coming soon, and I intend to hold the watch for them."

"Plenty on the wall doing that," said Wulfgar.

"Plenty who will welcome a drow elf into this place?" Catti-brie asked doubtfully, and that reminder had the other two looking to each other with concern.

"Girl's got a point," Bruenor admitted.

Wulfgar nodded and rose from his chair, hustling over to the long bar across the room. When Giselle had brought them in here, she had arranged for them to get a good meal—one well-deserved, she had told the innkeeper, and one paid for by the Riders.

Wulfgar motioned to the proprietor, who hustled over. "We'll need that meal now," he said.

"Cooking," the man replied.

"Give me what you have, if you'd be so kind," Wulfgar said. "We are in a great rush, it seems."

The man nodded and hustled away, returning quickly with three plates piled with bread and thick beef steaks, cooked rare.

Wulfgar piled them one atop the other, hoisted Aegis-fang over his other shoulder and started away, but for the door and not the table. He motioned to his companions, who hopped up and rushed to join him.

"Hey now!" the innkeeper cried. "But where do you think you're off to with my plates and silver?"

"We've business," Wulfgar called back, never slowing.

"You leave the plates," the innkeeper demanded, and to the other patrons, he yelled, "Here, stop them now!"

Bruenor and Catti-brie were beside Wulfgar then, as others rose to block the door.

"Ungrateful lot," Bruenor grumbled. "Not much's changed in a hunnerd years then."

Wulfgar, however, merely laughed, and turned to slide the plates onto a nearby table, sorting them as they dropped off his huge forearm. "We meant no harm, and surely no theft, and want no trouble," he said to the innkeeper. "Surely you have been a gracious host . . ."

He stopped at the sound of "Bwahahaha!" coming from over by the door, which banged open as a burly black-bearded dwarf entered Torch, shoving aside those sturdy men standing to block the way with ease—with such ease indeed, as if he was pushing aside a group of young children.

"By the bearded gods," Bruenor muttered when he turned that way.

"Athrogate," Bruenor whispered to his companions, for though he hadn't seen this one in many years, bawdy and bullish Athrogate was a tough fellow to forget. "Jarlaxle's friend."

The black-bearded dwarf waded through the patrons as easily as a ship skimming a glassy pond, so intent on Bruenor and the other two that he knocked Nesmé citizens all around.

"Strong fellow," Wulfgar remarked dryly.

"Strong as a giant, says his belt," Bruenor quietly replied, for he knew well the magical girdle Athrogate wore.

The dwarf bobbed up to stand before the three friends, and greeted them with a hearty, "Well met."

All around, patrons looked on curiously, and nervously, and none more so than the innkeeper behind the bar.

"Ye got yerself heroes here, Master," Athrogate called to the man. The black-bearded dwarf began walking a slow circuit about the trio, eyeing them studiously. "Great heroes, aye, greater than their age'd be showin'."

"Do I know ye, strange dwarf?" Bruenor asked.

"Aye, ye know me, and ye're thinkin' I'm not knowin' yerself, but I am." Athrogate replied, still stalking about.

"Bonnego Battl . . ." Bruenor started to say, but a great "Bwahaha!" cut that short.

"Still holdin' that name are ye?" Athrogate asked, and he leaned in close and added quietly, so only the three friends could hear, "Are ye then, King Bruenor?"

Bruenor stared at him hard. "Not knowin' what ye're about," he quietly replied.

"Jarlaxle," Catti-brie reasoned. "Is there anything that one does not know?"

"Didn't know how to find ye," Athrogate said to the woman. "When yer Da and Drizzt asked him to. Oh, but he tried—we tried. Looked across half the Realms for pretty Catti-brie, but not a sign. And here ye are, walkin' again."

The innkeeper had moved around the bar by then, and approached the group with a host of patrons flanking him.

"What are you about?" he asked, moving to collect his plates and silverware. Wulfgar moved quicker, gathering the meat and the bread, tearing the loaves in half and using them as plates for the steaks.

"Just came from Jolen Firth," Athrogate answered before Bruenor could. "He's looking to speak with these three."

"You know them, then?"

"Just that one," Athrogate said, pointing to Bruenor. "Bonnego's his name, and a fine young fellow he be."

"We would not steal your plates, good sir," Catti-brie added. "But we must be to the wall, for we've friends out in the night, who should be soon to your gate." When the innkeeper looked at her skeptically, she added, "Friends who battled beside us to save the Rider named Giselle. They stayed out to hold back any more of the monsters, that we could get Giselle and the horses to the safety of Nesmé."

The innkeeper nodded and seemed to shrink back a bit at that not-subtle reminder of how these three had come in here. He sheepishly handed the three plates up to Wulfgar, and helped the big man put the food back in place.

"Aye, and a poor lot am I to question," he said, seeming quite embarrassed. He glanced back over his shoulder and called to one of the townsmen leaning on the bar. "Three full tankards—nay, four," he ordered.

In short order, the now-four companions left Torch, their hands full of food and drink.

"The First Speaker's a tough one," Athrogate said to the others as soon as they were outside. "Suspicious fellow, and harsh with his words, though he's likely to be more kindly to yerselves than he was to meself. I killed a few trolls to death, and that makes 'em happy, but yerselves rescued the girl, did ye? Bwahahaha! Right back from the dead and ye're making yer legends anew."

Bruenor pulled him aside immediately. "How do ye know?" he demanded.

"Yer girl already telled ye how."

"Jarlaxle?"

"Aye, o' course."

"Where's he at?"

Athrogate shrugged. "Ain't seen him much in long tendays. Got me orders to get meself to Nesmé, and so I got meself to Nesmé. Didn't know why until I saw the three o' ye coming through the gate. Now here ye are and here I be."

"What is going on about these parts?" Wulfgar asked.

"Just got here," the dwarf explained. "Sky's dark, even in the day, and the trolls are thick as a birch tangle. Well, thinner now on the path me and Snort rode, bwahahaha!"

He cut the laughter short when he realized that none of the others had joined in. "They'll be coming to take ye to Speaker Firth."

"They'll find us at the wall, then, and we'll go when our friends have joined us," Catti-brie said, her tone brooking no debate, and she started off for the city gate.

"Friends?" Athrogate asked. "Tell me it's Drizzt, if ye will. Ah, but I'd be likin' to see that black-skinned hunter again."

He and the other two hustled to catch up to Catti-brie.

Before they ever made the wall, they were intercepted by a pair of Nesmé guards, informing them that First Speaker Jolen Firth requested an audience with them immediately.

"Then he can meet us on the wall by the gate," Catti-brie told the guards. "For that's where we'll be."

The guard shifted quickly about to block her path.

"I've spent the night killing orcs, ogres, and a frost giant," Catti-brie said evenly into the man's face. "And saving the life of Giselle, Rider of Nesmé. I am tired and worried for my friends who have not yet arrived to this most inhospitable town. We will await their arrival on the wall, by the gate, and if the First Speaker or any others wish to speak with us, he, they, will find us there."

The man looked to his companion, his expression unsure, and that hesitance gave Catti-brie all the room she needed to shove past him, the others following.

"But . . ." he started to argue, but was cut short by a riotous roar of "Bwahahaha!"

Regis sucked in his breath as Drizzt disappeared into the night, and Innanig immediately moved over to stand right beside him and glare down at him.

"You agree to this change in plan?" the orc shaman asked, his tone revealing that he didn't think the drow's orders should go unquestioned.

"You heard the dark elf."

"We are the western flank," Innanig replied. "One of three groups, and the smallest of them."

Regis tried to digest that information. There were hundreds of goblins, and scores of orcs and ogres. And if that wasn't enough, the northern patrol group returned right at that time, numbering a trio of giants among their ranks!

And this was the smallest of the battle groups? The halfling-turned-goblin swallowed hard as he grasped the size of the forces that had been arrayed against Nesmé.

"More glory to us in the morning, then, when we overrun the city ahead of our kin," he snapped at Innanig, bulling in and forcefully poking his hand to drive the orc shaman back a step. "Would you ignore the drow orders? Will you? Will you tell your orcs to stay behind?"

The shaman tried to stand strong against the aggressive posture, but it was clear that Regis had the upper hand.

"Then you and yours can join my goblins when we are in the city," Regis shouted, and the goblins began to cheer all around him, a growing wave of bloodlust. "And tell the drow RagHuw why you did not fight. Perhaps I will shrink your head, and Korock's too, and make a necklace. Yes!"

The goblins whooped and hollered, leaping about in a frenzy, and Regis feared he might have started a battle then and there.

It was settled before it could begin, though, when the frost giants stormed in and demanded to know what was going on.

"Your kin was killed in the west," Innanig, ever the troublemaker, cried, and the orc pointed at Regis as if to implicate him.

"And Korock is dead for it," Regis yelled back immediately. "Killed by a drow who demands that we attack at midday tomorrow."

"We cannot go without the other armies!" Innanig shrieked. "The plan was told!"

The giant swatted the orc aside as it finished speaking, and turned directly upon the diminutive goblin shaman. For a heartbeat, Regis thought his life was at its end, but the behemoth nodded approvingly.

"The main battle group is in position, east of our camp," the frost giant explained. "Three thousand orcs and a score of my kin. And hordes of ogres pulling war machines." The monster paused and turned to the other giants. "We move fast, yes," he said, nodding, and the others agreed.

"We will avenge our dead kin," the giant promised, turning back to Regis. "What battle groups would you have for the charge?"

The halfling-turned-goblin sputtered and stammered for a moment. "All at once," he blurted. "A full charge under the midday sky."

The giant began to question him, but Regis broke away and starting calling out glorious platitudes to the massed warriors. "We will beat the others to the city wall," he promised. "The victory will be ours."

The cheering mounted around him, and the goblin shaman played the part, leaping about enthusiastically. But inside, Regis was in knots.

If that second battle group reacted to the charge and moved fast, Nesmé might indeed be overrun, and in short order!

His friends were in there.

He thought about sneaking out soon after, when the goblins and orcs and others went to rest for the coming storm. Perhaps he should run off into the night, to Nesmé, to warn Drizzt and the others.

Perhaps he should go to the east, to see if there was some way he could deter or divert that main battle group.

Truly, though, he realized that there was very little he could do at this time. Even if he got to his friends, where would they go? Certainly the Companions of the Hall would not desert Nesmé with such a force arrayed against the city. And certainly the whole of that town could not be evacuated ahead of such a force.

He looked to the east and saw the flickers of campfires far, far afield.

He didn't know what to do.

CHAPTER 13

THE LONG GAME

"YOU ARE CERTAIN OF THIS?" THE DAMARAN SOLDIER ASKED THE YOUNG girl, standing at the side of the road named Wall's Around in the Damaran Capital of Helgabal, a city formerly known as Heliogabalus. Traditionally, Heliogabalus served as the principle city of the Kingdom of Damara, and certainly it was the largest city of the Bloodstone Lands. Other than the decades when King Gareth Dragonsbane had moved the seat of power to Bloodstone Village years before the advent of the Spellplague, this city had also served as the seat of power.

As it was again. The city's rightful place as the capital of Damara had been restored, and the King of Damara resided once more in the city now known as Helgabal.

The young girl blew a curly blond lock out of her face and sheepishly nodded.

"You saw it?"

"Yes sir," she said with the cutest of lisps.

Chewing his lip nervously, the soldier glanced along the lane to the curiosity shop the child had indicated, Mickey's Bag of Holding.

The child watched him, measuring him. The man was trying to muster the courage to investigate the story, she knew. But then, that was easier thought than done, particularly given the teasing hints she had dropped the soldier's way.

The soldier couldn't be sure, of course, but the little girl had taken great

197

pains to make it quite clear that the object of her story, if things were indeed as she had claimed to the soldier, could eat him.

In one bite.

"You stay away from there, child," the soldier scolded, and he pushed the girl along, hustling her away from the merchant area of Wall's Around and Mickey's. "Go on, now, to your home, and don't come down this way again."

Skipping as much as running, the little girl rushed off and turned a corner into an alleyway, disappearing into the shadows. The soldier passed by the entrance, hustling along the street away from Wall's Around—and who could blame him?

The little girl leaned against the stone wall of the building and put her cherubic little face in her pink hands. She took a deep breath, trying to digest yet again the startling changes that had come over this land of Damara. The line of Dragonsbane was dead—how had this gone unnoticed?—and the new king hardly seemed a worthy successor to the power, popular support, and righteousness King Gareth and Queen Christine had enjoyed!

The little girl had learned so much in the last few days, though many questions remained. What of the Monastery of the Yellow Rose, secluded along the high plateau between the Galenas and the Earthspurs?

The little girl meant to turn these surprising changes to her advantage, of course. She took another deep breath, trying to clear her pretty little head, trying not to think of how ridiculous and dangerous this perhaps too-clever ruse might prove.

Despite her innocent appearance, she was no stranger to danger.

"So be it," she said quietly, and he moved back out of the alleyway. She glanced to her left, to where the soldier had gone, and noted with a nod that the man was out of sight already. The little girl skipped down to the right, down to the merchant lane of Wall's Around, to Mickey's Bag of Holding and the shop across the street, A Pocketful of Zzzzs.

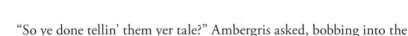

"So ye done tellin' them yer tale?" Ambergris asked, bobbing into the side wing of the great library of the monastery of the Yellow Rose.

Brother Afafrenfere looked up from the stacks of books and scrolls piled about him as he sat on the floor. He considered his friend curiously for a moment, then nodded in answer to her question.

"How did you get in here?" he asked.

"Brother Tadpole out there let me by," Ambergris replied. "He's still blushing from the kiss and little grab I gave him. Don't they let you brothers out to meet some girls once in a bit?"

Afafrenfere scowled at her.

"Present company excepted," she said with a gracious bow, and she hopped over to see what he was about.

"Are they treating you well?"

"Oh, aye," Ambergris said. "Feedin' me well, too! I'm a cleric o' the dwarf gods, and no enemy, so why not?"

"You have heard of these dark times in Damara, no doubt."

"Aye, tyrant king and whatnot," the dwarf replied with a dismissive wave of her hand. "Old story, different place."

"I only feared that they would be more suspicious of any newcomers, given the events in the Bloodstone Lands," the monk explained. "They are not on good terms with King Frostmantle. Not at all. And they interrogated me endlessly in an attempt to determine that I was not, after all, a spy from that suspicious and wary court—and wary because this king, by all accounts I have heard, is a craven tyrant, fearing every shadow."

"Most are."

"Even dwarves?"

"Aye, ye're knowin' me own tale, so I ain't to argue the point."

Afafrenfere nodded. "They appreciated my stories of our journeys."

"And ye telled them true o' yer time with Parbid in the Shadowfell, did ye? Ye telled that ye served Netherese warlords and such, and that ye were well on yer way to becoming a shade, throwing aside yer pledges and promises to their sacred order?"

"Would you prefer to walk out into the open chapel and scream that to all who would listen?" the monk asked dryly.

"Well, better to get it out o' yer own mouth in short order, I'm guessing," Ambergris replied. "This place's not without its own spies, now is it?"

"I told them everything," Afafrenfere admitted. "Honestly so."

"Brave monk."

"It is a tenet of my order that forgiveness can only be given upon one who is truly repentant, and one who is truly repentant presents the truth of his errors. To run from admitting a mistake is to deceive yourself into believing that no mistake was made."

"So it was a mistake for ye, then? Going to the Shadowfell with yer lover, fighting for the Netherese, joinin' the bounty hunters o' Cavus Dun? All a mistake and one ye're regretting?"

Afafrenfere stared at her calmly, and held his hand up to the sides in concession, indeed, in surrender. "A dwarf named Ambergris showed me the truth of that error."

Ambergris took a step closer and comfortingly dropped her hand on Afafrenfere's shoulder. "I know, boy," she said. "Been a long and hard road, and one that's gone awry. But ye're home now, in body and in heart. Ye never was one o' them bounty hunters. If I'd've thought different on that, I'd've killed ye on the ridge above the fallen Drizzt Do'Urden."

That brought a smile to Afafrenfere. He thought back to that day, when his band of bounty hunters had come upon Drizzt and Dahlia in Neverwinter Wood—and upon Artemis Entreri, they had learned the hard way. It rang as a painful memory for Afafrenfere, for he thought again of watching Parbid, whom he had loved dearly, die to the blades of Drizzt Do'Urden.

But it was a good memory as well, for in that fight, Ambergris had saved him and had pulled him away. And after that fight, Ambergris had saved him again, in spirit.

When he had left the Monastery of the Yellow Rose, Afafrenfere had thought the solemn place could never again be his home, but now he was here, and now it felt right. Indeed, a great serenity had come over him in simply entering these ancient halls of study and meditation.

"Jarlaxle might be back soon," Ambergris reminded and the monk nodded. "He'll be heading out on the road, and askin' us to go beside him."

"I cannot," Afafrenfere replied. "Not now."

"I'm knowing that."

The monk looked at her curiously. "But you are going with him," he reasoned from her posture and the resigned tilt of her head, and only as he spoke them did he realize that his words sounded a bit like an accusation.

"Nothing here for meself but yerself," the dwarf replied. "And if ye're to be staying, then ye're to be buryin' yer head in the books and the training and all the rest what goes with being a brother here. And a brother, err sister, here ain't what I'm meaning to be, no offense intended."

Afafrenfere wanted to argue, but he really couldn't. He steeled his jaw and tried not to cry, and nodded as he replied, "None taken."

The proprietor really was an attractive woman, with her copper-colored hair and those bright blue eyes shining in amazing contrast. Straight, tall and slender, she wore the finest clothes to accentuate every curve, to reveal enough of her breasts to tease. She wore a green dress this day, slit up high on one side to show the creamy skin of her strong and shapely leg.

Yes, this one was indeed a beauty.

The curly-haired little girl moved about the curiosity shop, making a point to lift and inspect every item. There were other shoppers milling about, but most wandering about briefly before exiting.

The child, though, lingered.

Soon she had the eyes of the copper-haired proprietor watching her from afar, she knew, and to confirm it, she fumbled one fabulous piece of blown and shaped glass, catching it as it started to tumble.

She found the copper-haired woman's gasp very telling.

At the same time, the door opened, the bells set atop it tinkling, as another woman entered the shop. She, too, was quite attractive, though dressed in plainer and more modest clothes. She was shorter than the other, and with strangely wide shoulders and a head that seemed a bit too small. Her hair was thick and rich and strawberry blond—which surprised the child, for she had remembered it being more gray than blond.

Then again, it was the woman's illusion, so she could do with it as she pleased, the little girl supposed.

The little girl moved along the aisles, trying to get closer to listen to the conversation, for the two were clearly agitated as they spoke in hushed tones.

"Too many guards," she heard the blond whisper, though she seemed to be too far away to hear a whisper.

The little girl's ears were keener than they now appeared, after all.

"All of a sudden," the other woman agreed.

"I warned you," said the blond.

Yes, she was always the more cautious of the two, the little girl remembered.

The other sighed and conceded the point with a nod. "Ever since that idiot Frostmantle decided to return to Heliogabalus," she lamented.

"Helgabal," the other corrected, and both of them sighed in apparent disgust.

"We could kill him and the whole of his court," said the tall copper-haired proprietor. "Such messy business."

"And with no guarantee that whoever replaced him would be any better, of course. More than a fair share of scalawags and fools among the Damaran nobility these dark days."

"There is that truth."

"There is always that truth with humans," the blond said with a shake of her head. "So self-important and thinking that they will have a lasting effect, and a shift of the wind blows them and their pathetic accomplishments away."

"Many of the Damarans might welcome his death."

The other sighed more dramatically and shook her head. "So much effort and so much risk," she lamented.

"Oh fie, let us just destroy the whole city and have fun doing it!" the proprietor exclaimed.

This time, the little girl's juggling wasn't faked and a piece of sculpted glass fell to the floor and shattered.

She swallowed hard, and before she could begin to say anything or do anything, the copper-haired woman was there, towering above her, glaring down at her.

Staring through her.

The child felt very small.

"What are you about, young fool? And where are your parents?"

She made a little whimpering noise, thinking the only road of survival surely lay in presenting a pathetic facade.

The copper-haired woman grabbed her by the ear and hoisted her up to her tip-toes. "I should swat you good," she said.

And likely launch me across the city, the little girl thought but did not say, for she knew the truth of these two women, of course. A truth she had hinted at to the soldier . . .

"Do you have the coin to pay for that?" the proprietor asked.

Of course she did, a thousand times over, but she wasn't about to admit that. She swallowed hard and whimpered pathetically.

"Oh, make the toddler work it off," said the other from the counter near the door. "The shop is a mess, as always. You could use the help."

"Bah!" said the copper-haired woman and she hoisted the little girl a bit more, gave a little twist to elicit a yelp, and dropped her back to her feet.

She really was exciting when she was angry, the little girl thought.

"Well?" the woman asked.

"Well, Ma'am?" she asked sheepishly.

Her words hit the copper-haired woman hard, apparently, for she straightened and stared at the little girl hard, and with great incredulity. Her expression seemed to say that she knew something wasn't right. She even sniffed at the air a bit, her pretty button nose crinkling, and she looked at the little girl even more curiously then.

Yes, she had recognized that something wasn't quite right, but she couldn't place it, the little girl realized, and she had to work hard to suppress her grin.

"You will clean," the tall woman insisted. "Every day until you have paid your debt in full."

"Yes Ma'am."

"Ma'am? What is Ma'am?"

"It is an expression, dear," said the other woman. "One usually reserved for older human women."

The vain copper-haired woman turned back on the little girl and gasped, and for a moment, the child thought she would slap her—which would likely take her head clean from her shoulders!

"Well, you cannot deny the passage of time, dear," the other woman said, injecting a much-needed bit of humor.

"There are rags in the back," the copper-haired woman said, and again she looked at the little one curiously, as if there was something she almost could make out, but not quite. "Not a speck of dust is to remain when you are done."

She moved back to the other woman, and the little girl ran to find the rags, a satisfied grin on her face.

Perfect, she thought, but did not dare say, did not dare even whisper. While her little ears were not human ears, and indeed were far superior, their ears, she knew, were much keener than her own!

He was the richest man in the Bloodstone Lands, a noble by inheritance and king by the deeds of those his money had bought. Even those closest to Yarin Frostmantle didn't like him very much, a fact that kept the man insecure, and kept the gold flowing from his coffers. Most kings had a spying network among their court, of course, but Yarin kept three at his call.

Everyone spied on everyone else. Informants were well-rewarded, while anyone smelling of treachery was thoroughly discredited if they were fortunate, thrown into a dungeon and tortured to death if not.

Long dead were any who dared to give voice to the rumor that Lord Yarin had ascended to the throne of Damara by murdering Murtil Dragonsbane, the last in the line of beloved King Gareth and Lady Christine.

Still, the circumstances of King Yarin's ascent remained an open secret in Damara these twenty years later, and in quiet corners of out-of-the-way reaches, the lament and the hope that another in the line of Dragonsbane might someday be found was oft-whispered.

Tapping his fingers nervously on the burnished wood, he sat on his throne this day, behind the huge and fortified table, faced, sided, and lined with glassteel windows to protect from arrows and the like.

"It is just a rumor," Queen Concettina reminded, drawing a scowl from Yarin that set her back in her seat. She dared say no more. She was the seventh queen of Yarin Frostmantle's reign, after all, and after three years in his bed, she had done no better than her predecessors in producing an heir.

She had heard the jokes whispered about the court. "Poor King Yarin. What foul luck to marry seven barren women. What odds!"

And if she had heard them, so too had he.

King Yarin had divorced his first four wives, and had sent them away to live in small homes on the borderlands of Vaasa, or even within that foul kingdom to the north. Apparently such arrangements had become too expensive for his appetite, or perhaps it was just his mounting frustration—and the rumors that at least two of those fallen queens had subsequently produced children of another man's loins, but the last two of his prior six wives hadn't fared as well.

King Yarin kept a guillotine in one of the hedge-walled gardens.

His fifth wife had been accused and summarily found guilty of treason for taking substances to prevent pregnancy. The claims against the sixth, Driella, were even more extraordinary, claiming that she had given birth to a son, but had murdered it in her bed. None of Driella's ladies in waiting spoke on her behalf—indeed, none of them spoke at all, and none of them had been seen again anywhere near the court of King Yarin Frostmantle!

Even the statues King Yarin had erected in the back gardens for those last two wives were now headless.

To serve as a poignant reminder to the most recent wife, to be sure.

Queen Concettina knew that the sands of the hourglass were fast-falling. She was a young woman, barely into her twenties and more than three decades younger than King Yarin. Her family wasn't from Damara, as she had come to Helgabal on a diplomatic mission her father had led from the port city of Delthuntle in Aglarond. Concettina's father, Lord Delcasio, had set up a lucrative trade agreement with King Yarin on that visit, and Concettina had been the guarantee of that agreement, binding the two families in marriage.

The young woman had accepted her father's choice and knew what was expected of her in her role. She attended Yarin's every need, and served the court with excellence, for she had been finely bred in a house of Delthuntle nobles. She was a diplomat and possessed of great charm and warmth, and all who met her, loved her.

None of that mattered, she had come to understand, in light of the greater events circulating around her.

King Yarin wanted an heir.

King Yarin did not much like being the butt of crude jokes.

If things worsened, the agreement between King Yarin and Lord Delcasio would not save her from disgrace, or worse.

The witness finally appeared before them, an elderly woman hustled in by a pair of King Yarin's personal elite guards, two brutish men as familiar with an executioner's hood as they were with the fancy caps favored for palace celebrations. They brought the old woman to stand right before the fortress-like table and backed away a step, then bowed and moved to the far end of the hall on a wave from King Yarin.

"You own a store along Wall's Around?" King Yarin asked her.

"Aye, m'lord."

"You are familiar with the proprietors of the two curiosity shops in question?"

"Aye, M'lord, Mickey and Lady Zee. I think they're sisters, though they don't let on."

"And why would you think that? They have run their shops in Helgabal for several years, I have been told, and have no family that anyone knows of."

"Several years now, but they been there before," the old woman said.

"I was not aware . . ." the king started to reply, but the woman inadvertently interrupted him, saying, "When I was . . ." as she tried to finish her previous answer. Realizing her error, she sucked in her breath, her eyes widening in terror, and she lowered her gaze immediately.

"Go on," King Yarin bade her.

"When I was a little girl," she said.

"When you were a little girl, what?" asked a confused King Yarin.

"They were there," the woman replied.

The King and Queen exchanged puzzled looks, for they knew of the woman in question, Mickey and the one known as Lady Zee, and neither were half this old crone's age.

"Where?" King Yarin asked incredulously.

"On the merchant row, in Wall's Around," the old woman answered. "My Da's Da owned my shop then . . ."

"Mickey's Bag of Holding and A Pocketful of Zzzzs were known in Wall's Around when you were a little girl?" the king asked loudly, and he looked to the side, to the Minister of Records, directing his question to that man, a monk from the Monastery of the Yellow Rose, as much as to this old woman.

The minister shrugged, clearly at a loss, and a scowl from King Yarin had him rushing away to his trove of records. The city had been quite fastidious in keeping these over the decades, back to the very beginning of the line of Dragonsbane. The paladin kings had desired order, and so had used the offered resources of the great monastery to record the histories, the families, the merchants, and many other details of the Damaran cities, particularly Heliogabalus.

"Don't know that they were called that, then," the old woman sheepishly replied.

That brought a scowl from King Yarin, and he slammed his hands on his great table and jumped up to his feet.

"You don't know?"

"No, M'lord."

"But there was a shop—or a pair of shops—run by these same two, you say? By, what, Mickey and Lady Zee?"

"Aye, M'lord, I'm thinking . . ."

"Thinking or knowing?" King Yarin demanded.

"It was so many years . . ." she started to answer, but Yarin had already motioned to his guards. They came running up and took the woman by the arms and hustled her away.

"This is a fool's chase," the king said as the Captain of his Court Guard moved up from behind to join him. "A puzzle of whispers and hints and nothing more. It is excitement for the sake of gossip, and gossip for the sake of excitement."

"My King, we must investigate," replied the Captain of the Court Guard, a slender fellow named Dreylil Andrus. "This gossip is serious . . ."

"That there may be a pair of dragons living in Helgabal?" the king asked skeptically, and he snorted with derision at the preposterous idea.

"Remember the line you succeeded," Captain Andrus warned. "Remember the name, Dragonsbane, and how well that name was earned. Little could be more damaging to your reputation among your citizens than these whispers."

"You believe them?" the king asked incredulously. "You heard the old fool." He swept his hand out to the woman, who was now at the far end of the grand hall. "Could she even remember her Da's Da's name, let alone those of two women from nearly a century ago who might have resembled these two now."

"It is a damaging rumor," Andrus warned. "Even if untrue."

"Am I to capture and execute a pair of merchants on such evidence? How might that entice future merchants to Helgabal, or comfort those now plying their wares here?"

Captain Andrus could merely shrug in reply, and offer, "It is a difficult situation."

"Learn more," the king demanded.

"My spies are about."

"Yes, and so are mine," said King Yarin, an open reminder that there were always forces at work on the forces at work in King Yarin Frostmantle's city of Helgabal.

CHAPTER 14

THE LURE

CATTI-BRIE WAS FIRST TO THE BATTLEMENTS NEAR TO THE NORTHWESTERN corner of Nesmé's wall. Before she got off that ladder, though, her way was blocked by an armored guard, a burly and brutish-looking man with his sword out of its scabbard and swinging threateningly at the end of one muscular arm.

"Here now, lass, you go back down and go find yerself a comfortable bed," he said.

"I came in with the group who saved the Rider of Nesmé known as Giselle," Catti-brie protested.

"Oh, I know who you are," said the guard. "I was in the gatehouse when you entered the city. But I tell you again, back down the ladder and find your way to a comfortable bed. There is no place on Nesmé's wall for those who are not of Nesmé's garrison."

"We've another two friends on their way in," Catti-brie replied.

"And we've the sentries to see them and open the gates for them," said the guard. Other soldiers moved closer to the pair up on the battlements, looking to the guard captain and nodding their support.

"Ah, ye dolt, move aside," came the call from behind Catti-brie, and Bruenor bulled his way up the side of the ladder, scrambling past her. "Got no time for yer foolishness. We're lookin' for our friends, and ye're owing us at least that."

The guard pointed his sword at the dwarf, but Bruenor never slowed, huffing and puffing up the last few rungs and hopping up to the top rung of the ladder to stand directly before the burly man, daring him to strike out.

On the ground at the base of the ladder, Athrogate bellowed a great laugh and Wulfgar clenched his warhammer, ready to take out the guard if the man moved on Bruenor.

"Ye stubborn fools o' Nesmé make an ass's cooperation seem more akin to that of a trained dog," the dwarf remarked. "Ye likely got a fight coming, don't ye know?"

At that proclamation, all the soldiers on the wall tensed.

"Not from us, ye orc-brained fools!" Bruenor said, noting their moves. "And ye'll be glad to have us on yer side when the fightin' starts if ye're not so stupid that ye're drivin' us away afore it."

"What fighting?" asked the burly guard blocking Bruenor's way, and he moved aside and allowed the dwarf up on the battlement.

"Giselle said you destroyed those orcs and their allies," said another.

"Their allies in the group that come against us, aye," said Bruenor. He helped Catti-brie off the ladder, and Wulfgar came up right behind her. "There'll be more, though we're not knowin' what they're about."

"That's what our friends are out there trying to learn," Catti-brie added.

"Indeed, do tell," came a request from below, and they all turned around to see a sturdy man dressed in fine armor moving up to the base of the ladder, soldiers flanking him on both sides—and pointedly moving Athrogate back from the man's path.

The expressions of those wall sentries around the trio of companions told them the truth of this one before one of the guards actually said, "First Speaker," in greeting.

"Ye're Jolen Firth?" Bruenor asked, hands on hips and a scowl on his face.

"First Speaker," the burly guard beside him corrected. But the man at the base of the ladder held up his hand to calm the excitable soldier.

"I am," he answered.

"Well, ye might want to be tellin' yer boys'n'girls here to turn their eyes out to the night, as there be monsters out there lookin' yer way."

"Yerself'd do well to listen to him," remarked Athrogate, standing by the First Speaker. "That one there, he's a lot more than he looks, I tell ye."

"Do tell me," Jolen Firth bade the dwarf, but Athrogate merely answered with a belly-shaking "Bwahahaha!"

"Or perhaps you would tell me, then," the First Speaker called up to Bruenor.

"Me friends're soon to be coming in," Bruenor replied. "We're up here waiting for 'em."

"Come and speak with me," Jolen Firth replied. "Nesmé's sentries will watch for your friends and bring them to us when they arrive."

"No they won't," said Catti-brie, drawing a curious look from the man.

"One's a drow elf," Bruenor said bluntly. "Are yer boys ready to let that one in?"

"A dark elf?" Jolen Firth replied, and it seemed as if the words would stick in his throat.

"Aye, and one once known in Nesmé, and not as any enemy."

The First Speaker held up his hands curiously.

"Drizzt Do'Urden," Catti-brie explained. "Once a great friend to Nesmé, once the champion of King Bruenor Battlehammer of Mithral Hall. He is out there, scouting, and will come to us with . . ."

"Battlehammer," the burly guard beside Bruenor spat with clear disgust. "Aye, Bruenor Orc-Friend, and curse his ugly face and curse his wretched name."

Catti-brie looked to Bruenor as if expecting him to simply throw the man from the battlements. Down below, Athrogate laughed all the louder.

"Drizzt Do'Urden?" Jolen Firth asked skeptically. "King Battlehammer?"

"Aye, the same and the same," Bruenor replied. "Once friends o' Nesmé."

"I do not believe that Nesmé ever considered King Bruenor a friend," said Jolen Firth.

Bruenor snorted at that, but before he could launch into the obviously forthcoming tirade, Catti-brie stepped before him.

"Galen Firth is your great-grandfather?" she asked.

"My grandfather's grandfather," Jolen Firth corrected.

The woman nodded, for the point would still stand. "When the first King Obould marched from the Spine of the World and Nesmé was overrun, her people sent fleeing across the open ground, Mithral Hall came to their aid, though Mithral Hall, too, was then under siege."

"I know the tale," the First Speaker replied. "But that was not King Bruenor."

"No, it was his Steward, because he had been gravely wounded battling Obould's orcs," said Catti-brie. "His steward and dear friend, the halfling Regis. A desperate Galen Firth went to him for help, and feared help would not come because Galen Firth and the Riders of Nesmé had ill-treated Bruenor's band when first they had come through Nesmé, and all because among that band was . . ."

"A dark elf named Drizzt Do'Urden," Jolen Firth admitted. "Aye, and you are clearly well-versed in the lore of the land, young woman."

"Still, Bruenor would have sent the same aid," Catti-brie insisted. "Galen Firth knew it, and you cannot dispute it. Mithral Hall was no enemy to Nesmé in the days of the first King Obould, and even after that fight, when Nesmé was reclaimed and rebuilt, and dwarves of Mithral Hall sent aid and skilled builders. The very stones of your wall were cut in Mithral Hall, were they not?"

Jolen Firth stared at her hard, but did not reply.

"The dwarves of Mithral Hall were good friends to Nesmé," Catti-brie finished.

"Until Bruenor signed the treaty," muttered the troublesome guard.

"Aye," others agreed.

"A treaty forced . . ." Bruenor started to interject, but he looked to his girl and checked himself—actually, it was when the dwarf looked back at the First Speaker, and more pointedly, at the large barbarian standing on the wall beside him, within easy range of Jolen Firth and clearly simmering with near-explosive rage.

Bruenor had never been fond of Nesmé, but Wulfgar had even less fondness for the town.

Looking at Wulfgar then, both of the companions on the battlements with him realized that they had to get past this debate—more pressing problems were staring them in the face at that time!

"Perhaps this discussion would be better suited to my private halls in the main keep," Jolen Firth offered.

"Aye, but at another time," Bruenor said. He turned and pointed out over the wall. "Our friends're out there, and coming in soon, we're hopin'. And we're meaning to meet them, and so should yerself. Aye, and one o' the two's Drizzt Do'Urden. Ye go and ask yer rider Giselle about that one and his cat. Ye go and ask her if she's alive now because o' Drizzt, and if she's not saying aye, then she's lying to ye."

"Enough, I beg," Jolen Firth said, holding his hands up in surrender. He started to continue, but a call from the wall of "Rider approaching!" interrupted him.

A moment later, the tinkling of bells could be heard drifting in on the night air, a sweet melody from the barding of a magnificent steed named Andahar.

"Drizzt," Catti-brie announced.

The guards looked to First Speaker Firth.

"Open the gates," he said to them.

The goblin shaman confidently strode out to stand before the orc group. He looked them over, up and down, then nodded.

"Where is Korock?" asked the orc leader, perhaps the ugliest and most imposing orc Regis had seen since the first King Obould himself. The tone of that question made it sound more like a command, and left no doubt in poor Regis that if he answered it incorrectly, the orc would murder him on the spot. Shaman Kllug might have been given some leadership role over the smaller group, but in the big scheme of things, he apparently wasn't as important as Regis had hoped!

Regis glanced back over his shoulder to the encampment, far in the distance. He had rushed out upon hearing that a sizable contingent from the main force was on its way across the leagues to speak with him.

Regis turned around—to find the orc even closer, towering over him. The creature's spittle and foul breath rained down on him, nearly gagging him. But a goblin wouldn't be put off by that stench, Regis reminded himself, and so he worked hard to not even crinkle his nose.

"Korock angered the drow," Regis answered.

The big orc put on a puzzled expression and snapped his hand down to grasp Regis—Shaman Kllug—by the front of his robe and easily hoist him from his feet.

"Drow?" the beastly orc asked.

"The dark elf who came to us," the halfling-turned-goblin squeaked. This orc's power amazed him; he thought he was about to be simply broken. A twist of the thick wrist and his neck would surely snap!

The huge orc looked around at his entourage, and that, too, was full of impressive physical specimens, as if they had been hand-picked from across the reaches of the Kingdom of Many-Arrows.

Indeed they had.

"Warlord Hartusk," said one of the others, "should I go and find the wizard Xorlarrin?"

Xorlarrin—Regis had certainly heard that name before. He swallowed hard, wanting no part of any dark elves other than Drizzt. He couldn't imagine his disguise would fool a drow wizard!

Hartusk tossed Regis from his grasp, sending him tumbling into the dirt. The imposter goblin pulled himself up quickly and hopped from foot to foot, as if ready to sprint away at first sign of threat. And indeed he was thinking exactly that. He glanced around at his companions, mostly goblins and a few orcs, including shaman Innanig, who was looking rather pleased at the treatment the goblin shaman was getting.

"Who is this drow?" Hartusk demanded.

"Of House Do'Urden," Innanig replied, and looking supremely satisfied, Innanig stepped past the goblin shaman to stand as a representative of the group.

Regis was more than happy to allow that. He had a feeling that Innanig had just inadvertently saved his life.

It became problematic, however, when the orc shaman began relaying all of Drizzt's orders regarding a midday attack. Hartusk's face twisted in anger as the orc shaman went on, and the beastly warlord was shaking his head forcefully by the end of the shaman's story.

"The third group is not in place," Hartusk said, grabbing Innanig and shaking him with such terrible force and terrible ease. "They are too near to Silverymoon and will not arrive for three days."

"We do not attack?" the suddenly not-so-confident Innanig asked.

"We will crush Nesmé in short order, when all three groups are in position," Warlord Hartusk replied.

"Yes, Warlord. All hail King Hartusk!" Innanig said, and as Hartusk let him go, the orc shaman fell to his knees.

Regis had to consciously remember to close his eyes a bit, as they were bulging. King Hartusk?

"Until my word, you stay in your hole," Hartusk ordered. "Have the goblin tribes arrived?"

"Yes, King Hartusk. Four tribes. They are in the tunnels and ready to come forth for the glory of Many-Arrows!"

The ugly and massive orc growled and nodded. The brute kicked Innanig hard, sending him sprawling. "Warlord Hartusk," he corrected. "Let the puny dwarves and humans have kings.

"Do you understand?" Hartusk bellowed. Innanig started to answer, but not quickly enough, for Hartusk stepped over and grabbed Innanig, yanking the flustered orc to its feet. After a rough shake, Hartusk slapped Innanig aside, which left the warlord's baleful stare falling squarely over Regis.

"Yes, Warlord Hartusk," the halfling-turned-goblin squeaked, and he genuflected repeatedly, and strategically backed a bit further away.

"Who is this drow?" Hartusk demanded, turning back to his own entourage, and all the orcs there shook their heads, shrugged and whispered among themselves. "Find Ravel," he ordered one group, and the orcs ran off into the darkness.

With a growl and a scan of the group that had come out with the orc and goblin shamans, Warlord Hartusk, too, turned around and began his return to the main battle group. He looked back only once, to toss a threatening stare back at the shamans, both goblin and orc.

With a look to Innanig, Shaman Kllug motioned for his band to head back the way they had come. Regis began barking out orders, but Innanig shoved him aside roughly and demanded that he shut up. "You do not lead anymore, puny goblin," the orc explained. "Warlord Hartusk has come with thousands of Many-Arrows orcs. You will do as Innanig demands." He widened his gaze to include the other goblins about. "All of you."

The battle group wasn't going to attack, Regis realized. The whole plan he had devised with Drizzt was disintegrating, leaving his friends trapped in Nesmé with an overwhelming force about to fall upon them.

He faded back from Innanig and the other orcs, moving among a group of goblins. "The orcs will kill us," he whispered to those about him. "They will send us in first to die, and any who do not fall to the arrows of Nesmé will be killed for the orcs' pleasure."

He filtered among the goblins, leaving them with astonished and nervous expressions.

He delivered his message of doom repeatedly, but said nothing directly about any action they should undertake.

No, he knew from his experience with goblins, it would be up to him to start anything definitive.

He waited until the whole of the troupe had started down the rim of a small, tree-filled dell. His hand moved under his robe and he felt the dirk on his right hip, taking some solace in the fact that both of the side catch blades had regenerated enough for use again.

He closed in on Innanig from behind.

The orc shaman wheeled about, as did the orcs flanking him left and right. One of Innanig's guards leaped immediately for the threatening goblin, but Regis's hand came fast out from under his robes, a tiny serpent flying through the air to land upon the orc, to scramble up its chest and wrap about its neck.

And the specter appeared and jerked the shocked creature back and to the ground, choking it with the garrote. Several nearby orcs noted that, but they fell back in fear.

Regis was still moving, his right hand coming out now, holding a hand crossbow, and he wasted not the blink of an eye in firing the bolt into Innanig's ugly face.

The orc shaman cried out in pain, the other orcs came forward.

A second serpent took down the closest as Regis dropped his hand crossbow to the end of its tether, his hand going fast back under the shaman robes, his hand coming back out almost instantly, this time holding a rapier that whipped across to turn aside the thrusting spear coming at him.

The halfling quick-stepped forward, past that attacking orc and up to Innanig, who stood there trembling—battling the drow poison, no doubt. And the poison became the least of its troubles as the hated rival goblin shaman strode forward and thrust, then retreated in perfect balance and came forward a second time, and a third and a fourth, and all so quickly that it seemed like a singular attack.

Blood streaming from four holes in his chest, drow poison coursing his veins, Innanig crumpled to his knees and fell over into the dirt.

And the orcs came on and Regis knew he was doomed.

But the goblins came on, as well, meeting the orc charge, fighting as if their very lives depended on victory here.

In the sudden tumult, Regis used his prism ring and warp-stepped past the closest orcs, rushing into the few in the trailing rank with fury and devastating stabs. Behind him the battle became a general melee, all chaos and confusion. In his little sphere, the first two orcs fell before they even realized he was there, and the third and last went down a moment later.

Regis turned back to the melee, looking to pick his spots.

Not to kill orcs, necessarily. He just wanted to keep it as even a fight as he could until both sides were whittled down.

The orcs fought fiercely, but the goblins outnumbered them. With

Regis's help and instructions, one group of three goblins finished off the last nearby orc, and it seemed as if the fight was won, with only a single orc remaining alive, though it was gravely wounded and down on one knee.

Regis reached into his pouch and produced a ceramic ball. He joined in a cheer with the goblins and sent them after the last orc, but barely had they gone past him when Regis crushed the ceramic ball, freeing the magic within the sealed container.

A globe of impenetrable darkness covered the goblins. They began calling out and, judging from the sounds, bumping into each other.

"Yes, drow," Regis lied, and to the goblins he added, "Stop! The drow have come."

The area inside the darkness went silent.

Regis disguised his voice and whispered something, then answered himself as Shaman Kllug. "Yes, Lord Do'Urden," he said, "I will throw down my weapon. We will explain."

He waited a moment, then reiterated loudly, "I will throw down my weapon!"

Still nothing, and the halfling-turned-goblin had to sigh and shake his head, muttering "idiots," under his breath. He shouted explicit instructions into the darkness, "Throw out your weapons!"

Two spears and a short sword came flying to the ground at his feet.

With a wry smile, Regis waded into the darkness behind the weapons, rapier and dagger in hand.

Very soon after, Shaman Kllug stabbed dead the last thrashing goblin and cut the throat from the last writhing orc. He ran off into the night and, terrified, almost veered south to make for Nesmé.

Almost.

He didn't stop running until he had come again into the orc and goblin encampment, where he deflected the many questions coming at him regarding the battle noises in the night with a stern warning that "Warlord Hartusk is there. Warlord Hartusk has come!"

"And Shaman Innanig will ride with the war chief," Regis told them, as would the others who had traveled out with him. He explained to the eager audience that those few goblins and orcs he had left behind would coordinate the movements of the massive central battle group in reinforcement of the glorious charge of this battle group.

"Glory will still be ours, but we must be quick," Shaman Kllug warned them all. "Warlord Hartusk will see us overrun Nesmé, and he will be grateful. Into the caves, everyone! Riders of Nesmé are about. If we are discovered, we will ruin Warlord Hartusk's glorious plans, and he will eat us, every one."

He got them all back into the caverns of the upper Underdark, below the boulder tumble.

Perhaps the hardest moment of either of Regis's lives came when the last of the giants went into the tunnel and he had to go in behind them.

"You have given me much to consider," Jolen Firth said to the companions after a short meeting in his audience chamber.

"We've given ye the chance to save yer city," Bruenor, still posing as Bonnego, replied. He shot a concerned look Drizzt's way, for the drow's tale of a huge enemy encampment ready to strike at Nesmé had unnerved him, as well. "Question's bein', are ye too thickheaded to hear it?"

Jolen Firth arched his eyebrows at that, and Athrogate gave another riotous laugh.

"Indeed," the First Speaker said a moment later. "I will consider what you have told me." He signaled to a guard, and as the woman came walking over, instructed her, "Set rooms for them and get them a meal."

"We will take your meal," said Wulfgar, the only one besides Drizzt who was using his real name—or at least, his real name from his former life. "But not your rooms. We've a friend out there in the night and so we'll stay out at the wall."

"Ready to go runnin' out if we're needed," Athrogate added, drawing curious looks from the others, to which he just shrugged and laughed.

"Get your sleep where you will," Jolen Firth said, for their expressions showed that there was no chance at changing their minds on this. "If what the drow claims is true, you will need it."

"If what the drow says is true, and it is, don't you doubt," said the woman who had been introduced as Ruqiah, "and you're not listening to his warning, then your town's lost . . . in one day."

"So I have been told," said the First Speaker, and he waved them away.

"At least he didn't chase us out of Nesmé," Wulfgar said when the group moved outside, heading for the northwestern corner of the wall. "A great improvement over our first journey through this town."

"Bah," Bruenor replied and he spat upon the ground. "Sooner meself's gone from here, sooner I'll be smilin' again."

"How many?" Wulfgar asked Drizzt.

"Hundreds," the drow answered. "At least. And more coming, by the thousands, no doubt. Nesmé will be hard-pressed." He paused and looked squarely at Bruenor as he finished, "For many tendays, likely."

"Then here we stay," Catti-brie said before Bruenor could argue against the drow's look.

"Nesmé's in the war," Bruenor replied, "and so Mithral Hall's in the war. Don't ye be tellin' me me place."

"We do not know that," said Drizzt.

The dwarf stormed past them, heading straight for the ladder, and Catti-brie and Drizzt grinned at each other knowingly. For all of his complaining, Bruenor would not forsake the folk of Nesmé.

The group of dark elves and Warlord Hartusk's orc entourage arrived at the scene of the fight, where goblins and orcs lay tangled in bloody death. Hartusk's scouts had alerted them to the grisly scene just after the dawn. They had come out expecting to find that the Riders of Nesmé had intercepted and slaughtered the troupe, but it was clear that these foot soldiers, goblins and orcs, had waged war against each other.

"Such vermin," a disgusted Ravel Xorlarrin said, drawing a severe look from Hartusk.

The drow wizard merely smiled at that and continued, "A foolish troupe." Again he paused, weighing the dangerous orc's response as he placed boundaries around his insult, taking it from a general insult to orc-kind, which it surely had been, to a more narrow complaint against this particular group.

Judging by the continuing scowl of Hartusk, the drow wizard wasn't much succeeding.

"Even the shaman," Tos'un Armgo called from the side of the battlefield, the north rim of the small dell where the goblins and orcs had waged their fight.

"The orc shaman," Doum'wielle added, surprisingly from above, for she had climbed into a tree to take a wider look at the area. "His name?"

"Innanig," said Warlord Hartusk. "Where is the dirty goblin shaman?"

His orcs began rummaging about the bodies, but came up shaking their heads.

"So perhaps they are not all dead, at least," said Ravel Xorlarrin. "And perhaps your orders were relayed to the battle group."

"Unlikely," came the call from above, and when all looked up, they saw Doum'wielle pointing to the southwest.

Hartusk and the two dark elves moved quickly to the southern rim of the small dell and climbed up to the highest nearby point. Before they even got to that high ground, however, they understood Doum'wielle's call, for a cloud of dust rose before them, far away, into the dim daylight.

An army was on the move, clearly.

Hartusk began to growl, clenching his huge fists as his sides.

"They march for Nesmé," Tos'un said before Ravel could flash him a hand signal to shut up.

Hartusk growled a bit louder. "It was a dark elf," he grumbled.

Tos'un looked to Ravel for some answers, for though the drow were marching under the common banner of House Do'Urden, the Xorlarrin Clan was most prominent in the Silver Marches at that time. The Menzoberranzan forces had arrived, but they remained in the north, other than Tos'un, Doum'wielle and Saribel, and Tiago and his group who had traveled back to the Sundabar siege. Ravel had been given the duty of magically transporting the orc warlord from force-to-force, taking the Armgo father and daughter with him.

The Xorlarrin wizard shook his head.

Which of your Xorlarrin brethren did this? Tos'un's fingers subtly flashed.

Ravel merely shrugged and shook his head again, having no answer. The Xorlarrins had many scouts out and about, of course, though few this far to the west. It was possible that the unpredictable Matron Mother Baenre had some of her own in the region, moving about secretly.

That was always the problem in coordinating a drow march, Ravel silently lamented. Excessive secrecy was no friend to complementary movements!

"This is not the plan," Doum'wielle called down. "The third battle group is not yet on the field."

"Saribel?" Ravel asked under his breath, as the half-drow's remark reminded him that his sister was leading that third group, and had attendants with her. Had she sent some scouts ahead to stir up trouble, perhaps?

Tos'un moved over to him, shaking his head, having caught the quiet question. "She does not know the land and would not be so bold as to order a charge."

"What do we do, drow?" Warlord Hartusk demanded, marching over to stand before the two.

"We could go back to your forces and begin our own charge beside them," Tos'un offered.

"Too far," Hartusk and Ravel replied together, and Hartusk's tone showed that he was not amused, and understandably so. The siege at Sundabar, a city many times the size of Nesmé, was proceeding according to plan. The Sundabar garrison was hard-pressed and could not hope to break out from the walled city, and the people inside, no doubt, were feeling the hunger pains as their rations diminished day by day. And the tunnelers were hard at work, and what a surprise it would be to the folk of Sundabar when a huge portion of their formidable high wall collapsed before them!

But while that was in process, Warlord Hartusk had grown restless, and so Tiago and the others had convinced the impatient orc to travel about the battlefields, perhaps to grab at the low-hanging fruit, such as Nesmé, with a population of barely three thousand and a garrison, though hardened by many fights with bog blokes and trolls, numbering no more than a few hundred.

The plan the drow leaders had set in motion back at Dark Arrow Keep was simple: first to isolate the three dwarf citadels, then to go against the line of Luruar's human cities, Sundabar, Silverymoon, and the least of them, little Nesmé. Little, but strategic, for with Nesmé down, the western flank of the war would belong to Many-Arrows, and when Sundabar fell soon after, the south-central cities of Silverymoon and Everlund would be isolated from any remaining allies in the Luruar alliance.

The war would be all but won, and Many-Arrows from that point forward could surely set the terms of any treaty—terms that would tear Silverymoon and Everlund away from the dwarf citadels in any meaningful way and allow the minions of rising Warlord Hartusk, with secret help from the drow, to pick off the dwarf fortresses one by one.

Much of the timetable depended on what would transpire here, at Nesmé. A swift and inexpensive victory would solidify the western flank and offer Hartusk a large and menacing force in the west, and curling back to Silverymoon. If the destruction of Nesmé could be accomplished quickly and completely, no aid for Hartusk's enemies would dare enter the Silver Marches from the west.

"They will be at Nesmé's wall before we muster the battle groups and begin our march in earnest," Doum'wielle lamented, lithely swinging down from her high perch to land on the ground near Ravel and the orc warlord.

"Go and stop them," Hartusk demanded, pointing back to the distant army.

"They are halfway . . ." Doum'wielle started to protest, but her voice trailed away under Hartusk's withering gaze.

The orc warlord dropped his demanding stare over Ravel.

"I've one spell," the wizard replied. "A teleport, to take you and our entourage back to our ranks outside of Sundabar."

Hartusk began a low growl.

"Perspective, Warlord Hartusk," Ravel said. "This is not the important battle, and it is one we will win despite the foolishness of those now charging Nesmé's walls. When Saribel's force is positioned in the east, Nesmé will surely crumble." He looked to the considerable cloud of dust in the southwest. "If it has not fallen beforehand."

"Let us lead the other group . . ." the orc began, but Ravel dared to interrupt.

"I understand your eagerness, for you are a creature of Gruumsh, a true orc warrior," he said, and knew it was likely the compliment had saved him a violent confrontation then and there. He pointed to the distant force running for Nesmé. "This," he explained, "is a flank, and one made mostly of goblins, who are surely expendable. Send runners to scout, I beg. They will not catch the charge in time to avert the fight, but they will return with news, either glorious or informative."

Ravel gave a little laugh, trying to put everyone at ease. "Indeed, perhaps this will play out for the best. Let this serve as our test assault—your commanders will better know the battlefield, and the strength of our enemies."

"I will see this town destroyed!"

Ravel nodded. "Then let the battles begin, and let the siege of Nesmé commence. Wear them down and wound them while Sundabar falls. Sundabar, King Hartusk, mighty Sundabar. Ten times the size of Nesmé, with walls thrice the height and fortitude. What might the great city of Silverymoon think when that is done, when Sundabar is in ruin?

"Yes, Warlord Hartusk, let Nesmé sit in siege and let the first shock be the greatest. Sundabar is hard-pressed, the plans are underway. They'll not hold. That is the prize to claim before winter."

Unbeknownst to his companions, Ravel had edged his voice with minor magical spells as he promised glory to the orc warlord. The wizard glanced at Tiago, who was nodding hopefully. Despite the earlier plans for burying Nesmé, Tiago wanted Saribel alone to claim this victory, and surely not the orc warlord. All of them, Tiago, Ravel, Tos'un, Doum'wielle and Saribel needed that prized feather in the cap of House Do'Urden, their House, to gain leverage with Matron Mother Baenre. Do'Urden was their House now, and a Noble House, eighth in the city.

Eighth. A position that could be improved, given the pedigree of the House Do'Urden nobles.

The orc warlord's assenting nods told the wizard that the magic, the argument, or a combination of both, was having the desired effect.

"Let us go and inform your commanders," Ravel coaxed. "And then back to Sundabar for us, to drive on the tunnelers that we might find a great victory before the snows settle on the land."

With one last look at the receding dust cloud in the southwest, King Hartusk grunted and started back to the east.

"If the goblin shaman is found alive after the battle, keep him alive," Ravel and his two companions heard Hartusk instruct one of the brutes marching beside him. "Bring him to me alive. His flesh will taste better if it is peeled while he still draws breath."

Doum'wielle cast a concerned glance at both her father and Ravel, but they each shrugged it away as if the orc warlord's gruesome demand was nothing out of the ordinary. They were drow, after all, raised in Menzoberranzan.

They had seen worse.

"Two thousand, at least," Wulfgar told his friends, who, along with hundreds of Nesmé citizens, crouched quietly behind the city walls. First Speaker Jolen Firth had heeded their warnings and in the dark of night had called up every able-bodied man and woman.

Scores of archers kneeled or sat behind the battlements. The entirety of the Riders of Nesmé, some hundred armored warriors, milled about near the gate, their horses saddled and ready. Every cleric in the city had been called up, placed strategically about the northwestern corner of the wall—a wall that was now thick with extra ladders, to get reinforcements up quickly and efficiently, and to get the inevitable wounded down to the courtyard to be healed. The handful of magic-users in the city had also been roused from their beds early that morning, and clustered now about Catti-brie, the woman who called herself Ruqiah.

Catti-brie had taken charge of that group. She showed them her spells-cars and told of her training among the Netherese in the City of Shade, and her extensive study with the Harpells of Longsaddle.

"Well, we'll likely all be inadvertently turned into frogs, then," one wizard in blue robes lamented playfully at her admission of the latter training, for wide indeed was the reputation of the exotic and eccentric Harpell clan.

Catti-brie shared in the mirth, but her face went grim immediately as she recounted the battle she had fought the previous night.

"Fireballs, and other spells of fire," she told them.

"My strongest spell is an ice storm," one replied.

"Keep it away from the giants, then," said the old wizard in the blue robes.

"Fire spells," Catti-brie reiterated. "A finger's wash of flames to clear a ladder top. A fireball to make a frost giant turn about."

"I've a spell of powerful digging at my disposal," an old woman boasted. "Let them put up their ladders and I'll drop them all in a hole! Haha!"

"Keep it far from the wall," another warned. "Sure that you'll collapse the stones of Nesmé, old fool."

"Aye," agreed the wizard in the blue robes, who seemed to Catti-brie to be a friend of the old woman. "If you undermine the wall, the giants will have no trouble knocking it down."

The old wizard-woman nodded and glanced about at the riders, who were moving to their horses. "Thousands, your friend said. Let's hope our warriors do not need to ride out from behind our walls."

"Let us hope that our arrows and spells will turn our enemies about and thin their ranks, that the riders might destroy them all," Catti-brie said, and she nodded across the courtyard, to where Drizzt was even then calling mighty Andahar to his side. He would keep the unicorn near him, below his place on the battlement. He'd put Taulmaril to good use this day, but if the Riders of Nesmé did go out from the walls, Drizzt meant to ride beside them.

The other mages, and everyone else watching, gasped at the magical appearance of the great unicorn. First it appeared tiny, as if far, far away, but it doubled in size with a running stride, then again and a third time, so that when it arrived beside Drizzt, it stood seventeen hands and more, with rippling muscles showing under its snowy coat all along its powerful neck. Andahar pawed the ground and tossed its head, the long ivory horn shining despite the dim light, as if in defiance of the darkened sky.

A pair of dwarves walked over to the mage group. "Girl, ye get me a mount for when them gates fling open," the one called Bonnego told Ruqiah.

"When needed," she answered. "We'll be hard-pressed here, I fear." She looked to the other dwarf and asked, "And you?"

Athrogate produced a small obsidian boar statue. "Snort," he said with a wry smile.

Catti-brie nodded and turned back to confer with the wizards.

"You've some colorful friends," the old wizard in the blue robes remarked.

"Colored red with orc blood by the end of the day, no doubt," Catti-brie answered.

Soon after, they heard the sound of the enemy charge, though they were still quite far away. They heard the shouts—the orcs and goblins weren't trying to disguise their attack at all. They had fallen for the ruse Drizzt and Regis had coaxed upon them. To their thinking, according to Drizzt, Nesmé was nearly deserted now, and with almost all of her warriors out to the south.

That was their chance.

Catti-brie looked around at the men and women up on the wall, shoulder-to-shoulder in this section. Every other one, it seemed, tapped an index finger over his or her pursed lips, calling for absolute silence.

She noted Drizzt climbing a ladder, Taulmaril in hand. He made the wall and peered out between the battlements.

He looked down to Catti-brie and pointed to another position on the wall, the one in line with the frost giants.

"There is our place," Catti-brie quietly instructed her wizard companions. "Kill as many of our enemies as you can, to be sure, but focus your strongest spells on the giants."

CHAPTER 15

FIELD OF BLOOD AND FIRE

Disguised as Shaman Kllug, Regis had patrolled the entrance to the Underdark caverns diligently that previous night, making sure that none of his monstrous minions slipped outside into the open air. He had to keep their morning charge a secret until they were well away from this spot, well away from the main battle group and Warlord Hartusk and the dark elves.

But would it all work anyway?

The halfling in the guise of the goblin shaman paced the corridors, mumbling to himself. Even if they were successful with the plan he and Drizzt had hatched, causing a rout of this group of monsters, what then? Thousands of orcs and other vicious enemies had assembled and more were on the way. How long could Nesmé, even if tomorrow brought an overwhelming victory, withstand the weight of the orc press?

Perhaps he should slip out in the night, he had pondered many times, and run to Nesmé with word for his friends and for all the townsfolk that it was time to flee that doomed place. Surrender the city—it had happened in the first Obould war—and flee to Silverymoon or Everlund.

The option seemed plausible to him, except that he knew he couldn't begin to execute it. He would never get to Nesmé in time to facilitate an evacuation, even if they would listen—and when had the stubborn people of Nesmé ever listened to anything? And if Hartusk's arrayed forces caught the folk out on the road, out from behind their high walls, the slaughter would be that much easier.

So Regis had found himself trapped here with no good options.

"Play for the day," he told himself. "Win the day, each day, and so you will win the war."

His resolve hardened, but later on, he found himself faltering yet again, when a huge tribe of ogres—scores of the brutes—came in to join the goblin and orc force. And not just any ogres, no. These giants were heavily armored and armed with fine weapons. And with them came ogrillon—so many of the squat and powerful troops. Ogrillon were the offspring of ogres and orcs, more the height of the latter, but thicker and stronger by far. These monsters, too, were wonderfully arrayed for battle.

Drow weapons. Drow armor.

The ogres spoke of Q'Xorlarrin, a drow city leading the glorious charge. It took Regis a while to decipher their incomplete information, but he gradually came to understand that Q'Xorlarrin was Gauntlgrym. Or near to Gauntlgrym, at least, and the name of Tiago came up often in his conversation with the ogre chieftain.

"We attack at midday," Regis told the brute. "A full charge at a nearly empty city. We will overrun it and prepare the way for the arrival of Warlord Hartusk and Tiago."

The ogre chieftain and his entourage seemed quite eager at that news.

They were hungry for blood and ready to go.

Regis breathed a sigh of relief at that. These brutes had come in without orders, other than to join in with this battle group, so they would not derail or even question the midday charge.

That sigh of relief became a wince of concern, however, as more ogres flowed in over the next hours.

Even with the trap set, Regis had to wonder if his monstrous force had grown so powerful that it would indeed overrun Nesmé, even without help from the larger battle group to the east!

He had no choice, however. The trap was set and had to be sprung.

They were out early the next day, swarming out of the tunnels and into the boulder tumble, forming into battle groups based on tribe and race. Regis called them together, group by group, blessed them in the name of Gruumsh, and sent them running to the south.

He went with the last group of goblins, huffing and puffing as they rumbled across the miles, trying valiantly to keep up. When he realized that he wouldn't be able to do so, the pretend shaman sent word to the trio of frost giants, and one came rambling back to gather him up.

Sitting on a giant's shoulder, then, Regis rode the miles to Nesmé.

When the walled town finally came in sight, the monsters ran all the harder, for it surely seemed as deserted as the drow informant had promised.

"Put me down," Regis ordered the giant.

"I can throw you over the wall," the giant replied with a laugh. "All glory to Kllug!"

Regis tried not to faint.

But the giant dropped him to the ground and thundered off, leaving the halfling-turned-goblin in the midst of a swarming sea of charging monsters. The phony Shaman Kllug began shouting out commands, this way and that, and if any of the bloodthirsty creatures had paused long enough to pay attention, it would likely have recognized the orders as nonsensical.

None were listening, though, for their goal was in sight and the charge had begun in full.

Regis breathed a sigh of relief and took a survey of the area about him. He had to stay out of the fight, obviously, and stay out of the way of retreating monsters when the ambush was sprung.

"If they retreat," he whispered with a wince as he noted the fury of the charge and that it was led by more than a hundred armored ogres.

The ground and walls shook around them from the thunder of the monstrous charge. Crouched on the wall behind the shielding battlements, Nesmé defenders nervously set and reset arrows to their bowstrings.

Drizzt Do'Urden snaked about them, whispering encouragement and reminding them to wait until the order. "Let them be near enough our walls so that every arrow will take one down," he said. "Our first volley will be the most important. Mark your target due north of your position and take the creature down."

Nods came back at him, but few inspired confidence. As seasoned as these warriors of the frontier city might be, the charge coming at them surely surpassed anything anyone in this region had seen in a century and more, since the assault of the original Obould and his orc thousands.

The ground shook more violently, the air filled with the war-whoops of orcs and goblins. Drizzt peeked over the battlement and his violet eyes widened indeed as he looked upon the hundreds and hundreds, the black swarm rolling for Nesmé's wall.

He noted the ogres most of all, running together with practiced precision, outfitted in armor and as one hoisting huge iron spears.

The drow ducked and scrambled to the edge of the parapet.

"Move! Move!" he shouted down to the many gathered there. "Near to the wall. Press in. Take cover!"

And not a moment too soon did the riders in the courtyard heed the call, for a great volley of spears and small arrows, and even a trio of giant-hurled boulders arched over the wall, filling the air like a swarm of angry bees. One boulder clipped the wall, sending pieces of stone flying, and a pair of soldiers, shocked by the thunderous retort, went rolling from the battlement to the ground below.

The drow peeked back over the parapet to see the monsters closing the last dozen strides to the base of the wall. He noted the ladders then, coming up amid the clusters of goblins.

And the ogres—so many ogres. And Drizzt understood what Regis had earlier discerned: that these had been trained and outfitted by a greater power, likely the drow.

"Shoot for volume," he told the archers. "Kill as many as you can, and quickly. For doom is upon us."

Up went the defenders of Nesmé, a line of bows between the rising stone crenellations of the wall, and off went scores of arrows, driving down into the throngs swarming to the base—so thick a swarm that the archers could not have missed a mark without consciously trying!

And up went Drizzt and Taulmaril, and he let fly for the nearest ogre, the lightning-streaking arrow crashing into its metal breastplate with thunderous force and an explosive shower of sparks. The ogre staggered back several steps under the weight of the blow.

But it did not go down.

The second arrow was on the way before the brute took another step forward, with the third arrow shooting out right behind.

It took a fourth to drop the stubborn brute, and the others were so much closer by then, and Drizzt knew that he was running out of time. He noted the giants, down to his right. They had originally been marked as his intended targets, but he could not afford that now, he knew. Not with so many armored ogres so very close. It would often take more than one shot to down an armored ogre, he had just learned, but it would take more still to down a giant.

Drizzt looked down the length of the wall and caught the stare of Catti-brie. He offered a grim nod and emphatically waved three fingers, one for each giant.

He would have to trust in her.

"The giants," Catti-brie whispered to the mages crouched about her. She looked to three in particular and asked, "Lightning?"

"Aye," one said and the others nodded.

"Draw them to us, then," Catti-brie whispered, and with a nod, she rose and looked out over the wall. Her heart almost failed her then, for she had not seen such a charge as this in her present lifetime. And the monsters were much closer than she had imagined. Arrows flew out all around her, monsters died by the dozens. She saw an ogre's head explode within its metal helm as one of Drizzt's devastating arrows drove through its faceplate.

But still the monsters came on, and responded with spears and arrows of their own, and the giants, so easy to spot hulking about the enemy lines, lifted huge rocks out of enormous sacks and sent them flying.

The sound of one of her fellow mages beginning his incantation spurred her and the other two to action, all casting the same spell, all holding forth tiny metal rods.

Lightning split the air, one burst, then three more in rapid succession. The timing, though partly inadvertent, proved perfect, for the first bolt stabbed out, drawing the attention of the monsters, and the remaining three confirmed the position of the mages to the giant enemies.

The nearest frost giant got stung by the first bolt, and then again, and its two hulking companions also each took a strike. Around them, goblins and orcs went squirming to the ground, teeth chattering, hair flying, limbs jerking in uncontrollable spasms. But frost giants were much hardier, of course, and the lightning stung them more than hurt them.

And angered them.

Catti-brie and her friends had gotten their attention!

In flew the boulders, sailing for the wall, and the four magic-users dropped to the stone. The wall shook under the weight of the blows, solid hits—one so solid that it rattled the teeth of all around and sent one of the wizards tumbling into the courtyard off the other side of the parapet!

"We've got to hit them again," cried the blue-robed mage, and he started up, only to catch an arrow in the face. Down he went, screaming in pain.

"Run away!" another cried.

"No, fight them," Catti-brie insisted. "There is nowhere to run and nowhere to hide. For Nesmé, fight them, now!" She scrambled over to the fallen wizard, a spell already on her lips. Blue mist came out of her other long sleeve, snaking about her and the man as she eased the arrow from his face, the wound closing from the magic of her spell as the bolt pulled free.

The other wizards looked on curiously.

"Fight them, I beg," Catti-brie said to them, and her actions had indeed spoken louder than her words. Up she jumped, the others climbing beside her, resolute.

Catti-brie dodged more than one arrow and spear as she cast the spell, and held her ground as a boulder soared in. It hit the wall just below her as her spell went off, a second lightning bolt erupting from her fingers to stab at the nearest giant—now barely three huge strides away—and send it staggering backward.

Catti-brie held her ground, just barely, under the weight of the boulder impact. She turned to the mages behind and about her. "Now!" she yelled at them. "With all force!"

They glanced to one another, uncertainty still clear in their expressions. This group was not battle-hardened, the woman knew.

Catti-brie turned to the old woman. "Your spell," she prompted. "They converge. Show us your power, for all of Nesmé."

Catti-brie turned around and sent off a volley of magical missiles, again at the nearest giant, trying to slow it.

She failed, but a trio of lightning bolts went out beside her, each slamming the behemoth and driving it back.

And the old woman was up beside her, furiously casting. The other giants rushed to their companion and the three moved as one for the mages, a trio of boulders leading the way, along with a host of spears and arrows from smaller humanoids running in support of their gigantic allies.

The old wizard woman almost broke in the face of that barrage, but Catti-brie enacted another spell, a shield before herself and her companion.

Missiles sparked and deflected all around them, but Catti-brie held her ground and continually coaxed the old woman to finish her spell. And so she did, and the ground just out from the base of the wall erupted in sudden tumult, dirt and stones flying around, right out from under the feet of the surprised frost giants, who could only tumble down into the hole the old woman had magically dug.

"Shields and fire, you defenders of Nesmé!" Catti-brie called to the others, and all began casting, all trepidation flown from their strong voices. "Else they will breach the wall and the hordes will pour in. And they will murder everyone in the town. Every man, every woman, every child. You can stop that. Now!"

She threw herself into her next spell, spitting the chant determinedly, and the other wizards, perhaps shamed by their initial hesitance, perhaps reminded of the stakes, perhaps terrified by the reality of no escape—perhaps a bit of all three—joined in with their own full-throated wizard songs.

Heartbeats later, Catti-brie's divine globe of fire appeared above the hole, roiling in the air. A moment later, a line of flames shot down at the brutes within.

A fireball exploded at the top of the hole, clearing goblins and orcs from the rim, and driving down the first giant as it tried to climb out.

A second fireball rent the air. Catti-brie began her own fireball spell, and as she wound through the chant, it felt different to her, and the words sounded different. She was well into her casting before she even realized that she was calling forth the spell using the language of the Plane of Fire, and that a great warmth was filling her, flowing through the ruby band on her finger. The fireball came forth, the most powerful of all, filling the top of the magical hole so beautifully that it almost appeared as if the hole was actually an erupting volcanic crater.

The flames rolled about and over each other, a brilliant dance, sensual and alive, and Catti-brie felt life within them indeed, and she reached out to them through her ring and called upon them.

Out of the mushrooming fires stepped forth a living beast, an elemental of fire, and on a nod from Catti-brie, it rolled over the edge of the pit like a lava flow, diving down at the three giants huddling on the bottom.

All eyes on the wall turned to Catti-brie, and the wizards shouted huzzahs at the display of power, and turned their cheers into action, spurred on to the heights of their own powers. And so it went, wizard after wizard throwing evocations of devastating power at, in, and around that hole, on and on, driving away the nearby goblins and orcs and ogres, or killing them outright, and keeping the giants trapped within the hole while the air about them seethed with magical fires.

From behind and from the side, goblin arrows did reach out at the wizard group, but like Catti-brie, most had enacted magical shields to ward such feeble missiles.

This part of the Nesmé wall had held, it seemed, and at the expense of the three frost giants trapped in a magical hole before the wall, as the wizards played out their wrath.

Death rained down from above, but in their bloodlust frenzy, the monsters did not break ranks. On they came, hoisting ladders, throwing spears, shooting bows. The ranks of archers atop Nesmé's wall did thin, inevitably.

The archers were not alone, however. At Drizzt's call, Bruenor, Wulfgar, and Athrogate scrambled up the ladders to the parapets and began running about the archery positions, swatting away ladders, or swatting away goblins that had managed to scramble up.

Drizzt continued to focus on the ogres—so many ogres. They did not need the ladders, he learned, as two turned and threw their backs against the wall, making a cradle by interlocking their fingers. In came a third, stepping onto their joined hands, and up they heaved, launching the brute to the wall top.

Drizzt was about to call out a warning as he furiously tried to set another arrow, but as the ogre landed on the wall, it was met by a swing of Aegis-fang. With all his strength behind it, Wulfgar sent the brute flying back down.

Drizzt laughed aloud at the sight, and lowered the angle of his bow, sending an arrow sizzling into the shoulder of the nearest ogre below.

He had to drop his bow and draw scimitars almost immediately, though, as an orc leaped in at him from behind. He fell away and spun to meet the charge, but the orc, almost to him, flew sidelong, smacking against the wall with a great grunt.

Only then did Drizzt notice one of the ball heads of Athrogate's morningstars. The second looped up high and came crashing down on the stunned orc, smashing its skull and shattering the bones in its neck. It fell away, or started to, but the dwarf dropped one of his weapons to the stone, grabbed the orc up in one hand, and hoisted it up high. With strength beyond the natural bounds of his dwarf frame, Athrogate hurled the dead orc down upon another nearing the top of a nearby ladder.

"Bwahaha!" he shouted, grabbing up his glassteel flail once more. "So many to hit, elf! Bwahahaha!"

And off he rambled.

Looking past him, Drizzt spotted Bruenor, caught in the corner of a turn in the wall, it seemed, and with an orc pressing him on one side, an ogre on the other. Drizzt started that way, then thought to grab his bow, then calmed and realized that his friend had lost nothing of his battle prowess in his return from death.

A swing of Bruenor's axe cut into the orc's side and had the creature lurching in pain. Hardly slowing, Bruenor reversed the momentum and flipped the blade over as he went around with a powerful backhand, just beating the ogre to the strike, his axe driving up into its ribs and skipping up off of bone to hook into its armpit. Drizzt could not help but recall the last time he had witnessed the dwarf in battle in Bruenor's previous life, on a ledge in a primordial chamber.

Entangled with a pit fiend.

Bruenor then had been infused with the power of the dwarven gods, and so he seemed now, his powerful strike easily lifting the ogre back over the wall to tumble down outside of Nesmé. And back the other way went Bruenor, his powerful swing taking out the next charging orc—indeed, nearly cutting it in half—and continuing through to finish off the one he had already chopped.

And now Bruenor began his own charge, down the line at more monsters pouring over the wall. His axe dripped blood with every step, but more blood replaced that, it seemed, with every other step.

The monsters had breached the wall, perhaps, but with Drizzt and his friends supporting the Nesmé defenders, it would be a short-lived victory.

"Drow!" came a cry from below, inside the wall, a few moments later, and Drizzt noted Jolen Firth astride his mount. Some of the riders had dismounted, and were even then scrambling up the ladders to support the archers, but the First Speaker showed no such movement, nor did the dozens on their powerful armored horses about him.

"Too many losses," Jolen Firth called up to Drizzt. "We must chase them from our walls, and quickly."

Drizzt glanced around, and as much as it pained him to desert the wall and Catti-brie and the others, he found that he couldn't disagree with that assessment.

He looked to the magical hole out before the wizard group, smoke pouring forth, and managed to put an arrow into the face of a giant as it tried yet again to climb out.

He called to Andahar, who waited nearby. He called to Bruenor and to Athrogate, who were side by side then. The dwarves exchanged some words and Athrogate howled happily and leaped down into the courtyard. He bounced to his feet and summoned Snort.

Bruenor nodded at Drizzt and grinned. "We'll hold 'em, elf!" he called.

That made Drizzt's choice much easier, and with a last look and a wave to Catti-brie, he shouldered his bow and swung down from the parapet, landing comfortably in the saddle of mighty Andahar.

Off they went behind Jolen Firth and the Riders of Nesmé, not for the nearest gate but beyond it, across the city to the east, where the main gate was not contested.

Arm in arm, helping each other, hoisting each other, the three giants at last climbed out of the hole. Smoke wafted from their singed clothing, blue-white skin glowed red under the great rash of burns inflicted by the rain of fire upon them and from the pummeling fists of the fire elemental.

They turned for the wall, and another magical barrage assailed them, including one last fireball from Catti-brie, this one fully immolating the trio, head to toe.

But when the roiling flames cleared, the giants stood, and it was obvious to all looking on that the wizards had nearly exhausted their magical energies.

Two of the giants had seen enough of this fight, though, and started stumbling away, but the third scolded them and demanded they halt. Stubborn to the end, that brute advanced to the wall. It didn't have its sack of rocks any longer—the sack had been burned away in the fiery hole—but it did have one remaining rock, jagged and dark, and it lifted it now like a bludgeon, and started for its tormentors.

Catti-brie hit it in the face with magic missiles.

But the behemoth walked through the barrage and on it continued, and like the giant, the woman would not back down. The behemoth was only a stride away, the rock lifted to smash her, when Catti-brie blasted it again.

But the brute didn't fall.

The blue-robed wizard tried to pull her away, but the woman wouldn't leave. Defiantly she stared at the behemoth.

"You have no place here," she told it. "Be gone."

The giant grimaced, then its head snapped hard to the side and the blue-robed wizard and several others gasped in surprise.

Not Catti-brie, though. She just smiled knowingly, for she had seen Wulfgar moving in fast and she knew well the nature of the missile that had so pulverized the giant's face.

Perhaps the brute figured it out, too, for it glanced down at the warhammer lying on the ground at its feet.

Then, like a cut tree, the behemoth tilted to the side and simply kept going, crashing to the ground, landing with a great "harrumph" as the last breath it ever took blew free from the impact.

Its two companions stumbled off with all speed, and the specter of the mighty frost giants fleeing in terror broke the will of the lesser monsters. Goblins, orcs, and even ogres in that area were swept up by the gravity of the behemoth's wake, and as that portion of the monstrous line broke apart, the infection of the retreat widened.

All along the wall, the monsters broke ranks and fled, and a wall of arrows chased them out.

And the horns of Nesmé blew loud and clear as the city's main gates swung open. Bows in hand, lances strapped and ready, tips and pennants proudly high, the Riders of Nesmé thundered onto the field. In armor shining despite the dim light, Jolen Firth led them, but it was the riders just to the side of the First Speaker that brought a hopeful smile to the lips of Catti-brie.

She saw the unicorn, Andahar, the bells of the steed's barding singing a sweet melody, and with the rider's green cloak and long white hair trailing. Beside Drizzt roared the fiery little hell boar, the wild black-bearded dwarf bouncing along atop it, flails in hand, ball heads spinning at the end of adamantine chains.

Drizzt let Jolen Firth and his closest riders lead for a short while, but then he veered slightly, Athrogate in his wake. Catti-brie smiled. The drow had seen the retreating giants.

As soon as Drizzt loosened Andahar's reins, the mighty unicorn leaped past the horses, churning the turf beneath his hooves with strides far longer than his mortal cousins could manage. Only one came close to pacing Drizzt and his mount, and the sight of Athrogate's fire-spewing boar, little legs spinning in a blur, speeding past a shocked Jolen Firth, brought a laugh to Catti-brie's lips.

"By the gods," muttered the blue-robed wizard beside her.

"The little one's riding an infernal beastie," said the old woman with the marvelous dig spell. "Guess you're to be running faster when you're being chased around by demons and devils all the day."

That brought a laugh all around, and indeed the day looked brighter.

"Conserve your spells now," Catti-brie bade the others. "The first fight is ours—few of our enemies will escape. But more may come and we must be ready. Go now and rest."

The other nodded. "And yourself," said the blue-robed wizard.

But Catti-brie looked around at the many wounded within the city and shook her head. "I am a priestess of Mielikki," she told them. "My work is only half done."

She moved for the ladder and found Bruenor and Wulfgar waiting for her.

"Give us a horse, girl," the dwarf said. "The fightin's out there now."

With a nod, Catti-brie began casting and a few heartbeats later, a large spectral steed materialized. Wulfgar leaped up and lowered his hand, easily hoisting Bruenor onto the magical horse behind him.

"Hurry up, boy," the dwarf demanded. "Damned drow's taking all our fun, I'm betting, or I'm a bearded gnome."

Wulfgar set the mount galloping before Bruenor even finished, but Catti-brie heard the words, and that old phrase threw her back in time so fully that it took her a moment to steady herself, as the weight of all that had transpired—not just here but in the magical forest and the passing of a century, in the rebirth and second life—nearly laid her low. She fell back against the ladder for support, and closed her eyes.

And the weight of memory and the sheer unreality pressed upon her.

She shook it away, though, and forced her eyes open once more, scanning about for clusters of the wounded. She had much work left to do.

Lines of lightning arched out from Taulmaril as Andahar bore down on the pair of stumbling, retreating frost giants. Smoke still wafted from their burned clothing and singed hair; their skin verily glowed red, angry red, from the punishment of wizard fires and the embrace of Catti-brie's elemental monster.

One staggered under the weight of Drizzt's barrage. It tried to move along faster, and its friend tried to pull it along, but of course, the arrows from the Heartseeker sped faster still.

After one particularly painful stab, the battered giant threw up its arms in outrage and shoved aside its companion, swinging about to face its tormentor.

Drizzt sat astride Andahar, the unicorn slowing and stopping and stomping the ground anxiously.

The giant roared. Drizzt looked it in the eye and casually leveled his bow.

To the side, Athrogate and his hell boar rambled past, but neither the drow nor the giant paid him any heed, their eyes locked in a hateful exchange.

Then, as the trance shattered, the giant roared and flung its last rock, and charged in behind.

Drizzt's arrow hit that spinning boulder, and with a thunderous retort, the rock broke in half, both pieces spinning aside harmlessly. And the drow let fly a second arrow, right behind the first.

It struck the giant in the face, and its angry roar became a pained scream. It slapped its huge hands over the wound and staggered.

Andahar charged and Drizzt lowered the bow and held on desperately.

To the side, the other giant rushed to support its friend, or started to, until it noticed the dwarf speeding in. With a growl, the behemoth lifted a foot, as if to stamp the dwarf and his strange mount flat, but that hell boar was having none of it, veering and springing at the last moment past the giant's supporting leg.

And the dwarf had one of his glassteel flails spinning above his head, like a cattleman with a lariat. The boar flew past, the giant stomped at it futilely, and the dwarf sent the weapon's heavy head smashing against the giant's knee.

The giant expected the hit and sucked in its breath, figuring it could withstand the blow as it turned.

But the giant did not understand the girdle-enhanced strength of this dwarf, Athrogate, nor the power of that morningstar, Whacker by name. Athrogate had called upon the enchanted weapon, and from the spikes on that balled head oozed magical liquid, oil of impact.

When the weapon struck the giant's knee, the tremendous force bent the giant's leg—sideways and to the ground.

The behemoth dropped, howling and grabbing at its shattered limb, and Snort landed and wheeled about for another pass, turning Athrogate just in time to witness the impact as Andahar, ivory horn lowered, crashed into the other giant's chest. The horn disappeared fully into the behemoth, the power of the unicorn smashing it through flesh and muscle and bone. The length of the horn reappeared, covered in blood, as the giant fell away to the ground, one hand grabbing its blasted face, the other now trying to stem the blood spurting from the hole in its chest.

Drizzt, too, went to the ground, the impact knocking him from his seat atop the unicorn. For a moment, Athrogate winced, as it looked like his friend would crash down hard. But Drizzt neatly tucked his head and rolled over, coming to his feet with momentum carrying him to the giant and with both his scimitars, somehow, already in hand.

"Bwahaha!" the dwarf roared, and all the louder when he noted a group of monsters, goblins and a pair of ogres, coming his way.

They slowed with each step, as the scene before them came clearer, as they understood, apparently, that these giants weren't going to help them.

They turned and ran away.

"Bah, ye cowardly dogs!" Athrogate cried after them, and he went to finish his giant, and quickly, for there were so many more things to hit!

From the back of the battlefield, Regis watched the slaughter unfolding before him. The Riders of Nesmé worked brilliantly, thin lines of cavalry weaving about the masses, carving out sections of the fleeing mob to slow them and turn them.

Arrows thinned each group as the stampeding charge thundered in, lances lowering to skewer and stab.

Some would escape, Regis understood. Indeed, many orcs neared his position even then, running for all their lives.

He had to stay in character, he knew, and he called to them, shouting orders as if to coordinate the retreat—though, once again as with the charge, any listening closely would have surmised that his blathering was more gibberish than anything else.

Mostly, he tried to stay out of the way—far out of the way, for these routed monsters were in a foul mood and any might decide to kill the shaman who had led them to this utter disaster.

Regis screamed orders and moved sidelong to a fallen log, then seemed to disappear, warp-stepping with his prism ring, and coming through the movement on his belly, crouched in tight against the wood.

Soon many more fleeing monsters passed him by, including a large contingent of ogres and ogrillon, some leaping atop the log and springing off, oblivious to him as they soared right over him.

One came down hard, crashing over the log, and Regis yelped, thinking it had dived for him!

But no, he realized when he saw the long arrow protruding from its back. Terrified, realizing that his allies were as likely to kill him as were the monsters, the halfling-turned-goblin pulled the orc the rest of the way over the log and covered himself with it.

Should he revert to his natural form? If he did so too soon, the monsters would cut him down. If he waited too long, an arrow would surely take him!

***

Farther back from Regis, much farther back and far to the side, a handful of orcs watched the disaster unfold. They saw the distant slaughter and the desperate retreat. They watched the Riders of Nesmé, in their shining mail, running down goblins and orcs. They saw ogres skewered by lances, then taken down under the press of armored horses.

And they saw the giants fall.

And with mouths agape, they watched the unicorn and the rider astride it, his skin black, his long white hair and green cape flying as he galloped his mount across the torn ground, his lightning bow dealing death with every shot.

"Are we betrayed?" one of them asked, for there could be no doubt here. This was a drow.

With a suddenness that tore a shriek from his lips, the orc covering Regis flew aside, and a strong hand slapped down and grabbed him by the front of his shaman robes and hauled him into the air.

He had to stab his attacker, he knew. But it was too sudden, too unexpected. He had to fight fast, but he could not. And then his senses returned enough for him to realize the truth of his attacker, and he cried out denials, "Stop! Stop! It's me."

And only as he heard his own words did Regis realize that he was shouting in the goblin tongue!

His lips flapped as he was shaken hard.

"Hey elf!" Athrogate bellowed, and he gave Regis another jostle. "I'm thinkin' I've found yer little rat friend! Bwahahaha!"

Regis nearly swooned, so overwhelmed with relief was he when he regained his senses enough to note the smile of Drizzt Do'Urden.

PART THREE

BOIL

IT ITCHES ON THE COLLECTIVE CONSCIOUSNESS OF A SOCIETY, NAGGING AND nattering, whispering unease.

The tiny bubbles of criticism appear, about the bottom of the pot at first, hanging on, secret.

Quiet.

They dart upward, roiling the surface, just a few, then a few more, then a cascade.

This is the critical moment, when the leaders must step forth as one to calm the brew, to lift the pot from the fire, but too often, I fear, it is the ambitious opposition to these leaders stoking the flames among the citizenry, poking the folk with one malicious whisper after another.

Veracity matters not; the emotional response takes hold and will not let go.

The bubbles become a boil, the heat flowing through the water and wafting up into the air on the souls of the many who will surely die in this symphony of hatred, this expression of rage seeking focus.

This war.

I have seen it over and over through the decades, in campaigns sometimes worthy, but most often involving nefarious designs beneath the lies and feigned purposes. And in that turmoil and misery and carnage, the warrior is held high and the flag is tightly wrapped—too tightly to allow for any questioning of purpose and method.

This is how society is convinced to plant the fireball beneath its own pot.

And when it is over, when the rubble replaces the homes and the graveyards overfill and still the bodies rot in the streets, do we look back and wonder how it came to this awful point.

That is the greatest tragedy, that the only time when questioning is allowed is when the ultimate failure of war has come to pass.

When the families are shattered.

When the innocent are slaughtered.

But what of war against monstrous intrusion, against the orcs and giantkind, would-be conquerors? Catti-brie, with Bruenor's loud echo, insisted to me that this was different, that these races, on the word of Mielikki herself, could not be viewed through the prism we hold to measure the rational and goodly races—or even the rational and not-so-goodly societies like that of my own people. Orcs and giantkind are different, so they assert, in that their malicious ways are not the teachings of an aberrant society but a matter much deeper, to the very soul of the creatures.

Creatures?

How easily does that pejorative flow from my lips when I ponder the orcs and goblins of the world. Even with my experiences telling me differently, as with Nojheim the goblin, the slave.

It is all too confusing, and in the heat of that boiling pot, I desperately want to hold onto Catti-brie's words. I want to believe that those I shoot down or cut down are unrepentant and foul, are ultimately intent on destruction and wholly irredeemable.

Else, how would I ever look in a mirror again?

I admit my relief upon entering the Silver Marches to find the Kingdom of Many-Arrows marching to war.

My relief upon finding war . . .

Can there be a more discordant thought? How can war—any war—be seen as a relief? It is the tragic failure of better angels, the loss of reason to emotion, the surrender of the soul to the baser instincts.

And yet I was relieved to find that Many-Arrows had marched, and I would be lying to myself to deny it. I was relieved for Bruenor, for he would have started a war, I am confident, and so the inevitable misery would then have weighed more heavily upon his shoulders.

I am relieved for Catti-brie, so determined in her declaration, her epiphany, that there can be no redemption for orcs.

This is her interpretation of the song of the goddess.

Her interpretation shakes my faith in the goddess.

She is not as sure of herself as she claimed; her voice before we faced this truth of war held steadier than now, as we huddle against Nesmé's wall awaiting the next charge, awaiting the next round of carnage. Her fireballs and fire pets have slain many these days, and have done so in gallant and correct defense of the city.

And still I see the perpetual wince in her fair face, the pain in her blue eyes, the frown beneath her mask of smile. She holds to Mielikki's words, her own proclamations, and hurls her spells with deadly force. But each death within and without Nesmé's walls takes from her, wounds her heart, crushes her hopes.

"It's what it be," Athrogate keeps saying as he stalks about the parapets.

Indeed, but "what it be" is not what Catti-brie wishes it could be, and so the battle pains her greatly and taxes her heart more than her body and mind.

For that I am glad. It is one of the reasons I so love her.

And so I can be relieved for my dear friends, for their hearts and the scars they will carry from this war—there are always scars from war—and still be dismayed by the carnage and brutality and the sheer stupidity of waging a war, this war, in the Silver Marches.

If we measure victory as a condition better than what was in place before the conflict, then there will be no winners.

Of that I am certain.

—Drizzt Do'Urden

CHAPTER 16

GRIM TIDINGS

Darkness fell fully over the lands of the Silver Marches. Within the walls of Nesmé, the horns began to blow, as they did every night.

The orcs came on again, and so familiar with their assaults were the hearty townsfolk that they could accurately gauge the strength of the various groups approaching by the sound of the footfalls.

Catti-brie and the wizards rushed to their assigned positions. They were not clustered any longer, though giants sometimes showed among the ranks of the orcs. Now they coordinated support for the archers, first by casting spells of light to illuminate the battlefield about the walls and so allow their cohorts to take deadly aim.

Arrows did not fly as thick from those walls as they had during the first attack. "Pick your shots carefully," was the order of the day, for supplies were dwindling after nearly two tendays of fighting. Each day, brave men and women went out to the south, into the Trollmoors, to gather wood, while bowyers worked long hours crafting arrows. But even that was a game of diminishing margins, as good wood became scarcer about the south wall, and more importantly, as trolls grew ever more present in that area. The foul beasts had smelled the blood of the battles, clearly, and so now Nesmé was being pressed on all sides.

Few were the hours of quiet within the city each day, and sometimes the defenders would find no rest at all.

Drizzt stood beside Catti-brie, and his magical quiver would not run out of arrows, and so his deadly bow sang throughout each fight, sending flashing arrows out from the wall, a steady stream that seemed more a wizard's fireworks than the play of an archer.

All along the wall ran Wulfgar, Bruenor, Regis, and Athrogate, shouting encouragement, tossing ladders and ogres aside. Whenever a breach seemed inevitable, these four arrived, with Drizzt close behind, and so the point of weakness was strengthened and the monsters driven away.

When daylight came, meager as it was, it revealed to them a field blackened with bodies and carrion birds, the dead piling deep, the birds growing fatter—so fat that Regis wondered whether they would not be able to fly away before a coming charge, to be trampled in the midst of their gluttony.

Mid-morning on the twenty-first day of the siege of Nesmé came the urgent cries from the southern wall. Drizzt was the first of the companions to arrive on the wall, amid a group of Nesmé defenders, all pointing out to the south and calling support to a small band, a handful, of humans trying to approach the city.

But still far away.

Trolls followed that group in close pursuit. More of the monsters filtered through the skeletal trees left and right, angling in from the sides to cut the humans off, and it seemed clear that the humans would not make it to Nesmé's wall.

"Set fires outside the gate," Drizzt ordered the Nesmians, and to a pair, he added, "Go find my friends—find the black-bearded dwarf. And Catti-brie."

Some of the sentries began asking questions back at him, but Drizzt wasn't listening. He vaulted over the battlement and dropped the fifteen feet to the soft ground below, landing lightly and racing off to the south, bow in hand. A sparkling lightning arrow flew off with every stride, some ahead and to the right, some ahead and to the left.

He hit more than one troll, though most of the shots skipped off bony branches of the dead trees that so marked this region. But near misses were just as important, for his intent was to slow these closing forces.

Drizzt shouldered his bow, drew his blades, and sprinted ahead with all speed for the desperate humans.

They staggered and scrambled, trying to stay ahead, but knew they could not. A pair had drawn weapons, ready to turn about and die fighting.

"Keep running!" Drizzt yelled to them. "To Nesmé. To Nesmé!"

The drow put his head down and charged forward. The nearest humans, too, drew weapons, aiming his way, for what were they to think with trolls chasing them from behind and a drow bearing down on them from the other direction?

A sword leveled to stop him, but Drizzt rolled his scimitar under it and took it harmlessly aside. "Keep running. To Nesmé!" he shouted again as he passed those first two men.

The next in line, a woman, put up her blade, staring at him incredulously.

"Run!" he told her as he flashed by, and then he leaped right over the trailing two, a man and a woman, who had stopped and turned to face the pursuing trolls.

Drizzt landed in full stride, two running steps launching him into the surprised trolls. His scimitars worked in a blur, stabbing and slashing, up high and down low, hitting the first pair of trolls many times before they ever realized that a drow had arrived.

And Drizzt bored through that pair, fell into a slide through the muddy ground and cut off the leg of the next troll in line.

The drow came up and turned a sharp right, now pursued from behind and with many more monsters closing in on him from ahead. He sprinted to a pair of trees, slowing slightly to allow the nearest troll to almost catch him, then sped up and raced around.

The troll just kept going straight, crashing through the trees, sending splinters flying. And when it came through the other side and managed to straighten, it found the drow waiting, the scimitars dancing.

Off sprinted Drizzt, now back to his bow. He let fly at the flanking trolls in that direction, drawing their attention and turning many to come at him.

He veered, running deeper into the moors, trolls coming at him from behind and from both flanks. He was caught, surely, except that he had those anklets, those brilliant, magical anklets that sped his stride, and with a sudden burst, he came out ahead of the closing vise and continued on with a score and more of trolls close behind.

Spurred by the words of the drow, and more so by the actions of the drow, the Nesmians scrambled to the city's southern gate and flung the doors wide.

"Firewood!" echoed the cries across the town, and more folk came running, and soon many were carrying logs from fireplaces, even wooden chairs—anything that could be burned.

A pile grew in heartbeats, and one man bent over it, striking flint to steel, blowing at the fledgling flames to coax them to life.

"Quicker!" urged his friends, and others fell with their own flint and steel.

"Someone get a torch!" yelled one man, a call echoed back into the city.

But then the fire-builders were drawn aside by the touch of a woman, and Catti-brie took their place. She brought her hands up before her, thumbs touching, fingers extended, and whispered through her magical ring to the plane of living flames. A cone of fire shot forth from her fingers and the wood blazed to life.

The woman rose and turned to the south, to see the party of humans all racing for their lives, a few trolls still directly behind them and with other hideous beasts coming on to intercept.

"Out o' me way!" she heard behind her, coming through the gates, and she nodded and did not need to turn about to know what that meant. A heartbeat later, Athrogate and Snort thundered past her, the boar's hooves puffing smoke with every stride.

"Not so many now," one of the Nesmians cried. "Come on, fellows, fight them and win!"

"For Nesmé!" shouted another.

Wulfgar, Bruenor, and Regis came running out soon after, to stand beside Catti-brie, who had closed her eyes and was well into her spellcasting.

To slow down was to die, Drizzt knew, for he was far from the city now, and far from any who might help. He veered left and right about the trees, occasionally turning to let fly an arrow into the nearest troll in pursuit.

He could outrun the trolls.

But then he heard wolves, and not so far away, and he couldn't outrun wolves.

He veered to the left to begin his wide circuit to get him back to the city, but then had to change directions as he made for a tangle of trees, for they were not trees, but bog blokes, malicious living creatures hungry for his flesh.

"Guen, I need you," he called, drawing out the onyx figurine.

He realized before the gray mist began to form that he needed more than Guenhwyvar, though, for what had seemed like a simple pursuit of an unfortunate party by some trolls was actually a part of a larger assault on Nesmé.

The trolls and bog blokes, and surely the wolves he had heard and now could see, worked in concert with the besieging orcs.

Drizzt cursed under his breath and ran on.

What choice did he have?

The five humans knew they were doomed, for the trolls closing on their right had them beaten to the spot and they could not reach the city!

They tightened ranks, weapons in hand, side-by-side, and prepared to die.

"Fight through them—one of us must get to Nesmé," the leader of the party demanded, and four nods returned the order.

"Open for Brewer, he's the fastest," one of the women advised.

"I'll not leave you to die," Brewer huffed in reply.

And as if to end the debate before it could begin, a tremendous fireball erupted, just ahead and to the right, engulfing the leading trolls in biting, killing flames.

The five humans ran on through the smoking carnage.

Athrogate rushed by them, laughing wildly, morningstars spinning, Snort snorting flames. The dwarf charged into the pursuing trolls with glee. A moment of explosive swings and hell boar fireballs later and the trolls, at least, weren't so happy about his arrival.

The five humans ran on.

He ran for his life, trolls all around.

Guenhwyvar sprang upon one, her claws digging deep ridges as she leaped away, tackling a second beast. And then on she sprang, tearing free of the troll's grasp and darting before another pair, tripping them up as only a feline could.

Whenever she passed through Drizzt's field of vision, the drow nodded appreciatively. Guenhwyvar was keeping him moving, keeping the trolls away.

Even so, as he turned back for a straight run to Nesmé, Drizzt knew it wouldn't be easy. A few heartbeats later, a huge two-headed troll leaped out in the path before him to block his way.

He put an arrow into its belly, staggering it backward, but only a step.

Drizzt didn't slow and didn't draw his scimitars. With every step, he sent off another lightning arrow. One went for the beast's left head and up came its thick hand to block. But the arrow went right through the fleshy limb and exploded into the troll's face, and that head began crying out in outrage that it had been blinded.

Drizzt kept charging, and kept shooting, every arrow going to a head. Sparks flew and missiles stabbed. Barely five feet away, the beast reaching for him, Drizzt held his course and held his nerve and let fly again, his arrow splitting the troll's other head in half.

Still the stubborn beast reached for him, but blinded now, it could not react to his dodge, and could only cry out in surprise when Drizzt sprang upon its huge arm and used that to springboard higher, tucking into a roll right over the troll's shoulder.

He landed behind it, running still, and the blinded troll tried to turn about to pursue, but got slammed by a second troll that had been in close pursuit of Drizzt. Then a third piled in behind and the group went down in a heap.

The drow ran on. He found open ground, but saw then the wolves, off to the side.

He couldn't beat them to the wall.

He lifted the whistle about his neck to his lips and blew out a call to Andahar.

The wolves closed. Drizzt shot the lead one dead, but the others, trained by orcs, did not break and flee.

He shot a second. He saw Andahar, so far away it seemed, striding for him.

A third wolf fell to Taulmaril's lightning.

Andahar loomed closer . . . another stride.

Drizzt fell into a forward roll, a leaping wolf going right over him. He came to his feet with his bow shouldered.

He turned for Andahar, hoping the unicorn was close enough.

He grimaced, nearly cried out, when a wolf leaped for him, too quick for the unicorn, he knew, too close for him to block.

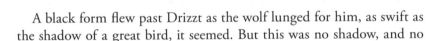

"They are all around," Wulfgar cried to Catti-brie and the others. "A force approaches Nesmé from the north. A full attack!"

Bruenor charged out from the wall, his friends and many Nesmians close behind, to clear the last expanse for the human party rushing in.

"Take 'em in, Rumblebelly," he bade Regis, for the halfling's weapons were all but useless against the huge and mighty trolls.

Wulfgar swatted a troll aside, clearing the last expanse, and the five humans linked up and were ushered through, hurried to the gates.

"Break and go," Bruenor ordered all around, and he and Wulfgar fought a retreating action, axe and warhammer keeping the trolls at bay. And a giant fire elemental came up beside them to help do battle—and how the trolls shied from Catti-brie's pet!

"The dwarf!" Wulfgar cried, pointing to Athrogate.

The black-bearded dwarf came on in full retreat, his spirited boar scrambling back to the city with a host of enemies close behind.

"But where is Drizzt?" Catti-brie cried.

"He'll find his way," Bruenor and Wulfgar answered together, and Bruenor added, "In we go, all. And shut the gates behind us."

Catti-brie couldn't argue, not with the great enemy force approaching the city from the south, not with the horns blowing all around Nesmé as the orcs and goblins and ogres and giants came on. She looked to the south, to the Trollmoors, and whispered a prayer for Drizzt, and reminded herself to trust in that one.

A black form flew past Drizzt as the wolf lunged for him, as swift as the shadow of a great bird, it seemed. But this was no shadow, and no bird, but Guenhwyvar, six hundred pounds of fighting feline, leaping into the canine with such force that she sent the wolf spinning aside, twisting about in the air sidelong. She landed beside it and fell over it in a rolling ball of fury, claws raking, her jaw clamped down upon the beast's neck.

"Run off, Guen," Drizzt cried, for so many more wolves approached. The drow leaped and caught hold of the unicorn's mane as Andahar thundered by, and nimbly pulled himself into his seat.

"Guenhwyvar!" he called out, turning the unicorn to cut between the incoming wolf pack and the battling panther. "Be gone. To your home, my friend."

Andahar leaped away, half the wolves nipping at his flanks, and Guenhwyvar melted away into a gray mist, leaving the other half of the pack spinning around, yapping and nipping in confusion.

With just a few great strides, the unicorn pulled away from the wolf pack, hooves churning up the muddy ground. Drizzt thought to pull forth Taulmaril, but for the immediate run, at least, he could do no more than hold on desperately, as Andahar skidded on the soft ground and nearly toppled many times in that flight.

The orcs had come against Nesmé every day since the first attack, but to Bruenor, this one seemed different, and not just because it was larger, to be sure, with trolls and bog blokes joining in from the south.

Archers let fly, wizards dropped the fireballs, and hurled boulders and volleys of spears and javelins flew against and over Nesmé's battered walls.

But something was different.

Moving to the northeastern corner, where the fighting was heaviest, Bruenor watched the movement of the enemies across the fields. Athrogate and Regis flanked him—they had left Catti-brie back at the south wall, that she could direct her fire elemental, for the beast proved of great value there. Trolls, who could regenerate any wound save that of fire, would not approach it and indeed fled before it. Wulfgar was there beside Catti-brie, in support, and in the hopes that Drizzt would return.

The two dwarves and the halfling passed by some wizards preparing their next magical barrage as a group of goblins approaching their position.

Bruenor put a hand on one of the wizard's shoulder and gave a shake, then a second. "Hold yer spells," he cautioned.

"What? Dwarf, are you mad?" a second wizard exclaimed.

But Bruenor just held his hand up to silence the man and kept looking out, now nodding as he recognized what this was about.

"Hold yer spells," he told them more forcefully, and he yelled out to all around. "Hold yer spells and pick yer shots only when ye know ye canno' miss."

Protests came back at him, but Bruenor, confident now in what he was seeing, would not relent. He ran around, shouting down any wizards he saw beginning some spellcasting, and berating archers who were pulling back far and angling high, sending arrows far out from Nesmé to, usually, land harmlessly into the churned fields.

"They ain't coming," he cried, and the dwarf made such a spectacle of himself that he soon found Jolen Firth standing before him.

"What is this about, fool dwarf?" the First Speaker demanded. "Would you weaken our response—?"

"I'd be savin' yer fool skin, ye mean," Bruenor shot back, and when Jolen Firth started to argue, the dwarf grabbed him by the arm and dragged him to peer out over the battlement. "What d'ye see?" Bruenor demanded.

The First Speaker seemed at a loss. The field before them trembled under the stamp of monstrous boots, the black waves of Many-Arrows' army swarming to and fro.

"Who's in front?" Bruenor clarified, and when Jolen Firth didn't immediately respond, the dwarf yelled, "Goblins. Just goblins!"

"They're baiting us," Athrogate agreed.

"Aye, all our fire and lightning and most 'o the arrows flung out against the fodder," said Bruenor. "Ye see any ladders in them front ranks, Firth? Ye see any rams?"

It was true enough, and soon the First Speaker began nodding his agreement. The fight in the south was real enough, but this main assault was simply a ruse.

"They're trying to exhaust our defenses, mostly the wizards," Regis agreed. "The goblins charge sideways as much as forward."

"What do we do?" Jolen Firth asked Bruenor.

"They're not to come against us fully, but to hoot and holler in the fields as our arrows get spent," the dwarf explained. "Seen this before from the dogs." He didn't add when he had seen it, because few around him would have believed him to be more than three hundred years old, but it hardly mattered.

"And yet," Bruenor finished, "we're still wantin' to kill 'em, eh?"

"Bait 'em back," Athrogate said with a wry smile.

"It's what I'm thinking," said Bruenor.

Jolen Firth looked from one to the other curiously.

"Open yer gates," Bruenor told him.

"Are you mad?"

"Ye boys keep sayin' that and I'm sure to get me feelings hurt," Bruenor replied. "Put yer riders all about and open yer damned gates. Get yer wizards all on the wall above 'em and when enough of them goblins have come in, fill the place outside with fire to stop the press, and shut the gates. Then ye got a fishbowl full o' goblins for easy killing."

Jolen Firth wore a skeptical smile.

"Or are ye as stubborn as them what went afore ye?" Bruenor asked.

But Jolen Firth wasn't, and he offered a nod to Bruenor and rushed down from the wall, calling his elite riders together and moving them off to the sides of the courtyard before the main gates.

A handful of wizards joined Bruenor and his two companions along the parapets topping the two main guard towers, and all around held their breath when the gates creaked open.

"Ye hold yer fireballs until I'm tellin' ye," Bruenor said.

"Moths to the flame," Athrogate said with a laugh. "Fool goblins are sure to be getting their wings burned, bwahahaha!"

It was true enough, they could see, for the goblins, despite their orders to serve as dancing decoys, simply could not resist the invitation. Like water finding a low channel they swarmed about the gates of Nesmé, pressing into the city by the score.

They flooded the courtyard inside the wall, archers turning around to rain death upon them. Then came the horns and the Riders of Nesmé, bursting from the shadows in tight cavalry groups to surge into the crowd, cutting apart the goblin ranks. And how much stronger was that counterpunch when mighty Andahar, bells singing sweetly, thundered up the southern boulevard, bringing Drizzt into the fray!

Up on the wall above the gates, Bruenor and his two friends smiled widely at the drow's devastating charge, at the ranks of goblins fleeing before him, or falling dead to his spinning blades, or getting crushed under Andahar's powerful hooves, or gouged by the unicorn's horn to be thrown high into the air!

"Burn 'em," Bruenor told the wizards, and all five fell into spellcasting, their fireballs erupting one after another right outside of the gates, like a solid dam of flames to hold back the tide.

Jolen Firth's men pressed in to get to those gates and close them. Archers concentrated their fire on the goblins nearest the portal, breaking resistance.

Then down went Bruenor, Athrogate, and Regis, leaping from the parapet into the midst of the swarm, centering the counterpunch that cleared the gates. It was Bruenor himself, with an assist from giant-strong Athrogate, who set the great locking beam back in place, sealing the city, and sealing the fate of the goblins caught inside.

Andahar galloped up to the dwarves, but Drizzt only had time for a quick nod as he leaped from the unicorn's back up to the battlements, Taulmaril in hand. Following the drow's lead, the archers and wizards turned their attention back outside the walls, driving back the monstrous press with furious volleys of missile and magic.

And the courtyard filled with blood, and not just goblin blood.

Soon after, the outside enemy forces turned and fled, and Bruenor nodded at the retreat, and warned Jolen Firth and all around that the enemy would be back for real next time, and in short order.

And so it came, the great assault, for indeed that first attack had been a ploy to expend the city's magical defenses, to wear down wizard and archer alike.

For hours the defenders battled as the city was pressed on all sides, and the fields blackened with orc and goblin dead, with fallen ogres and giants and trolls alike.

Many times were the walls breached, and yet, the Companions of the Hall were always there to meet the enemy, the five friends and Athrogate, and Andahar and Snort, and Guenhwyvar, too, for Drizzt needed her once more.

And when it was done, at long last, the walls of Nesmé stood tall.

Catti-brie's work had just begun, as had that of the other clerics of the city, and of the gravediggers and the groups assigned to throw the dead monsters back over the wall.

"Piling 'em so deep, the wall's getting shorter," Bruenor lamented at one point, standing beside Drizzt and Wulfgar on the north battlement. "The dog's'll be just walking over soon enough."

It was an exaggeration, of course, but not as great an exaggeration as Drizzt wished.

"What's his call, elf?" Bruenor asked, nodding to Athrogate, who searched among the carnage in the courtyard, helping to find the wounded city defenders.

"He is a powerful ally."

"Aye, that much I'm knowin', but why's he here?"

"For Jarlaxle," Drizzt said with a shrug, for he could hardly know the depth of it.

"Then where's Jarlaxle?"

"Watching and soon to come, let us hope."

"Or maybe not," said Wulfgar and the other two looked to him, intrigued by the sly tone of his voice. The barbarian directed their stares out over the wall, to the campfires of the besieging army. "Led by drow, we were told," he reminded them.

"Not Jarlaxle," Drizzt assured him, and he looked to the bloody courtyard again, then out over the wall. "No, not Jarlaxle," he repeated, as much to convince himself as the others, for if indeed Jarlaxle was a part of this tragedy, then everything Drizzt had believed about the mercenary was surely a lie.

A whistle from below directed their attention to Regis. "Jolen Firth will speak with us," the halfling called up.

"Good news, I'm sure," Bruenor muttered.

His sarcasm proved well-placed, they learned a short while later, when they went to meet with the First Speaker, to find him sitting with the five humans that had been chased through the Trollmoors.

Grim-faced, Jolen Firth looked to the woman at his side and nodded.

"Sundabar is besieged," she explained. "By thousands."

"Silverymoon, too," said another.

"Sundabar will not hold much longer," said the first, and she turned her gaze over Bruenor most especially, "And no dwarves will come to her aid. Not Felbarr, nor Mithral Hall. And the enemy count giants among their ranks—hundreds—and aye, they've dragons, too."

"Alas for Luruar," said yet another.

Drizzt noticed the twitch in Bruenor's eye, and realized that his poor friend could hardly draw breath.

Bruenor said not a word as the tale unfolded, the five newcomers detailing the slaughter of the Knights in Silver at the Crossings of the Redrun, the rumors of the death of a dwarf king in the disastrous Battle of the Cold Vale, and the black sky and foul work of the drow—House Do'Urden, they all declared, and one after another cast a stern look Drizzt's way.

"The Silver Marches are lost," one flatly stated, and he might as well have added, "on the signature of a dead dwarf king," Drizzt understood as he studied the grave mask Bruenor's face had become.

"I told ye, elf," Bruenor said as they made their way from the First Speaker's keep. "Smelled it when I was through here a few years ago. Smell o' war, orc war. Ah, but I seen this one comin', don't ye doubt."

He ended with a strange sound, half a growl, half a laugh, and aptly reflecting the look on his face. Studying that expression, Drizzt realized that Bruenor was not dismayed by the events at hand. Far from it, he was seeing this as his chance to make things right.

But he was angry, too, and likely at himself almost as much as at the orcs.

With a look back at Drizzt, gray eyes narrowing and another little growl coming forth, Bruenor slapped his axe over one shoulder and strode away.

"There is not enough orc blood in the world to satisfy him," Wulfgar remarked, and he dropped his hand on Drizzt's shoulder.

Drizzt didn't have an answer for that. He bid Wulfgar a good night then went to his room in the inn called Torch and collapsed on the bed. He let himself fall into a deep reverie, the elven sleep, too exhausted and emotionally overwhelmed to battle the slumber.

He awakened some time later, how long he could not tell, to find Cattibrie against his side, curled about him.

"It's ugly," she whispered.

"It's not just Nesmé."

"I know. I spoke with the others. They remain out at the wall." She snuggled closer, and Drizzt felt her shoulders bob a bit, as if she was stifling a sob.

"What is it?" he asked and kissed her forehead.

She shook her head. "It is me being a fool, and nothing more."

"You have seen much suffering this day."

"I have facilitated much suffering this day."

There it was, a frank admission, a feeling from the heart, and one that had Drizzt sucking in his breath. She had sounded so confident back in Icewind Dale, decrying the orcs and evil giantkind, speaking the word, she claimed, of Mielikki. But now, in the heat of battle, with the harsh realities of burning flesh and the screams of the dying, the pain was clear.

"How many were saved, my love," he whispered. "Should we have let the giants crash through the walls?"

"No," she said weakly, then repeated more forcefully, "No! Of course not." She rolled up over him a bit, looking down at him, her long auburn had tickling his bare shoulder and chest. "My magic should be to create and to heal," she explained. "Not to destroy."

"By destroying evil in the world, are you not facilitating goodness and the peace you seek?"

"Is that not the foolish claims of every general . . ."

" . . . in every war," Drizzt finished with her, for that was one of his favorite sayings.

"They are orcs," the drow went on, thinking to take it back to Mielikki and the divine guidance. "By your own admonishments to me . . ."

Catti-brie kissed him to silence him, and as she pulled back, her fingers gently stroking his cheek, she whispered, "Shut up," but in a sweet voice.

CHAPTER 17

THE MOCKERY

DAHLIA SAT ON THE EDGE OF THE GRAND CANOPIED BED, LOOKING EVERY bit the part of a House Matron Mother in Menzoberranzan in her silky, revealing nightgown, the lace patterns creating spider-like revelations of her flesh.

Looking every bit the part except for the color of her skin, of course. The elf woman's hair had grown out a bit, thick and black and rolling about her strong but delicate shoulders. She had kept the red streaks in that raven mane, for Dahlia now had plenty of time and unlimited resources for such vanities, and indeed, such trivialities seemed the only thing upon which she could focus her thoughts.

Indeed, unless summoned by Matron Mother Baenre to Council, Dahlia had nothing at all to do. She was the leader of House Do'Urden in rank, but not in any practical manner. Not that she understood any of that, in any case.

And so too did Kimmuriel, who hid in the shadows at the edge of Dahlia's room, know. Most of the soldiers in the House held fealty to Bregan D'aerthe, complemented by a sizable force on loan from House Baenre, and with both answering to Andzrel Baenre, the First House's weapons master.

This was all a temporary situation, of course, with the appointed nobles of House Do'Urden—Tiago Baenre and his wife Saribel, patron Tos'un Armgo and his daughter Doum'wielle, among others—off in the east on the surface, directing the war of the Silver Marches.

258

Kimmuriel didn't expect that much would change for Dahlia when the warriors returned, though. She was a mockery in the city, and nothing more. Oh, when Tos'un returned, Dahlia would be called upon to perform as his marital partner, no doubt, and it was likely that Tiago, too, would demand such privileges with Dahlia, as Matron Mother Baenre and Matron Mother Mez'Barris battled over which might produce the heir to Dahlia's unlikely, and likely soon enough to be vacant, throne.

Was Dahlia aware of that?

Was Dahlia aware of anything, really?

Kimmuriel had secretly visited this chamber several times in the last tenday, and had secretly invaded Dahlia's mind, and still he could not be sure.

The psionicist sent out waves of mental energy, imparting suggestions of sleep to the elf woman, and soon after, she rolled herself back onto her bed and sank into deep reverie.

Kimmuriel was there almost immediately, by her side on the edge of the bed. He placed his fingers on her forehead and face, gently, delicately, and created a deep connection.

A swirl of discordance swept about his brain as he melded with the woman. The threads of her thoughts wound and knotted, rolling over each other and going nowhere. Even in her reverie dreams, often the most intense moments of concentration for an elf, Dahlia could not follow a thought anywhere near to conclusion.

He saw a flash of Drizzt, and of Entreri—she was reaching back for a memory, he knew.

And then there was a tunnel, a dead goblin, a pit of writhing snakes . . .

It made no sense, because that was exactly as Dahlia's enemies had planned. In these sessions, Kimmuriel had learned nothing more than the unrelenting confusion swirling within the woman's destroyed mind.

And yet, Matron Mother Baenre was using Dahlia on the Ruling Council. Angry whispers throughout Menzoberranzan spoke of Baenre's power grab by putting nothing more than her own echo in the eighth chair.

With that in mind, Kimmuriel took a different route and used the connection to impart a thought into Dahlia. He gave her an image of Drizzt, violet eyes shining in the starlight, sliding into bed beside her, kissing her, touching her.

He felt the memory unwind within Dahlia, the visceral, telepathic prompting carrying her to a place beyond confusion. She grabbed at Kimmuriel —she believed him to be Drizzt, he knew from her own thoughts.

And she relived a memory, and the knots of discordant thoughts couldn't block her or turn her aside.

She took Kimmuriel with her through that memory.

It wasn't quite what he had intended, but it did answer some questions for Kimmuriel as Dahlia became the aggressor and shoved him over onto his back, climbing atop him with a hunger that denied the fog that had been injected into her mind.

With a blast of psionic energy, he could have blown her aside like a leaf in an autumn gale, but he found himself mesmerized by that which he was witnessing in Dahlia's mind. Her thoughts were jumbled, a piled of interwoven night-crawlers, but he had cleared a path through the knotted worms now, it seemed, and Dahlia ran along it furiously.

"Why, Kimmuriel, I had no idea that you were interested in such carnal pleasures," Gromph Baenre said to the psionicist when Kimmuriel had finished with Dahlia and was preparing to leave House Do'Urden. With the new insight he had gained into the morass that was Dahlia's jumbled mind, Kimmuriel had thought it time to depart Menzoberranzan for a bit and see to his business on the surface. His intended teleportation journey was interrupted, however, by the rather powerful psionic intrusions of Methil El-Viddenvelp, the illithid standing at Gromph's side when the archmage met Kimmuriel in the ante chamber just outside of Dahlia's room.

"I was learning," Kimmuriel replied dryly, "as the subject of an experiment."

"One for which I am sure you could find many willing subjects," Gromph teased.

Kimmuriel stared at him blankly, revealing his boredom. "What do you want, Archmage?"

"I?" Gromph asked innocently. "Why, Master Oblodra, you are the one who is where he does not belong."

Kimmuriel hardly failed to miss the unsubtle reference to his surname—the name of a House Gromph's mother, with the power of the Spider Queen flowing through her, had utterly obliterated. "Bregan D'aerthe has been ordered to serve in House Do'Urden, has it not? I lead that band."

"I am sure that Dahlia . . . Matron Mother Do'Urden, is pleased with your service."

"Your unrelenting quips waste my time, Archmage. Is there something of substance you wish to discuss? Like, perhaps, why you instructed Methil to interrupt my attempt to be gone from this place?"

"Because I wished to speak with you, of course."

"Then speak of something worthy of my attention."

The illithid's tentacles waggled then, and Gromph heard Methil's silent call and nodded.

"Were you impressed with Methil's work on that pathetic creature?" the archmage asked.

"He has twisted her brain in circles," Kimmuriel replied. "That which was Dahlia, the consciousness, the memories, the thought patterns, the expected behaviors, has been wound into indecipherable knots, for the most part. He has driven her quite insane." Kimmuriel cast a disgusted look at the torn and battered illithid.

"Perhaps for Methil El-Viddenvelp, that could be considered propagation," Kimmuriel quipped.

Methil's tentacles wagged at that—Kimmuriel could feel the creature's confusion, then just a hint of anger—and Gromph laughed aloud.

"Well played," the archmage congratulated. "I do not believe that I have ever seen a mind flayer angered before."

I would very much like to discuss with you your actions against Dahlia, Kimmuriel imparted telepathically to the illithid. A most impressive . . . knotting. You have made great gains into the pattern of thoughts and memories, Methil, and for this I salute you and wish to learn from you. Both with Matron Mother Quenthel and now with Dahlia, your work has been magnificent.

Kimmuriel keenly felt the response, which was not humble and not appreciative of the compliment, but rather, was simply an acknowledgement that Methil believed Kimmuriel quite correct in his assessment.

Gromph looked from one to the other, and arched an eyebrow when the illithid bowed to Kimmuriel.

"Do you plan to enlighten me?" asked the archmage, who sensed the exchange but could not quite decipher it.

"Our discussions are quite beyond your understanding at this point in your training, my student," Kimmuriel answered.

Leave us, Kimmuriel silently requested of Methil, and the illithid bowed again and complied. Methil walked to the door, then dematerializing to pass right through the closed door as only a powerful psionicist might.

"Brilliant," Kimmuriel said as he watched Methil leave.

"Rather showy, I think," Gromph said.

Kimmuriel looked at him incredulously.

"Shall I weave a dimensional door to take me from this place when I desire to leave?" the archmage asked.

Kimmuriel shrugged and shook his head, his expression still incredulous, even belittling. "If you so desire."

"And will I then be brilliant in the eyes of Kimmuriel?"

"Showy," the psionicist was quick to answer, and now Gromph wore a confused expression.

"Methil exists more in his mind than in the physical world," Kimmuriel explained. "He exited the room in that manner for the sake of expediency, nothing more."

Gromph glanced back at the door. "Are you saying that it was less effort for the mind flayer to walk through the door than to reach out and open it?"

"Brilliant," Kimmuriel replied, and when Gromph looked back at him, he added, "And brilliant in a manner unlike your magical dweomers each day. For Methil the powers are nearly inexhaustible."

"Will I come to that point, my teacher?" Gromph asked slyly.

"If you do, I will envy you."

Gromph tilted his head to study Kimmuriel. "You cannot do so?"

"Of course I can, but for me, alas, it would be easier to open the door. Not so for Methil."

"Or for many mind flayers, I expect."

"Even among that group, this one is powerful," Kimmuriel answered. "Insane, dangerously so, but powerful. He escapes the bonds of the physical coil with ease, and I believe that his work with your dead mother's head has taught him much of the workings of thought, even above what others of his kind might know." He shook his head and glanced back at Dahlia's bedroom door. "He has piled a million worms in a jumble, and that jumble is Dahlia's mind."

"A jumble in which you took advantage."

"Advantage?" Kimmuriel asked skeptically. "Hardly."

"Ah, yes," said Gromph sarcastically. "You were learning."

"I am always learning. That is why I am the master, and you the student."

Gromph's red eyes flared for just an instant. He was not used to being talked to in that manner, Kimmuriel knew.

"Now that you have learned, you will leave? Or am I to have another lesson?"

If you have the time, Kimmuriel imparted into Gromph's thoughts, then added, Why is Dahlia still here in the city?

"Where should she . . ." Gromph started to respond, but Kimmuriel assailed him with a sudden jolting blast of psionic energy to silence him.

Where should she be? Gromph silently asked him, and he imparted to Kimmuriel that the other nobles of House Do'Urden—Patron Tos'un and his half-breed daughter, Weapons Master Tiago and High Priestess Saribel—were all away at war.

And House Do'Urden Wizard Tsabrak?

Gromph shook his head and laughed. "In Q'Xorlarrin," he said, "with Matron Mother Zeerith, where he will remain, it seems."

Kimmuriel looked at him curiously, trying to unwind that information in light of the timber of Gromph's voice. There was some not-subtle hint there of amusement.

Yes, of course, Kimmuriel realized, Gromph would be glad to see Tsabrak remain outside of Menzoberranzan. The Xorlarrin had channeled the power of Lolth directly, something no drow in Menzoberranzan had done since Matron Mother Baenre had dropped House Oblodra into the chasm of the Clawrift. In enacting the Darkening, Tsabrak Xorlarrin had become a rival to Gromph—though in knowing the two as he did, Kimmuriel doubted that the Xorlarrin would survive the first volleys of a magical battle against Gromph Baenre.

Quenthel, who was the matron mother, had wanted Tsabrak here in Menzoberranzan, Kimmuriel knew, and Gromph had not fought her on that matter. Indeed, from his earlier discussions with Gromph, Kimmuriel had come to believe that it would be a relief to this old drow to have someone else relieve him of much of his responsibilities to the city, particularly as he delved deeper into the art of psionics, the pure magic.

But now the amusement?

"Matron Mother Baenre and Matron Mother Zeerith . . ." Kimmuriel started to ask.

"I'll not speak of it," Gromph replied, then added slyly, "Just so we understand each other."

It was a curious phrase coming from this one, one of those nonsensical surface structures often bandied about by the less intelligent races, but in this context it was, more than that. A hint?

Kimmuriel sent his probing thoughts into Gromph's mind. There were few drow more intelligent than Gromph Baenre, and he could easily defeat such psionic intrusions from afar. Indeed, Kimmuriel wondered whether even an illithid could gain much from stubborn Gromph directly through the meld of its probing tentacles if the archmage mentally tried to block it.

But now those guards were down. Gromph was allowing him in.

Gromph kept it focused, his disciplined mind allowing no side-journeys for the psionicist, who felt almost as if he had mentally entered a long and illustrious hallway, full of statues with teasing placards.

Yes, the psionicist knew immediately, Quenthel and Zeerith were arguing over the disposition of Tsabrak Xorlarrin. With the death of her House's First Priestess, her eldest daughter Berellip, Matron Mother Zeerith had insisted that the Lolth-blessed Tsabrak remain with her as the Archmage of Q'Xorlarrin.

Quenthel had not been amused by this unexpected development, but Gromph surely was.

"Ravel Xorlarrin will become the Wizard of House Do'Urden," Kimmuriel asked as much as stated.

"He is friend to Tiago, and is the brother of Saribel," Gromph replied. "And he is a potent mage in his own right."

"A student of Gromph," Kimmuriel said, and then he learned from his continuing probing of Gromph's mind that the relationship between Gromph and Ravel was more than that, and indeed, that Gromph had helped Ravel find Gauntlgrym. The new wizard of House Do'Urden was indebted to Gromph.

And so it all made sense . . . the archmage's light step and amused tone.

"Well enough," Kimmuriel said and he broke the connection. "But that does not answer my original question as to why Dahlia remains in Menzoberranzan. To serve as your Matron Mother's second on the council, no doubt, but could that not be arranged from afar?"

"She is too valuable to Quenthel," Gromph replied, "and to Lady Lolth."

That last part put the normally unshakable Kimmuriel on his heels a bit.

With a beckoning wave, Gromph invited him back in, and in his thoughts, the archmage revealed to him the battle of the goddesses, Lolth and Mielikki. Dahlia had served Lolth, inadvertently, as the temptress of the rogue, Drizzt Do'Urden.

Drizzt had rejected her.

Mielikki had won.

Lolth did not like losing.

Through Gromph's thoughts—images put there by Methil, Kimmuriel understood—Kimmuriel saw the proxy fight between the goddesses in the primordial chamber of Gauntlgrym, where Mielikki's chosen, Catti-brie, defeated Dahlia in the end.

"And so it is House Do'Urden that leads the charge in the Silver Marches," said Gromph. "The House of heroic Drizzt turning against the kingdoms that once named him as friend, but now will believe that all of it, including the peace with the orcs that Drizzt had counseled King Bruenor to sign, was naught but a longer plan to conquer the region."

Are you implying that this war is nothing more than the petulant fit of a goddess to destroy the reputation of a single rogue? Kimmuriel imparted, but did not dare speak aloud.

"Even Tos'un Armgo," Gromph said with a laugh. "He was placed among the elves of the Glimmerwood with the aid of Drizzt, and he has betrayed them utterly. It is beautifully diabolical, is it not? The edges of Lolth's web have rolled together, and look, she has caught a fly named Drizzt."

Kimmuriel shook his head.

"All of that is merely an added benefit," Gromph assured him. "The war is Lolth's means to unite her people under the matron mother once more, and more fully than at any time since the fall of Yvonnel the Eternal. The city is Quenthel's, wholly. Her alliances are strong and well-placed. None will dare move against her wishes, let alone her House."

"Your House," Kimmuriel corrected, and Gromph's responding shrug spoke volumes to the perceptive psionicist. Gromph was ambivalent about it—all of it.

But why?

He thought of Jarlaxle, who had ever been possessed of a similar malaise regarding the matters of the Menzoberranzan's Houses, and, in general, of the dispossession of drow males, for these were matters for the priestesses and matron mothers . . .

Kimmuriel considered that the eighth month had begun, and the significance of that month to this drow, who served still as the archmage, and thus, the Master of Sorcere, the drow academy of magic.

"The Spider Queen uses the war to unify her people," he said quietly, and Gromph nodded. "The Spider Queen wishes to unify her people at this time because she is engaged in a struggle—not the sideshow that is her fight with Mielikki but a greater struggle to command the domain of Mystra, the domain of Magic, of which Gromph is her most accomplished practitioner."

He nodded again, for this one did not ever feign humility—which was a quality Kimmuriel shared with Gromph.

"And now Gromph seeks the higher magic of the mind, and without, I expect, the blessing of the Spider Queen."

The archmage shrugged.

"You have the lists of the new students entering Sorcere," Kimmuriel said. Gromph nodded.

"More daughters of noble Houses than sons," Kimmuriel guessed, "for the first time in memory, perhaps the first time ever."

"Ever," Gromph confirmed.

"And many more females than males."

Gromph did not need to respond, for now Kimmuriel understood. Almost all of the accomplished wizards of Menzoberranzan were males. True, there were female wizards, but most of those were primarily priestesses who had learned the arts arcane in addition to their long training at Arach-Tinilith. And so, Lady Lolth's move to secure the domain of Mystra had brought hope to many of the males of Menzoberranzan, had brought apparent freedom to House Xorlarrin, the one Noble House where males had been able to achieve such prominent stature, because it was the one noble House where arcane magic did not remain wholly subservient to the divine magic of the priestesses.

The arts arcane had remained the domain of the males throughout the history of Menzoberranzan, their one rung on the city's hierarchical ladder, but now even that was being preempted by the matron mothers. Their daughters would dominate Sorcere, and all that would be left for the males was Melee-Magthere, the school of warriors.

Gromph's sister, Matron Mother Baenre, was strong now, as Gromph had said. The addition of House Do'Urden on the Ruling Council had given her, in essence, two votes of the eight, and the alliances she had formed with the other sitting Houses guaranteed her near absolute control.

"Enough control to make a mockery of it all," Gromph answered, and

Kimmuriel was pleased by the fact that the archmage had just read his thoughts. He had not put up any defenses, for he could have stopped the intrusion easily, and the lack of a psionic block was an invitation indeed, and one that Gromph had been able to answer.

"A mockery of House Do'Urden, a mockery of the Ruling Council," Gromph explained. "They all know it, Matron Mother Mez'Barris of Barrison Del'Armgo most especially. Matron Mother Baenre has shown them that she will pull the strings and they will serve as puppets, and nothing makes that more obvious to the Matron Mothers than when Dahlia, Matron Mother Darthiir Do'Urden, walks into the Ruling Chamber and takes her seat at Lolth's table."

None would go against her, Kimmuriel thought. Not then.

"It is always a temporary thing in Menzoberranzan, is it not?" Gromph asked, reading that thought, and Kimmuriel found the old wizard's words and tone interesting, inviting even.

Quenthel's power would solidify with a victory in the Silver Marches, but perhaps there were some in Menzoberranzan—and indeed, given the dispute over Tsabrak, some in Q'Xorlarrin—who were not thrilled with that possibility.

And perhaps there were some in Lolth's flock who were not quite as hopeful that she would claim Mystra's domain as her own as they once had been.

"Matron Mother Zeerith is adamant about Tsabrak remaining in her fledgling city," Kimmuriel reasoned.

"Her son, Ravel, will replace him in House Do'Urden."

With a wave of his hand, Kimmuriel ended all telepathic intrusions Gromph might attempt from that point on. The psionicist wore a pensive expression as he tried to unwind the subtle hints and inferences of this most surprising meeting. Two of Zeerith's children would sit in high standing in House Do'Urden, then, with Ravel as House Wizard and Saribel as the First Priestess.

It occurred to Kimmuriel that such an unusual arrangement would not grant Zeerith the power she might anticipate, however.

Because Dahlia, named Matron Mother Darthiir, ruled House Do'Urden, and such was the power of the mockery Matron Mother Baenre had enacted that anyone making an attempt on Dahlia's life would surely risk the overwhelming response from House Baenre, perhaps even from Lady Lolth, who was obviously—since it was such a mockery of all that Menzoberranzan knew and believed—pleased with Matron Mother Baenre's choice for the Eighth seat on the Ruling Council.

And Matron Darthiir was the unquestioning puppet of Matron Mother Baenre.

Kimmuriel cast a sly look at Gromph, the companion of Methil El-Viddenvelp.

Or was she?

CHAPTER 18

A DRAGON'S ROAR

THE CITY HAD BEEN BUILT BY DWARVES IN A TIME BEYOND MEMORY, AND
so it remained as one of the strongest fortresses above ground in all
of Faerûn. Double walls surrounded Sundabar, with a deep moat full of
ravenous giant carnivorous eels between them, and ladders and walkways
were properly placed connecting the sentry positions, and easily dropped
if a section of the city was ever lost—which had not happened in the
proud history of the place.

And so mighty Sundabar had withstood the tendays of bombardment,
the continual attacks from the masses of orcs and other foul monsters,
and even the occasional strafing of the white dragons. A thousand were
dead, thrice that number seriously wounded, and twice again that number
carrying injuries that would have sent them running for a cleric in times
when a cleric could be bothered. Indeed, almost half of the twenty-five
thousand citizens of Sundabar bore some wound, and all found their
stomachs growling in hunger as supplies continued to wither.

The great granary caverns below the city had been opened, but mini-
mally, as Knight-Captain Aleina Brightlance, a Knight-in-Silver commander from neighboring Silverymoon, had taken command of the city's
defenses upon request from King Firehelm. It was an unlikely and unusual
request, of course, but one facilitated by an event of extraordinary bad
luck. A huge stone dropped by a great dragon had landed squarely upon
the headquarters of the Sundabar garrison commander, and at a time of

intense planning. The stone had flattened the building, and flattened, too, the Captain of the Guard of Sundabar and most of his officers!

Aleina, fresh from the disaster at the battle known as the Crossings of the Redrun, had been pressed into service, and she went about her tasks with steely determination.

She was not impervious to the cries of the hungry, nor was King Firehelm, son of Frosthelm, son of Helm Dwarf Friend, but Aleina knew, and had convinced the kindly king, that no help would be forthcoming from Sundabar's allies and neighbors. The city had to hold strong until the winter, and then they had to hope that the snows and freezing winds would convince the orcs to give up their siege and return to the north.

Aleina rode the length of the wall as twilight descended over the city this day, the 6th of Eleint, on her magnificent white stallion, calling huzzah to the brave men and women—human and dwarf mostly—who stood tall on the battlements. She winced subtly and did not show her dismay at the fact that many of those guards were not really men or women but children.

The orcs were preparing another charge this day, Aleina believed. They would get to the outer wall, climbing over their dead. Many would gain the wall, and many defenders would die expelling them. The siege had run for six tendays, through midsummer and now into the ninth month.

Aleina passed by a pair of her Silverymoon companions, fellow Knights-in-Silver who had fled the carnage at the Crossings of the Redrun and turned for Sundabar, guessing the course of the orc horde. An elf, Plenerond Silverbell, and his human companion Doughty called back to her with a responding, "Heigh-ho!" and lifted their bows in salute.

Aleina noted the bandages wrapping the fingers of the duo, digits rubbed skinless by a thousand bowshots a day. She grimly nodded as she rode on, taking heart that most of those arrows had probably found a mark. On her last trip to the city's outer wall, she had seen a frost giant lying dead in a heap, its body so thick with arrows that it more resembled a giant porcupine than any humanoid creature. Aleina had noted the fletching on some of those arrows, and had recognized several at least that had come from Plenerond Silverbell's quiver.

King Firehelm awaited her in the city's grand central citadel, a fortress within the fortress. As she rode up to the main door of that massive and impregnable keep, she spotted the king on a balcony, hands gripping an iron rail as he stared out over the city courtyard, the walls, and the bloody fields. He took note of her and looked down with an approving nod, but his eyes went right back to the fields, to the carnage.

His shoulders had slumped under the weight of it all, Aleina thought.

She handed the reins to an attendant at the door and bounded up the stairs to the king's chamber, entering through the door from the hallway just as Firehelm was coming back in from the balcony.

He was a middle-aged man, muscular and tall, with long arms, a thin waist, and broad shoulders, so that when he stood upright with his arms hanging free at his sides, his forearms were far out from his hips indeed. He wore a full beard, still more brown than gray, and had a powerful brow, ridged by what seemed to be a singular eyebrow, knotted above his large and thick nose and beneath his curly long brown locks.

He was dressed in shining plate armor, a thick purple cape above it, and with a thick and heavy bastard sword with an enormous ball pommel set in a scabbard on his right hip—for the King of Sundabar was left-handed. Looking at the formidable weapon, Aleina was amazed he could even draw it, despite his long arms.

But he could, and Firehelm's prowess in battle was well-known to Aleina, though she had rarely ventured to Sundabar before this troubled occasion. The strong man did not shy from battle, and indeed had led many scouting parties against orc raiders over the years.

"My liege," she said with a curt bow.

"Knight-Captain," he replied courteously. "May I extend again my gratitude to you for your service to Sundabar?"

"You were in need and ever has Sundabar been ally to Silverymoon," the Knight-in-Silver replied.

"In need?" he echoed with an amused chuckle. "Truly you have a gift with understatement. I am out of commanders, Knight-Captain," He moved to a seat before the flaming hearth and bade her to sit across from him, and as she made her way over, he retrieved a fancy bottle of fine brandy and poured them both a glass.

"Not true," Aleina said. "Many veterans line your walls, skilled with weapons and in strategy. They were not moved to higher ranks only because your commanders had been in place for so long, until . . ."

She paused, for she didn't want to upset him.

"Until the dragon dropped a stone on the lot of them, eh?" the king

R.A. SALVATORE

finished, and he handed her the glass then lifted his own in a silent toast to the men and woman crushed in that tragedy.

"You have many who are capable, King Firehelm," she said after a sip, "and undeniably, fanatically loyal to king and city. All around the wall, you are well-served by fine warriors."

"Even fine warriors need a fine leader," he said. "Do not underestimate your worth to Sundabar in these dark days for the sake of humility. I'll not hear it, I tell you. Even in the duties of rationing . . ." He paused and smiled as she winced.

"Aye, it wounds you to tell a child to ignore the grumbling in his belly," King Firehelm went on. "And yet you do it, because you have put the counters to work and know the limits of the rations you must enforce to get us to winter. But what then? Will food not be harder to find when the snows lay deep on the land?"

"If the orc siege is broken, then we will find allies," Aleina answered. "The dwarves of . . ."

Firehelm held up his hand. "Speak not of them to me," he warned. "They left your kin—they left you—to die at the Redrun. They huddle in their holes unscarred. And this is their fault to begin with, the fault of old King Bruenor . . ."

"My King, I beg of you to focus your energies on the problems at hand," Aleina dared to interrupt.

"The actions of the dwarves, now and then, are relevant to those problems."

"Indeed, but I trust in King Emerus and King Connerad. If they can find their way from their embattled gates, they will come to Sundabar's aid."

"If they find their way," the king said, his emphasis on the first word revealing his doubts that such would be the case. She understood his frustration—he had expressed it to her several times in recent days as the food grew scarcer and the casualties mounted.

In turn, Aleina had pointed out to Firehelm that a third of Sundabar's citizenry were dwarven, and many had familial connections to the dwarf kingdoms, particularly in Citadel Felbarr.

"In any event, we must hold our ground," Aleina said. "I am concerned with the wizards most of all."

"The shudders of their lightning bolts have rattled my bones," the king replied. "And left many enemies smoking on the field."

"Their strikes have been deadly, indeed," Aleina agreed, "but I have asked them to prepare more defensive magic and they have refused."

"Kabbledar is a stubborn one," King Firehelm admitted, referring to the mage who led Sundabar's small but skilled wizard's guild. "Their lightning strikes down giants and keeps the dragons up high. Their fireballs melt goblins and orcs by the score. What would you have them do?"

"The outer wall is in need of repair at many points," she said and she put her glass down on the small table between the chairs. "We can hold back the hordes for one day while the wizards cast spells of creation, for stone and iron walls, for . . ."

She paused as she followed the king's gaze to her glass, to see the remaining liquid shivering like the waters of a disturbed pond. A moment later, before Aleina could ask what that might be, she felt the tremor, deep within the roots of the citadel, deep within the foundations of Sundabar.

A long and low vibration, it continued and grew in power, like the rumble of a beginning avalanche.

Out on the wall, the defenders also felt the tremble, and knew at once that it was from more than the charge of the orc hordes, who indeed were coming on once more.

"There," Doughty said to Silverbell, grabbing his companion by the arm and turning him about. "By the gods!"

The cry of disbelief reflected well Silverbell's initial reaction, for a strange and terrifying sight indeed was revealed to them at the city's main guard tower beside the northern gate. Tendrils of sparkling lightning climbed up the stone walls, crackling in and out of the arrow slits, blue sparks in the dying daylight. Through one window, the pair caught a glimpse of a soldier scrambling past, trembling and smoking, sparkles of magical lightning biting at him. Atop the tower, the guards watched the magic climb and knew they were doomed—so much so that two leaped from the battlement, flying fifty feet to crash to the ground.

To the side of the tower, further from the two Silverymoon warriors, the wall itself began to shake and tremble, and a great crack appeared in the thick stone.

"They tunneled," Silverbell said, his voice barely audible.

The web of magical lightning crested the tower walls and loosed its fury on the poor soldiers still atop the tower, archers and spotters and a catapult crew. They jolted about weirdly, several fell from the tower, and their clothes began to smoke.

Beyond the tower, the wall collapsed, folding in on itself, stones scraping and smashing against each other, crashing to the ground and splashing into the moat. One large section fell outward, slamming the outer wall, and it too had clearly been compromised.

Their enemies had tunneled under the walls and to the base of the guard tower, and had compromised the substructure!

Cries erupted within the guard tower, as those who had survived the lightning barrage now met living foes, the sounds of battle coming forth.

A barrage of giant boulders slammed against the compromised outer wall, just beyond the fallen inner wall.

And Silverbell spotted it first, a dragon swooping down from on high, wings folded as it fell into a speeding dive and aimed, the elf knew at once, for the compromised wall.

"Wizards!" he cried. "Wizards! Oh archers! To the breach! To the breach!"

He looked out over the wall, to the worg-riding orcs, the giants, and the armored ogres all speeding for that same area, the spot the dragon, a living battering ram, would soon open wide, and Silverbell knew then that Sundabar, this day, was doomed.

They had the guard tower. The city gates fell open and the hordes poured through.

Silverbell and Doughty fired off their remaining arrows, then drew their swords and leaped down to join the wild melee.

But they knew they could not win.

Sundabar could not win.

"To the citadel. To the citadel!" came the cries from every corner of the city, and the infirm and the elderly and the young scrambled to get to the King's Keep, the great citadel that centered the circular city of Sundabar.

And those who could fight, like Silverbell and Doughty, held back the hordes as long as they could, and fought on when the city began to burn about them.

King Firehelm rushed out onto his balcony, and knew despair. A third of the buildings were ablaze, and orcs and goblins swarmed through the streets like a spreading flood.

"Hold the doors!" he shouted down to Aleina and the others, dwarves mostly, battling on the wide stone steps immediately before the great citadel. Every heartbeat they could keep the approach to the great iron doors open meant that another citizen of Sundabar could get in behind the massive walls.

"The caverns," the king remarked, more to himself than to the two guards flanking him. "We must get into the Everfire Caverns and fight our way through the Underdark, yes."

Nodding, that thought in mind, King Firehelm retreated into his room to find his maps for those tunnels flowing from the granaries below the citadel.

No sooner had he left the balcony when a dark shadow passed over it, and the two guards he had left behind were so mesmerized by the sight of the dragon passing so low over the city that neither saw its rider leap free into the air, plummeting to the citadel roof in a death-defying freefall.

At the last moment, barely twenty feet above the building and dropping like a stone, Tiago Baenre tapped his House emblem, thus enacting the magical levitation spell. His descent slowed immediately, but did not end, and he hit the roof hard but fell into a roll both to absorb the shock, and to send him to his desired target.

He came to the edge of the roof directly above the king's balcony and went over without hesitation, pressing his shield underneath the lip of the overhang and calling forth its web-like magic to hold him up as he rolled over and got his feet down over the balcony, still a dozen feet below them.

"Hey!" one of the guards cried out, at last noticing him.

Tiago released the magic of the shield and dropped before the man, and even as he lightly touched down, his sword Lullaby was already in swift motion, taking aside the guard's thrusting spear with practiced ease, then rolling over the shaft to slash at the man's upper arm.

The guard grunted and leaped back, blood showing on his sleeve just below his shoulder. He called to his companion, who rushed to his side, and thrust forth again with his spear.

Tiago blocked it with Spiderweb, his shield, and drove it down low and to his left, then chopped down with his sword along the shaft, splintering the spear in half.

To his credit, the guard played the hand perfectly, ignoring the break and stabbing ahead again with the makeshift spear that was the sharp shaft. He thought he had a hit, and against a lesser warrior he surely would have, but Tiago continued his turn behind the sword chop, rolling right around just a hand's breadth ahead of the pursuing weapon.

The drow went down low as he turned, then crouched even lower, bending over at the waist, as he came around, lifting his left leg up fast in a diagonal kick that caught the pursuing and overbalancing guard under the ribs and drove him up and over the railing. He grabbed for it futilely, but toppled over, plummeting to his death.

Tiago paid him no heed at all, coming around with Lullaby slashing forward in perfect timing to take aside the sword of the second guard.

Tiago cut straight across, right to left, then backhanded down on the return, interrupting the flow before the blade went too low, to stab the sword straight ahead. Pressing furiously, the drow rushed ahead behind the stab, and the sentry, up on his toes and with his hips thrown back, barely got his own shield in line to brace against the weight of Tiago's bull rush. Spiderweb and the guard's shield crashed together hard, though given the cushiony composition of Tiago's shield, it was a muffled sound.

The guard moved to leap back and get his feet under him, but he didn't understand the properties of Tiago's shield, for it held on, and as he jumped back, Tiago tugged hard.

The guard landed on his toes and stutter-stepped in an attempt to fully regain his balance, but on came the drow. Tiago released the shield's grip with a mere thought and raced ahead, stabbing low, rolling his sword over the desperate parry.

Down came the guard's shield right behind his diving sword, and wisely so, but again, the superior Tiago simply retracted his blade and rolled about over the shield, sending Spiderweb around to bat the shield further across the guard's body.

Tiago stabbed out to the side, right under his own shield arm, Lullaby slashing into the guard's elbow.

The man yelped in pain and leaped away, but the drow was with him, Lullaby poking in again over the drooping shield—drooping because of the wounded elbow and because of the insidious poison Lullaby injected. A great weariness fell over the guard and his movements slowed, just a bit.

Even at full speed, the guard was no match for Tiago. Sluggish as he now was, with drow poison coursing his veins, Tiago simply overwhelmed him.

Lullaby flashed in under the guard's raised shield, then again above it as the guard, stabbed in the gut, reflexively brought the shield slamming down.

Out to the left went Lullaby, a feint that fooled the guard, who over-reacted in his mounting desperation, throwing both his sword and shield out that way to try to block.

But the drow's sword wasn't there, and it came in fast behind the double block, opening the man's throat.

The poor guard staggered back, gasping and coughing, and his legs gave out before him.

"By the gods," came a cry from inside the room, King Firehelm fast returning, huge sword in hand. "Murderous drow!"

As if to confirm the accusation, Tiago shrugged and spun, Lullaby coming across perfectly, the fine blade slicing through flesh and bone with ease.

As King Firehelm leaped onto the balcony, the dead guard fell face down to the floor.

"Dog!" the king howled and leaped in, a great two-handed overhead chop crashing down for Tiago's head.

Up went Spiderweb above Tiago's head to block, and a lesser shield would have shattered under the weight of the blow. But not only did Spiderweb survive the impact, its magical properties helped mitigate the weight of the blow, and that, along with Tiago's perfectly timed drop to his knees, left the drow fully uninjured from the powerful attack.

Convinced this brute of a man would simply hoist him from the ground with his next swing, Tiago didn't even try to stick Spiderweb to that huge sword. Instead he turned Firehelm's strength against the man.

Up and around went the large blade, now sweeping in from Tiago's left. The drow swung about and brought Spiderweb down at the last moment to catch the attack, and Firehelm's follow-through actually lifted Tiago back to his feet, and there, the drow stepped back and slid off as the sword passed before him harmlessly.

Tiago rolled around it with sudden ferocity, and out shot his sword as he came fully around, stabbing Firehelm in the chest. Tiago retracted immediately and sent his blade in a short vertical spin just as Firehelm let go of his own sword with one hand and reached out to throttle Tiago.

Fingers went flying free and Firehelm howled and retracted his hand, then tried to get his sword back in line as Lullaby came ahead once, twice, and thrice, stabbing hard.

Finally, Firehelm was in position to block, but Tiago wasn't there.

The drow rolled right around the staggering, wounded king, and on the completed turn, Lullaby swept down across the back of Firehelm's knees.

And around Tiago went again, a complete spin, and this time the fine blade slashed the King of Sundabar across the lower back.

Down went Firehelm to his knees, falling forward to brace himself on the floor with a fingerless hand. Growling, the stubborn warrior king feebly stabbed out underneath his horizontal torso with his sword. The blade hit nothing, for there was nothing to hit, and the confused Firehelm waved it about.

But Tiago was back the other way, on the other side and up near Firehelm's shoulder, Lullaby up high.

With unerring aim, Tiago brought it down.

He sheathed Lullaby and picked up the head of King Firehelm from the floor of the balcony, then leaped to the stone railing overlooking the citadel's front gates, far, far below.

But not so far that the city defenders down there didn't hear the drow's victorious cry, or didn't see the specter of Tiago Baenre, standing tall on the balcony, holding high the head of the King of Sundabar.

In the room behind Tiago, the doors banged open and many soldiers charged in. The dark elf turned to regard them, and then looked at them with a bit of amusement.

With a smile and a salute, Tiago stepped back off the railing and dropped from their sight.

A moment later, as the furious court guards rushed out onto the balcony and to their fallen, headless King, Tiago came back into view, but now astride the dragon, and now with the white horned head of Arauthator staring at the fools.

Icy breath bit at them and drove them back and froze the blood in their veins.

Across the burning city went Tiago and his flying mount, all the while with the head of King Firehelm held high for all to see, for orcs and goblins, ogres and giants to cheer, and for humans and dwarves and other citizens of Sundabar to look on and despair.

Many citizens of Sundabar got into the safety of the citadel that day, including Aleina Brightblade, and the great impregnable iron gates banged closed. They had escaped, momentarily at least.

But the city was lost and in flames, and nearly ten thousand citizens of proud Sundabar lay dead, or were trapped outside to be hunted down and slaughtered.

The flames rose high from every corner of the city.

Black smoke curled into the sky, rising up through that long night to thicken the Darkening and dimming the morning's sun even more.

CHAPTER 19

UNDRESSED

Deliver this to Zee," the copper-haired Mickey told the little girl. She handed over a fairly large box, and it was far from empty.

The child, who had told Mickey that her name was Catti, took the box and immediately bent low under the weight, then fought to ease it down to the floor. "Too heavy, lady," she whimpered.

Mickey measured every movement, the sinking box of goods, the struggle to stop it from merely crashing to the floor. An impressive performance, she thought, so natural and even-flowing.

With a disgusted snort, the shopkeeper reached into the box and pulled forth a large metal candelabra. "There," she said. "You can carry it now. Tell Zee I will return her candelabra at a later time, and that you were too pathetic to carry it all."

"Yes, lady," Catti whispered and she gathered up the box and pushed her way out the door.

Mickey watched her go, shaking her head and wondering what the child would taste like. She went to the secret stairs at the back of her shop and down to the basement, then through a concealed door and the tunnel she had dug under Wall's Around to the basement of A Pocketful of Zzzzs.

Moments later, she was in her natural form, crouched in a wide chamber behind a curtain colored to look like a basement wall. She heard the stairs creaking under footfalls, heard Lady Zee's voice.

"My but you are so clean for a waif without a home," she said. They were in the room beyond the curtain now, not far.

"I try to bathe where I can find water, lady. Miss Mickey would not approve."

"And your teeth are so straight and white!" Lady Zee exclaimed. "I would not expect that of a homeless waif."

"They . . . they hurt, lady," the child stammered.

"It is a minor mistake," Lady Zee explained. "Nothing to fret about."

"Mistake?"

Mickey gave a toothy grin at the slight hint of doubt in the little girl's tone. She reached forth with one deadly claw and hooked the curtain, pulling it taut.

"You disguised so much and so well," Lady Zee went on. "But the scent . . . ah, the unusual scent, and one that is surely that of a male and no little girl."

The curtain came down and the little girl whirled about, and stood face to-snout with a dragon, a true dragon, copper scales glistening in the meager candlelight of Lady Zee's basement.

The child didn't shriek and didn't attempt to flee, and didn't even tremble in terror.

She merely sighed.

"Well?" Lady Zee asked and the little girl who was not a little girl turned around to regard her.

Behind her, the dragon inhaled and blew forth a cone of heavy breath, one that would slow down its targets as if they were running, or striking, underwater.

"Garlic," the little girl mouthed as the dragon's breath washed over her.

"I have a different cloud I can put over you," Mickey the dragon warned, and the little girl nodded, slowly, her expression showing that she was well aware of the line of acid a copper dragon could spit from its mouth.

She looked around, her movements exaggerated and sluggish. The basement was full of crates and items of many shapes and sizes, as Lady Zee, often changed her wares. She pointed to a fancy dressing screen, looked to Lady Zee and shrugged questioningly.

The woman extended her hand, inviting the girl to go behind it.

Mickey and Lady Zee watched the shadow of their captive behind the screen. She pulled the dress up over her head and tossed it over the top. The two looked to each other with a shrug, noting that the little girl wasn't moving slowly at all, and her earlier drawl and movements had been certainly faked.

Faked, like everything else about this curious little creature.

From nowhere, it seemed, the little silhouette brought forth a gigantic hat with a gigantic feather sticking from it, and she crouched as she put it on her head, then slid her hands down the side of her face and seemed to be removing a mask. When she stood up straight once more, she was fully a foot taller, at least, and when she came out around the screen, more than her height and clothes had changed, indeed!

Her gender had changed, as the dragons had expected, but so had her hair color, blond to white, and her skin color, fleshy pink to ebon black.

"Ladies, it has been far too long," Jarlaxle said with an exaggerated bow, sweeping his hat across the floor.

"Jarlaxle, Jarlaxle," laughed Lady Zee as a swirling wind engulfed the dragon beside her, and within the tumult of the swirl, the beast became a human woman once more, but now one without any clothes, which didn't seem to bother her in the least.

"I should eat you just for deceiving us," said the former dragon.

"And I should insult you for your silly names," the drow mercenary replied. "Mickey? Really Tazmikella, that is a name more fitting a halfling."

"I told you as much, sister," Lady Zee said to Tazmikella.

"And you, Ilnezhara," Jarlaxle said. "Lady Zee?"

"Enough, drow," Tazmikella warned. "I am still considering the method of your demise."

"Beautiful Tazmikella, you wound me," Jarlaxle said.

"I could . . ."

"And to think that I have come here out of concern for you," the drow dramatically added. "The idiot king is stirring, I fear, and he is no Dragonsbane, but wishes to be, whatever the course to get there."

"You came here to warn us of King Frostmantle?" Ilnezhara asked skeptically.

"No," Jarlaxle admitted. "But once here, I have learned that he is watching you two with concern. Why I came here in the first place will also concern you, I assure you."

"Do tell," the dragon sisters said in unison.

Brother Afafrenfere kept his head down as he walked into the candlelit private prayer chamber of the masters of the Monastery of the Yellow Rose.

They were in there, all of them, and before he even moved to the solitary chair set before the long table, he heard the voice of Perrywinkle Shin, Master of Summer, the highest ranking active monk in the grand monastery.

They talked among themselves even after Brother Afafrenfere took his seat—and two minor masters came over to crouch on either side of him, chanting into his ears so that he could not eavesdrop on the conversation at the table. Still, Afafrenfere could make out the tone of the gathered leaders, and it was a somber one indeed.

Were they going to dismiss him for his indiscretions? He had betrayed the order, after all, and others had been banished for less.

Or perhaps they would go further than that, the monk wondered, and worried. The Order of the Yellow Rose was not a vindictive group, nor particularly vicious, but they adhered to their laws and rules—if Afafrenfere's betrayal warranted a severe punishment, the masters would oblige.

If it warranted a sentence of death, he would be killed, mercifully perhaps, but he would be put to death.

The monk found it hard to draw breath, and he felt foolish indeed for returning to this place. What was he thinking? He had run to the Shadowfell and forsaken his vows. He had committed acts unlawful by the rules of the Order of the Yellow Rose, and he had admitted as much, in great detail, upon his return.

"Fool," he whispered under his breath.

"Brother Afafrenfere," Master Perrywinkle called down from the table, which was on a stage raised as high as Afafrenfere's waist, putting its floor at eye level for the seated monk.

Afafrenfere looked up to regard the man, who was past middle age, but had stayed lean and strong, clearly. His hair was silver, receding far back on his head now, but his eyes remained sharp and sparkling blue, and seemed to look right through Afafrenfere. Afafrenfere held no illusions. With his training, Perrywinkle could leap over that table and fall over Afafrenfere, and easily throttle him in a matter of heartbeats.

"Stand," Perrywinkle instructed, and Afafrenfere popped up straight. The monks flanking him moved back several steps.

"For days now, we have watched your progress, young brother," Perrywinkle went on. "Your friend is intemperate and will not remain here much longer."

"Yes, Master."

"You understand?"

"Of course, Master."

"But what are we to do with you?" asked the woman to Perrywinkle's left, Savahn, who was Mistress of the East Wind.

"I accept whatever you choose, Mistress," Afafrenfere humbly replied.

"Indeed," said Perrywinkle, "and that humility and honesty is the only reason you were allowed back into the monastery in the first place. And it is the only reason that you are to be allowed back into the Order at all."

"Master?" Afafrenfere asked, though he could hardly breathe.

"We will reinstate you, fully," Perrywinkle replied, and then he cut short the smile widening on Afafrenfere's face by adding, "in time and on condition."

"Yes, Master," Afafrenfere said, and he lowered his gaze to the floor.

"You have lived an interesting life, young one," came a voice from the side, a voice Afafrenfere did not recognize, but one that spoke of glory and the higher planes of existence, a voice so sweet, though it was not, and so solid, though it was not, that it seemed a disembodied, almost godly thing.

Despite his better judgment, Brother Afafrenfere glanced to the side, to the speaker, and he sucked in his breath in shock.

There stood a man, and yet not so, as this figure didn't seem to quite fit in the corporeal surroundings, as if he could walk through the wall, or fall through the floor. He seemed less than human, and yet so much more, a man who had ascended to a higher level of being. He was old, so old, old enough to know the years before the Spellplague. He was so thin, little more than skin and bones he seemed, beneath the white robe he wore, and yet, there was a solidity about him that mocked Afafrenfere's muscular frame.

"Grandmaster Kane," Brother Afafrenfere meekly whispered.

"Young Brother Afafrenfere," Kane replied bending at the waist. His legs remained perfectly straight, and yet the impossibly nimble man went so low that he tapped his forehead on the stone floor—and all in perfect balance!

Afafrenfere didn't know what to do. This was Kane, friend of King Gareth Dragonsbane, a legend in the Bloodstone Lands who had done battle with Zhengyi the Witch King, who had fought three dragons at Goliad in the triumphant victory of King Gareth over the undead legions of Vaasa. That was a hundred and thirty years before, and even then, Kane had been an old man!

It was a common rumor about the monastery that death had never found Kane, that the Grandmaster of Flowers had transcended the mortal coil through sheer meditation and force of will, to become a creature akin to the immortals of the higher planes. It was said that still he walked the halls of the Monastery of the Yellow Rose in the early hours of the morning, taking in the smells and sights to remind himself always of his previous existence in the realm of mortal men.

But those were rumors, whispered campfire tales told to younger brothers, Afafrenfere had thought, and nothing literally true.

Now he knew better. This was Kane. This had to be Kane.

Afafrenfere felt the urge to fall back into the chair, then out of the chair to his knees, and he did not fight it, and soon prostrated himself on the ground, his head to the distant specter.

There came some mumbling among those masters at the table on the dais, but Afafrenfere couldn't make it out—and didn't care anyway.

This was Grandmaster Kane. Any less a show of devotion and humility before this man who was greater than a man rang as an insult in the ears of Brother Afafrenfere.

He heard no footsteps, but he felt a light touch on the back of his head. "Rise," Kane bade him.

Before Afafrenfere could move, he felt himself doing just that, lifting off the floor to stand upright before the Grandmaster, as if some telekinetic power had simply hoisted him.

Kane motioned to the chair, and Afafrenfere fell back into it.

"I have listened to your conversations with your dwarf friend," Kane explained. "I watched your arrival before our gates, the drow elf beside you, sitting astride a steed of the lower planes."

Afafrenfere's eyes went wide.

"Jarlaxle, yes?" Kane asked.

Afafrenfere swallowed hard and managed a slight nod.

"I know him," Grandmaster Kane explained. "Indeed, I once battled him and his companion, a man named Artemis Entreri."

Afafrenfere swallowed hard again to steady himself, and managed to squeak out, "I know Entreri."

"He is still alive?"

The young monk nodded.

"Resourceful," Grandmaster Kane remarked. "No doubt Jarlaxle the trickster has played a role in that."

"Grandmaster," Afafrenfere said, "I did not know that he was an enemy . . ."

"He is no enemy," Kane replied. "Be at ease, brother. As I said, I have listened to your conversations with the dwarf. More than that, I have peered into your soul. You have returned here repentant, with good intentions and a desire to redeem yourself."

"I have, Grandmaster."

Grandmaster Kane turned to Perrywinkle. "You have prepared the items?"

The Master of Summer motioned to Savahn, who rose and moved around the table, lightly hopping down to the floor and moving on bare feet to Grandmaster Kane. In trembling hands—trembling hands from a Mistress of the East Wind—she held forth a pair of clear gems, diamonds perhaps, set on fine silken cords, which Kane took, and motioned her away.

"Jarlaxle will return for you," Kane went on. "And he will not be alone."

"He will return for Ambergris . . . the dwarf," Afafrenfere quickly corrected.

"For both of you."

Afafrenfere, his expression nearing one of panic, looked up to Master Perrywinkle. "I wish to remain here, in the monastery," he gasped.

"The choice of course will be yours," Grandmaster Kane answered. "But you would be doing a great service to us all if you went with Jarlaxle."

Afafrenfere's incredulous expression was all the query Kane needed.

"This is a time of great upheaval," the Grandmaster of Flowers explained. "Titanic events gather momentum beyond our walls, beyond the Bloodstone Lands, indeed, beyond this plane. There are greater stories being written around the edges of the conflicts Jarlaxle seeks than those he understands. Stories of dragons, stories of gods. He will be there, in the middle of it, no doubt, because that is his way."

Afafrenfere's mouth moved as he tried to form words, as he tried to find some answer, or some question even, to this remarkable and cryptic hint.

"It will be your penance, brother," Master Perrywinkle said from the table.

"We would have eyes in the midst of this storm, brother," Grandmaster Kane explained. "Good fortune has returned you to us at just this time."

"You wish me to go with Jarlaxle?"

"Yes."

"Then I will go, without question."

"Tell him, Grandmaster Kane, I beg," said Perrywinkle.

Kane nodded deferentially. "It is unlikely you will survive," he said.

Afafrenfere stiffened and set his jaw. "If that is my fate and it is for the good of the Order, then so be it," he said without a quiver in his voice.

"Though you may," Kane went on, and he gave a little laugh and held out one of the circlets to Afafrenfere. "You will be with Jarlaxle, after all, and that one has escaped more certain death than perhaps any mortal alive."

He motioned to the silken cord. "Tie it about your head, with the diamond set here," he said, and poked Afafrenfere in the center of his forehead.

As Afafrenfere tied the circlet about his head, Kane did likewise.

"You will not be alone, brother," Grandmaster Kane said. "You will be as my eyes and ears, and I will help guide you as you walk the path of the Yellow Rose."

"I am filled with envy," Master Perrywinkle admitted, and the others at the table murmured similar sentiments, and with sincerity, Afafrenfere believed.

"What am I to do?" the confused young brother asked.

"That which is right," Kane answered simply, and he bowed and simply dematerialized, his body shattering, it seemed, into a cascade of small sparkling lights, like the wet petals of a flower floating down through the crystalline light of a magical chandelier.

To the floor, they settled, and then through the floor, and Kane was gone.

Afafrenfere stood silent, mouth hanging open, but at the table, expressions of cheer and awe, even some clapping, commenced, the masters leaping up as one and rushing to the spot where the Grandmaster of Flowers had vanished.

"Envious, oh I must pray," one master said, patting Afafrenfere on the shoulder.

"Good fortune has found its way to you this day," said Mistress Savahn. "That you are friends with that rogue dark elf, who will stick his inquisitive nose into the midst of events far greater than he." She walked up and kissed Afafrenfere on the cheek. "If you survive this," she whispered so that only he could hear beyond the murmur of the others, who were studying the spot where Kane had disappeared, "you will return here much greater in knowledge and power than you can imagine." She looked to the dais. "You will find a seat at that table, young brother."

Afafrenfere's expression did not, could not, change.

"If you survive," Mistress Savahn added, and she moved to join the others.

"Whites?" Tazmikella asked. The two dragons and Jarlaxle were out of the city now, and settled into the manor house the dragon sisters shared beyond Helgabal's walls.

"So I am told," Jarlaxle replied. "I have not seen them, but given the location, and the monsters in questions, it would make sense."

"Arauthator and Arveiaturace," Ilnezhara said with obvious disgust.

"Not Arveiaturace, but more likely one of their foul offspring," said Tazmikella. "Arauthator, certainly, considering the region in question and that one's undying savagery and insatiable hunger."

"And the other," Ilnezhara remarked. "Young and full of mischief."

"Young and ambitious, you mean," Tazmikella corrected. "Seeking the favor of his or her vicious father, and in Arauthator's own lands."

Jarlaxle noted the dragon's incredulous tone, and understood that such an event was not common. White dragons were not as gregarious as some of the other dragonkind, he knew, and, given Tazmikella's tone, this Arauthator was solitary even beyond that reputation.

"Both ambitious, it would seem," Tazmikella said.

"They seek the favor of that five-headed abomination," agreed her sister.

It wasn't often that anything shocked Jarlaxle, who had lived many centuries and had seen most of what the world could offer, so he believed, but as he digested Ilnezhara's words, and recognized the being to which she referred, his jaw did droop open.

"If they gather enough treasure, they believe they can bring it all back," Tazmikella explained to him, with his stunned expression.

"They?"

"Our chromatic cousins," Ilnezhara said with clear distaste.

Jarlaxle was not very well-versed in dragonkind, but he knew enough to understand the delineation. There were many different kinds and flavors of dragons in Faerûn, but they fell into two distinct types: chromatic and metallic, with five major variations of each: black, white, blue, green, and the great red dragons for the former; bronze, brass, silver, gold and, like the sisters before him, copper, for the latter—though the drow had heard rumors of strange hybrid offspring between the ten primary forms.

"It all?" Jarlaxle weakly prompted.

Ilnezhara and Tazmikella looked at him and sighed.

"Tiamat?" he asked in a whisper. Indeed, he could hardly speak the name. Tiamat was the hurricane, the earthquake, the volcano, the blizzard, and the poison. The goddess of dragons, who could unmake the world, or lay it all to waste, at least!

"Perhaps we should investigate this, sister," Ilnezhara remarked.

"We have our lives here," Tazmikella argued. "We have barely returned for this new adventure in Heliogabalus . . ."

"Helgabal," Jarlaxle corrected, drawing stern looks from the both of them.

"But already they are suspicious," Ilnezhara reminded. "Frostmantle is a weasely king, but not without his resources, you must admit. Were he to determine the truth of us, he would use every warrior at his disposal to strike at us, for if he could slay us, or even drive us from his city, then he would better fit the crown of Dragonsbane."

"Dragonsbane was no enemy to us."

"Dragonsbane tolerated us when he learned the truth, and nothing more," Ilnezhara scoffed. "And only because he needed us to help him keep a watchful eye on Vaasa in the late years of his life. Why, he even refused your offer to bed him."

"Fool!" Jarlaxle interrupted loudly, again drawing stern glances, but this time, he merely grinned and tipped his hat in honest salute to the sisters.

"Jarlaxle thinks himself charming," Tazmikella said, turning back to her sister.

"He is," said Ilnezhara.

"He hopes to charm us now, perhaps to be rewarded for his flattery."

"Oh, he will be," Ilnezhara replied, and she tossed a wink at the drow, who sat back and folded his hands behind his head.

"Except," Ilnezhara went on as soon as Jarlaxle got comfortable—perhaps a bit too comfortable.

"Yes," her sister prompted.

"It is an amazing coincidence, is it not, that Jarlaxle comes back to us at precisely the moment that King Frostmantle's guards grow curious?"

"Oh, I had not thought of that, sister," Tazmikella agreed, though of course, she had, and both swiveled their heads, very reptile-like, to regard the drow.

"A fortunate break for both of us," Jarlaxle said with a grin.

"Do tell," they said together.

"The fates have found for you a path out of here, and to greater adventure and more important duties, apparently, and just at a time when perhaps you should be taking leave of this miserable city and her miserable king."

"Oh, good fortune indeed," they both said together, with dripping sarcasm.

Jarlaxle shrugged and smiled.

He knew they wouldn't kill him.

He hoped they would reward him.

"Are ye to pray the whole o' the day then?" Ambergris asked her friend when she caught up to him in the garden on the flat roof of one of the side wings of the grand monastery. She had to ask him four times before he opened an eye and seemed to register that she was even there.

"Not prayer," he replied, coming slowly from his trance. "I am meditating on the teachings of my order."

"Readin' yer own mind, are ye?" the dwarf asked, and laughed heartily.

"You wager on me when I am fighting," the monk reminded.

"Seems a good bet."

"I wage those battles a thousand times in my mind for every one I fight," Afafrenfere explained. "I see the movements of my enemies. I see my responses and put them into my arms and legs as surely as if I were waging physical battle instead of mental."

Ambergris shrugged. "Well, whate'er ye're doing, it works, I admit. But what's it about now? Since ye met with them masters, ye've not been much seen."

Afafrenfere held up his hand to stop her, and she quieted and regarded him curiously.

"I prepare myself," he replied. "I will depart this place when Jarlaxle returns, to take to the road with you once more."

"Heigh-ho!" Ambergris blurted and she clapped her thick hands together loudly. "We'll find a road o' profit and adventure, don't ye doubt."

"Adventure," Afafrenfere agreed.

Ambergris looked at him curiously. "Ah, but ye're one of them robe-wearers takin' a vow o' poverty, are ye?" She paused and nodded, then smiled toothily. "Well good. More for Ambergris. Haha!"

Afafrenfere closed his eyes and let her voice fade away as he fell once more into his thoughts to prepare himself for the road ahead.

You are not alone, young brother, he heard in his head, the comforting thoughts of Grandmaster Kane, and the diamond pressed against his forehead glowed with warmth.

CHAPTER 20

BEST OF BAD CHOICES

ＴHE HORDE CAME ON AGAIN, ROARING WITH GLEE AS THE ARCHERS AND
wizards of Nesmé cut them down by the score. Every day, the carnage
repeated, and yet, despite the mounds of bodies blackening the fields on
every side of the city, the orc ranks did not greatly thin.

Indeed, now the trolls and bog blokes had joined in, and Nesmé was as
often pressed from the moors of the south as from the north and east.

Inside the city wall, however, attrition mounted.

Drizzt, Catti-brie, and the others relaxed together in the shadow of the
southern gate tower during one of the few true respites.

"Nesmé's a dead town if none're coming to help," Bruenor lamented.

"Hold until the first snows and th'orcs'll be running away," Athrogate replied.

"Eleasis's turned to Eleint," Bruenor reminded, referring to the eighth
and ninth months of the year. "Another month at least, more likely two,
afore we're seeing the first o' the snows, and another month after that when
the turn to winter's enough to chase the hungry dogs away."

"Pray for an early winter then," said Regis.

"Even a month might be too long for Nesmé," Wulfgar added. "All
the priests in the city are busy with folk already wounded, day and
night, and more join those ranks with every attack. More are laying
down than standing up, I fear."

"Help'll come," Bruenor said determinedly, and he looked to the north,
the direction of Mithral Hall, they all knew.

"That doesn't look promising," Regis remarked, and they all turned to him, then followed his gaze and nod across the courtyard, to First Speaker Jolen Firth and one of the wizards who had stood with Catti-brie in the first assault, the older woman so proficient with the spell of digging. The grim expressions on the faces of the pair explained Regis's words, surely.

"What news?" Drizzt asked as they approached.

Jolen Firth turned to the mage.

"I have gone out this day with spells of far-seeing," the old woman explained. "Won't be no help coming, to be sure."

"The dwarves remain in their holes," said the First Speaker. "And each with an army camped about their gates. Is there no end to the number of orcs in the world?"

"One's too many for me own tastes," Bruenor muttered, and Drizzt noted an accusatory look coming his way from his dwarf friend. That treaty, Drizzt understood, continued to play hard on poor Bruenor in these difficult days.

"Silverymoon is sorely pressed, and has suffered greatly." Jolen Firth went on. "And Sundabar . . ." He paused and swallowed hard and the companions understood the gravity of what might come next by the moisture apparent in the proud man's eyes.

"Sundabar has fallen," he said. "The city is burning, the walls destroyed. I know not how many thousands have perished—many took refuge in the great citadel that centers the city, it is rumored."

"Aye, I've seen them in there, with thousands of orcs all around, just outside the place," said the old woman. "They're not to get out."

"They will abandon the citadel in short order, no doubt," Jolen Firth explained, "for the Everfire Caverns below. They cannot hold long, and now that Many-Arrows has taken the city about them, the winter will not drive the orcs away."

"And so the orcs will gain the citadel," Regis reasoned.

"Aye, and so we've a new orc fortress in our midst," said Bruenor, and he kicked at the ground.

"We might break out to the west," Regis offered.

"To the Uthgardt tribes, out from under this unnatural darkness," Wulfgar added.

"Surrender Nesmé?" Jolen Firth asked, his voice full of doubt, even hints of outrage.

"How long can you hold?" Regis asked. "And even if winter brings respite, with Sundabar . . ."

"No," Jolen Firth replied evenly and with finality. "We would die here, to a man, before we would surrender."

"When Obould first came, the city was abandoned," Drizzt reminded.

"A different time," Jolen Firth immediately argued. "And in that time, Silverymoon could come to our aid, and so the city would be retaken in short order."

"Nesmé was but a town in those days," the old mage added. "With barely a wall to speak of. Ah, but we didn't go and build the fortress just to run away."

"Well, we can't all be sitting still and hopin' for snow," Bruenor decided. "We got to go, elf." He looked about to his friends, and to Athrogate. "We'll fight our way to Mithral Hall and help King Connerad shake off th'orc stench. Then we'll hit them orcs, and hard, and each town freed will add to our numbers."

"A fine plan," said Jolen Firth.

"You'll not get near to Mithral Hall if you take the whole of Nesmé with you," the old woman said. "In my spells, I have seen that place, too, and the orcs are thick about it. Thousands and thousands! Many march south to Silverymoon, but many more come back from the front lines to settle about the halls of the dwarves. Nay, you'll get nowhere near those gates, and the dwarves wouldn't open them if you did."

Bruenor looked to Drizzt.

"West," Drizzt said, to Bruenor and to Jolen Firth. "It seems the only way."

The First Speaker was about to argue once more, his expression growing angry, when Regis interjected, "We can get to Mithral Hall."

All eyes turned on him, and he seemed surprised by the revelation he had just shared.

"You can, perhaps, in disguise," said Drizzt. "Will a goblin shaman make the trek? Perhaps with a drow escort?"

"They'd not open the doors," Bruenor and Jolen Firth said together.

"No, the five of us," Regis said, and he looked around at his friends and corrected it to "six," as he noted Athrogate. "We can get there, but it won't be easy. Do you remember the orc encampment?"

Drizzt shrugged. He hadn't even really entered the place, but had seen it from afar.

"There is a boulder tumble and a deep cave," Regis explained.

"How deep?" Drizzt asked, and he was beginning to understand.

"The goblin tribes and the ogres who reinforced that orc assault came to the camp through the tunnels," Regis explained. "They tap into the Underdark. I know this to be true, for I was in them."

Drizzt looked to Bruenor. "We ain't but fifty miles from Mithral Hall, elf," he said hopefully.

"As a bird flies," Drizzt replied. "In the winding ways of the Underdark . . ."

"She's straight north," Bruenor argued.

Drizzt spent a long time considering it. The Underdark was no safe journey, of course, but with his powerful friends about him, surely they could survive a tenday in the upper tunnels.

"It is worth a try," Jolen Firth remarked.

"We might even find a back door for me kin to break out," said Bruenor. "The Battlehammer boys sneak out and crush these dogs about Nesmé, then Nesmé comes north and helps Mithral Hall clear her gates."

He looked to Jolen Firth, who nodded—but noncommittally, Drizzt understood, and so too did Bruenor recognize that hesitance, likely, given the history between Mithral Hall and Nesmé. If the siege of Nesmé was broken, the Riders would turn east, no doubt, to go to the aid of Silverymoon.

Still, their prospects here were nothing but dark, Drizzt understood. He doubted that Nesmé would hold until the winter, and if Jolen Firth refused to attempt to break out to the west—and even that would likely prove disastrous, then the thousands here would surely die.

"We can get there," Regis said again.

Drizzt looked to Catti-brie, who nodded her agreement.

"It is a desperate plan," the drow said.

"Ye got better, elf?" asked Bruenor.

"No, and so we go."

The orc reclined against the boulder, staring up at the clouds, fantasizing about the spurting blood of some human.

Ah, yes, the walls of Nesmé would fall, and then the people of Nesmé would fall to jagged blades!

The beast came out of its trance when a deerskin boot appeared on the stone beside its ear, and then another on the other side of its head. The orc arched its back a bit to look up and behind, to see a huge man standing there, straddling its head, and with his arms up high.

The orc started to leap up, but the warhammer came down faster, the barbarian chopping down as if he was splitting wood.

The orc's arms shot out to the sides, fingers waggling, as Aegis-fang collapsed its chest. Its eyes bulged as if they would fly from the sockets, and its life-force did fly, straightaway, from the blasted corpse.

Wulfgar glanced to the side and nodded, and Regis and Drizzt sprinted out from around another boulder, leaving the three orcs they had just slain, and darted into the small cave within the boulder tumble.

The barbarian turned around and waved the all clear to Bruenor, then Catti-brie, then Athrogate, who had taken perimeter positions around the boulder tumble.

A commotion drew Wulfgar's attention and he glanced back down before him to see a goblin rushing out of the tunnel in full flight. He hoisted his warhammer to throw, but hesitated.

"Regis?" he called.

Out of the hole came the halfling. "Real one," he explained, pointing to the fleeing monster.

Aegis-fang went spinning out and the goblin went spinning down.

"Bwahaha!" Athrogate roared with delight, coming in fast from the side upon Snort, for he too had noted the fleeing goblin. "Full o' bluster, humans be, all boast'n'bluster'n'yammer, but this one here, ogre tall and giant strong, sure can throw a hammer."

Wulfgar jumped down from the stone, Aegis-fang returning to his grasp. He stared at Athrogate incredulously, which made the dwarf laugh all the harder.

"He is easily amused," Regis remarked.

"Might be because I'm smarter than the rest of ye, eh?" Athrogate said, walking by the pair to join Drizzt in the cave. "Make yer laughs where ye can, little one, because yer tears'll chase ye and catch ye where they will."

Regis started to respond, but held back and found himself nodding instead.

"A lesson worth learning," Wulfgar remarked, and tossed a wink the halfling's way, then started into the cave. "A pity, then, that the dirty dwarf's songs aren't more entertaining."

"Bah!" Athrogate snorted.

Drizzt led the way down the hole into the tunnels below, and a series of large chambers that were now abandoned, but had been full of goblins and orcs very recently, judging by the debris and waste.

"They're probably off attacking Nesmé again," Regis remarked, and the others nodded.

"Relentless," Catti-brie agreed.

"I told ye, elf," the dwarf said to Drizzt. "They been wanting a war, and so war they're getting!" He looked around, nodding, but none of the others, except perhaps Athrogate, seemed to be sharing his obvious enthusiasm at that moment. "Bah, but it's the way o' things," Bruenor said.

"With all speed to Mithral Hall, then," said Catti-brie. "The sooner we get to the dwarves, the better Nesmé's chances of survival." She took an arrow from Drizzt's quiver and cast a quick spell, and the head of the missile lit up with a light as strong as a torch, and indeed, Catti-brie held it forth as if it was just that.

She looked to Drizzt, they all did, and the drow nodded and moved about the chambers, peering into the tunnels to try to discern the most northerly route. They started along one, but after some hours of walking, Drizzt paused and shook his head.

"What do ye know?" Bruenor asked.

Drizzt waved the dwarf up beside him and sniffed the air. Bruenor did likewise.

"Deeper tunnels," Drizzt explained. "This course will take us down, too far down, I fear."

"Bah, but ye're wanting to go all the way back to find another path?" Bruenor asked skeptically.

"That is the way of the Underdark," Drizzt explained. "We will find many dead ends and many wrong turns. This will not be an easy journey, nor a quick one, likely." He pointed to the magical belt pouch Regis wore, which the party had stuffed with many days worth of rations for just this possibility.

"Might be branching tunnels ahead," Athrogate added.

Bruenor looked to Drizzt, who shrugged.

"We can't be knowin' until we look," said the orange-bearded dwarf.

"We could lose another day."

"Or save a couple."

Drizzt looked to the others, who of course had no answers and could merely shrug in response.

297

"Mithral Hall's mines go deep, eh?" Athrogate asked.

"Aye," said Bruenor.

"We ain't far from the surface," the black-bearded dwarf reasoned. "Tunnels takin' us lower're more likely to find a strand o' Mithral Hall, then." He nodded into the darkness ahead, and Drizzt, too, could only shrug. Then the drow took up the lead once more, skipping ahead beyond the glow of Catti-brie's magical light, slipping along the dark tunnels.

They camped in a shallow alcove to the side of that tunnel, Catti-brie dismissing her light and Drizzt and the two dwarves, all three possessed of superior lowlight vision, taking turns on watch.

Many times that first night did Drizzt go to the others, mostly Wulfgar and Catti-brie, to comfort them, for he knew that they were all but blind in the near-darkness, and realized that must be an unsettling thing indeed.

They did find side-passages the next day in their hike, and many more passages off of those, and surely even the dwarves might have become lost in the maze of the upper Underdark. Not the drow, though. This was Drizzt's natural domain, the home he had known for the first decades of his life, and few had walked more Underdark corridors than he.

Confident in their general direction, if not in their chances to actually find some familiar ground, he led them along, day after day.

"To live here," Regis whispered incredulously to Wulfgar during one of their camps.

The barbarian couldn't see his halfling head shaking his head, but he knew as much from the sound of Regis's voice.

"It is worse when you are blind in the near darkness," Wulfgar replied.

"I'm not," said the halfling. "My lowlight vision is strong now—stronger than it was in my previous life."

"Yet you avoid guard duty," Wulfgar said with a snicker.

"I go out from the encampment each night—Drizzt knows," Regis surprised him by saying. "Hunting for fungus and lichen. If we ever find a proper chamber in which to camp, I'll set up my workshop and brew some more potions."

"You are full of surprises, my little friend."

"Still, to live here, year after year," Regis said. "Surely I would lose my sanity. And it is not simply the darkness, though that is pressing enough."

"I understand," Wulfgar answered. "Whenever I think of the mountains of stone above our heads . . . It presses on my thoughts as surely as the weight would crush my body."

"Too many corners," Catti-brie added, sliding over to join in the conversation. "You must always be on your guard, for every turn in the passage could bring you face to face with an enemy. A goblin or orc, an umber hulk, a displacer beast . . ."

"A drow," Wulfgar added.

"Aye, and might be a dwarf waiting to slug ye," came another voice, Bruenor's voice. "A dwarf angry and tired because his friends wouldn't shut their mouths when he was trying to sleep."

"True enough," Athrogate added from the other side, for Drizzt was out on watch at that time. "Might be two of 'em, bwahaha! Four fists!"

The group took several side passages the next day, and had to backtrack twice when they came to a dead end at one tunnel, and another that ended in a large chamber centered by a deep, deep hole.

The next few days of travel proved much the same, with so many tunnels before them. Drizzt continued to lead, and did well to keep them from any Underdark denizens, though the upper tunnels of the Underdark were not typically rife with monsters, other than the orcs, most of whom were out with Warlord Hartusk's forces, no doubt.

They lost track of time, but knew they were nearing a tenday out from Nesmé, when at last they came into regions that sparked some recognition in Bruenor.

"It's the smell," he remarked to the others when they came into a series of wider tunnels, many with natural side chambers. "Smell o' home."

"Then yer home's smelling like orc," Athrogate replied.

The others looked to the black-bearded dwarf curiously.

"Aye," Bruenor agreed. "There's a bit o' that stench in the air. But it's more than that, I tell ye. I'm knowing this place."

Soon after, Athrogate's words seemed prescient, for they began to find signs that orcs indeed haunted these tunnels. Around one corner in a winding and narrow passage, they found Drizzt waiting for them, some dozen steps ahead, with his hand up to halt their progress.

"Wire," the drow said quietly, pointing down at the floor.

Catti-brie bent low with the lighted arrow, revealing that a trip wire had been strung across the breadth of the corridor.

"Pressure plate on the wall," Regis added, noting a slab of stone that seemed slightly different in hue than the other stones of the corridor.

Athrogate went to investigate, gingerly stepping over the trip wire. He tested the slab of stone Regis had indicated, then stepped back, nodding.

"What's it do?" Bruenor asked.

"Not for knowing," Athrogate admitted. "Not for finding out, either."

On they went, more quietly then, and with Catti-brie shielding the magically illuminated arrow. Drizzt continued to lead the way, but remained much closer to the others. They found more traps, many more, along with goblin sign: scat and scattered items, even a plate of half-eaten food that was not very old, clearly.

They said nothing, and were reminded to stay very quiet when they heard whispers, echoing off the rocky walls, bouncing around them confusingly.

Orcs were all around them, they knew, but it was impossible to determine how many, or how far away, for the echoes of whispers in the crisscrossing, multileveled tunnels came at them from every conceivable angle. They went into a battle formation, Drizzt still leading, Bruenor and Athrogate side by side behind him, with Wulfgar and Regis bringing up the rear and Catti-brie in the middle, that she might launch her magic in any direction as needed.

They could feel the pressure growing against them. They remained as quiet as they could, but they were not silent, obviously, and the corridors magnified the sound and carried it to many ears, they feared.

Soon after, the tunnel became a combination of natural tube and worked walls, dwarf walls, and lined with larger chambers on the right-hand wall, connecting to shorter tunnels and more chambers beyond.

Bruenor's eyes lit up at the sight. "We're close," he whispered. "The western deep mines o' Mithral Hall, I tell ye."

Drizzt came back to the group. "We go to the right, then?" he whispered to Bruenor. "There are many enemies that way, I fear."

The dwarf considered it, trying to recall the layout. They were deep, clearly, well below the great forges of Mithral Hall, down near the lowest tunnels. There weren't many ways to get into the corridors that would lead to Mithral Hall proper from this region, he knew, and by design, keeping these areas secluded for defensive purposes.

"Stay to the long tunnel another thousand steps," the dwarf advised. "She'll bend back to the east, I'm thinking, and there we might find our way."

With a nod, Drizzt pressed ahead once more. He kept his hand near his belt pouch, expecting that he might soon need to call Guenhwyvar to his side.

They could smell the orcs now, and no doubt, the orcs could smell them.

The corridor narrowed and the party slowed. They went over a series of traps, three trip wires spanning the corridor, the second two strides beyond the first, the third two strides beyond the second.

Drizzt found himself more lucky than clever as he crossed the second, barely missing a small pressure plate that had been deviously placed in the center of the corridor. When he noted it, the drow sucked in his breath; they were barely moving along as it was, and now they'd have to be doubly careful, every step of the way.

Up ahead, the corridor bent sharply to the right, the east, and split in a tight fork, also continuing along to the north.

With a look to Bruenor, the drow went to the right, the others rolling in behind.

The corridor tightened, the smell of orc thickened about them. In the distance, they heard drums, and chanting.

Up in the front, Drizzt called in Guenhwyvar and sent her running ahead.

"We've been herded," Regis whispered, sorting it all out. He grabbed Wulfgar to halt the man, then pushed ahead and similarly bade Catti-brie to stop.

"Herded," he said to the dwarves, and even as he spoke the word, they heard the roar and the cry as Guenhwyvar, long out of sight of them, engaged some unseen enemy.

"Drizzt!" Regis called in warning, for he saw the seams in the walls and the ceiling, and he realized that the orcs had wanted them in this very place!

The dwarves turned around to regard him, but the halfling yelled for them to turn back immediately—and just in time as a stone panel in the ceiling fell aside and a quartet of orcs came leaping down at them.

Up ahead, Drizzt, too, found enemies as secret side panels slid aside, orcs leaping at him left and right.

And dying to his spinning blades, left and right.

Regis managed to poke his rapier in between the two battling dwarves to stab at an orc. He considered throwing a serpent at another, when a cry from behind spun him about. He darted away underneath Catti-brie's reaching hands, the woman throwing a fan of flames over the dwarves and into the faces of the taller orcs.

Past Catti-brie, Regis spotted Wulfgar, his hammer whipping side to side furiously as orcs pressed in at him.

"I'm coming!" the halfling called to his large friend, and he pushed past Catti-brie, leaping back to Wulfgar. He had barely begun that charge, though, when he heard the sound of stones scraping and sliding.

"What?" Catti-brie asked, glancing back over her shoulder, just in time to see a section of the wall to the left of Regis come sliding out, slamming the halfling and driving him to the right hand wall.

"Wulfgar!" she cried.

The barbarian swept aside the closest orc and spun back, and he and Catti-brie both sucked in their breath, expecting Regis to be splattered against the corridor wall by the sheer weight of the sliding block!

But no, that section of wall fell away just before impact, revealing a steep decline, and into it tumbled Regis.

His cry slipped away with him.

"No!" Wulfgar yelled. He swept aside the stubborn orcs pressing in at him once more, then leaped for the wall, sealed now by the block that had come sliding across the corridor.

"Regis!" Catti-brie yelled. "Wulfgar!" she added, seeing a host of orcs bearing down at him from behind.

The stones ground again, the slab from the left-hand corridor wall slid back the other way, and for a brief moment, before the second wall could slide back into place, the hole into which Regis had tumbled came clear.

"Wulfgar, no!" Catti-brie cried, but too late, for the barbarian was already moving, diving fearlessly to the floor, going into the side hole up to his waist and reaching into the darkness for his friend.

"A deep hole!" he cried, or tried to cry, for the second slab crashed into him then and began to crush the life out of him. He groaned and reached down for it, but his angle was all wrong and he couldn't begin to press it back. Desperately, the barbarian jammed the head of Aegis-fang in between the slab and the wall.

But still it pressed at him, and he had no choice but to go forward, into the side passage. He squirmed and tugged.

"Wulfgar!" Catti-brie cried, and she grabbed the edge of the stuck slab and tried to pull back, to no avail. She couldn't continue, for more orcs appeared around the corner, bearing down at her. She fell back and began a new spell.

And Drizzt was beside her somehow, having cut through an orc battling Bruenor, then leaping the dwarves. The drow ranger sped right past Catti-brie to meet the orc charge, scimitars spinning in a blur to take aside a thrusting spear and cut the throat out of the first in line.

"Wulfgar!" he cried at the partially-blocked side passage, where only the head of Aegis-fang was now wedged, preventing the slab from sealing off the exit. "Regis!"

Out stabbed Twinkle, taking the second orc in the gut, and Drizzt rolled past it to engage the next two in line. Fury drove his strikes as he considered his fallen friends—fallen from view, at least, and taken from his side.

The tunnel began to tremble and vibrate.

Drizzt drove back the pair of orcs before him.

"Go left!" Catti-brie called, and the drow immediately threw himself against that left-hand wall.

A flash of magical lightning exploded past him, blasting the orcs backward, and Drizzt thought immediately to turn and go at the slab, perhaps to use the leverage of the wedged warhammer to pry it back open.

Even as he turned, however, the images so briefly revealed in the brilliance of the lightning bolt screamed at him to flee.

The tunnel shook more violently, and there came a rumble like an avalanche, for back at the corner came a most diabolical war machine, a cylindrical wheel as tall as a dwarf and as wide as the corridor, tons of worked stone wrapped with sheeted steel and wickedly ridged.

Drizzt knew this contraption, for it was no orc design. He grabbed the lighted arrow from Catti-brie and flung it down the hall, in time to see the war machine mow down an orc, squishing it flat beneath its weight and chopping it apart with its ridges. Ogres pushed the monstrous contraption—many ogres—and little would stop them.

"Oh run," Drizzt told Catti-brie, and shouted it again, louder.

"Juicer!" Bruenor cried when he managed to look back. "They got a juicer. Run!"

Drizzt went for the warhammer, one last desperate chance to open a way to his lost friends, but even as he reached for it, it disappeared, and the slab slammed into place with a resounding thud, sealing the passage.

The drow dived into a roll past it, sheathing his scimitars as he went, and he came up holding Taulmaril, and so fought a retreating action, launching a line of arrows behind him to kill orcs, and hopefully, to slow the ogres and their juicer.

Up in front, Bruenor and Athrogate worked wildly to clear the way, but the orcs battling them wanted no part of the coming machine of slaughter, which would not distinguish friend from foe, and they too fled with all speed.

"Juicer!" Bruenor shouted repeatedly, for surely the word held powerful meaning for him, Drizzt understood. This was a dwarf machine, a Mithral Hall design, and so at least part of the complex had fallen to the orcs.

"Run, ye durned fools, for all yer lives!" Bruenor cried.

And so they did.

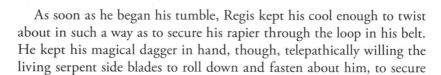

As soon as he began his tumble, Regis kept his cool enough to twist about in such a way as to secure his rapier through the loop in his belt. He kept his magical dagger in hand, though, telepathically willing the living serpent side blades to roll down and fasten about him, to secure the weapon to his hand.

He stabbed at the stone of the floor and the walls with it, hoping to hook it in a crease and somehow slow his descent.

He bounced and tumbled, sometimes on a slide, other times dropping over a short ledge into a painful fall. Welts and bruises covered him, he was sure, he tasted blood in his mouth, and he had to tuck his arms and legs in tight, trying to prevent an awkward tumble that would break his bones.

On sudden impulse, he reached into his magical belt pouch—how he wished he could just crawl into that extra-dimensional space at that moment—and mentally called for his potion pouch. His fingers worked fast, counting the places, his thoughts worked fast, trying to recall the order of the vials in the line of leather loops under the flap of that pouch.

Over another drop he went, crying out as he flew through the blackness. He banged his head on the ceiling, then tumbled down with a groan, rolling around a bend in the descent.

He brought forth a small potion vial and simply stuffed it into his mouth and cracked the glass with his bite, releasing the contents.

Too late, he feared. He saw the last expanse before him, marked by fires, torchlight, at the end of a long and steep slide.

He stomped his feet, left and right, trying to slow his descent, and then his left foot stuck, the potion taking effect, and he nearly tore out his knee as he awkwardly rolled up and over that anchored foot.

Then he moved, the potion giving him control, and he heard something tumbling down from behind and had no choice but to climb up the side wall of this tunnel, scrambling desperately.

He got to the ceiling, crouching there inverted, and now could see what awaited him at the bottom of the decline: a host of orcs and thick-limbed ogrillon.

He heard the crash and recognized the grunt, and tried to swing about, and even tried to grab at Wulfgar as the big man bounced and tumbled beneath him, though he surely had no chance of even slowing huge Wulfgar's crashing descent.

"Oh no," he whispered as Wulfgar covered the last lengths of the slide, to pitch out through the ceiling of that lower corridor and fly down hard to the floor.

The monsters fell over him, punching at him, kicking at him, swatting him with clubs.

"Oh no," Regis whispered. He wanted to go to Wulfgar, but the horde was over the barbarian. Too many. Regis inched down for a better view.

But there was nothing he could do.

The mob moved off, dragging Wulfgar by the ankles. And the way he bounced, so limply, so lifelessly, made Regis fear that the poor man was already dead.

The monsters hoisted him onto their shoulders, and cheered and danced as they made their way down the corridor, Wulfgar's battered body bouncing in tune with their running strides.

"Oh no," Regis breathed. He looked back up the tunnel, then shook his head. His potion wouldn't last long enough for him to get all the way back to the upper corridor, and he had no other elixirs of this type.

Nor could he leave his fallen friend.

He crept down, poking his head through the hole and into the tunnel, and knew immediately that he was in the heart of a complex thick with orcs, with several in sight, and a few goblins besides.

"Oh no," he whispered again.

CHAPTER 21

THE GHOST OF DWARF KINGS PAST

THE TUNNEL SHOOK WITH THE THUNDER OF THE ROLLING JUICER AND the heavy footfalls of the ogres pushing it. Drizzt trailed the others, firing arrows at the contraption, or over the contraption, skipping them off the ceiling to put them in behind the gigantic, crushing wheel to try to slow down the determined charge of the ogres. He had scored a couple of hits, he figured from the yelps and grunts coming from behind the war machine, but he hadn't slowed it.

All of the orcs between the companions and the war machine were dead now, shot down by Drizzt or splattered by the rolling contraption—juiced, as Bruenor would put it. But it hardly mattered because the enemy at that moment wasn't an orc but a cylinder of heavy stone.

The drow thought of dropping the bow and drawing blades, but the expanse between the top of the rolling war machine and ceiling was too tight for him to hope to get through. He scanned the ceiling ahead, looking for a high spot where he might get over the wheel, or perhaps a slim alcove he might squeeze into, coming out behind the crushing wheel when it rambled past.

The orcs and ogres had chosen their corridor of death well, it seemed, for Drizzt saw no such opportunities. He looked back to the closing wheel, skipped an arrow off the ceiling above it and considered the size of the opening as the flashing lightning arrow illuminated it more clearly.

He had to shake his head; there was no way he could get through.

But the corridor continued, long and straight and with no side passages, and even though the orcs before Bruenor and Athrogate were more interested in running away than in trying to slow the group, the juicer was gaining on them, and too quickly. They couldn't outrun it, they couldn't stop it.

If Drizzt could just buy some time so that Catti-brie could cast some spell, perhaps . . .

He shot his next arrow into the ceiling, trying to dislodge a chunk of stone to fall before the rolling crusher. Bits did fall, but the juicer turned them to pebbles as it bounced across.

"Faster! Faster!" the drow implored his companions, for he couldn't slow the thing, and surely they were doomed.

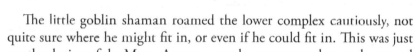

The little goblin shaman roamed the lower complex cautiously, not quite sure where he might fit in, or even if he could fit in. This was just another legion of the Many-Arrows army, he came to understand, camped here outside of the tunnels of Mithral Hall as surely as their orc kin were camped outside the dwarf doors on the surface above.

He found a large chamber where crude forges were working, hot fires blazing, orc blacksmiths pounding at spear tips and wicked swords. Off to the side, some ogres were being fitted with thick breastplates.

He could not deny the truth: They were organized, methodical, and determined.

Dozens of tunnels spider-webbed out of the forge room, and from many, the goblin shaman heard the rhythmic sound of picks hitting stone. The goblins and orcs were mining, and smelting, and fashioning their weapons. Surely they couldn't match Bruenor's kin in such endeavors, but orcs were clever creatures when it came to making implements of pain.

On went the halfling-turned-goblin, through a door and along the complex. He passed many common rooms with scores of beds, rows and rows of weapons set on racks, a dining hall, even a great auditorium or chapel of some sort, filled with benches set in a semicircle around a raised stage, and with a large fire pit breaking the semicircle in half.

The halfling-turned-goblin swallowed hard when he considered that stage, with a blood-stained table on the lip of it and several large posts set in place behind it, each hung with heavy shackles. He thought of Prisoner's Carnival in the old city of Luskan, where magistrates brought forth the criminals captured in the city and exacted cruel punishment, torture, and horrible death upon them, to the cheers of hundreds of onlookers.

If humans were capable of such viciousness, what might these orcs do?

He moved to the stage, curious, and noted the piles of slop on the dirty stone floor. Entrails, brains, pools of blood . . .

Gagging, he rushed out of the chamber, scouting the area, looking for something, anything.

"Run! Run!" Drizzt implored the others, for the rambling juicer was then barely five strides behind him, and closing fast!

He heard a horn blow, a note so discordant that he immediately thought that it must be some instrument of the ugly orcs, and indeed sounded more like a belch than a melodic note.

The cry of "Me king!" jogged his memory, though, and the drow recalled the source of that belching note and what it foretold.

Drizzt stumbled past the specter of Thibbledorf Pwent, who stood with hands on hips staring at the approaching calamity. Five steps later, the fleeing Drizzt saw the juicer plow into Pwent.

Or rather, plow through Pwent.

Or rather, plow through the fog Pwent became.

The specter trapped in Bruenor's horn had retained some of his vampiric properties, so it seemed!

And yes, Pwent became corporal once more on the other side of the rolling calamity, Drizzt knew, and the others knew, and surely, the ogres knew!

"Keep yer runnin'," Bruenor shouted. "He'll not be holdin' them for long!"

Drizzt sprinted up beside Catti-brie and caught her by the arm. "A spell," he bade her, and the pair stopped and turned back.

"Run on!" Bruenor scolded them.

"Something, anything," Drizzt said to the woman.

Catti-brie searched her memory, counting on her fingers as she considered the enchantments at her disposal this day, and what spells she had available that might help, The fighting behind the juicer wheel sounded intense now, with ogres roaring and grunting and squealing, and the occasional "Me king!" coming forth from the battleraging dwarf specter.

Catti-brie nodded and turned back to fully face the now-distant juicer. She began to cast.

Behind the wheel, the sound of battle stopped, and almost immediately, the fog of the defeated dwarf specter drifted up and over the juicer wheel, flying back for the magical horn. A heartbeat later, the heavy wheel creaked and began to roll once more, very slowly now as the ogres tried to gain momentum.

"Quickly," Drizzt implored her.

Catti-brie closed her eyes and brought her ruby ring up to her lips, whispering her enchantment into it, asking the Plane of Fire for more strength and clarity.

Her line of fire began at her feet and rolled back down the hallway the way she had come. She put the fiery source line right near to the right hand wall, the roiling flames reaching out across the corridor from there.

As soon as the spell roared to life, Drizzt grabbed the woman's arm and sped her along.

The corridor trembled again under the weight of the war machine.

But then came cries of surprise and pain, as the brutes rolled it right into the area of Catti-brie's conflagration, and the great crushing contraption stopped once more.

The companions ran on.

Guenhwyvar rejoined them some time later, when at last they came into an area of side tunnels and side chambers. Before they could decide which way to go, the decision was made for them, for enemies appeared, so many enemies, too many enemies to even think of making a stand.

Each of the companions in turn cast a forlorn glance back down the main tunnel, back in the direction of where they had lost Wulfgar and Regis.

There was nothing they could do but run.

And so they did, through rough-hewn chambers mostly dug by Bruenor's clan in days long past. They were in the old, lower mines now, they knew, still outside the complex of Mithral Hall, but not far away.

Other hands had worked these chambers as well, including the gray dwarves, the duergar, who had inhabited the bowels of Mithral Hall in the centuries of Clan Battlehammer's exile, after the dragon Shimmergloom had chased young Bruenor and his clansdwarves from their home.

The companions went through doors and around corners, through chambers narrow and wide, and down hallways that split in many directions. But because of pursuit, never was there a choice for them regarding their course, they came to realize. And they quickly came to understand, too, that they were being herded, for orcs and ogres, ogrillon and goblins, were always there, blocking every passage but one.

Side-by-side and at a full run, Athrogate and Bruenor shouldered a door, crashing through into what seemed to be a storeroom. Ancient mining implements sat on a rusted old rack against one wall, and pegs lined the other wall. Three doors were in the room, each heavily reinforced with rusted metal beams.

"A safe room," Bruenor said to no one in particular. In days long past when these mines were in use, the dwarves would come here to sleep and take their breaks—Bruenor could well imagine the wall to his left thick with cloaks and miner's aprons. In the event of a cave-in, this room would likely stand strong, a sanctuary.

But it was no sanctuary for the friends at that time, with monsters so close on their heels.

On they went, through the door directly across from the one they had broken in. They came into a mine, then, a long and worked tunnel, sloping gradually upward before them.

"Run! Run, we're there!" Bruenor cried, picking up his pace.

There were no side-passages to be seen now, just a single metal door at the top of the tunnel ahead. Bruenor burst through it and roared in apparent victory. All four and Guenhwyvar scrambled in and Drizzt slammed the door shut, and good luck was with them, for while the door had not been barred before them, there was indeed a locking bar leaning against the wall beside it.

Athrogate already had the bar in hand, and he and Drizzt were quick to secure the door.

Old iron carts, ore carts, sat scattered about this chamber, a pair sitting on rails that ran under the room's other, higher door.

"Ah, me hall and me boys," Bruenor said, moving for that closed door. "We'll be back, ye dog orcs, and we'll find me boy and Rumblebelly."

Through the second door was a short passage, sloping up steeply. On the far wall hung crank winches, come-alongs, with piles of heavy, rusted chain on the floor beneath them. The rails continued up the expanse, to what once had been the portal to the main complex of Mithral Halls mines.

But now those rails ran into a solid wall, an iron wall.

"They sealed it," Bruenor mumbled, hiking up the incline to the blocked exit. He put his hand up against the metal. "By Moradin's hairy arse, they shut them orcs out, and so shut us out."

He turned back to his friends, his crestfallen expression aptly reflecting the mood, and at that very moment, came the first resounding crash as a heavy hammer slammed the barred metal door in the room behind them.

"We got nowhere to run, elf," Bruenor said.

"Aye, and no supplies," said Catti-brie, and she mouthed "Regis" when Bruenor shifted his gaze to regard her.

A thunderous slam shook the floor beneath their feet and sent streams of dust dropping down around them.

"They've got a ram," Athrogate said, and he gave a little laugh, seeming quite amused at how easily they had been herded, cornered, and caught.

The click of a shackle brought Wulfgar back to consciousness, somewhat at least. His shoulder throbbed—something in there was torn, surely. One shin was broken and would not support him, and the other leg, too, was battered, so much so that he really couldn't support his weight.

And so he hung to the limit of the chains, the metal shackles tearing at his wrists. Eventually they would eat right through and one of his hands would fall off, he suspected, and then he'd hang for a bit from the remaining hand, until that one, too, was sawed away.

Then he'd fall in a heap to the floor, and who could guess what tortures would be exacted upon him.

He couldn't see out of one eye, so swollen was the side of his face, and it took him a long, long while to finally manage to crack the other blood-crusted eyelid open. And then he winced, though it hurt him greatly to even move his face.

He was in a large and shadowy area, about mid way along one of the longer walls in the rectangular chamber. Torches were set about the walls haphazardly, leaving vast swaths of the place in darkness. It was a two-tiered chamber, with a higher floor running the length of the longer side walls, and the main middle swath of the room down lower. Far down to the left, in the middle of the shorter wall, loomed a dark tunnel opening.

Tables and shackling posts and racks of unpleasant-looking implements were scattered about, some with the rotted remains of some unfortunate still strapped in place. Only in noting those rotting corpses did Wulfgar become aware of the awful stench hanging about the room.

There was a pit in the middle of the lower area, fairly large, and Wulfgar marked some movement within it, far below, though he couldn't make out what horrid creatures might be in there.

Wulfgar saw that his weren't the only shackles set into the stone along the wall he was chained to, and he wasn't the only prisoner. In fact, he was one of many. He noted several dwarves, hanging from the ground, battered and wretched, too short to put their feet on the floor, and a few humans as well, all sprinkled in between many shackled goblins, also too short for the shackles, and so hanging like the dwarves.

It seemed to Wulfgar that many of the prisoners were long dead.

An ugly brute roamed the room, a pair of sniveling goblins following its every move. Too short to be an ogre, too wide to be an orc, Wulfgar recognized it as an ogrillon. He had battled a few of those brutes in his day, and thought them to be the stupidest and most vicious of creatures, a most horrible blend of the worst traits of the orc and ogre parents, with the viciousness of the former and the intelligence of the latter.

The ogrillon grabbed something under a tarp on a cart far down to Wulfgar's left, near the tunnel opening. Hardly considering its cargo—which it was holding by the ankle, Wulfgar soon realized, the brute lumbered down the middle of the room. A torn and battered orc carcass came out from under the tarp, to fall with a splat onto the stone floor. It dragged behind the ogrillon, and led a long line of entrails behind it, smearing the floor with blood and bile.

The brutal torturer walked right up to the edge of the pit in the center of the floor and swung the goblin in. Barely had it crashed down when Wulfgar heard the ravenous sounds of monstrous beasts, biting and gnawing and slurping.

The goblins trailing their torturer boss seemed especially pleased with this, hopping and laughing excitedly. One grabbed up the trailing entrails and began dancing about—then almost went flying into the pit as one of the monsters within gave a great tug, or perhaps it was slurping the stringy thing into its mouth.

The goblin let go at the last moment, flopping to the floor, and its ugly little companion laughed crazily.

Wulfgar didn't know what to make of any of this. He felt as if he had been thrown into the middle of a caricature of evil, some gruesome collection of monsters a child might imagine hiding under his bed. He recalled his long slide and the beasts waiting for him, and knew that all was lost. He could only hope that his friends had escaped.

And that he would die quickly.

He started to nod off again—perhaps he did indeed, for he could not be sure of how much time had passed—when he was brought back to alertness by the sound of the brutish ogrillon leaping up to the raised floor right beside him. The brute sniffed at him and growled, then moved down the other way, past a dwarf, then a goblin.

It stopped before another dwarf, and poked at the poor bearded fellow.

The dwarf kicked out with a dirty and bare foot, hitting the ogrillon, but to little if any effect.

Down snapped the ogrillon's hand, grabbing the dwarf by the ankle and lifting the foot once more. How the poor fellow squirmed and tried to kick out with his other foot, but the ogrillon turned into the dwarf, moving too close for the poor fellow to have any real effect.

With the strength of its ogre heritage, the jailor yanked the leg up and up, and the dwarf squirmed and groaned in pain.

The jailer looked the poor prisoner in the face, then bit off the dwarf's toes.

And how the poor fellow screamed, and the ogrillon, chewing away, giggled with amusement and moved along the line.

Two goblins and a dwarf were selected, their chains lifted over the hooks above with a long pole that looked much like a fireplace poker. The ogrillon tugged them along, the goblins trailing with whips cracking.

One of the goblin prisoners, whining, resisted, and with frightful strength, the ogrillon jailer lifted its arm and snapped it down, and the chain rolled with tremendous force, cracking up and jerking the goblin wildly as it snapped like a heavy whip.

The ogrillon gave a sudden tug, and the goblin, off-balance from the snap, went flying face-first to the floor.

The goblin jailers leaped atop it, kicking and biting and punching until the boss ogrillon ordered them back.

Then it started along once more, tugging the three chains, dragging the battered goblin along with ease, to the cart, where the prisoners were roughly piled. Into the tunnel they all went.

Wulfgar slumped down. He almost envied the three prisoners who were being taken, no doubt, to a horrid and torturous death.

His turn at whatever macabre carnival lay at the other end of that tunnel would come sooner or later, and the sooner the better, he figured.

"When they get through, we've got to make a run," Bruenor explained to the others, his sentence interrupted by a resounding boom and an earthquake-like shudder about the room as the monsters drove their ram into the heavy door.

"Cut through 'em, elf, and we'll break clear," the dwarf added.

"Stay together or split apart?" Drizzt asked, and Catti-brie looked at him with a horrified expression.

"Together," she answered before Bruenor could.

"Ah, but the elf's got a better chance o' findin' our friends," Bruenor argued.

Another booming impact shook the room, and strangely, another came immediately after it, though much less profound.

And, the trio realized a moment later, the second crash had come from the other direction. The three ran out of the cart room into the higher chamber, to see Athrogate standing before the iron wall, his morningstars spinning all around. He came around with a left-handed swing, the heavy glassteel ball smashing into the iron, to no apparent effect.

"Save yer strength, ye dope!" Bruenor yelled, but Athrogate went at it again, and again with his left, and then a second and third time in rapid succession.

Bruenor led the others up the incline. "Ye ain't to break through an iron wall," the dwarf declared, but his voice trailed off as he came to realize that the section of the wall before Athrogate had changed in hue.

"Bwahaha!" Athrogate roared and spun around to face the others. "Ain't

I, then?" he swung the ball of his left-hand weapon in a spin before them. "Cracker!" he explained.

Another tremendous boom shook the room. Behind Drizzt Guenhwyvar's ears went flat.

"They're breaking through," the drow warned.

"Bwahaha!" Athrogate roared all the louder, and now he presented the morningstar in his right hand, letting the friends see the ball, which appeared wet. "And . . ."

"Whacker," he and Drizzt said together, the drow, smiling now, catching on.

Athrogate went into a spin. Drizzt tugged Catti-brie back, and not a moment too soon. When Athrogate bashed Whacker's head into the iron wall, right where Cracker had prepared the metal, there came an explosion that sounded as loud as the ogre-manned ram behind them, shaking the chamber and sending great chunks of rusted metal flying around.

Cracker would coat with a peculiar substance, the essence of the rust monster, and, not to be outdone, its sister flail, Whacker, could exude oil of impact from its metal nubs.

In went Cracker again, driving its metal-destroying goo deeper into the wounded wall.

In went Whacker right behind, the next coat of oil of impact exploding mightily under the weight of the blow.

After a third round, Athrogate's swing drove right through the metal, blasting a fair-sized hole.

Back in the other room, the ram hit again. Guenhwyvar roared and a monster squealed in agony.

"They've got it open enough to grab at the bar," Drizzt warned, and he leaped back the other way, Taulmaril in hand, and began launching a line of arrows at the small opening around the edge of the battered door.

"Stay with me," Athrogate yelled back, and in went Cracker, with Whacker right behind, widening the hole in the iron wall. "Haha, keep yer faith in Athrogate!"

But out of that hole in the iron wall came a crossbow quarrel, skipping off the seam of the iron wall and nearly clipping Athrogate as it flew past.

"Hey now!" he roared, falling away.

"No, ye dolts!" Bruenor yelled, using the Delzoun language of the dwarves. "No goblins. It's meself, and ye're knowin' me!"

"Eh, who's that now?" came a cautious reply, and within the shadows beyond the hole, Bruenor noted some movement.

"Yerself's a Battlehammer?" asked another voice, full of incredulity.

"Aye, and soon to be dead," Bruenor cried back, figuring he hadn't the time to explain. "And sooner to be dead if ye're to shoot me."

A jumble of noise and movement came from the other side of that iron wall, with hammers coming up to bang wider the hole Athrogate's powerful weapons had created, and to dull the sharp edges of the break. Then a tarp came through, dwarf hand reaching about to quickly smooth it. "Come on, come on!" the dwarf called from beyond.

Athrogate tossed his weapons through and leaped for the hole, reaching his arms in. On the other side, dwarves took his hands and tugged him through, and barely had his heavy boots disappeared into the hole when Bruenor shoved Catti-brie in right behind.

"Come on, elf," he called to Drizzt.

"Don't wait for me!" Drizzt replied.

"Hey, ye Battlehammer, get in here!" yelled a dwarf from the other side.

With a glance and growl back the other way, Bruenor realized that the best thing he could do for Drizzt was to clear the way. So in he went, rolling through into the hallway beyond, and he hopped to his feet and moved the others out of the way.

"Elf coming," he explained.

"Drow!" shouted one of the Battlehammer dwarves and he lifted his crossbow.

Bruenor grabbed it immediately and drove it down.

"Drizzt Do'Urden!" Bruenor yelled at him, at them all. "Friend o' Mithral Hall."

Drizzt came up with a running dive, gracefully rolling through Athrogate's hole, and turning right over as he did, to come up to his feet, bow in hand, and swinging right back around.

"Guen!" he yelled, and he let fly a series of arrows. "They're through!"

He fell back then, to the side, and the panther sprang through the hole. And how the poor, confused dwarves fell away!

"She's a friend, too," Bruenor assured them, and he grasped the cat's muscled neck and gave a rough shake to prove his point.

Drizzt went right back to the hole, Taulmaril singing its song of death as his line of lightning arrows drove back the orcs and ogres.

"Plates and stones," one of the Battlehammer dwarves bellowed to his companions. "Get it patched afore we're thick with monsters."

The dwarves went into a frenzy then, running all around, seemingly haphazard to an untrained onlooker. Bruenor knew better, though, for they were working in brilliant coordination, some rushing back to collect hammers and rivets, others going for steel plates they could bolt to the wall, still others returning with heavy stones to bolster the repair.

These were his clansdwarves, his Battlehammers, and they had lost nothing in terms of skill and training in the decades Connerad had served as their king.

Bruenor managed a little grin of pride then, but only for a short while. Only until the steel plate went up against the iron, sealing off the monsters.

And sealing off, too, any chance for Bruenor and his friends to get back to Wulfgar and Regis.

CHAPTER 22

THE GRIN BEHIND THE EXECUTIONER'S HOOD

THEY HOWLED AND THEY WHOOPED, TAKING PLEASURE IN THE MISERY on display before them. Up on the stage, the ogrillon torturer, wearing an executioner's hood, bounced about with great showmanship, lifting his thick arms to bring the crowd more fully into the performance.

He pulled a curious glove from his pouch and held it up to the crowd.

Regis, posing as a goblin among the gathering, thought it something Thibbledorf Pwent might have worn, for a single barbed spike protruded from the back of the garment. With seductive deliberation, bringing a hush from the crowd, the ogrillon slipped the glove over his fat-fingered hand, then snickered and turned to the nearest prisoner, an unfortunate goblin hanging two feet from the floor, shackled to a post.

The ogrillon waved the spike right before the goblin's face, and the creature squirmed about and turned its head, whimpering pitifully.

The ogrillon laughed, as did the crowd.

The brute moved, a very short punch, but a very accurate one, and the spike went into the goblin's eye.

The goblin sucked in its breath, and the crowd hushed, knowing a vocal explosion of agony was about to ensue.

The ogrillon tugged back, the barbs of the spike dislodging the goblin's eyeball, which fell out of the socket and rolled about on the miserable creature's cheek.

And then came the screams, and oh, how it screamed!

And oh, how the gathered orcs and ogres and goblins cheered!

Regis joined in, despite his revulsion, because he suspected—and rightly so—that a couple of the four miserable creatures up there on that stage had gotten themselves in the path of the sadistic ogrillon for offenses less than not properly cheering. Three were goblins—the one screaming, a second tied down on the table at the front of the stage, and surely to soon be disemboweled, and a third hanging limply from a second post, likely already dead—and the fourth a dwarf, hanging quietly, his lips moving.

Singing himself an old song, Regis figured, putting his mind to a place far removed from this living hell.

How Regis wanted to go to him, to fight and die beside him. Or maybe just to stab the poor fellow in the heart and be done with it, for there was no way they could hope to escape. Better to die quickly, surely.

The halfling-turned-goblin came out of his trance when the ogrillon moved in front of the poor dwarf. The brute turned to the crowd and held up a large waterskin.

The cheering reached new heights.

The ogrillon grabbed the dwarf's head and yanked it back and began pouring the liquid down its throat, and how they cheered!

It must be some poison, Regis thought, and a particularly fast-acting and horrid one, judging by the way the dwarf began to thrash.

No, not poison, the halfling realized to his horror as the dwarf's beard began to smoke. Not poison, but acid.

The ogrillon moved back, but the dwarf kept thrashing. A garish red wound appeared on the poor fellow's throat, and blood began to drip, then a larger wound appeared just below the poor fellow's bare chest, his skin disintegrating wherever a spot of the foul acid collected.

He lived for a long, long while, gurgling, occasionally emitting some strange screaming sounds, and thrashing wildly, insane with agony. Regis had to hide his revulsion through it all, had to cheer and whoop and pretend to be like those around him.

He wanted to get out of these tunnels and out into the battles above. At that moment, Regis wanted nothing more than to slide his rapier through the chest of a goblin, or orc, or any of the other monstrous beasts he might find.

He was horrified, but mostly, he was angry, so angry, murderously angry.

He didn't know that poor dwarf's name, of course, but he silently vowed then and there that he would avenge the fellow.

"Bah, but take the frown off yer face," Bruenor said to the dwarves when the hole was finally sealed and secured, the monsters locked outside the tunnels of Mithral Hall proper once more.

Now the dwarves had turned their focus on Drizzt, it was clear, and they didn't seem too happy about him being in the complex. At first, the four companions had thought it to be a general nervousness among the Battlehammers regarding the presence of a most extraordinary six-hundred pound black panther, but even after Drizzt had dismissed Guenhwyvar back to her Astral home, the dwarf scowls had remained.

"Ye breaked yer helm," one of the dwarves noted, and Bruenor reflexively reached his hand up to feel.

"Ha, now it's looking like the helm o' King . . ." another started to say, but she stopped abruptly and sucked in her breath.

"Hey, yer shield!" said a third.

More dwarves gasped, and they ringed the companions, spears and swords leveled.

"Ye'd best be tellin' us where ye're coming from," said the dwarf who had noted the broken helm—broken only in the one horn, so much like the one horn that had been knocked from the legendary helmet of the legendary King Bruenor centuries before.

"From the west, the Sword Coast," Bruenor answered.

"From the upper chambers o' Mithral Hall, ye mean," accused the female, and she prodded her spear at Bruenor. "Ye grave-robbing pig!"

Athrogate turned to Bruenor to regard him, then looked back at the others, then back to Bruenor, trying to sort it out.

And he did sort it out, just enough to roar, "Bwahahaha!"

"No, it is no such thing," Catti-brie said loudly, stepping before the others. "And it will be explained, in full and to the satisfaction of King Connerad."

"Aye, that it will be, or the four o' ye will be finding more trouble than ye can know," said the first, who was apparently the commander of this patrol group. "Now, ye give me that helm and shield," he ordered Bruenor, and then his eyes went wide and he gasped out, "And that axe! Oh, but ye took it from me dead king's cold hands."

"Are ye old enough to remember that dead king?" Bruenor asked him.

"I fought in the Obould War," the dwarf shot back. "Under Banak Brawnanvil hisself!"

Bruenor smiled and took off the helm, then moved closer to the dwarf, and more into the light. "Then ye're knowin' me," he said. "Unless yer memory's dead past a few years gone."

The dwarf looked at him curiously.

"All o' ye!" Bruenor roared. "None o' ye are knowing me? I trained with yer Gutbusters, out o' Felba—"

"Little Arr Arr!" exclaimed the female, and she tried to continue, but found herself sputtering.

"Aye, Ragged Dain's protégé," said the first dwarf. "What're ye doing back, little one, and . . . and where'd ye get that battle gear? Yer reputation didn't name ye as a thief."

"No thief," Bruenor said. "Nay, ne'er that. Ye take us to yer King Connerad and ye'll be knowing the truth, I promise ye."

"Bah, but ye're sorcerers, all o' ye, sneakin' in to kill Connerad," the female warrior said accusingly, and she prodded her spear at Bruenor once more.

Bruenor snorted at her.

"How're we to know ye're not?" the commander demanded.

"Bwahaha!" Athrogate bellowed. "Ha, but we thought them orcs were tough!"

"Ye know me as Little Arr Arr, Reginald Roundtree o' Citadel Felbarr, friend to Mithral Hall, honorary Gutbuster," Bruenor declared. "And aye, but I've got another name, I'm admitting, but one that names me as friend to Mithral Hall as sure as the one yerselfs're knowing. More sure than the one yerselfs're knowing. Now, ye take me and me friends here to see yer king—we'll go in naked and gagged, and with a circle o' spears about each of us, if that's what it's taking. But we got things to tell yer king and things yer king's needin' to know."

"Ye give over yer weapons," the female demanded.

"Aye," agreed the leader.

Bruenor looked to Drizzt, who shrugged, then to Athrogate, who laughed all the harder, and surprisingly, the black-bearded dwarf was the first to turn over his prized flails.

"Don't ye be licking them," he said to the dwarf who took them. "One'll rot yer teeth, th'other'll give ye a surprise next time ye chomp down on a mutton bone, don't ye doubt."

Bruenor handed his axe to the commander, then slipped off his shield—or started to, but he paused and pulled a flagon of beer out from it, drawing curious looks from all around. "Damn good shield," he said with a wink, handing it over.

"That helm, too," the dwarf demanded.

"Nah, not that," Bruenor said.

"Bah, but let him keep it," the female said. She slung Taulmaril over one shoulder, Drizzt's scimitar belt over the other.

"If we find another fight, you will want to get those back to me quickly," Drizzt said to her, and she nodded, for she had just seen the drow put that devastating bow to action, driving back the orcs from the breached iron wall.

Off they went, through the lower mines of Mithral Hall and eventually into the great undercity of the dwarven complex. Athrogate took in the sights with interest and relief, simply glad to be away from the outer tunnels. He had been in Mithral Hall before, several decades past—acting as a spy and secret emissary for Jarlaxle—to coax Drizzt and the others out.

For the other three companions, the journey through Mithral Hall was much more than mere relief at being free of the monsters. Bruenor recalled his last visit to the place, only a few years previously, when he had been known as Little Arr Arr. He thought of the graves, of his own empty cairn and the tombs of his father and his father's father, and of old Gandalug, First King of Mithral Hall, who, like Bruenor, had returned from the grave to lead again as the Ninth King of Mithral Hall.

He looked to his beloved daughter as he considered two other cairns, hers and the one for Regis. How would Catti-brie feel when she looked upon her own grave, he wondered, for he had looked upon his own, his real one, in the upper audience hall of Gauntlgrym, and the sight of it had profoundly affected him.

And oh, the grave of Regis. And now it might be needed again, he knew.

That last thought hung over him and weighed his shoulders, dimming the determination a bit and dulling the joy at returning home once more. Not just for Bruenor, but for Drizzt and Catti-brie, too, and even Athrogate's step fell a bit heavier.

They had left two beloved and valued companions behind.

"Trust in them," Drizzt whispered when they moved through the undercity, to the tunnels leading to the audience chamber of King Connerad Brawnanvil. He said no more—he didn't have to—for the others understood who he was referring to.

And yes, they all knew, they had to trust in Regis and Wulfgar. Those two had tumbled out of the passageway and fallen far from the fight, at least.

It was not time for the other Companions of the Hall to surrender hope.

He flitted in and out of consciousness, unaware of the passage of time. Every time he woke up, Wulfgar was surprised that he was still alive.

Sometimes it was a scream that brought him back, sometimes a loud metallic banging from the pit in the center of the rectangular room—he didn't know what beast was in there, but it was clearly powerful, monstrously so. The whole of the room would shake with its slamming.

So it was now, and Wulfgar managed to turn his gaze enough to see the ogrillon torturer, trailed by a pair of goblins, walking away from that pit. Considering the blood and guts on the floor before the lip of the pit, Wulfgar guessed that the brutal ogrillon had fed another tortured soul to its monstrous pet.

An orc dressed in shaman's robes entered the room and rushed over to talk to the ogrillon. Wulfgar couldn't hear what they were saying, and wouldn't have understood the language anyway, but for some reason, he had a bad feeling about this one that only grew worse when the orc pointed up at him and started his way, the other three in tow.

"Who are your friends?" the orc demanded, slapping him across the face. "The drow, the dwarves, the woman wizard? Who are they?"

"I have no friends," Wulfgar replied, his voice barely audible, and his answer, clearly, unacceptable, for the orc unloaded a series of heavy punches, battering him about the ribs. And oh, but the wicked creature wore metal knuckles, and with little nubs that ground Wulfgar's bones beneath their crush.

"Who are they?" the orc demanded. "How did they get out?"

Wulfgar could barely hear him, barely knew where he was or how he had gotten here, but that last line rang as sweet music in his ears.

His friends had escaped!

Despite the pain and the beating, a smile erupted on his bloody face.

"Take him!" the orc screamed to the ogrillon. "To the carnival. Take him. Tear him apart!"

The orc ended with a straight right cross into Wulfgar's face, jerking the barbarian's face back so that he slammed the back of his head on the stone wall behind him, and his thoughts and vision flew away.

He was vaguely aware of his chains coming down, then felt the explosions of pain as his weight pressed down on his battered legs. He crumpled to the floor and was dragged along. He managed to open one eye when he landed in the back of the cart, though he couldn't see much, and even less when a goblin prisoner was pitched in atop him.

He saw the ogrillon behind the wagon, heard it yelling something he couldn't understand at the goblins.

A goblin shouted back and the brute roared in anger.

Then came a sharp *click*—perhaps it was a bone breaking, perhaps his own, or one from the goblin lying atop him.

The ogrillon moved away , and looking under the prisoner goblin's legs, Wulfgar could see it running back to the center of the room. Then it shouted, and seemed to slip and fall, pitching forward weirdly.

But it was too far away, and with his angle, and under the goblin, Wulfgar lost sight of it. He heard some screaming, ogrillon and goblin, he thought, then a crash.

And more screaming, horrified and shrieking, and the room shook and the monster in the pit thrashed.

Wulfgar didn't know what to think. He tried to rise, but couldn't, tried to turn more to get a better view back near the room's center, but could not find the strength even for that.

It seemed a moot point a moment later, in any case, as the ogrillon torturer returned—and so did the orc shaman and some of its beastly friends, all screaming angrily from the hallway just beyond the jail. The ogrillon brute lifted the goblin's leg and looked in on Wulfgar, grinning at him from behind the executioner's hood it now wore.

Then it was gone, and darkness fell over Wulfgar once more as the wagon started its roll.

CHAPTER 23

MY FRIEND, THE TORTURER

HE CUPPED HIS HANDS ABOUT HIS FACE TO BLOCK OUT THE REFLECTION of the high sun. Inside, all seemed normal about the curiosity shop, except of course that the door was locked and the place was empty.

The guard turned around and glanced past the many soldiers accompanying him, to the shop entrance across the street, where a second group of Helgabal soldiers had found a similarly locked door. Like Mickey's Pouch of Holding, A Pocketful of Zzzzs seemed quite abandoned.

"Break it in," ordered an old dwarf named Ivan, the commander of this force, who stood in the middle of Wall's Around with hands on hips and a scowl on his lips. "Both o' ye!"

A few shoulder blocks had both feeble doors opened. In swarmed the forces, into the curiosity shops, weapons drawn.

Priests and wizards followed closely, but not too closely, and with another line of warriors between them and the potential enemies they might find, these two women who had set up shop in Helgabal.

These two women rumored to be much more than simple humans.

All around the area, wizards, priests, and archers took up their positions. If dragons came forth from the shops, they would be met with a barrage of magic and missiles immediately and brutally. Ballistae had been set up on several roofs, ready to throw huge barbed spears laden with heavy chains.

From a rooftop even farther away, Dreylil Andrus leaned on a rail and shook his head. "This is madness," he said to his companion, a tall and hawkish-looking fellow called Red Mazzie, arguably the most accomplished wizard in all of Damara.

"So we take the women away in chains, torture them until they admit they are dragons, and execute them to the cheers of the onlookers," the wizard replied, and he seemed almost bored by it all.

"While you and your associates explain that you are magically preventing them from transforming into their natural forms, of course."

"Of course," answered Red Mazzie.

"That lie doesn't seem obvious to you?"

"Of course, again," the wizard answered with a laugh. "But then, I am a wizard, and schooled in such matters. I would know the truth, of course, that if we had before us Mystra reborn, we still would not likely stop a dragon in so simple a maneuver as reverting to its own beastly form. But the common folk will believe it—they will believe whatever we tell them. Is that not all that truly matters?"

Captain Andrus wanted to argue, but really could not. The mage spoke the truth.

"So we will capture these two shopkeepers and take them away in chains, and what a spectacle it will be!" Red Mazzie went on, rather dramatically, indeed overly so.

"And King Frostmantle will earn his title as Dragonsbane and at long last exorcise that ghost from his castle," said Andrus. "And only at the price of the lives of two innocent women."

"Bah, but they are merchants, shopkeepers, barely above the peasantry."

Andrus sighed. "Do you think there might be a way to spare them?"

"A dangerous ruse?" Red Mazzie asked.

"It is all a ruse!" Andrus roared back, and the wizard laughed.

"Indeed. How long have you served King Yarin?"

"Indeed," Andrus agreed, ignoring the rhetorical question.

"King Yarin will have his glorious victory over the dragons of Wall's Around," the mage said. "And yes, the lives of two innocent women will serve as the price of that victory."

Andrus sighed again and leaned heavily on the railing, facing the distant shops. He saw the guards coming out now, from both doors, meeting with the dwarf in the center of the boulevard. They had collected many items from the respective stores, but the two women were not among those gathered items, apparently.

"Suppose they are dragons," Andrus remarked. "What then?"

"Dragons? True dragons?"

Andrus turned to Red Mazzie, delighted that his supposition had put the wizard back on his heels. "Yes. True dragons. Perhaps the old crone spoke truly when she claimed that these same sisters were here on Wall's Around back when she was a little girl, nearly a century ago. Surely Damara and Vaasa teemed with the wyrms in those days, during and immediately following the reign of the Witch King in Vaasa. Perhaps a pair made their way to Heliogabalus to mingle with the populace, in disguise."

"Under the nose of the paladin King Dragonsbane?"

Andrus shrugged. "Why not?"

"And under the nose of Olwen Forest-friend, and Grandmaster Kane, and Emelyn the Gray, as powerful a wizard as Damara has ever known?"

"Perhaps, yes."

"Dragons?" Mazzie's incredulity did not abate.

"Are all dragons evil?"

The wizard laughed and shook his head at the preposterous suppositions.

The roof door banged open then, and the dwarf leader of the battle group came out onto the roof. "Not there. Not been there for a bit."

"It is a fine day, late in the season," Captain Andrus replied. "Why would a merchant close her shop on such a day, particularly with winter so close?"

"Ain't just that the shops're closed, Captain," the dwarf answered. "We found a tunnel connecting the two, running right under Wall's Around."

That piqued the interest of both men.

"Do tell," Red Mazzie bade Ivan.

"Aye, and that ain't all," the dwarf answered. "I been in those shops afore, me brother buys many the goods from Lady Zee and Mickey, and can tell ye that them two ladies were well-versed in appraising. Fine items, the best o' quality, don't ye doubt. Oh, they had many the cheap pieces scattered about—what merchant won't be taking the coin of a fool who can't be telling the difference, eh?"

"And?" prompted an annoyed Captain Andrus, who figured he had wasted too much of his time on this distasteful business already.

"But they knowed a good piece when they saw one," the dwarf answered. "And had many o' them scattered about on their shelfs."

"And?" Andrus prompted again.

"Weren't none o' them good pieces in there now, neither place," said Ivan. "Just junk, all junk. Worthless, save to a blind fool."

"So they sold their better wares," Andrus started to reply, but Red Mazzie cut him short.

"You think they took all of the fine pieces with them," the wizard reasoned. "They abandoned their shops and absconded with the valuable items?"

"That'd be me own guess, aye."

"They simply rode out of Helgabal in the middle of the night with a wagon full of plunder?"

"No," the dwarf and Andrus said together.

"We asked that o' the gate guards afore we came here," Ivan explained. "Both o' them ladies were in the city yesterday, or the day before that, or sometime recent. But they ain't gone out, neither, that anyone's seen."

Red Mazzie turned to Andrus and shook his head. "Then they're still about in the city," the wizard said.

"Or perhaps they flew out in the dark of night," Andrus replied, and he was only half-joking.

"Carryin' half a store o' goods with 'em?" asked the dwarf.

Neither man offered an answer.

"Search the town, all of the town," Captain Andrus ordered, and the dwarf heaved a long sigh.

"Big town," he said.

"And post guards about both shops, and with other guards in sight to relay their cries of alarm should Mickey or Lady Zee return," Andrus commanded.

The captain and Red Mazzie left the roof then, leaving Ivan to wonder how far they would carry this absurd hunt to satisfy the idiocy of King Yarin Frostmantle. "Dragons," the dwarf muttered, shaking his head.

He had ridden a dragon once, a great red in a faraway land in a long-ago time.

And he had fought another one, a dead one, a dracolich, and that ride had been wilder still.

Ivan Bouldershoulder smiled widely as he thought of those foregone days. Often did he tell those tales in the taverns of Helgabal. And so many others—who would believe that he had caught a fleeing vampire in a bellows?

Ah, but that story got him a round of drinks every time!

It was a good life.

The ogrillon paraded about the stage, an eager smile behind its executioner's hood as it lifted one implement of torture after another for the huge gathering to see. Each wicked item elicited a tremendous cheer, and shouts in several languages, all calling for a painful and cruel death to the human.

It wasn't often that they got a human to their carnival so fresh from the battle now, and this large barbarian had inflicted quite a bit of damage to orc-kind in the last few tendays.

The ogrillon scanned the room—there were hundreds in here, he estimated. Many more than the last time. In between the sections of benches in the semicircular amphitheater, a huge bonfire lifted its flames high into the cavern, and about it danced goblins and orcs, all eager to see the pain inflicted on the prisoners.

The ogrillon moved to a small fire on the stage and lifted a hot poker from its glowing embers. With a wicked smile, the skilled torturer turned for the goblin and took a step that way.

The crowd cheered, but not as crazily as before, for they had seen many puny goblins murdered, and this one seemed hardly alive—would it even squirm when the poker went against its pallid flesh?

Hearing that muted response, the ogrillon threw down the poker and waved at the goblin dismissively, turning around and pinching his own nose in clear disgust.

The crowd laughed heartily.

Yes, this executioner was a fine showman.

Over at the center altar on the stage, the ogrillon lifted an acid-filled waterskin up high, and while the audience's eyes were drawn up, the torturer subtly shifted a second waterskin into place on the gruesome sacrificial table.

The brute went to the goblin quickly, his back to the crowd, the acid-filled waterskin up high, and his free hand going to his belt, producing a fine dagger. He crashed right up against the hanging goblin, then backed away a step, paused for a few heartbeats, then roughly poured the acid down the creature's throat.

The wretched creature gurgled, but did not squirm.

A splotch of blood appeared on the goblin's throat. Another was already flowing from its heart, from a quiet stab wound that had ended the goblin's life before the acid ever got near its lips

More bloody splotches appeared, the acid eating the creature from the inside, through its lungs and upper belly.

But no screams came forth, and no wild thrashing as one would expect.

The goblin was already dead, the crowd realized, and a chorus of boos and jeers came at the torturer from every part of the audience chamber.

Wulfgar managed to open his working eye at that time, and he glanced over just as the goblin's torso fully collapsed from the corrosive fluid, spilling its contents over the floor. Now the crowd did cheer and dance and scream with wicked glee.

Wulfgar watched the torturer rush back to the table and grab up another waterskin. The brute held it up and half the crowd cheered—but the other half, thinking such a tactic would create too quick a kill, screamed for the ogrillon to stop. The acid was supposed to be the finale, after all.

The ogrillon did not stop or even slow, however, but spun around and charged at Wulfgar.

Wulfgar's eye widened with horror. He had to fight it!

Up came his legs—one, at least, for the other was too swollen and pained for him to lift. He twisted and thrashed about in his shackles, but he could not pull his arms free.

The ogrillon slapped aside his leg and came up right against him, one bloody hand to his throat, the other lifting the waterskin to his lips.

Desperately, the barbarian turned his head—as much as he was ready to die, as much as he preferred death to this horrible imprisonment, in that moment of truth, his instincts made him fight, and fight for all his life.

The waterskin chased him about; he snapped his head back the other way, but some liquid got into his mouth. He tried to spit it out, but the waterskin was back to his lips, blocking his attempted spit and pouring more liquid!

Some slipped down his throat, and he felt . . . warmth.

"Scream, you fool," the ogrillon whispered in his ear, and in a voice that was strangely familiar.

The brute stepped back. It took Wulfgar a moment to register what might be happening here. There was blood on his lip and on his throat, but it was not his. The ogrillon torturer had put it there with his bloody hands!

His bloody hands and his familiar voice.

So Wulfgar screamed, and he thrashed. He gave the audience the show it so dearly craved.

The waterskin came back to his lips, and he pretended to try to get away from it, but no, he was quickly caught, and he drank deeply.

The torturer's free hand, holding a small implement, went up to the shackle as the ogrillon pushed in closer, as if to hug Wulfgar and stop him from turning away.

"Don't pull your hand free," came the instruction, and Wulfgar felt one shackle loosen as skilled fingers deftly picked the crude lock. "Grab the chain, keep your hand up high."

The ogrillon pulled away and swung about. "And keep screaming," he said above the roar of the crowd.

And so Wulfgar did, screamed and thrashed as if in horrid, burning agony.

In truth, he felt his bones knitting, his wounds closing, his eyes clearing. He had consumed half the waterskin, several powerful potions of healing. He almost felt as if his legs could hold him upright once more.

A moment later, he knew they would!

The ogrillon torturer paraded about the room, holding the waterskin, rousing the orcs and goblins. The barbarian cried in feigned agony. The gathered orcs and goblins, ogres and ogrillon, cheered wildly and spat curses, and threw small stones at the hanging barbarian warrior.

"Go slack," the ogrillon in the executioner's hood quietly demanded as he passed the prisoner on one of his parades, and Wulfgar fell to the length of his chains, now seeming overwhelmed, spent.

The crowd booed.

The ogrillon leaped against the man and moved as if to bite his ear, telling him to scream again, and so he did.

"You'll know when," the torturer promised, moving back and lifting the waterskin once again to Wulfgar's lips, draining its healing contents down his throat, while his free hand went up to pick the second shackle.

Wulfgar screamed wildly, and the crowd followed with cheers of equal intensity. The barbarian noted a slight nod from the torturer, and so he fell slack again, holding himself by the chains above the shackles, his legs apparently useless beneath him.

The crowd grew quiet, orc-kind glancing all around, wondering, obviously, if the show had ended.

But the ogrillon executioner's smile defeated that notion, and the brute reached under its filthy robe, brought forth a small vial, and held it up for all to see. The nearest creatures leaned forward in anticipation, not sure what to make of the item. Was this some new torture liquid, perhaps? Acid or poison, or maybe something to revive and partially repair the fallen human, that he could be tortured again for their pleasure?

But no, it wasn't for him, they came to realize when the ogrillon started to turn, but swung back and hurled the small bottle out from the stage.

It soared out over the heads of the closest onlookers, past a hundred curious gazes, and crashed into the base of the bonfire, where the oil of impact promptly exploded, launching flaming logs and kindling, gouts of flame and stinging sparks, all around the back of the hall.

"Now!" the executioner, who was not an executioner, implored his barbarian friend, and Wulfgar put his feet under him and leaped away from the wall, his shackles falling free.

The ogrillon executioner lifted his hand again, displaying a cluster of small ceramic balls, though few in the confused and crazed and outraged audience noted the newest presentation.

Goblins screamed and orcs gasped, and few had sorted things out enough to make a move.

But some did, including an ogre near to the stage, who leaped up in one powerful movement.

Out went the executioner's hand, ceramic pellets flying in a wide spread, and those balls hit and shattered, their concealed contents radiating light, magical light, divine, brilliant light!

The last of the ceramic balls hit the floor right in front of the approaching ogre, who growled in protest and hunched back, shielding its eyes, which had not seen such light in months!

"Follow! Run!" the ogrillon called to Wulfgar, and the barbarian did indeed.

But he paused after only a couple of steps, noting the crowd, dodging a spear that was flying his way, and focusing on one large orc in particular. That creature, large and fierce, seemed to be organizing the others, rallying it to its banner, which, held high as a standard, proved to be a most curious weapon indeed.

The ogrillon moved to the right side of the stage, to the tunnel that would take it from this place. Noting that the barbarian wasn't right behind, the brute spun around—just in time to see Wulfgar, Aegis-fang somehow in hand, smash the ogre across the face and send it flopping from the stage onto a group of orcs that were trying to get up at him.

Hardly slowing, Wulfgar flung the hammer out into the audience, spinning it for one particularly large orc who stood there staring at its empty hands, hands that only a few moments before had held the very same warhammer that now caved in the side of its head.

Wulfgar and Regis, the phony ogrillon, rushed out of the room and down the hall to the torture chamber, a hundred monsters roaring in protest and charging in pursuit.

CHAPTER 24

ON THE WINGS OF DRAGONS

Today," Tiago promised Warlord Hartusk, the drow's long white hair blowing with every downbeat of great Arauthator's wings. The ancient white dragon hovered above them, above the courtyard before the huge metal gates of the citadel of Sundabar.

Tiago looked up the side of the citadel, to the many ropes reaching out from it to the gigantic tree trunk Arauthator held in his powerful hind claws.

"Indeed, now," the drow assured the warlord, and he moved Hartusk aside and looked up to, and called up to the dragon.

With a shriek that had orcs and goblins covering their ears for miles around, Arauthator dived down and away from the citadel, and when the ropes tugged, the dragon let go. The gigantic log, which sped down and swung in at the end of those many tethers, slammed full force into the doors of the keep.

The dragons had already weakened those portals, and now they tumbled in, both great doors and the metal jamb holding them plunging inward to the marble floor with a resounding crash.

In poured the goblin fodder, and behind them, Hartusk's elite orc warriors, brandishing fine swords.

But the place was empty, as they had expected.

"The humans, dwarves, and their allies have fled," came the reports, filtering back out from every possible location within the massive structure.

"Seal every exit from those granaries," Hartusk ordered, nodding and

334

unsurprised, for this had been predicted. Firehelm's cowardly folk had fled to the Everfire Caverns below the granaries that lay beneath the great citadel. "Construct heavy doors within the tunnels, guard chambers all around. And heavier doors still at the granary entrances."

Beside him, Tiago Baenre nodded his approval. They had anticipated this flight, and Hartusk, of course, had declared that he would chase after the fleeing Sundabar citizenry. But Tiago had offered a different course, this course, to secure the city, to seal the Underdark routes fully and claim the great Citadel of Sundabar for Many-Arrows.

"We will have the whole of the winter," Tiago had explained to Hartusk, and so he and his fellow drow explained again at the first meeting within the citadel. "Let us block any return by Firehelm's minions. Let us rebuild the walls of Sundabar."

The orc warlord nodded, but still didn't seem overly thrilled with the idea.

"Let us rebuild the walls of Hartusk Keep," Tiago offered, and Hartusk seemed more amenable to the idea.

So it was, and so it went, with goblins and orcs working furiously to repair the walls and blasted structures of proud Sundabar for their own filthy uses.

In short days, the plan was going along splendidly, better than the drow could have hoped. This was the third city of Luruar, behind Silverymoon, which was also under heavy siege, and Everlund, sitting nervously just to the south.

"Conquering Sundabar so efficiently allows us to hold the siege," Tiago explained to his fellow dark elves, Ravel and Tos'un, and to Doum'wielle and Hartusk and the great orc's advisors. "From here, we can easily resupply and reinforce our hordes about Silverymoon's gates throughout the deepest of the winter snows. There will be no reprieve for Luruar."

"None," Warlord Hartusk agreed, slamming his fist down hard on the oaken table, the same table King Firehelm and his commanders had often used, and from the same throne Firehelm had sat upon, and Frosthelm before him, and great King Helm before him.

"It is unfortunate that so many escaped," Ravel Xorlarrin put in, and Tiago shot him an angry look. "We could have put them to use in rebuilding Warlord Hartusk's city," the wizard explained.

"Our victory is no less complete," Tiago insisted. "In short months, we have trapped the dwarves in their three holes. We have slain King Bromm of Adbar and taken his head to Dark Arrow Keep."

He marched about the table now, growing more animated with every word.

"We have thrown aside the line of Obould, for the greater glory of Gruumsh and his chosen, Warlord Hartusk."

That brought cheers from the orcs.

"Nesmé is caught and held, Silverymoon besieged and helpless, and Sundabar has fallen. Already fallen!"

"Victory," Warlord Hartusk growled, and the other orcs echoed.

"All of Luruar is doomed," Tiago told them. "Soon after the spring melt, the only city above ground to remain in the hands of our enemies will be Everlund, and they will beg for mercy."

"They will find no mercy," said Hartusk, and the orcs cheered more wildly.

Ravel cast a sidelong glance at Tiago at that, however, for they had discussed this very matter privately. Menzoberranzan's goals were not directly aligned with those of Warlord Hartusk. He wanted war, wanted blood, and there would never be enough to satisfy the brutal warlord.

But the drow understood the balance and the timing they must find. If they pushed too far—and Everlund might indeed be that one city too far—they would invite the wrath of outside powers, great kingdoms who themselves would feel threatened by an expanding orc empire. How might the Kingdom of Many-Arrows, even with her gains, fare against the forces of Waterdeep and Mirabar, or the armies of Cormyr?

Tiago shook his head to comfort his companion. It did not matter. As they had discussed, Warlord Hartusk was their pawn and not the other way around. The white dragons would not side with the orcs above the commands of Gromph Baenre and Matron Mother Baenre herself. The giants would adhere to the orders of the phony three brothers of their god Thrym, and those three, too, were mere puppets of Gromph, and fully under the control of Methil.

Hartusk's forces would go as far as the dark elves allowed, and if beyond that, they would be on their own.

"The Silver Marches will be ours," Tiago promised anyway. "From the throne room of Silverymoon will we plot the fall of the dwarven kingdoms Adbar, Felbarr, and filthy Mithral Hall. And when they are ours, from their mines will come fine metals, and from their forges will come greater power. By the turn of 1486, Warlord Hartusk will know seven great cities in his domain, three from the dwarves and three from the humans, to complement Dark Arrow Keep."

The orc warlord let out a long and low growl of approval at that promise.

"But only," Tiago warned, "if we strictly adhere to the designs my war-skilled brethren have lain before us."

Warlord Hartusk narrowed his yellow eyes at that not-so-subtle reminder of who was directing this war.

The very next day, Tiago's proclamation was put to a great test, as drow couriers arrived from the west into Hartusk Keep, the new city of orcs.

Tiago caught up to the dark elf scouts as they entered Warlord Hartusk's throne room. Across the way, the huge orc seemed quite at home, bedecked in a thick purple robe and a crown of jewels.

"What news?" Tiago asked as he made his way with them to the seated orc leader.

"From Nesmé," explained a female Tiago recognized as one of Saribel's handmaidens.

Tiago reached for her arm to slow her, but wisely deferred from touching her. She was a priestess of substantial rank, judging from her dress, and likely, he prudently reminded himself, a noble of House Baenre. He could not touch her without permission.

"Cousin?" he asked, and stopped, and the woman stopped, too, and turned to regard him.

"You are Do'Urden now, and not Baenre," she reminded.

"I am always Baenre," he dared to respond, and he stiffened his jaw with resolve. "I serve the matron mother first, Matron Darthiir second."

The smile on the female's face told him he had passed the test.

"What news from Nesmé?" he quietly asked. "Pray tell me before we inform the orc."

"From Saribel," the priestess explained. "Nesmé holds strong, and has found mighty heroes among her ranks."

"We were warned that it was a stout town, not unused to battle."

"What is the delay?" Warlord Hartusk shouted from the other end of the hall, but Tiago held up his hand to bid patience from the brute. Hartusk, of course, immediately sent his soldiers to gather the pair.

"A drow is named among those heroes," the priestess quickly and quietly explained. "One with purple eyes, who rides a unicorn and throws lightning from his mighty bow."

Tiago found it hard to draw breath.

"Drizzt?" he whispered as the orcs gathered him and the priestess up and hustled them to stand before Warlord Hartusk.

The priestess grinned at him, all the answer he needed.

"What news?" Hartusk demanded.

"Fine news," Tiago said before the priestess could speak. He could hardly get the words out, for he was trembling with excitement. "Nesmé is near to surrender, Warlord. My wife Saribel has softened their walls. Before the first snows, Nesmé, too, will be ours."

Hartusk slammed his fist upon the arm of his throne, his eyes shining hungrily. "I wish to stomp them under my own boots," he growled, seeming more angry than pleased.

"And so you shall," Tiago assured him. "You and I—the dragons will take us there. We will see the fall of a second Luruar city before the first snows descend upon the land."

Later that same day, Hartusk and Tiago stood in the courtyard before the citadel, the Old White Death, Arauthator, crouched on the cobblestones before them.

"Plunder, you promised, and so there is," the dragon warned, seeming less than pleased by Tiago's demands that they fly far to the west. "Jewels and gems are here, in this place, and they are mine."

Warlord Hartusk narrowed his yellow eyes and turned a baleful glare over Tiago.

"Indeed, they are, great wyrm of the north," the drow answered, ignoring the brutish orc. What was Hartusk about to say, after all, in the face of an angry dragon? "Will you convey them, or will your son Aurbangras fly the load to your lair in the mountains?"

The dragon tilted its head, staring at him curiously. Up above, gliding back and forth across the city, the younger wyrm roared.

"Only one will be needed in the west, in Nesmé, the city of the marketplace of Luruar," Tiago explained, making sure to accentuate the word "marketplace" to the insatiable wyrm.

"Spread a thick net wide across this square," Arauthator ordered. "Fill crates with gems and jewels and gold, and cover the net with these crates. If I deem it enough, I will grant your passage to Nesmé."

"And if not?" Hartusk said before Tiago could make the foolish orc shut up.

Arauthator let out a low growl that rumbled through the foundations of every house and structure in Sundabar. Far away from that central square, the vibrations dislodged a huge slab of stone from the wall Arauthator had smashed. It slid free, cleaving a goblin mason in half before splashing down in the eel-infested moat.

"If not, perhaps I will eat the crown from your head, puny orc," the dragon answered, and Arauthator smiled—or perhaps it was more a mere display of the dragon's massive teeth than an actual smile!

Whatever the source of that wicked grin, the effect proved immediate and complete.

Before the sun was halfway to the western horizon, Aurbangras lifted away from Sundabar with a huge net of crates. To the north, the son of Arauthator flew to the cavern lair of Old White Death.

Arauthator's journey was to the east. The dragon would never admit it to Tiago, certainly, but Arauthator was quite enjoying this play. For too long, Arauthator had remained high in the Spine of the World, away from the civilized lands. Now the wyrm enjoyed again the smell of battle and the thrill of slaughter.

With Tiago, Ravel, and Hartusk upon its back, the Old White Death set off for the east, for Nesmé.

"And Drizzt," Tiago whispered, thinking that his moment of ultimate glory would soon be upon him.

He would find the favor of Lolth, the blessing of the matron mother, the honor of Menzoberranzan, and the burning envy of Andzrel.

Glory to Tiago, glory to House Do'Urden, for the head of its wayward son.

Ambergris and Brother Afafrenfere walked out of the Monastery of the Yellow Rose one crisp and sunny autumn morning, the dwarf dragging a litter of supplies behind her. The drow named Jarlaxle was waiting for them, Master Perrywinkle Shin had informed them, when he had personally roused them from their slumber.

All of the masters of the Monastery of the Yellow Rose were there to bid farewell to the departing Afafrenfere, forming a long line to the great doors leading out of the main building. Each offered good thoughts and blessings as the monk passed, Mistress Savahn even went up on her tiptoes to kiss the man on the cheek.

"Be well and be wise," she said to him. "We wait anxiously for your return, young brother. I do expect to learn from you, as you learn from your spirit guide."

It was an odd remark, Afafrenfere thought, and he almost reached up to touch the gem set in the middle of his forehead. He couldn't help but smile as he considered again the beauty of Grandmaster Kane, who had dissolved to butterfly lights, sprinkling to and through the floorboards. And even that had not been the end of the man, they all knew. Afafrenfere lifted his eyes to the heights of the grand foyer of the monastery, imagining Kane up there, walking his rounds.

Or perhaps even watching the departure, he realized, and he thought he did note some movement on one of the higher balconies.

Determination carried the monk out of the monastery and down the long trail to his destiny. He looked back only once, to see the masters watching him from the porch of the great building.

He lifted his gaze, and noted, too, another witness, in one of the high windows. Yes, he was not alone, he knew, not even excluding Jarlaxle and Ambergris.

Kane, Grandmaster of Flowers, who had transcended death itself, watched him from that high window, but also walked with him, walked within him.

The pair spotted the drow down the trail, sitting astride his nightmare, and as they approached, Jarlaxle turned around and walked his mount away, leading them far from the monastery's gates, indeed long out of sight of the place, before he allowed them to catch up.

"Ye know, elf, ye might've slowed to let me hitch this durned litter to yer horse." Ambergris grumbled when at last Jarlaxle turned his mount back to the pair.

"I would not want your masters to see our mounts," the drow explained, slipping down from the saddle.

"They could see you from the doorway," said the monk.

Jarlaxle smiled, and to the surprise of the other two, dismissed his nightmare, picking up the onyx figurine it left behind and dropping it into a deep belt pouch.

"Why, then?" the dwarf asked. "What?"

"Not that mount," Jarlaxle replied, and he slowly turned to the side, to his left, and the others looked that way, too.

The trees shook and branches crackled, and through the tangle came their mounts, apparently.

Ambergris dropped her litter, and nearly dropped to her knees.

Afafrenfere, too, sucked in his breath.

Courage, the voice in his head assured him.

"Wondrous experiences," the monk whispered aloud.

"Oh, indeed," Jarlaxle agreed with a laugh. "Are you to faint away, dwarf?"

"Dragons," Ambergris mouthed, barely able to speak, as the two copper dragons, Tazmikella and Ilnezhara, crawled into the clearing and shook away the branches they had dislodged in their trek.

"Say it with respect, dwarf," Tazmikella replied, and her voice still sounded like that of a human woman, which put the dwarf and the monk off-kilter a bit as they tried to make sense of the amazing scene before them.

"I give you the ladies Tazmikella and Ilnezhara," Jarlaxle said. "There are great happenings in the wider world, my friends, and these two would like to accompany us on our journey."

"Saddles?" Afafrenfere heard himself say as he noted the leather harnesses the dragons wore, including a two-seated one on the dragon Jarlaxle had introduced as Ilnezhara.

"We're to ride them things?" Ambergris asked incredulously.

"They have most graciously offered," said Jarlaxle.

The dwarf began to titter, just a bit, then it became a giggle, then erupted into a full-force belly laugh. "Do ye steer it like a pony, then?" she asked Jarlaxle.

The reaction surely showed Ambergris that she had asked the wrong question.

The drow sucked in his breath and fell back, and in the blink of an astonished dwarf eye, Ilnezhara's face was there, quick as a serpent strike, stopped barely a finger's breath from Ambergris's now-wide eyes.

"You hold on," the dragon explained. "You do nothing more than hold on. You are my guest and not my rider. If you ever forget that . . ."

She paused and opened wide her maw, and poor Ambergris nearly fainted away as she stared at the rows and rows of jagged teeth, many longer than her forearm!

"Note the flatter teeth in the back," Tazmikella added wickedly. "They will hold you and grind you, but oh so slowly. Our kind are known to digest rather . . . painfully."

"Acid breath," Jarlaxle explained with a wink.

Ambergris swallowed hard.

The drow moved around Ambergris and the grinning dragon, over to Tazmikella, where he nimbly pulled himself into the saddle.

"Courage," Afafrenfere whispered, echoing the voice in his head. He moved to stand before Ilnezhara.

"With your permission, magnificent Ilnezhara," he asked, and he bowed low in respect.

"Do," the dragon answered with a deferential nod.

Up went the monk, into the saddle, and he called to his companion.

"Might I be joinin' him?" Ambergris asked quietly.

"Just hold on," Ilnezhara replied.

With every step, it looked as though poor Ambergris might simply topple over, but she somehow made it to the side of the great wyrm. She took Afafrenfere's hand and he pulled her up behind him.

Barely had she settled into her seat when Tazmikella leaped straight up with a great swirl of air, and flexed her wings out wide, banking and drifting away down the side of the high mountain pass.

"Hold on," Afafrenfere warned the dwarf, and he had guessed right, for up leaped Ilnezhara, much like her sister.

In mere heartbeats, the dragon sisters and their trio of "guests" soared up high, very high, higher than archers could shoot, where cold winds buffeted Jarlaxle, Afafrenfere, and Ambergris.

All fear flew away from the dwarf then, and she shrieked with glee as the world spread wide before her and below her.

She looked across the way to Jarlaxle, who nodded and returned her smile. At first, Ambergris was surprised that his reaction seemed so muted as compared to her own, but when she thought about it, about him, she could only nod. Ambergris believed that her life had been eventful, but she knew it would seem positively mundane to that particular drow, after all.

In fact, few in the Realms had seen, bartered, battled, befriended, or copulated with a more impressive array of powerful beings and monsters than Jarlaxle.

Afafrenfere remained quiet, but was no less elated than the dwarf behind him. So many wondrous things would he experience, he knew, not the least of which being the insights he would find from the spirit of Kane.

His heart sang to him, and he knew beyond doubt that the adventures he had known already paled in comparison.

And this road had only just begun.

From the courtyard of Hartusk Keep, Doum'wielle and Tos'un watched the trio fly away on the back of Arauthator.

It is a brilliant adventure, is it not?" Tos'un asked, wrapping his arm about his daughter's slender and strong shoulders. "Ah, but it is good to be back where I belong, among my people—our people—and in the midst of such glorious campaigns."

Doum'wielle nodded and offered a smile to her father, but inside, she was much less certain of this course. She had seen, she had done and caused, terrible things and horrific suffering. Her own homeland would soon be razed, she knew, her own mother murdered. Or worse, captured.

She thought of her brother, whom she had murdered.

These changes in her life, so abrupt, so stark, so brutal . . .

Her doubts only lasted a few moments, however, as a wave of ecstasy coursed through her body. Ugly things seemed pretty things, her movements, she thought, were pre-ordained and of a higher purpose. She was a blessed thing.

Without even thinking of the movement, Little Doe put a hand to the hilt of her fabulous, sentient sword.

Her fabulous, evil sword.

On and on came the waves of monsters, goblins and orcs and ogres throwing themselves against the walls of the battered town. Even without the five heroes who had set off to find help from Mithral Hall, the defenders of the city fought valiantly and repelled the attackers.

But more monsters came on and more died.

Giants milled about the back ranks of the monstrous force, heaving their boulders against and over the wall. From the south came the trolls and bog blokes.

"Fight on!" Jolen Firth rallied his charges. "Every arrow is a goblin dead. Heigh-ho!"

And the hardy warriors of Nesmé cheered back at him and set the next arrows to their bowstrings, and indeed, more monstrous corpses piled outside of Nesmé's strong wall.

Along the south wall, a blue-robed wizard ran the length of the archer line, enchanting their arrows with magically flaming tips.

Trolls didn't like fire. Neither did bog blokes, monsters the folk of Nesmé often referred to as "self-delivering kindling."

An hour into the attack, the enemy dead piled thick.

Two hours into the attack, the defenders continued to rally.

Three hours into the attack, the wall was breached, but the Riders of Nesmé were to the spot in short order, running down the monsters, chasing them back out or slaughtering them within the city.

Four hours into the attack, the weary defenders held on, though the mages had little magic left to throw, the clerics had healed all that they could heal, and the archers' fingers bled, rubbed more than raw.

But still they held, and still Jolen Firth rode about the ways of the town, rallying his warriors, telling them that this would be their most glorious day. And indeed, they seemed to be holding, and Nesmé commanders even whispered that perhaps they could quickly recover and then break out against their battered enemy when this assault was through, and drive the orcs from their fields.

For a brief moment, the defenders knew hope.

It fell from on high, barely a speck against the roiling blackness of the Darkening, tumbling, tumbling. Soon after, it began to make a whistling sound, falling so fast that the air screamed about it.

The rock—and it was a rock, a huge rock, a rock the size of a giant—landed atop Jolen Firth's own keep, crushing down with such force that it shattered the roof and plunged through, the sheer weight and force of the explosion blowing out the walls of the building as the rock crashed down to the ground.

A few were killed, many more wounded, but that alone could not have turned the battle.

However, the source of the falling stone surely could, and surely did.

It, too, came down from on high, folding its leathery wings in a great stoop that had the cheeks and lips of its rider flapping in the press of wind, and had his white hair flying out behind him with such force that it seemed as if he would be a bald drow by the time he and Arauthator reached the ground.

The Old White Death had come, unfolding its wings at the last moment and leveling out to sweep above the city, low enough for the dragon's killing claws to tear some defenders from the wall as it passed, low enough for the dragon to breathe its killing frost over a group of Riders as they huddled near the breach, trying to hold back the monstrous hordes.

The defenders of Nesmé saw the dragon and knew their doom had come.

The attackers of Nesmé saw the dragon and knew they could not lose.

On the monsters charged again, ferociously, and now the giants joined in the assault, a score of the behemoths coming on in a group from the west, confident that the city's wizards had exhausted their killing fiery magic. Barely five long strides from the wall, the giant legion pulled up as one and hurled their boulders, each stone slamming the wall right near the previous, and under that concentrated attack, the center of Nesmé's western wall buckled and tumbled.

The dragon rushed past south-to-north along that same expanse, at just that time, its murderous breath scattering defenders, widening the breach.

In poured the monsters, the goblins and orcs and armored ogres, and behind them came the giants, staying close in their group, rocks in hand.

Jolen Firth led the Riders of Nesmé to the newest breach, trampling goblins, battling ogres.

But down came Arauthator and Tiago astride the wyrm, and the horses reared in terror, and even fled before the power of the dragon. No training and no rider, no matter how skilled, could stop them in their terror.

And so the brilliant coordination of the city defense was shattered.

And so did Nesmé die.

EPILOGUE

Apair of burly orcs dragged Giselle across the courtyard and
uncremoniously dropped her in the mud at the base of the dais that
had been constructed to seat the two dark elves, who had proclaimed
themselves as Duke and Duchess of Nesmé.

One was a high priestess of Lady Lolth, so the whispers said, and the
other, the dragon rider, with his starry sword and a strange shield that could
widen for full protection and contract to mere buckler size on command.

To the side of the stage, Jolen Firth stood chained to a post, barely alive.

To the other side, a huge pile of bodies, many of whom Giselle had
known as friends.

"You are a Rider of Nesmé?" the male drow asked, though it took Giselle
a few moments to decipher his words, given his strong accent.

"I am Giselle . . ." she started to say, but the orc beside her kicked her
in the ribs.

"You are a Rider of Nesmé?" the drow asked again.

"Yes," she answered through gritted teeth.

"Where is the drow?"

Giselle looked at him curiously.

"The drow who fought for Nesmé," the dragon rider clarified.

Giselle stared at him dumbfounded, her thoughts spinning.

"Drizzt Do'Urden?" he asked.

"Who?" she asked, or started to ask, but the orc bent low and chopped
its fist across her face, dropping her down to the mud.

The orc grabbed her by the back of the head and began rubbing her
face in the muck. It tugged her head back and face-slammed her down,
once and then again, until the drow finally said, "Enough."

346

"Drizzt Do'Urden?" he asked the mud-spitting Giselle again.

"I do not know . . ." she started to reply, but the orc grabbed her roughly once more.

"No, no," the drow called and the orc held.

"That will not make her answer," the drow prompted, but then he smiled wickedly. "Well, go on for a bit, perhaps, for my pleasure."

The orc slammed her face in the mud again and pummeled her about the ears. The brute tugged her head back painfully and slammed her down hard, then pressed on the back of her head so that she could not breathe, so that her nostrils and mouth filled with mud.

She flailed desperately and tried to reach back to break the hold, but she could not, and she was sure she would die.

But then the orc relented, yanking her head back so that she was looking at the drow couple once more.

"You still do not know the answer to my question, I am sure," the male drow said.

Giselle stared at him, offering nothing. He motioned to the side, and a young child was dragged out before her, a boy who could not have been more than seven or eight years of age.

"Drizzt Do'Urden?" the drow asked.

Giselle stared at the child.

Too long.

"Kill him," the drow said, matter-of-factly.

"No!" Giselle shouted in a mud-filled cry as an orc near the boy lifted its wicked blade to his throat.

"Drizzt Do'Urden?" the drow asked again.

"He left," she said. "Days ago."

"To where?"

Giselle hesitated.

"To where?" the drow shouted, coming forward now to the edge of the dais. When Giselle didn't immediately reply, he motioned to the orc.

They had a lot of children waiting in the wings, Giselle knew.

"North!" she cried. "He went north, to find allies to come to Nesmé's aid."

"Drizzt Do'Urden?" the drow asked. "A dark elf? You know him as Drizzt Do'Urden?"

"Drizzt, yes," she admitted. "He saved me in the forest, him and his companions. They came to Nesmé and aided us in our time of need.

And he went out north, days ago, to find help, to beg of the dwarves of Mithral Hall, perhaps."

The drow did not seem pleased, not at all. He sat back in his chair, mulling and muttering.

"You should have answered sooner," he said to Giselle, and then to the orc to the side, he added, "Kill him."

"No!" Giselle cried, but it was muffled as the orc securing her slammed her down into the mud again. That proved merciful, for she did not have to witness the execution of the young boy.

She heard his cry, though, and saw him lying in the mud, so still, when the orc holding her yanked her head back once more.

"I will have him," the drow Duke of Nesmé told the priestess at his side. "He will not escape me again."

Another dark elf came up to the stage then. "We've six hundred prisoners," the drow reported. "The rest are dead."

"Too many," the Duke of Nesmé replied. "Choose the hardiest half to serve as slaves. Do as you will with the other half."

Giselle's head fell back to the mud, the woman overwhelmed by the casual evilness of this dark elf before her. She had seen many battles in her twenty-five years of life, but she simply could not fathom this level of cruelty, this level of atrocity, particularly from a creature so strangely beautiful.

"What of him?" asked the orc, and the brute pointed to Jolen Firth.

"Crucify him before the city's main gate," the drow answered without hesitation.

"And her?" asked the orc, who tugged Giselle by the hair.

"She lives," she heard the Duke order the orc guarding her.

To Giselle, those might have been the cruelest words of all.

The halfling-turned-ogrillon went right past Wulfgar's former prison and sped further down the corridor, turning into a side passage, one much narrower. Regis had scouted this area well, and with orcs and other monsters closing in fast, with spears flying to skip across the floor not far behind their running feet, he and Wulfgar got through a door.

Regis slammed it shut and dropped a locking bar in place.

"Follow," he told his friend, and on they ran.

"How?" Wulfgar asked many footsteps later, through a dozen more doors, several side passages, and into a more natural area of the upper Underdark—and still pursuit was not far behind!

Regis pulled off the executioner's hood, threw it aside, and tapped his head where his disguised magical beret was. He immediately reverted to his true halfling look, but remained much larger than he had been, as tall as Wulfgar and still much thicker, so that he looked like a strangely gigantic human child.

"You may have to pull me along," the giant halfling said. "The potion . . ." He grimaced and there came a popping sound in his hip, another in one shoulder, as the magical effects of the potion began to wear away.

"Regis?" Wulfgar asked, grabbing him to steady him, for indeed it seemed as if the halfling would pitch over headlong to the floor.

"I hate this potion . . ." Regis stuttered, and he even bit his lip as his face twisted. Then he pitched away from Wulfgar, stumbling to the side as he tried to take a step—with a shortened leg.

Behind them, a goblin shrieked, "There! There!"

Wulfgar, though still unsteady himself, his wounds not fully healed, hoisted the halfling right over his shoulder and awkwardly charged along. Regis continued to squirm and twist strangely.

"It . . . doesn't . . . grow or . . . shrink all at once . . ." the halfling gasped.

Wulfgar pulled the halfling from his shoulder and held him out at arm's length. The barbarian's face screwed up in shock as the halfling twisted weirdly. Half of Regis seemed too small, or the other half too big—Wulfgar couldn't sort it out!

"Keep . . . running . . ." Regis stammered. "Left . . . door . . ."

Wulfgar leaped ahead and several strides down, shouldered the door the halfling had indicated, then rushed down a long and winding passageway. With the door long out of sight, they heard the flopping feet of goblin pursuit, and Wulfgar looked back over his shoulder, expecting to see a spear already flying his way.

"I . . . I can run now," Regis said, his voice returning to normal.

Wulfgar set him down and hustled him along.

"I hate that potion."

"Then why use it?"

"Because I'm a bit too short to be a proper ogrillon torturer," the halfling explained. "And I feared that if my disguise was not proper, I would not have struck terror into the heart of Wulfgar."

"Terror," Wulfgar echoed with a laugh. "You are full of surprises, my friend."

"The orcs agree," said Regis. He tugged Wulfgar's arm as they passed another side passage, and down that one they ran.

Soon after, they went under an archway, exiting into a wider, sloping and more natural tunnel.

Wulfgar looked to Regis, but the halfling was beyond the area he had scouted. To the left, the tunnel deepened, a fairly steep decline.

"Right, then," Wulfgar reasoned, seeing the halfling's perplexed expression. "We are quite deep enough. I can barely see as it is."

"That direction might bring us right back to the goblins," Regis warned, but Wulfgar shrugged, willing to take the chance.

To the right they went, climbing steadily, but barely had they gone a hundred strides and around one long corner when they came upon a mob of monsters, orcs and ogrillon, too many to fight.

And so the chase was on anew.

In a few moments, the pair passed the side passage again, and didn't dare turn back for fear of getting caught between the two groups. Down they ran, and the glowing lichens grew sparser and the tunnel dimmer.

"I am running blind," Wulfgar warned, and he was only exaggerating a little bit, Regis feared. The big man was slowing.

But they couldn't stop and they couldn't turn back!

Regis pulled him down another side tunnel, this one running level at least, and glowing a bit more, comparatively, with illuminating lichen. Perhaps the orcs would run past, perhaps the ogrillons would throw up their fat hands in frustration and turn about.

They sped along, Regis looking back as much as forward. He turned back at the last instant, and a good thing he did!

"Wulfgar!" he cried, grabbing the man's arm and dropping to the stone. Still Wulfgar pulled him along for another stride, skidding to a stop as he started to look down at his friend.

Started to look down, but did not continue, for even in the nearly nonexistent light, Wulfgar understood Regis's cry.

The tunnel ended right at Wulfgar's toes, and in a deep, deep drop. They stood on the edge of a vast cavern, its floor far below.

They heard the monstrous pursuit, closing fast.

Regis glanced all around. "Always an answer," he whispered, more to himself than to Wulfgar.

"Aha!" he cried when he looked past Wulfgar, to the left, to a small ledge that went only a few steps along the rim of the chamber.

"Go," he bade the man. "Stay against the wall."

Wulfgar stared that way doubtfully, barely discerning the ledge, but understanding that it only went a stride or two.

Not far behind, an orc spotted them and screamed.

"It won't work," Wulfgar insisted. "We are seen!"

"Go," Regis told him and shoved him. "Just go!"

"It only travels a short way," Wulfgar protested. "Better to fight them . . ."

"That's all we need," Regis implored him. "Just go!"

With no options before him, Wulfgar eased his way along the narrow ledge. Barely five feet along it, he had nowhere left to go. He looked back to Regis, to see his friend standing in the larger corridor.

An orc cried out, and the voice was not far at all!

Regis growled back at it. "I will kill you!"

The halfling sidled onto the ledge beside Wulfgar, his back to the wall. "This is how I killed the ogrillon torturer," he explained to the confused barbarian, and he held up a vial of some sort.

Regis winked and as the footfalls of the pursuit closed in, the halfling peeked around the corner, came up straight, took a deep breath, then casually tossed the vial back into the main passageway. The glass shattered when it hit the stone floor, and Wulfgar noted a sudden and brief shimmer.

"What?" he started to ask, but was interrupted by the surprised shout of an orc, followed by the sound of a heavy tumble and more voices calling out in surprise.

The orc slid right past Regis, pitching from the ledge and over the cliff. And behind it came the others, all in a tangle, clawing futilely at the floor, but unable to break their unexpected slides. One stabbed hard with a dagger, and in the dim illumination, Wulfgar noted a shower of tiny sparkles.

But even that scrape didn't slow the creature enough to prevent it from pitching over the ledge.

Over they went, first the orc, then another, and a third wrestling with an ogrillon. And more behind and more behind them, slipping and falling, sliding and flying out into the open cavern.

The chamber before them echoed with screams, and the sickening sounds of flesh and bone crashing down to unyielding stone.

Then all was quiet, so quickly, save a single whimpered cry far down in the cavern, for one of the creatures, at least, had apparently survived the fall.

"Come along," Regis said. "Dive back the other way." Around the corner went the halfling, bending low and pushing off into a headfirst slide away from the ledge.

Wulfgar came to the edge tentatively and bent low, touching the ground. Ice.

With a glance back at the drop, the barbarian similarly dived and slid to safety, to Regis, waiting for him on the other side of the slippery trap.

"The ogrillon jailer?" Wulfgar asked.

"I was one of the goblins, of course," Regis explained. "I shot the other with a crossbow dart, and the ogrillon took exception."

"He charged at you," Wulfgar reasoned, trying to remember what little he had seen of that scene, back in the prison when he had been on the cart under a near-dead goblin.

"I was standing back by the middle of the room."

"Before the pit," said Wulfgar, catching on. "And so you created your . . . ice." He looked back at the trap behind them. "And the ogrillon torturer slipped and fell and was carried into the pit."

"With his pet umber hulks," the halfling added, and he started back along the corridor, Wulfgar at his side.

"Umber hulks?" Wulfgar asked incredulously.

"Small ones," Regis explained. "Stuck in a metal-floored and metal-walled pit, and quite out of their minds with rage. Their reaction to the ogrillon flying in at them made me believe that he had not treated his pets very well."

Wulfgar digested it all with his head shaking and a grin set upon his face. "You fed them the other goblin, too?"

"Of course," Regis replied dryly. "I treat my pets well."

"Grave robbing?" Bungalow Thump asked as soon as the foursome were brought before King Connerad, before they had even been formally announced and King Connerad had greeted them. "What're ye thinking, Little Arr Arr?"

"Well met once more, Drizzt Do'Urden," Connerad said. "And yerself—mayhap—Reginald Roundshield, though it seems ye've a bit o' explaining to do."

"Nothing for me, good king?" asked the woman standing beside the drow, and Athrogate chuckled.

Connerad looked at her curiously, not quite knowing what to make of her.

"Ye'll get yer say," promised the female dwarf flanking the king on the right, who wore the garb of a high-ranking officer in the Mithral Hall garrison.

"Ye sneaked into King Bruenor's own grave when ye were here as our guest?" Bungalow Thump asked incredulously.

"Ah, but King Emerus is sure to be disappointed in ye," said the woman, General Dagnabbet.

"King Bruenor's grave in Mithral Hall is empty," the dwarf they knew as Reginald Roundshield sternly replied, and he stared right at Bungalow Thump as he declared, "King Bruenor's grave in Mithral Hall has never been anything but empty."

The battlerager stared back at him hard, and seemed on the edge of a tirade, clearly taking the claim as some sort of an insult.

But that didn't stop Bruenor. "Ain't that the truth, King Connerad?" he asked.

Connerad looked to Drizzt, who of course, had been in on the ruse when Bruenor had secretly abdicated the throne to Connerad's father, Banak Brawnanvil, those many years before.

The drow nodded slightly in reply.

"Bruenor fell in Gauntlgrym," Bruenor declared. "Aye, ye've heared the whispers, and know 'em to be true. Yer King Bruenor found Gauntlgrym, and there he fell and there he was buried."

The trio—and more than a few dwarf guards about—looked to each other in confusion and excitement.

"So ye went out from here to Gauntlgrym," King Connerad said to the dwarf. "And there you robbed the grave o' King Bruenor?"

"I didn't rob anything," the dwarf replied.

"Surely the helm you wear, and the shield and axe—aye, I'd know that axe as well as if it was me own . . ." Connerad said.

"Aye, and that's Bruenor's helm or I'm a bearded gnome," said Bungalow Thump, using one of his old king's favorite lines for effect.

"I didn't rob anything," Bruenor insisted, and he came forward slowly, shaking his head. He put his hands on the arms of Connerad's throne, drawing a gasp from both dwarves flanking the king. But they didn't intervene as Bruenor said again, "I didn't rob anything." He moved closer to Connerad, staring the king in the eye, moving so close that their long noses almost touched.

Very deliberately, Bruenor went on. "I . . . taked . . . what . . . was . . . me . . . own."

King Connerad tried to digest that for a long while, as did the others, and gradually, Bruenor backed off.

Connerad looked to Drizzt, his expression showing the poor dwarf to be fully at a loss.

The drow nodded again, slowly and deliberately.

"Ye've seen it before," Bruenor insisted. "When I gived me throne to Gandalug."

King Connerad clearly didn't know what to make of any of this. He looked to Bruenor, then to Drizzt, and back to the dwarf.

"Bwahaha!" Athrogate roared at the show.

Clarity finally came to the dwarf king when he settled his gaze once more on the woman. He had looked into Bruenor's eyes, and yes that had sparked some recognition, but now, in that context, looking at the woman, King Connerad knew.

In his heart, he knew the truth.

"Catti-brie," he mouthed, barely able to push the words past the lump in his throat.

The woman smiled.

"By the gods' hairy arses," the stupefied Bungalow Thump muttered, and General Dagnabbet gasped.

Exhausted, Wulfgar and Regis sat against some corridor wall in some area they did not know, and with tons and tons of rock hanging over their heads, for they had traveled much lower in the unending maze of the Underdark. Soon after the halfling's deadly trap at the ledge, they had encountered yet another band of stubborn enemies, and had run on for what seemed like hours.

Finally, in a mossy cavern, they had found a reprieve, but it would not last long, they knew, and determined enemies were not far away.

"I pray that you have many more tricks," Wulfgar said.

"So do I," the halfling answered.

"And many more potions."

"Few," Regis answered. "So few. If we find a safe spot, I will try to brew some more, perhaps."

"Is there a safe spot to be found in any of these dark places?"

The halfling didn't answer, but he did tap the barbarian's arm, and handed over a large piece of salted meat. They had rations, at least, and enough for a party much larger, for Regis had carried almost all of them for the group in his magical, weightless pouch.

"Do you think the others escaped?"

Wulfgar smiled as he recalled the ranting of the orc shaman who had come to him before he had been dragged out to the carnival.

"Of course," he answered. "There are not enough orc-kind in the world to defeat our friends."

"Or us," Regis answered hopefully, but all that came back at him was a long silence.

And indeed, sitting in a tunnel, lost in the Underdark and with hordes of monsters hunting them, his optimism seemed quite out of place.

"We'll not get out of this alive, you know," Wulfgar told him a long while later.

"You seem content with that." Regis didn't mean it as an accusation, but it surely sounded like one.

"Borrowed time," the barbarian explained with a resigned shrug. "I was, and should be, long dead."

Regis managed a smile—there was truth to Wulfgar's words, of course, but the halfling wasn't sure he could agree with the sentiment. He thought of his second life, of Doregardo of the Grinning Ponies and mostly of Donnola Topolino. He imagined the potential adventures, the grand love, he had yet ahead of him, the life he might have known.

"Maybe we'll find our way," he said, his voice thick with lament.

Wulfgar dropped a comforting hand on his shoulder.